"The quest...
what are you...

"I've been trying to explain it to you. We have a community of ladies here in Spindle Cove, and we support one another with friendship, intellectual stimulation, and healthful living."

"No, no. I can see how this might appeal to a mousy, awkward chit with no prospects for something better. But what are *you* doing here?"

Perplexed, she turned her gloved hands palms-up. "Living happily."

"Really," he said, giving her a skeptical look. Even his horse snorted in seeming disbelief. "A woman like you."

She bristled. Just what kind of woman did he think she was?

"If you think yourself content with no man in your life, Miss Finch, that proves only one thing." In a swift motion, he pulled himself into the saddle. His next words were spoken down at her, making her feel small and patronized. "You've been meeting all the wrong men."

A Night to
Surrender

Tessa Dare

AVON
An Imprint of HarperCollinsPublishers

AVON BOOKS
An Imprint of HarperCollins*Publishers*
195 Broadway
New York, NY 10007

Copyright © 2011 by Eve Ortega
Excerpt from *A Week to Be Wicked* copyright © 2012 by Eve Ortega
ISBN 978-0-06-204983-4
K.I.S.S. and Teal is a trademark of the Ovarian Cancer National Alliance.
www.avonromance.com

First Avon Books mass market printing: September 2011

Avon Trademark Reg. U.S. Pat. Off. and in Other Countries, Marca Registrada, Hecho en U.S.A.
HarperCollins® is a registered trademark of HarperCollins Publishers.

Printed in the U.S.A.

HB 11.01.2023

For my mom, with love.
Healer, scholar, writer, role model, friend.

Acknowledgments

irst and foremost, I'm deeply grateful to my husband and children. Having a writer in the family can't be easy, but they seem to take it all in stride. As do the staff at my children's wonderful childcare center. Leave it to the romance author's daughter to liven up a chapel lesson on "temptation."

My editor, Tessa Woodward, and my agent, Helen Breitwieser, have my infinite gratitude for their patience, faith, and excellent advice. I am indebted, as always, to Courtney Milan and Amy Baldwin for their friendship and support. Bren, I could not have finished this book without you! Thanks for listening, and for making all those long days and nights in "the office" so much fun.

I'm grateful to Elyssa, Leigh, Jennifer, and Jackie for offering critique and subject expertise. Ben Townsend, thank you for pointing the way on all matters military. Thanks to copy editors Eleanor Mikucki and Martha Trachtenberg for catching all my many mistakes, and to Kim Castillo for keeping my act together. Everyone at Avon has been wonderful.

Finally, I want to thank my chaptermates in the Orange County Chapter of Romance Writers of America. I can't list every name, but you know who you are. Our chapter motto might be "One hand reaching forward, one hand reaching back," but while I was writing this book, I know I felt both arms wrapped around me. I'm truly blessed to be part of such a generous, talented group.

Chapter One

Sussex, England
Summer 1813

ram stared into a pair of wide, dark eyes. Eyes that reflected a surprising glimmer of intelligence. This might be the rare female a man could reason with.

"Now, then," he said. "We can do this the easy way, or we can make things difficult."

With a soft snort, she turned her head. It was as if he'd ceased to exist.

Bram shifted his weight to his good leg, feeling the stab to his pride. He was a lieutenant colonel in the British army, and at over six feet tall, he was said to cut an imposing figure. Typically, a pointed glance from his quarter would quell the slightest hint of disobedience. He was not accustomed to being ignored.

"Listen sharp, now." He gave her ear a rough tweak and sank his voice to a low threat. "If you know what's good for you, you'll do as I say."

Though she spoke not a word, her reply was clear: *You can kiss my great woolly arse.*

Confounded sheep.

"Ah, the English countryside. So charming. So . . .

fragrant." Colin approached, stripped of his London-best topcoat, wading hip-deep through the river of wool. Blotting the sheen of perspiration from his brow with his sleeve, he asked, "I don't suppose this means we can simply turn back?"

Ahead of them, a boy pushing a handcart had over-turned his cargo, strewing corn all over the road. It was an open buffet, and every ram and ewe in Sussex appeared to have answered the invitation. A vast throng of sheep bustled and bleated around the unfortunate youth, gorging themselves on the spilled grain—and completely obstructing Bram's wagons.

"Can we walk the teams in reverse?" Colin asked. "Perhaps we can go around, find another road."

Bram gestured at the surrounding landscape. "There *is* no other road."

They stood in the middle of the rutted dirt lane, which occupied a kind of narrow, winding valley. A steep bank of gorse rose up on one side, and on the other, some dozen yards of heath separated the road from dramatic bluffs. And below those—*far* below those—lay the sparkling turquoise sea. If the air was seasonally dry and clear, and Bram squinted hard at that thin indigo line of the horizon, he might even glimpse the northern coast of France.

So close. He'd get there. Not today, but soon. He had a task to accomplish here, and the sooner he completed it, the sooner he could rejoin his regiment. He wasn't stopping for anything.

Except sheep. Blast it. It would seem they were stopping for sheep.

A rough voice said, "I'll take care of them."

Thorne joined their group. Bram flicked his gaze to the side and spied his hulking mountain of a corporal shouldering a flintlock rifle.

"We can't simply shoot them, Thorne."

Obedient as ever, Thorne lowered his gun. "Then I've a cutlass. Just sharpened the blade last night."

"We can't butcher them, either."

Thorne shrugged. "I'm hungry."

Yes, that was Thorne—straightforward, practical. Ruthless.

"We're all hungry." Bram's stomach rumbled in support of the statement. "But clearing the way is our aim at the moment, and a dead sheep's harder to move than a live one. We'll just have to nudge them along."

Thorne lowered the hammer of his rifle, disarming it, then flipped the weapon with an agile motion and rammed the butt end against a woolly flank. "Move on, you bleeding beast."

The animal lumbered uphill a few steps, prodding its neighbors to scuttle along in turn. Downhill, the drivers urged the teams forward before resetting their brakes, unwilling to surrender even those hard-fought inches of progress.

The two wagons held a bounty of supplies to refit Bram's regiment: muskets, shot, shells, wool and pipeclay for uniforms. He'd spared no expense, and he *would* see them up this hill. Even if it took all day, and red-hot pain screamed from his thigh to his shinbone with every pace. His superiors thought he wasn't healed enough to resume field command? He would prove them wrong. One step at a time.

"This is absurd," Colin grumbled. "At this rate, we'll arrive next Tuesday."

"Stop talking. Start moving." Bram nudged a sheep with his boot, wincing as he did. With his leg already killing him, the last thing he needed was a pain in the arse, but that's exactly what he'd inherited, along with all his father's accounts and possessions: responsibility for his wastrel cousin, Colin Sandhurst, Lord Payne.

He swatted at another sheep's flank, earning himself an indignant bleat and a few inches more.

"I have an idea," Colin said.

Bram grunted, unsurprised. As men, he and Colin were little more than strangers. But during the few years they'd overlapped at Eton, he recalled his younger cousin as being just full of ideas. Ideas that had landed him shin-deep in excrement. Literally, on at least one occasion.

Colin looked from Bram to Thorne and back again, eyes keen. "I ask you, gentlemen. Are we, or are we not, in possession of a great quantity of black powder?"

"Tranquillity is the soul of our community."

Not a quarter mile's distance away, Susanna Finch sat in the lace-curtained parlor of the Queen's Ruby, a rooming house for gently bred young ladies. With her were the rooming house's newest prospective residents, a Mrs. Highwood and her three unmarried daughters.

"Here in Spindle Cove, young ladies enjoy a wholesome, improving atmosphere." Susanna indicated a knot of ladies clustered by the hearth, industriously engaged in needlework. "See? The picture of good health and genteel refinement."

In unison, the young ladies looked up from their work and smiled placid, demure smiles.

Excellent. She gave them an approving nod.

Ordinarily, the ladies of Spindle Cove would never waste such a beautiful afternoon stitching indoors. They would be rambling the countryside, or sea bathing in the cove, or climbing the bluffs. But on days like these, when new visitors came to the village, everyone understood some pretense at propriety was necessary. Susanna was not above a little harmless deceit when it came to saving a young woman's life.

"Will you take more tea?" she asked, accepting a fresh pot from Mrs. Nichols, the inn's aging proprietress. If Mrs. Highwood examined the young ladies *too* closely, she might notice that mild Gaelic obscenities occupied the center of Kate Taylor's sampler. Or that Violet Winterbottom's needle didn't even have thread.

Mrs. Highwood sniffed. Although the day was mild, she fanned herself with vigor. "Well, Miss Finch, perhaps this place can do my Diana some good." She looked to her eldest daughter. "We've seen all the best doctors, tried ever so many treatments. I even took her to Bath for the cure."

Susanna gave a sympathetic nod. From what she could gather, Diana Highwood had suffered bouts of mild asthma from a young age. With flaxen hair and a shy, rosy curve of a smile, the eldest Miss Highwood was a true beauty. Her fragile health had delayed what most certainly would be a stunning *ton* debut. However, Susanna strongly suspected the many doctors and treatments were what kept the young lady feeling ill.

She offered Diana a friendly smile. "I'm certain a stay in Spindle Cove will be of great benefit to Miss Highwood's health. Of great benefit to you all, for that matter."

In recent years, Spindle Cove had become the seaside destination of choice for a certain type of well-bred young lady: the sort no one knew what to do with. They included the sickly, the scandalous, and the painfully shy; young wives disenchanted with matrimony, and young girls *too* enchanted with the wrong men . . . All of them delivered here by the guardians to whom they presented problems, in hopes that the sea air would cure them of their ills.

As the only daughter of the only local gentleman, Susanna was the village hostess by default. These awkward young ladies no one knew what to do with . . . she knew what to do with them. Or rather, she knew what *not* to do with them. No "cures" were necessary. They didn't need doctors pressing lancets to their veins, or finishing school matrons harping on their diction. They just needed a place to be themselves.

Spindle Cove was that place.

Mrs. Highwood worked her fan. "I'm a widow with no sons, Miss Finch. One of my daughters must marry well, and soon. I've had such hopes for Diana, lovely as she is. But if she's not stronger by next season . . ." She made a dismissive wave toward her middle daughter, who sat in dark, bespectacled contrast to her fair-haired sisters. "I shall have no choice but to bring out Minerva instead."

"But Minerva doesn't care about men," young Charlotte said helpfully. "She prefers dirt and rocks."

"It's called geology," Minerva said. "It's a science."

"It's certain spinsterhood, is what it is! Unnatural girl. Do sit straight in your chair, at least." Mrs. Highwood sighed and fanned harder. To Susanna, she said, "I despair of her, truly. This is why Diana must get well, you see. Can you imagine Minerva in Society?"

Susanna bit back a smile, all too easily imagining the scene. It would probably resemble her own debut. Like Minerva, she had been absorbed in unladylike pursuits, and the object of her female relations' oft-voiced despair. At balls, she'd been that freckled Amazon in the corner, who would have been all too happy to blend into the wallpaper, if only her hair color would have allowed it.

As for the gentlemen she'd met . . . not a one of them had managed to sweep her off her feet. To be fair, none of them had tried very hard.

She shrugged off the awkward memories. That time was behind her now.

Mrs. Highwood's gaze fell on a book at the corner of the table. "I am gratified to see you keep *Mrs. Worthington* close at hand."

"Oh yes," Susanna replied, reaching for the blue, leather-bound tome. "You'll find copies of *Mrs. Worthington's Wisdom* scattered everywhere throughout the village. We find it a very useful book."

"Hear that, Minerva? You would do well to learn it by heart." When Minerva rolled her eyes, Mrs. Highwood said, "Charlotte, open it now. Read aloud the beginning of Chapter Twelve."

Charlotte reached for the book and opened it, then cleared her throat and read aloud in a dramatic voice. " 'Chapter Twelve. The perils of excessive education. A young lady's intellect should be in all ways like her undergarments. Present, pristine, and imperceptible to the casual observer.' "

Mrs. Highwood harrumphed. "Yes. Just so. Hear and believe it, Minerva. Hear and believe every word. As Miss Finch says, you will find that book very useful."

Susanna took a leisurely sip of tea, swallowing with it a bitter lump of indignation. She wasn't an angry or resentful person, as a matter of course. But once provoked, her passions required formidable effort to conceal.

That book provoked her, no end.

Mrs. Worthington's Wisdom for Young Ladies was the bane of sensible girls the world over, crammed with insipid, damaging advice on every page. Susanna could have gleefully crushed its pages to powder with a mortar and pestle, labeled the vial with a skull and crossbones, and placed it on the highest shelf in her stillroom, right beside the dried foxglove leaves and deadly nightshade berries.

Instead, she'd made it her mission to remove as many copies as possible from circulation. A sort of quarantine. Former residents of the Queen's Ruby sent the books from all corners of England. One couldn't enter a room in Spindle Cove without finding a copy or three of *Mrs. Worthington's Wisdom*. And just as Susanna had told Mrs. Highwood, they found the book very useful indeed. It was the perfect size for propping a window open. It also made an excellent doorstop or paperweight. Susanna used her personal copies for pressing herbs. Or occasionally, for target practice.

She motioned to Charlotte. "May I?" Taking the volume from the girl's grip, she raised the book high. Then, with a brisk *thwack*, she used it to crush a bothersome gnat.

With a calm smile, she placed the book on a side table. "Very useful indeed."

"They'll never know what hit them." With his boot heel, Colin tamped a divot over the first powder charge.

"Nothing's going to hit them," Bram said. "We're not using shells."

The last thing they needed was shrapnel zinging about. The charges he prepared were mere blanks—black powder wrapped in paper, for a bit of noise and a spray of dirt.

"You're certain the horses won't bolt?" Colin asked, unspooling a length of slow-burning fuse.

"These are cavalry-trained beasts. Impervious to explosions. The sheep, on the other hand . . ."

"Will scatter like flies." Colin flashed a reckless grin. "I suppose."

Bram knew bombing the sheep was reckless, impulsive,

and inherently rather stupid, like all his cousin's boyhood ideas. Surely there were better, more efficient solutions to a sheep barricade that didn't involve black powder.

But time was wasting, and Bram was impatient to be moving on, in more ways than one. Eight months ago, a lead ball had ripped through his right knee and torn his life apart. He'd spent months confined to a sickbed, another several weeks clanking and groaning his way down corridors like a ghost dragging chains. Some days during his convalescence, Bram had felt certain *he* would explode.

And now he was so close—just a mile or so—from Summerfield and Sir Lewis Finch. Just a mile from finally regaining his command. He bloody well wouldn't be thwarted by a flock of gluttonous sheep, whose guts were likely to burst if they weren't scared off that corn.

A good, clean blast was just what they all needed right about now.

"That'll do," Thorne called, embedding the last charge at the top of the rise. As he pushed his way back through the sheep, he added, "All's clear down the lane. I could see a fair distance."

"There *is* a village nearby, isn't there?" Colin asked. "God, tell me there's a village."

"There's a village," Bram answered, packing away the unused powder. "Saw it on the map. Somesuch Bay, or Whatsit Harbor . . . Can't exactly recall."

"I don't care what it's called," Colin said. "So long as there's a tavern and a bit of society. God, I hate the country."

Thorne said, "I saw the village. Just over that rise."

"It didn't look charming, did it?" Colin raised a brow as he reached for the tinderbox. "I should hate for it to be charming. Give me a dank, seedy, vice-ridden pustule of a village any day. Wholesome living makes my skin crawl."

The corporal gave him a stony look. "I wouldn't know about charming, my lord."

"Yes. I can see that," Colin muttered. He struck a flint and lit the fuse. "Fair enough."

"Miss Finch, what a charming village." Diana Highwood clasped her hands together.

"We think so." Smiling modestly, Susanna led her guests onto the village green. "Here we have the church, St. Ursula's—a prized example of medieval architecture. Of course, the green itself is lovely." She refrained from pointing out the grass oval they used for cricket and lawn bowls, and quickly swiveled Mrs. Highwood away, lest she spy the pair of stockinged legs dangling from one of the trees.

"Look up there." She pointed out a jumble of stone arches and turrets decorating the rocky bluff. "Those are the ruins of Rycliff Castle. They make an excellent place to paint and sketch."

"Oh, how perfectly romantic." Charlotte sighed.

"It looks damp," Mrs. Highwood pronounced.

"Not at all. In a month's time, the castle will be the site of our midsummer fair. Families come from ten parishes, some from as far away as Eastbourne. We ladies dress in medieval attire, and my father puts on a display for the local children. He collects ancient suits of armor, you see. Among other things."

"What a delightful notion," Diana said.

"It's the highlight of our summer."

Minerva peered hard at the bluffs. "What's the composition of those cliffs? Are they sandstone or chalk?"

"Er . . . sandstone, I think." Susanna directed their attention to a red-shuttered façade across the lane. Wide window boxes spilled over with blossoms, and a gilt-lettered sign swung noiselessly in the breeze. "And there's the tea shop. Mr. Fosbury, the proprietor, makes cakes and sweets to rival any London confectionery's."

"Cakes?" Mrs. Highwood's mouth pursed in an unpleasant manner. "I do hope you aren't indulging in an excess of sweets."

"Oh no," Susanna lied. "Hardly ever."

"Diana has been strictly forbidden to indulge. And that one"—she pointed out Minerva—"is tending toward stoutness, I fear."

At her mother's slight, Minerva turned her gaze to her feet, as if she were intently studying the pebbles beneath them. Or as if she were begging the ground to swallow her whole.

"*Minerva*," her mother snapped. "Posture."

Susanna put an arm about the young woman, shoring her up. "We have the sunniest weather in all England, did I mention that? The post comes through two times a week. Can I interest you all in a tour of the shops?"

"Shops? I only see one."

"Well, yes. There is only one. But it's all we have need of, you see. Bright's All Things shop has everything a young lady could wish to buy."

Mrs. Highwood surveyed the street. "Where is the doctor? Diana must have a doctor nearby at all times, to bleed her when she has her attacks."

Susanna winced. No wonder Diana's health never fully returned. Such a useless, horrific practice, bleeding. A "remedy" more likely to drain life than preserve it, and one Susanna had barely survived herself. Out of habit, she adjusted her long, elbow-length gloves. Their seams chafed against the well-healed scars beneath.

"There is a surgeon next town over," she said. A surgeon she wouldn't allow near cattle, much less a young lady. "Here in the village, we have a very capable apothecary." She hoped the woman would not ask for specifics there.

"What about men?" Mrs. Highwood asked.

"Men?" Susanna echoed. "What about them?"

"With so many unwed ladies in residence, are you not overrun with fortune hunters? Bath was teeming with them, all of them after my Diana's dowry. As if she would marry some smooth-talking third son."

"Definitely not, Mrs. Highwood." On this point, Susanna need not fudge. "There are no debt-ridden rakes or ambitious officers here. In fact, there are very few men in Spindle Cove at all. Aside from my father, only tradesmen and servants."

"I just don't know." Mrs. Highwood sighed, looking about the village once again. "It's all rather common, isn't it? My cousin, Lady Agatha, told me of a new spa in Kent. Mineral baths, purging treatments. Her Ladyship swears by their mercury cure."

Susanna's stomach lurched. If Diana Highwood landed in a spa like that, it might truly be the end of her. "Please, Mrs. Highwood. One cannot underestimate the healthful benefits of simple sea air and sunshine."

Charlotte tugged her gaze from the ruined castle long enough to plead, "Do let's stay, Mama. I want to take part in the midsummer fair."

"I believe I feel better already," Diana said, breathing deep.

Susanna left Minerva's side and approached the anxious matriarch. Mrs. Highwood might be a misguided, overwrought sort of woman, but she obviously loved her daughters and had their best interests at heart. She only needed a bit of reassurance that she was doing the right thing.

Well, Susanna could give her that reassurance truthfully. All three of the Highwood sisters needed this place. Diana needed a reprieve from quack medical treatments. Minerva needed a chance to pursue her own interests without censure. Young Charlotte just needed a place to be a girl, to stretch her growing legs and imagination.

And Susanna needed the Highwoods, for reasons she couldn't easily explain. She had no way to go back in time and undo the misfortunes of her own youth. But she could help to spare other young ladies the same friendless misery, and that was the next best thing.

"Trust me, Mrs. Highwood," she said, taking the woman's hand. "Spindle Cove is the perfect place for your daughters' summer holiday. I promise you, they will be healthy, happy, and perfectly safe."

Boom. A distant blast punched the air. Susanna's ribs shivered with the force of it.

Mrs. Highwood clutched her bonnet with a gloved hand. "My word. Was that an explosion?"

Drat, drat, drat. And this had all been going so well.

"Miss Finch, you just claimed this place was safe."

"Oh, it is." Susanna gave them her most calming, reassuring smile. "It is. No doubt that's just a ship in the Channel, sounding its signal cannon."

She knew very well there was no ship. That blast could only be her father's doing. In his day, Sir Lewis Finch had been a celebrated innovator of firearms and artillery. His contributions to the British army had earned him acclaim, influence, and a sizable fortune. But after those incidents with the experimental cannon, he'd promised Susanna he would give up conducting field tests.

He'd *promised.*

As they moved forward into the lane, a strange, low rumble gathered in the air.

"What is that noise?" Diana asked.

Susanna feigned innocence. "What noise?"

"*That* noise," Mrs. Highwood said.

The rumble grew more forceful with each second. The paving stones vibrated beneath her heeled slippers. Mrs. Highwood squeezed her eyes shut and emitted a low, mournful whimper.

"Oh, *that* noise," Susanna said lightly, herding the Highwoods across the lane. If she could only get them indoors . . . "That noise is nothing to be concerned about. We hear it all the time here. A fluke of the weather."

"It cannot be thunder," Minerva said.

"No. No, it's not thunder. It's . . . an atmospheric phenomenon, brought on by intermittent gusts of . . ."

"Sheep!" Charlotte cried, pointing down the lane.

A flock of deranged, woolly beasts stormed through the ancient stone arch and poured into the village, funneling down the lane and bearing down on them.

"Oh yes," Susanna muttered. "Precisely so. Intermittent gusts of sheep."

She hurried her guests across the lane, and they huddled in the All Things shop's doorway while the panicked sheep passed. The chorus of agitated bleats grated against her eardrums.

If her father had hurt himself, she was going to kill him.

"There's no cause for alarm," Susanna said over the din. "Rural life does have its peculiar charms. Miss Highwood, is your breathing quite all right?"

Diana nodded. "I'm fine, thank you."

"Then won't you please excuse me?"

Without waiting for an answer, Susanna lifted her hem and made a mad dash down the lane, weaving around the few lingering sheep as she made her way straight out of the village. It didn't take but a matter of seconds. This was, after all, a very small village.

Rather than take the longer, winding lane around the hill, she climbed it. As she neared the top, the breeze delivered to her a few lingering wisps of smoke and scattered tufts of wool. Despite these ominous signs, she crested the hill to find a scene that did not resemble one of her father's artillery tests. Down at the bottom of the lane, two carts were stalled in the road. When she squinted, she could make out figures milling around the stopped conveyances. Tall, male figures. No short, stout, balding gentlemen among them.

None of them could be Papa.

She took a relieved gulp of acrid, powder-tinged air. With the burden of dread lifted, her curiosity took the fore. Intrigued, she picked her way down the bank of heather until she stood on the narrow, rutted road. In the distance, the figures of the men ceased moving. They'd noticed her.

Shading her brow with one hand, she peered hard at the men, trying to make out their identities. One of the men wore an officer's coat. Another wore no coat at all. As she approached them, the coatless man began to wave with vigor. Shouts carried up to her on the breeze. Frowning, Susanna moved closer, hoping to better hear the words.

"Wait! Miss, don't . . . !"

Whomp.

An unseen force plucked her straight off her feet and slammed her sideways, driving her off the lane entirely. She plowed shoulder-first into the tall grass, tackled to the turf by some kind of charging beast.

A charging beast wearing lobster-red wool.

Together, they bounced away from the road, elbows and

knees absorbing the blows. Susanna's teeth rattled in her skull, and she bit her tongue hard. Fabric ripped, and cool air reached farther up her thigh than any well-mannered breeze ought to venture.

When they rolled to a stop, she found herself pinned by a tremendous, huffing weight. And pierced by an intense green gaze.

"Wh—?" Her breath rushed out in question.

Boom, the world answered.

Susanna ducked her head, burrowing into the protection of what she'd recognized to be an officer's coat. The knob of a brass button pressed into her cheek. The man's bulk formed a comforting shield as a shower of dirt clods rained down on them both. He smelled of whiskey and gunpowder.

After the dust cleared, she brushed the hair from his brow, searching his gaze for signs of confusion or pain. His eyes were alert and intelligent, and still that startling shade of green—as hard and richly hued as jade.

She asked, "Are you well?"

"Yes." His voice was a deep rasp. "Are you?"

She nodded, expecting him to release her at the confirmation. When he showed no signs of moving, she puzzled at it. Either he was gravely injured or seriously impertinent. "Sir, you're . . . er, you're rather heavy." Surely he could not fail to miss *that* hint.

He replied, "You're soft."

Good Lord. Who was this man? Where had he come from? And how was he still *atop* her?

"You have a small wound." With trembling fingers, she brushed a reddish knot high on his temple, near his hairline. "Here." She pressed her hand to his throat, feeling for his pulse. She found it, thumping strong and steady against her gloved fingertips.

"Ah. That's nice."

Her face blazed with heat. "Are you seeing double?"

"Perhaps. I see two lips, two eyes, two flushed cheeks . . . a thousand freckles."

She stared at him.

"Don't concern yourself, miss. It's nothing." His gaze darkened with some mysterious intent. "Nothing a little kiss won't mend."

And before she could even catch her breath, he pressed his lips to hers.

A kiss. His mouth, touching hers. It was warm and firm, and then . . . it was over.

Her first real kiss in all her five-and-twenty years, and it was finished in a heartbeat. Just a memory now, save for the faint bite of whiskey on her lips. And the heat. She still tasted his scorching, masculine heat. Belatedly, she closed her eyes.

"There, now," he murmured. "All better."

Better? Worse? The darkness behind her eyelids held no answers, so she opened them again.

Different. This strange, strong man held her in his protective embrace, and she was lost in his intriguing green stare, and his kiss reverberated in her bones with more force than a powder blast. And now she felt different.

The heat and weight of him . . . they were like an answer. The answer to a question Susanna hadn't even been aware her body was asking. So this was how it would be, to lie beneath a man. To feel shaped by him, her flesh giving in some places and resisting in others. Heat building between two bodies; dueling heartbeats pounding both sides of the same drum.

Maybe . . . just maybe . . . this was what she'd been waiting to feel all her life. Not swept her off her feet—but flung across the lane and sent tumbling head over heels while the world exploded around her.

He rolled onto his side, giving her room to breathe. "Where did you come from?"

"I think I should ask *you* that." She struggled up on one elbow. "Who *are* you? What on earth are you doing here?"

"Isn't it obvious?" His tone was grave. "We're bombing the sheep."

"Oh. Oh dear. Of course you are." Inside her, empathy twined with despair. Of course, he was cracked in the head. One of those poor soldiers addled by war. She ought to have known it. No *sane* man had ever looked at her this way.

She pushed aside her disappointment. At least he had come to the right place. And landed on the right woman. She was far more skilled in treating head wounds than fielding gentlemen's advances. The key here was to stop thinking of him as an immense, virile man and simply regard him as a person who needed her help. An unattractive, poxy, eunuch sort of person.

Reaching out to him, she traced one fingertip over his brow. "Don't be frightened," she said in a calm, even tone. "All is well. You're going to be just fine." She cupped his cheek and met his gaze directly. "The sheep can't hurt you here."

Chapter Two

You're going to be just fine," she repeated.

Bram believed her. Wholeheartedly. At the moment, he was feeling damned fine indeed. He had a road cleared of sheep, a functioning leg, and a fetching young miss stroking his brow. Why the devil should he complain?

Granted, the fetching young miss thought he was a blithering idiot. But that was a mere quibble. Truth be told, he *was* still gathering his wits.

In those moments following the blast, his first, admittedly selfish thought had been for his knee. He was almost certain he'd ripped the joint apart again, what with that ungainly rescue attempt. Before his injury, he would have managed to scoop this girl off the road with more grace. She was lucky he'd been standing to the side of the lane and not down the hill with the others, or he never could have reached her in time.

Once a few moments' assessment and a trial flex or two had assured him his knee remained intact, his thoughts had all centered on her. How the irises of her eyes were the same blue as . . . well, irises. How she smelled like a garden—a whole garden. Not just blossoms and herbs, but the juice of crushed green leaves and the rich, fertile essence of the earth. How she made the perfect place to land, so warm and so soft. How it had been a stupidly long time since he'd had a woman under him, and he couldn't recall one ever caressing him so sweetly as this.

God, had he truly kissed her?

He had. And she was lucky he hadn't done more. For a moment there, he'd been well and truly dazed. He supposed the blast was to blame for that. Or maybe it was just her.

She sat up a bit further. Wisps of loosened hair tumbled about her face. Her hair was a striking shade of gold, touched with red. It made him think of molten bronze.

"Do you know what day it is?" she asked, peering at him.

"Don't *you*?"

"Here in Spindle Cove, we ladies have a schedule. Mondays are country walks. Tuesdays, sea bathing. Wednesdays, you'd find us in the garden." She touched the back of her hand to his forehead. "What is it we do on Mondays?"

"We didn't get to Thursdays."

"Thursdays are irrelevant. I'm testing your ability to recall information. Do you remember Mondays?"

He stifled a laugh. God, her touch felt good. If she kept petting and stroking him like this, he might very well go mad.

"Tell me your name," he said. "I promise to recall it." A bit forward, perhaps. But any chance for formal introductions had already fallen casualty to the powder charge.

Speaking of the powder charge, here came the brilliant mastermind of the sheep siege. Damn his eyes.

"Are you well, miss?" Colin asked.

"I'm well," she answered. "I'm afraid I can't say the same for your friend."

"Bram?" Colin prodded him with a boot. "You look all of a piece."

No thanks to you.

"He's completely addled, the poor soul." The girl patted his cheek. "Was it the war? How long has he been like this?"

"Like this?" Colin smirked down at him. "Oh, all his life."

"All his life?"

"He's my cousin. I should know."

A flush pressed to her cheeks, overwhelming her freckles. "If you're his cousin, you should take better care of him. What are you thinking, allowing him to wander the countryside, waging war on flocks of sheep?"

Ah, that was sweet. The lass cared. She would see him settled in a very comfortable asylum, she would. Perhaps Thursdays would be her day to visit and lay cool cloths to his brow.

"I know, I know," Colin replied gravely. "He's a certifiable fool. Completely unstable. Sometimes the poor bastard even drools. But the hell of it is, he controls my fortune. Every last penny. I can't tell him what to do."

"That'll be enough," Bram said. Time to put a stop to this nonsense. It was one thing to enjoy a moment's rest and a woman's touch, and another to surrender all pride.

He gained his feet without too much struggle and helped her to a standing position, too. He managed a slight bow. "Lieutenant Colonel Victor Bramwell. I assure you, I'm in possession of perfect health, a sound mind, and one good-for-nothing cousin."

"I don't understand," she said. "Those blasts . . ."

"Just powder charges. We embedded them in the road, to scare off the sheep."

"You laid black powder charges. To move a flock of sheep." Pulling her hand from his grip, she studied the craters in the road. "Sir, I remain unconvinced of your sanity. But there's no question you are male."

He raised a brow. "That much was never in doubt."

Her only answer was a faint deepening of her blush.

"I assure you, all the lunacy is my cousin's. Lord Payne was merely teasing, having a bit of sport at my expense."

"I see. And you were having a bit of sport at *my* expense, pretending to be injured."

"Come, now." He leaned toward her and murmured, "Are you going to pretend you didn't enjoy it?"

Her eyebrows lifted. And lifted, until they formed perfect twin archer's bows, ready to dispatch poison-tipped darts. "I'm going to pretend I didn't hear that."

She tugged on her glove, and he swallowed reflexively. A few moments ago, she'd pressed that hand to his bared throat, and he'd kissed her lips. All pretending aside, they'd shared a moment of attraction. Sensual. Powerful. Real. Perhaps she'd prefer to deny it, but she couldn't erase his memory of her sweet, lush mouth.

And she couldn't hide that hair. God, that hair. Now that she stood tall, wreathed by midday light, she all but blazed with beauty. Red flames and golden sunlight, each striving to outshine the other.

"You never did tell me your name," he said. "Miss . . . ?"

Before she could answer, a closed-top coach hurtled over the crest of the hill, headed their way. The driver didn't bother to slow, just whipped the team faster as the coach and four bore down on them. All present had to scramble to one side, to avoid being crushed beneath its wheels.

In a protective gesture, Bram positioned himself between the lady and the road. As the carriage went by, he glimpsed a crest painted on its side.

"Oh no," she breathed. "Not the Highwoods." She called after the coach as it rumbled off into the distance. "Mrs. Highwood, wait! Come back. I can explain everything. Don't leave!"

"They seem to have already left."

She turned on Bram, flashing him an angry blue glare. The force of it pushed against his sternum. Not nearly sufficient to move him, but enough to leave an impression.

"I do hope you're happy, sir. If tormenting innocent sheep and blowing ruts in our road weren't enough mischief for you today, you've ruined a young woman's future."

"Ruined?" Bram wasn't in the habit of ruining young ladies—that was his cousin's specialty—but if he ever decided to take up the sport, he'd employ a different technique. He edged closer, lowering his voice. "Really, it was just a little kiss. Or is this about your frock?"

His gaze dipped. Her frock had caught the worst of their encounter. Grass and dirt streaked the yards of shell-pink muslin. A torn flounce drooped to the ground, limp as a forgotten handkerchief. Her neckline had likewise strayed. He wondered if she knew her left breast was one exhortation away from popping free of her bodice altogether. He wondered if he should stop staring at it.

No, he decided. He would do her a favor by staring at it, calling her attention to what needed to be repaired. Indeed. Staring at her half-exposed, emotion-flushed breast was his solemn duty, and Bram was never one to shirk responsibility.

"Ahem." She crossed her arms over her chest, abruptly aborting his mission.

"It's not about me," she said, "or my frock. The woman in that carriage was vulnerable and in need of help, and . . ." She blew out a breath, lifting the stray wisps of hair from her brow. "And now she's gone. They're all gone." She looked him up and down. "So what is it you require? A wheelwright? Supplies? Directions to the main thoroughfare? Just tell me what you need to be on your way, and I will happily supply it."

"We won't put you to any such trouble. So long as this is the road to Summerfield, we'll—"

"Summerfield? You didn't say *Summerfield*."

Vaguely, he understood that she was vexed with him, and that he probably deserved it. But damned if he could bring himself to feel sorry. Her fluster was fiercely attractive. The way her freckles bunched as she frowned at him. The elongation of her pale, slender neck as she stood straight in challenge.

She was tall for a woman. He liked his women tall.

"I did say Summerfield," he replied. "That is the residence of Sir Lewis Finch, is it not?"

Her brow creased. "What business do you have with Sir Lewis Finch?"

"Men's business, love. The specifics needn't concern you."

"Summerfield is my home," she said. "And Sir Lewis Finch is my father. So yes, Lieutenant Colonel Victor Bramwell"—she fired each word as a separate shot—"you concern me."

"Victor Bramwell. It *is* you."

Sir Lewis Finch rose from his desk and crossed the office in eager strides. When Bram attempted to bow, the older man waved off the gesture. Instead, he took Bram's right hand in both of his and pumped it warmly.

"By the devil, it's good to see you. Last we met, you were a green captain, just leaving Cambridge."

"It has been a long time, hasn't it?"

"I was sorry to hear of your father's passing."

"Thank you." Bram cleared his throat awkwardly. "So was I."

He sized up the graying eccentric for any signs of displeasure. Sir Lewis Finch was not only a brilliant inventor, but he'd become a royal advisor. He was said to have the ear of the Prince Regent himself, when he chose to bend it. The right word from this man could have Bram back with his regiment next week.

And idiot that he was, Bram had announced his arrival in the neighborhood by tackling the man's daughter in the road, rending her frock, and kissing her without leave. As strategic campaigns went, this one would not be medal-worthy. Fortunately, Sir Lewis seemed not to have noticed his daughter's bedraggled state on their arrival. But Bram had best conclude this interview before Miss Finch returned and had a chance to relate the tale.

He couldn't be faulted for not making the connection. Save for the blue eyes they shared, she could not have been more different from her father. Miss Finch was slender and remarkably tall for a woman. By contrast, Sir Lewis was thick in the middle and short of stature. His few remaining wisps of silver hair would scarcely brush Bram's epaulet.

"Be seated," the man urged.

Bram tried not to betray much visible relief as he sank into a studded leather chair. When Sir Lewis handed him a drink, he rationed the whiskey in small, self-medicating sips.

As he drank, he studied his surroundings. The library was unlike any gentleman's library he'd ever seen. Naturally, there was a desk. A few chairs. Books, of course. Whole walls of them, populating several floor-to-ceiling mahogany bookshelves. The shelves themselves were separated by plaster columns with Egyptian motifs. Some resembled stalks of papyrus. Others were carved into the shape of pharaohs and queens. And to one side of the room, occupying most of the open space, sat an enormous coffin of solid, cream-colored stone. Its surface was etched, inside and out, with row upon row of tiny symbols.

"Is that marble?" he asked.

"Alabaster. It's a sarcophagus, from the tomb of King . . ." Sir Lewis ruffled his hair. "I forget his name at the moment. I have it somewhere."

"And the inscriptions?"

"Hexes on the outside. On the interior, directions to the underworld." The old man's hoary eyebrows rose. "You can have a lie-down in the thing, if you like. Good for the spine."

"Thank you, no." Bram shuddered.

Sir Lewis clapped his hands. "Well, I don't suppose you've brought two wagons through eight turnpikes just to discuss antiquities over a fine whiskey."

"You know I haven't. Idle chatter isn't my purpose, ever. But I will take the whiskey."

"And dinner later, I hope. Susanna will have already informed the cook."

Susanna. So, her name was Susanna.

The name suited her. Simple, pretty.

Susanna. Susanna Finch.

Rather like the refrain of a song. A cheerful, stubborn sort of song. The sort of tune that persisted, dug a trench in a person's mind and kept merrily chirping there for hours, days . . . even when that person would rather be rid of it. Even when that person would slice off his own great toe just to turn his attention to something, *anything* else.

Susanna. Susanna Finch. Susanna fair with brazen hair.

He turned his gaze to the window, which overlooked an immaculately tended garden. With each herb and shrub he glimpsed, he identified another element of her intriguing, garden-infused perfume. He saw lavender, sage, hyacinth, rose . . . a dozen other plants he couldn't name. But through the open window, the breeze carried their scent to him. Lifting his hair with gentle fingers, just as she had.

He gave himself a shake. She was Sir Lewis's daughter. He could not think of her this way. Or any way.

"So," he said, addressing the older man. "You received my letter?"

Sir Lewis took a seat on the opposite side of his desk. "I did."

"Then you know why I'm here."

"You want your command back."

Bram nodded. "And while I'm here, I wonder if you'd be interested in an apprentice. My cousin has a knack for destruction, and not much else."

"You refer to Payne?"

"Yes."

"Good Lord. You want me to take on a *viscount* as an apprentice?" Sir Lewis chuckled into his whiskey.

"He may be a viscount, but for the next several months he's still my responsibility. Unless someone gives him a useful occupation, he'll have ruined us both by year's end."

"Why don't *you* give him a useful occupation?"

"I won't be here," Bram said, leaning forward and giving the older man a pointed look. "Will I?"

Sir Lewis removed his spectacles and set them aside, rubbing his temples with thumb and forefinger. Bram didn't like the looks of this. Temple rubbing wasn't the sign of a decision going one's way.

"Listen, Bramwell . . ."

"Bram."

"Bram, I admired your father a great deal."

"So did I. So did the nation." Bram's father had distinguished himself in India, rising to the rank of major general and earning a great many honors and awards. "My father admired you and your work."

"I know, I know," Sir Lewis said. "And I was grieved indeed when news reached me of his death. But our friendship is precisely the reason I can't help you. Not the way you've asked."

Bram's gut turned to stone. "What do you mean?"

The older man ruffled his few remaining wisps of silver hair. "Bram, you were shot in the knee."

"Months ago now."

"And you know very well, an injury of that nature can take a year or more to heal. If it heals completely at all." Sir Lewis shook his head. "I cannot, in good conscience, recommend you for field command. You are an infantry officer. How do you propose to lead a battalion of foot soldiers when you can barely walk?"

The question struck Bram in the solar plexus. "I can walk."

"I've no doubt you can walk across this room. Perhaps to the end of the pasture and back. But can you cover ten, twelve, fourteen miles at a grueling pace, day in and day out?"

"Yes," he said firmly. "I can march. I can ride. I can lead my men."

"I'm sorry, Bram. If I sent you back into the field like this, I would be signing your death warrant, and perhaps those of others in your command. Your father was too good a friend. I simply can't."

His palms went damp. Devastation loomed. "Then what am I to do?"

"Retire. Go home."

"I don't have a home." There was money enough, to be sure, but his father had been a second son. He hadn't inherited any property, and he'd never found time to purchase an estate of his own.

"So buy a home. Find a pretty girl to marry. Settle down and start a family."

Bram shook his head. Impossible suggestions, all. He was not about to resign his commission at the age of nine-and-twenty, while England remained at war. And he damned well wasn't going to marry. Like his father before him, he intended to serve until they pried his flintlock from his cold, dead grip. And while officers were permitted to bring their wives, Bram firmly believed gently bred women didn't belong on campaign. His own mother was proof of that. She'd succumbed to the bloody flux in India, a short time before young Bram had been sent to England for school.

He sat forward in his chair. "Sir Lewis, you don't understand. I cut my teeth on rationed biscuit. I could march before I could speak. I'm not a man to settle down. While England remains at war, I cannot and will not resign my commission. It's more than my duty, sir. It's my life. I . . ." He shook his head. "I can't do anything else."

"If you won't resign, there are other ways of helping the war effort."

"Deuce it, I've been through all this with my superiors. I will not accept a so-called promotion that means shuffling papers in the War Office." He gestured at the alabaster sarcophagus in the corner. "You might as well stuff me in that coffin and seal the lid. I am a soldier, not a secretary."

The man's blue eyes softened. "You're a man, Victor. You're human."

"I'm my father's son," he shot back, pounding the desk with his fist. "You cannot keep me down."

He was going too far, but to hell with boundaries. Sir

Lewis Finch was Bram's last and only option. The old man simply couldn't refuse.

Sir Lewis stared at his folded hands for a long, tense moment. Then, with unruffled calm, he replaced his spectacles. "I have no intention of keeping you down. Much to the contrary."

"What do you mean?" Bram was instantly wary.

"I mean precisely what I said. I have done the exact opposite of keeping you down." He reached for a stack of papers. "Bramwell, prepare yourself for elevation."

Chapter Three

usanna, pull yourself together.

After excusing herself to hurriedly tame her disheveled hair and exchange her torn, muddied frock for a fresh blue muslin and matching gloves—in the process, speaking more sharply to Gertrude than the poor maid deserved—she joined Lieutenant Colonel Bramwell's companions in the Red Salon.

As she entered, she stole a quick glance in the hall mirror. Her appearance was repaired, as much as it could be. Her composure, on the other hand, remained splintered in a thousand jagged pieces, all of them rubbing and chafing within her. Some jabbed at her pride. Others stirred up the familiar well of dread that always opened whenever Papa and black powder were mingled. The rest made her prickle all over with awareness. It wasn't a nice feeling.

And it was all *his* fault. The beastly, teasing, handsome sheep-bomber. Who was the man, and what did he want with her father? Hopefully just a polite social call. Though she had to admit, Bramwell didn't seem the type for polite social calls.

The downstairs maid brought in the tray, and Susanna

directed her to place it on a rosewood table with legs carved in the shape of long-whiskered goldfish.

"Tea, gentlemen?" she asked, pulling her gloves snug as she reached for the pot. Pouring tea was just what she needed right now. Such a civilizing force, tea. She would nip sugar with little silver tongs. Stir milk with a tiny spoon. Tiny spoons were incompatible with a state of sensual turmoil.

The thought comforted her. Yes. She would give the men tea, and perhaps a nice dinner. Then they would be on their way, and the world would return to rights. At least her corner of it.

The formerly half-dressed gentleman—Lord Payne, as she now knew him—had located his coat and cravat, and smoothed his hair. He made a suitably aristocratic ornament, at home among the lacquered cabinets and glazed green vases.

As for the officer—a corporal, she'd gathered from his patches—he stood near the plate window, the picture of unease. He glared suspiciously at the dragon-emblazoned carpet, as if expecting the embroidered beast to strike. If it did, she had no doubt he'd kill it handily.

"Will you take tea, Corporal?"

"No."

It occurred to her this might have been the first—and only—word she'd heard from his lips. He was the sort of man one knew, just from looking at him, had an interesting story to tell. She also felt, just as certainly, he would never tell it. Not at knifepoint, much less over tea.

She handed Lord Payne a steaming cup, and he took an immediate, reckless draught. A devilish smile curved her way. "Gunpowder tea? Well done, Miss Finch. I do enjoy a lady with a sense of humor."

Now this one . . . he was a rake. It was written all over

him, in his fine dress and flirtatious manner. He might as
well have had the word embroidered on his waistcoat, between the gold-thread flourishes. She knew all about men
of his sort. Half the young ladies in Spindle Cove were
either fleeing them or pining for them.

Susanna flicked a glance at the closed door to her father's library, wondering what could be keeping him so
long. The sooner these men left, the easier she would
breathe.

Payne reclined in his chair, tilting his head to regard
the brass chandelier. "This is quite a room." He indicated
a display case mounted on the wall. "Are those . . ." His
head cocked. "What *are* those?"

"Rockets, from the Ming dynasty. My father is an avid
collector of antiquities. He takes a particular interest in
historical weaponry." Pouring her own tea, she explained,
"Summerfield has an eclectic theme. This room is in the
chinoiserie style. We have an Austrian morning room,
an Ottoman parlor, and an Italianate terrace. My father's
study takes inspiration from Egypt and the great library
of Alexandria. His medieval collections are housed in the
long hall. Oh, and there's a Grecian folly in the garden."

"Sir Lewis must be a great traveler."

She shook her head, stirring sugar into her cup. "No,
not really. We'd always talked of a Grand Tour, but circumstances were against it. My father brought the world
to Summerfield instead."

And how she loved him for it. Sir Lewis Finch would
never rank among the most attentive or observant of fathers, perhaps. But when she'd needed him most, he'd
never failed her. He'd moved all their possessions and
his entire laboratory to Summerfield, turned down innu-
merable invitations and opportunities to travel over the
years . . . all for Susanna's health and happiness.

"Good, you're all assembled." Her father emerged from the library. Rumpled, as always. Susanna smiled a little, battling the urge to go smooth his hair and straighten his cravat.

Lieutenant Colonel Bramwell followed like a thunder-cloud, dark and restless. Susanna had no urge whatsoever to touch *him*. At least, none that she would admit to. As he moved across the room, she noted that he favored his right leg. Maybe he'd done himself an injury earlier, when he'd tackled her to the ground.

"I have an announcement," her father said, brandishing a sheaf of official-looking papers. "Since Bramwell has failed to muster the appropriate enthusiasm, I thought I would share the good news with you, his friends." He adjusted his spectacles. "In honor of his valor and contributions in the liberation of Portugal, Bramwell has been made an earl. I have here the letters patent from the Prince Regent himself. He will henceforth be known as Lord Rycliff."

Susanna choked on her tea. "What? Lord Rycliff? But that title is extinct. There hasn't been an Earl of Rycliff since . . ."

"Since 1354. Precisely. The title has lain dormant for nearly five centuries. When I wrote to him emphasizing Bramwell's contributions, the Prince Regent was glad of my suggestion to revive it."

A powder blast in the Red Salon could not have stunned Susanna more. Her gaze darted to the officer in question. For a man elevated to the peerage, he didn't look happy about it, either.

"Good God," Payne remarked. "An earl? This can't be borne. As if it weren't bad enough that he controls my fortune, my cousin now outranks me. Just what does this earldom include, anyhow?"

"Not much besides the honor of the title. No real lands to speak of, except for the—"

"The castle," Susanna finished, her voice remote.

Her castle.

Of course, Rycliff Castle didn't belong to her, but she'd always felt possessive of it. No one else seemed to want the pile of ruins, after all. And when they'd first taken this house and she'd been so weakened from fever, Papa had called it hers. *You must get well, Susanna Jane*, he'd said to her. *You have your very own castle to explore.*

"Susanna, show them all the model." Her father looked pointedly at a high shelf on the room's southern wall.

"Papa, I'm sure the lieutenant colonel wouldn't be interested in—"

"He's Lord Rycliff now. Of course he'll be interested. It's his castle."

His castle. She couldn't believe it. Why hadn't her father told her anything about this?

"The model, dear," her father prompted. "I'd fetch the thing on my own, but you know you're the only one tall enough to reach that shelf."

With a quiet sigh, Susanna dutifully rose from her chair and crossed the room to retrieve the clay model she'd made of Rycliff Castle more than a decade ago. Sometimes life could be astonishingly efficient in dispensing mortifications. In the space of a minute, she would be exposed before three male visitors to be both freakishly tall and an abominably poor sculptor. What would come next? Perhaps her father would invite the men to count her freckles, one by one. They'd be here until moonrise.

Suddenly, Bramwell was at her side.

"This?" he asked, touching a finger to the model's edge. She cringed, wishing she could deny it. "Yes, thank you."

As he retrieved the model from the shelf, she stole

glances at him out of the corner of her eye. She had to admit, the Rycliff title suited him. Give the man a mace and a chain mail vest, and she could easily have mistaken him for a medieval warrior, squeezed through some rocky gap in the centuries to emerge in modern day. From the sheer size of him, large and solid all over, to that squared jaw, shadowed with a day's or more growth of whiskers. He moved with more power than grace, and he wore his dark hair long, tied back at his nape with a bit of leather cord. And the way he'd looked at her just before that kiss—as though he would devour her, and she would enjoy it—was straight from the Dark Ages.

As he presented the crumbling mess of sun-dried clay and pasted-on moss, Susanna fought the urge to blow dust off the thing. Evidently the maids couldn't reach this shelf, either.

"Isn't it clever?" Her father took the model from Bramwell's hands and held it up. "Susanna made this when she was fifteen years old."

"Fourteen," she corrected, cursing herself a moment later. Because "fourteen" somehow made it better?

With a flourish, her father placed the model on a table in the center of the room. The men reluctantly gathered around it. Bramwell glowered at the lumpy gray diorama.

"It may not look like much," her father said, "but Rycliff Castle's history is legend. Built by William the Conqueror himself, then enlarged by Henry the Eighth. It's situated on a bluff, right on the sea's edge. Below is the cove, see?" He pointed. "And the water's a lovely color in truth, not this murky gray."

Susanna touched her ear. "There was blue paint, once. It's flaked away."

Sir Lewis went on, "The cove was a bustling medieval

port. Then, in the thirteenth century, there was a terrific landslide. The result of storms, erosion. No one knows. Half of the original castle fell into the sea, and what's left is in ruins. But come along, Bramwell." Sir Lewis prodded the officer. "Look happy. Haven't you always wanted a castle?"

At his side, Susanna watched the man's massive hand gather into a fist. She heard knuckles crack.

"Sir Lewis, I'm honored, and I appreciate your recommendation, but this"—he waved at the model—"is not what I had in mind. I'm not interested in playing at knights and dragons."

Ignoring him, Sir Lewis jabbed his forefinger on the table's lacquered surface, to what would have been the castle's western side. "The village would be just about here, down in the valley. Charming little place." Then he turned and squinted at the far corner of the room. "And just about where that jade medallion is displayed"—he pointed—"would be Cherbourg, on the northern coast of France."

Bramwell glanced toward the jade, then looked back at Sir Lewis. His brow rose in silent question.

Sir Lewis clapped a hand on the officer's shoulder. "You did want a command, Bramwell. Well, you've just been granted a castle on England's southern coast, not fifty miles distant from the enemy. As the new lord, you'll raise a militia to defend it."

"What?" Susanna blurted out. "A militia, here?"

She must have misheard, or misunderstood. These men were meant to take tea—perhaps a nice dinner—and then leave. Never to be seen again. She could not become *neighbors* with the sheep-bomber. And heavens . . . a militia? What would become of the ladies and Mrs. Nichols's rooming house? There were no men like these in Spindle Cove. The absence of rakes and officers was the village's primary attraction.

"Papa, please stop jesting," she said lightly. "We don't want to waste the gentlemen's time. You know very well, a militia would be useless here."

"Useless?" Bramwell cut her a look. "Militias aren't useless. To the contrary, they're essential. In case you were unaware, Miss Finch, England is at war."

"Naturally, I'm aware of that. But everyone knows the threat of French invasion has passed. They've had no real naval clout since Trafalgar, and Bonaparte's forces are so depleted after that drubbing in Russia, he hasn't the strength to invade anyone. As matters stand, it's all he can do to hold Spain. With Wellington's forces on the march, even that grasp is tenuous."

The room went silent, and Bramwell frowned at her, intently. Yet another instance of *Mrs. Worthington's Wisdom* proved wrong. If a woman's intellect was in any way analogous to her undergarments, men should thrill to see it revealed. Strangely enough, Susanna had never known it to work that way.

"You know a great deal about current events," he said.

"I am an Englishwoman with an interest in the war's outcome. I take the trouble to inform myself."

"If you're so well informed, you should also know we're at war with not only France, but America. Not to mention, the coastline is rife with privateers and smugglers of every stripe." With a single fingertip, he drew the model toward him. "I'm astonished this Rycliff Castle has gone unsecured so long."

"There's nothing astonishing about it." Reaching out, she tugged the model right back. "No one would attempt to come ashore here. As my father said, the coast has changed since the Normans invaded. The landslide formed a sort of reef. Only the smallest fishing boats can navigate it, even at high tide. Many a ship has foundered and wrecked in that cove. Not even the smugglers trouble with it." She looked up at him, pointedly. "Nature affords us protection enough. We don't need uniformed men. Not here."

Their gazes locked and held. Something defensive flared in those bold green eyes, and she wondered at the thoughts crossing his mind. Not thoughts of kissing her, she'd wager.

"I'm afraid," Sir Lewis said, chuckling, "this happens to be a disagreement of the most vexing sort."

Susanna smiled. "The sort where the woman has the right of it?"

"No, my dear. The sort where both sides have equal merit."

"How do you mean?"

Her father motioned toward the chairs, directing them all to sit. "Susanna, you are correct," he said, once all were settled. "The chances of any enemy invading Spindle Cove are so small as to be infinitesimal. However—"

Suddenly, Lord Payne choked and sputtered, replacing his teacup with an abrupt crack.

"What's the matter with you?" Bramwell asked.

"Nothing, nothing." Payne dabbed at his spattered waistcoat. "Sir Lewis, did you say Spindle Cove?"

"Yes."

"This place, here. Is Spindle Cove."

"Yes," Susanna echoed slowly. "Why?"

"Oh, no reason." Payne rubbed his mouth with one hand, as if massaging away a laugh. "Please, do go on."

"As I was saying," Sir Lewis continued, "chances of invasion are slim indeed. However, Bramwell here will tell you that a solid defense is based on the appearance of readiness, not the probability of attack. Similar points along the coast have been fortified with Martello towers, defended by local volunteer militias. Spindle Cove cannot appear to be the weak link in the chain."

"There's nothing weak about our village, Papa. Visitors know it to be perfectly safe. If this militia comes to pass, that reputation can only suff—"

"Susanna, dear." Her father sighed loudly. "That's quite enough."

It wasn't nearly enough. *Papa, do you know what kind of man this is?* she longed to argue. *He's a bomber of defenseless sheep, an enemy of flounced muslin frocks, and a kisser of unsuspecting women! A perfect beast. We can't have him here. We can't.*

Only deep, abiding respect for her father kept her quiet.

He went on, "To be perfectly honest, there is another reason. I am the only other local gentleman, you see. This duty should have been mine. The Duke of Tunbridge is responsible for the Sussex militia, and he's been hounding me for over a year now to provide a display of our local readiness." His eyes fell to the carpet. "And so I have promised him one, at this year's midsummer fair."

"The midsummer fair? Oh, but that's not even a month away," Susanna said, dismayed. "And we've always made the fair a children's festival. Suits of armor, crossbows. A few melons fired out to sea with the old trebuchet."

"I know, dear. But this year, we'll have to treat our neighbors—and the duke—to a proper military review instead." He leaned forward, bracing his arms on his knees. "If Bramwell agrees, that is. If he doesn't embrace the Rycliff title and take on this militia as his duty . . . the task will fall to me."

"Papa, you can't." The thought alone made Susanna

wilt. Her father could not be responsible for embodying a militia company. He was aging, and his heart was weak. And he was her only family. She owed him her life, in more ways than one. The prospect of welcoming this horrid Bramwell and his friends into their safe, secure community filled her with dread. But if the only alternative would endanger her father's health, how could she argue against this militia scheme?

The answer was plain. She couldn't.

Her father addressed the officer. "Bramwell, you've led entire regiments into battle. I'm asking you to train a company of four-and-twenty men. Believe me, I know full well this is like asking an African lion to serve a barn cat's purpose. But it *is* a position of command, and one I'm free to offer you. And it's only a month. If you do well with it . . . after midsummer, it could lead to something more."

A meaningful look passed between the men, and Bramwell—now Lord Rycliff, she supposed—was silent for a long moment. Susanna held her breath. A half hour ago, she'd wished for nothing more than to see the back of this man and his party. And now, she found herself forced into a most unpleasant occupation.

Hoping he would stay.

At length, he stood, pulling on the front of his coat. "Very well, then."

"Excellent." Rising to his feet, Papa clapped his hands together and rubbed them briskly. "I'll write to the duke forthwith. Susanna, you're always fond of walking, and there's ample time before dinner. Why don't you show the man his castle?"

"This is the way," Susanna said, leading the men off the dirt lane and onto an ancient road grown over with grass.

The path was a familiar one. Over the years she'd resided in Spindle Cove, Susanna must have walked it thousands of times. She knew each curve of the land, every last mottled depression in the road. More than once, she'd covered this distance in the dark of night with nary a misstep.

Today, she stumbled.

He was there, catching her elbow in his strong, sure grip. She hadn't realized he was following so close. Just when she thought she'd regained her balance, his heat and presence unsteadied her all over again.

"Are you well?"

"Yes. I think so." In an effort to dispel the awkwardness, she joked, "Mondays are country walks; Tuesdays, sea bathing . . ."

He didn't laugh. Nor even smile. He released her without comment, moving on ahead to take the lead. His strides were long, but she noticed he was still favoring that right leg.

She did what a good healer ought never do. She hoped it hurt.

Perhaps, with that swooping tackle in the road, he had saved her from losing a few toes. But if not for him, there would have been no danger in the first place. If not for him, right now she would be seeing the Highwoods settled in at the rooming house. Poor Diana. Poor Minerva, for that matter. Charlotte was young and resilient, at least.

They climbed the rest of the way in silence. Once they crested the sandstone ridge, Susanna pulled to a stop. "Well," she said between deep inhalations, "there it is, my lord. Rycliff Castle."

The castle ruins sat perched at the tip of an outcropping, an arrowhead of green heath jutting over the sea. Four stone turrets, a few standing arches . . . here and there, a bit of wall. This was all that remained. In the background spread the English Channel, now turning a lovely shade of periwinkle in the dimming afternoon.

Silence reigned for a long minute as the men took in the scene. Susanna kept quiet, too, as she tried to see the ancient fortress through fresh eyes. As a young girl, she'd been taken with the romance of it. When one viewed the castle as a picturesque ruin, the absent walls and ceilings were the best features. The missing parts were invitations to dream; they inspired the imagination. Looking upon this as a prospective residence, however, she could only imagine the missing parts would inspire grave misgivings. Or perhaps hives.

"And the village?" he asked.

"You can see it from here." She led them through a standing fragment of arched corridor, across an open expanse of grass that had once been the castle's courtyard, to the bluff, where they could overlook the crescent-shaped cove and the valley that sheltered her beloved community. From here, it looked so small and insignificant. With any luck, it would remain beneath his notice entirely.

He said, "I'll be needing a closer look tomorrow."

"It's nothing special," she hedged. "Just an average English village. Hardly worth your time. Cottages, a church, a few shops."

"Surely there's an inn," Lord Payne said.

"There is a rooming house," Susanna said, leading them back from the edge of the bluff. "The Queen's Ruby. But I'm afraid it is completely occupied at this time of year. Summer visitors, you understand, come to enjoy the sea." *And to escape men like you.*

"An inn won't be necessary." Lord Rycliff walked slowly about the ruins. He propped a hand against a nearby wall and leaned on it, as if to test the wall's soundness. "We'll be staying here."

This statement was received with universal incredulity. Even the stones seemed to throw it back at him, rejecting the words as false.

"*Here*," the corporal said.

"Yes," Lord Rycliff said. "Here. We'll need to begin settling in, if we're to make camp before nightfall. Go see to the carts, Thorne."

Thorne nodded his compliance and quit the place immediately, descending the way they'd come.

"You can't mean to stay *here*," Lord Payne said. "Have you *seen* here?"

"I have," Rycliff answered. "I'm looking at it. So we'll be camping. That's what militiamen do."

"I'm not a militiaman," Payne said. "And I don't camp."

Susanna would guess he didn't. Not in those fine boots, at least.

"Well, you camp now," Rycliff said. "And you're a militiaman now, as well."

"Oh no. Think again, Bram. You're not pulling me into your tin soldier brigade."

"I'm not leaving you a choice. You need to learn some discipline, and this is the perfect opportunity." He cast a glance around. "Since you're so fond of setting blazes, see if you can start a fire."

Susanna put a hand on Rycliff's sleeve, hoping to claim his attention.

She got it. His full, unwavering attention. His intent gaze ranged over her face, searching out her every feature and flaw.

"Forgive the interruption," she said, releasing his sleeve. "But surely camping isn't necessary. My father may not have made the express invitation as yet, but I'm certain he intends to offer you lodging at Summerfield."

"Then give your father my thanks. But I will respectfully decline."

"Why?"

"I'm meant to be defending the coast. Difficult to do that from a mile inland."

"But my lord, you do understand this militia business is all for show? My father's not truly concerned about an invasion."

"Perhaps he should be." He glanced at his cousin, who was currently snapping dead branches from an ivy-covered wall. With a tilt of his head, Rycliff drew her aside. "Miss Finch, it's not wise for officers to quarter in the same house with an unmarried gentlewoman. Have a care for your reputation, if your father does not."

"Have a care for my reputation?" She had to laugh. Then she lowered her voice. "This, from the man who flattened me in the road and kissed me without leave?"

"Precisely." His eyes darkened.

His meaning washed over her in a wave of hot, sensual awareness. Surely he wasn't implying . . .

No. He wasn't implying at all. Those hard jade eyes were giving her a straightforward message, and he underscored it with a slight flex of his massive arms: *I am every bit as dangerous as you suppose. If not more so.*

"Take your kind invitation and run home with it. When soldiers and maids live under the same roof, things happen. And if you happened to find yourself under me again . . ." His hungry gaze raked her body. "You wouldn't escape so easily."

She gasped. "You are a beast."

"Just a man, Miss Finch. Just a man."

ram told himself he was looking out for Miss Finch's safety as he watched her picking her way down the rocky slope. He told himself a lie. In truth, he was utterly entranced by her figure in retreat, the way her curves gave a saucy little bounce with each downward step.

He would dream of those breasts tonight. How they'd felt trapped beneath him, so soft and warm.

Blast. This day had not gone as planned. By this time, he was supposed to be well on his way to the Brighton Barracks, preparing to leave for Portugal and rejoin the war. Instead, he was . . . an earl, suddenly. Stuck at this ruined castle, having pledged to undertake the military equivalent of teaching nursery school. And to make it all worse, he was plagued with lust for a woman he couldn't have. Couldn't even touch, if he ever wanted his command back.

As if he sensed Bram's predicament, Colin started to laugh.

"What's so amusing?"

"Only that you've been played for a greater fool than you realize. Didn't you hear them earlier? This is Spindle Cove, Bram. *Spindle. Cove.*"

"You keep saying that like I should know the name. I don't."

"You really must get around to the clubs. Allow me to enlighten you. Spindle Cove—or Spinster Cove, as we call it—is a seaside holiday village. Good families send their fragile-flower daughters here for the restorative sea air. Or whenever they don't know what else to do with them. My friend Carstairs sent his sister here last summer, when she grew too fond of the stable boy."

"And so . . . ?"

"And so, your little militia plan? Doomed before it even starts. Families send their daughters and wards here because it's safe. It's safe because there are no men. That's why they call it Spinster Cove."

"There have to be men. There's no such thing as a village with no men."

"Well, there may be a few servants and tradesmen. An odd soul or two down there with a shriveled twig and a couple of currants dangling between his legs. But there aren't any *real* men. Carstairs told us all about it. He couldn't believe what he found when he came to fetch his sister. The women here are man-eaters."

Bram was scarcely paying attention. He focused his gaze to catch the last glimpses of Miss Finch as her figure receded into the distance. She was like a sunset all to herself, her molten bronze hair aglow as she sank beneath the bluff's horizon. Fiery. Brilliant. When she disappeared, he felt instantly cooler.

And then, only then, did he turn to his yammering cousin. "What were you saying?"

"We have to get out of here, Bram. Before they take our bollocks and use them for pincushions."

Bram made his way to the nearest wall and propped

one shoulder against it, resting his knee. Damn, that climb had been steep. "Let me understand this," he said, discreetly rubbing his aching thigh under the guise of brushing off loose dirt. "You're suggesting we leave because the village is full of spinsters? Since when do *you* complain about an excess of women?"

"These are not your normal spinsters. They're . . . they're unbiddable. And excessively educated."

"Oh. Frightening, indeed. I'll stand my ground when facing a French cavalry charge, but an educated spinster is something different entirely."

"You mock me now. Just you wait. You'll see, these women are a breed unto themselves."

"The women aren't my concern."

Save for one woman, and she didn't live in the village. She lived at Summerfield, and she was Sir Lewis Finch's daughter, and she was absolutely off limits—no matter how he suspected Miss Finch would become Miss Vixen in bed.

Colin could make all the disparaging remarks he wished about bluestockings. Bram knew clever women always made the best lovers. He especially appreciated a woman who knew something of the world beyond fashion and the theater. For him, listening to Miss Finch expound on the weakened state of Napoleon's army had been like listening to a courtesan read aloud from her pillow book. Arousing beyond measure. And then he'd made the idiotic—though inevitable—mistake of picturing her naked. All that luminous hair and milky skin, tumbled on crisp white sheets . . .

To disrupt the erotic chain of thought, he pressed hard against the knotted muscle in his thigh. Pain sliced through the lingering haze of desire.

He pulled the flask from his breast pocket and downed

a bracing swallow of whiskey. "The women aren't my concern," he repeated. "I'm here to train the local men. And there *are* men here, somewhere. Fishermen, farmers, tradesmen, servants. If what you say is correct, and they're outnumbered by managing females . . . Well, then they'll be eager for a chance to flex their muscles, prove themselves." Just as he was.

Bram walked to the gateway and was relieved to see the wagons approaching. He couldn't remain lost in lustful thoughts when there was work to be done. Pitching tents, watering and feeding the horses, building a fire.

After one last sip, he recapped his flask and jammed it in his pocket. "Let's have a proper look at this place before the dark settles in."

They began in the center and worked their way out. Of course, the current center wasn't truly the center, since half the castle had fallen into the sea.

Turning back toward the north, Bram now recognized the arch they'd entered through as the original gatehouse. Walls spread out from the structure on either side. Even in spots where the walls had crumbled, one could easily trace the places where they'd stood. Here in the bailey area, low, moss-covered ridges served to mark interior walls and corridors. To the southern, waterfront side, a four-leafed clover of round turrets hugged the bluff, connected by sheer, windowless stretches of stone.

"This must have been the keep," he mused, walking through the arched entryway to stand in the center of the four soaring towers.

Colin stepped inside one of the dark, hollow turrets. "The staircases are intact, being stone. But, of course, the wooden floors are long gone." He tilted his head, peering toward the dark corners overhead. "Impressive collection of cobwebs. Are those swallows I hear chirping?"

"Those?" Bram listened. "Those would be bats."

"Right. Bats. So this inches-deep muck I'm standing in would be . . . Brilliant." He stomped back into the court-yard, wiping his boots on the mossy turf. "Lovely place you have here, cousin."

It *was* lovely. As the sky turned from blue to purple, a sprinkling of stars appeared above the castle ruins. Bram knew he'd made the right decision to decline quarter at Summerfield. All concerns of duty and restraint aside, he never felt comfortable in stuffy English manor houses. Their door lintels were too low for him, and their beds were too small for him. Such homes weren't for him, full stop.

The open country was where he belonged. He didn't need a place like Summerfield. However, his empty stomach was beginning to argue he should have accepted a meal at Sir Lewis's table, at least.

A low bleat drew his attention downward. A lamb stood at his feet, nosing the tassel on his boot.

"Oh look," said Colin brightly. "Dinner."

"Where did this come from?"

Thorne approached. "Followed us up. The drivers say it's been nosing around the carts ever since the blasts."

Bram examined the creature. Must have been separated from its mother. By this time of summer, it was well past the age of weaning. It was also well past the age of being adorable. The lamb looked up at him and gave another plaintive bleat.

"I don't suppose we have any mint jelly?" Colin asked.

"We can't eat it," Bram said. "The beast belongs to some crofter hereabouts, and whoever he is will be miss-ing it."

"The crofter will never know." A wolfish smile spread

across his cousin's face as he reached to pat the lamb's woolly flank. "We'll destroy the evidence."

Bram shook his head. "Not going to happen. Give up your lamb chop fantasies. His home can't be far. We'll find it tomorrow."

"Well, we do have to eat something tonight, and I don't see a ready alternative."

Thorne strode toward the fire, carrying a brace of hares, already split and gutted. "There's your alternative."

"Where did you get those?" Colin asked.

"On the heath." Crouching on the ground, Thorne drew a knife from his boot and began skinning the animals with ruthless efficiency. The rich smell of blood soon mingled with smoke and ash.

Colin stared at the officer. "Thorne, you scare me. I'm not ashamed to say it."

Bram said, "You'll learn to appreciate him. Thorne always comes up with a meal. We had the best-stocked officers' mess on the Peninsula."

"Well, at least that satisfies one type of hunger," Colin said. "Now, for the other. I've an insatiable craving for female companionship that must be addressed. I don't sleep alone." He looked from Bram to Thorne. "What? You've just returned from years on the Peninsula. I'd think you two would be positively salivating."

Thorne made a gruff sound. "There's women in Portugal and Spain." He set aside one skinned carcass and reached for the other hare. "And I've already found one here."

"What?" Colin sputtered. "Who? When?"

"The widow what sold us eggs at the last turnpike. She'll have me."

Colin looked to Bram, as if to say, *Am I to believe this?*

Bram shrugged. Thorne was nothing if not resource-ful. At every place of encampment, he'd always ferreted out the local game and found a local woman. He hadn't seemed particularly attached to any of them. Or perhaps the women simply didn't attach themselves to Thorne.

Attachments were Bram's problem. He was an offi-cer, a gentleman of wealth, and, all things being equal, he preferred to converse with a woman before tupping her senseless. Taken together, these qualities seemed to encourage a woman's attachment, and romantic entangle-ments were the one thing he couldn't afford.

Colin straightened, obviously piqued. "Now wait just a minute. I will happily be outdone when it comes to hunting game, but I will not be . . . outgamed, where the fairer sex is concerned. You couldn't know it, Thorne, but my reputation is legendary. Legendary. Give me one day down in the village. I don't care if they *are* ape-leading spinsters. I'll be under skirts in this neighborhood long before you are, and far more often."

"Keep your pegos buttoned, both of you." Bram gave the sleeping lamb at his knee a sullen nudge. "The only way we'll accomplish our task and be quit of this place is if the local men cooperate. And the local men won't be eager to cooperate if we're seducing their sisters and daughters."

"What precisely are you saying, Bram?"

"I'm saying, no women. Not so long as we're encamped here." He cast a glance at Thorne. "That's an order."

The lieutenant made no reply, save to skewer the two skinned hares on a sharpened branch.

"Since when do I take orders from you?" Colin asked.

Bram leveled a gaze at him. "Since my father died, and I came back from the Peninsula to find you stickpin-deep in debt, that's when. I don't relish the duty, but I hold your fortune in trust for the next several months. So long as I'm paying your bills, you'll do as I say. Unless you get married, in which case you'd spare us both the better part of a year's aggravation."

"Oh yes. Marriage being a fine way for a man to spare himself aggravation." Colin shoved to his feet and stalked away, into the shadows.

"Where do you think you're going?" Bram called. Colin was welcome to have his adolescent sulk, but he should take care. They hadn't checked the soundness of the entire castle, and there were those steep bluffs nearby . . .

"I'm going to have a piss, dear cousin. Or did you want me to keep my pego buttoned for that, too?"

Bram wasn't any happier than Colin about this arrangement. It seemed ridiculous that a man of six-and-twenty, a viscount since his tender years, should even require a trustee. But the terms of his inheritance—meant to encourage the timely production of a legitimate heir—clearly stipulated that the Payne fortune was held in trust until Colin either married or turned twenty-seven.

And so long as Colin was his responsibility, Bram knew of no better way to handle the situation than to make his cousin a soldier. He'd taken far less promising fellows and drilled a sense of discipline and duty into them. Deserters, debtors, hardened criminals . . . the man seated across the fire, for one. If Samuel Thorne had made good, any man had hope.

"Tomorrow we'll start recruiting volunteers," he told his corporal.

Thorne nodded, turning the roasting hares on the spit.

"The village seems the likely place to begin."

Another barely perceptible nod.

"Sheepdogs," Thorne mused sometime later. "Perhaps I'll find a few. They'd come in useful. Then again, hounds are better for game."

"No dogs," Bram said. He wasn't one for pets. "We'll only be here a month."

A rustling sound in the shadows had them both turning their heads. A bat, perhaps. Or maybe a snake. Then again, he supposed it was just as likely a rat.

"What we need in this place," Thorne said, "is a cat."

Bram scowled. "For God's sake, I am not acquiring a cat."

Thorne looked to the woolly beast at his knee and cocked a brow. "You seem to have acquired a lamb, my lord."

"The lamb goes home tomorrow."

"And if he doesn't?"

"He's dinner."

Chapter Five

n a village of women, secrets had shorter life expectancies than gnats. The moment she opened the door of Bright's All Things the next morning, Susanna was inundated with queries and questions. She ought to have known she would be besieged. Young ladies crowded around her like hens after corn, pecking for bits of information.

"Is it true, what we've heard? What they're saying, is it true?" Nineteen-year-old Sally, the second eldest of the Bright children, leaned eagerly over the counter.

"That would depend." Susanna lifted her hands to untie the ribbons of her bonnet. As she worked the knots loose, anticipation in the shop built to a palpable fever.

"Depend on what?"

"On who 'they' are, and precisely what it is they're saying." She spoke calmly. Someone had to.

"They say we've been invaded!" Violet Winterbottom said. "By *men*."

"What else would we be invaded by? Wolves?"

Susanna looked about the shop, taking a moment to collect her thoughts and enjoy the familiar splendor. This sight never failed to enchant her. The first time she'd entered Bright's All Things shop, she'd felt as though she'd stumbled upon Ali Baba's treasure cave.

The shop's front was lined with south-facing diamond-paned windows, which admitted an abundance of golden sunlight. Each of its other three walls was stacked, floor to lofty ceiling, with shelves—and those shelves were crammed with colorful goods of every sort. Bolts of silk and lace, quills and bottles of ink, buttons and brilliants, charcoal and pigments, comfits and pickled limes, tooth powder, dusting powder, and much, much more—all of it sparkling in the midday sun.

"The inn's scullery maid had it all from her brother." Sally's cheeks were pink with excitement. "A band of officers have encamped on the bluffs."

"Is it true there's a lord in their party?" Violet asked.

Susanna removed her bonnet and laid it aside. "Yes, some officers are temporarily encamped on the castle bluffs. And no, there is not a lord in the party." She paused. "There are two."

The squeal of excitement occasioned by this pronouncement quite pained her ears. She looked to Sally. "Could you show me those two spools of lace again? The ones I looked at Thursday last? I couldn't decide between the—"

"Hang the lace," Sally said. "Tell us more of these gentlemen. Cruel thing, you know we are dying of anticipation."

"Miss Finch!" A most unexpected woman pushed her way to the fore. "Miss Finch, what is this I hear about lords?"

"Mrs. Highwood?" Susanna blinked at the lace-capped widow in disbelief. "What are you still doing here?"

"We're all here," Minerva called, standing behind her mother, arm-in-arm with Charlotte. From the counter, Diana gave a shy wave.

Somehow, Susanna had missed them in the initial crush. "But . . . But I saw your carriage leaving yesterday."

"Mama sent it to fetch all our things," Charlotte said, bouncing on her toes. "We're to stay here in Spindle Cove for the summer! Isn't it marvelous?"

"Yes." Susanna laughed with relief. "Yes, it is. I'm so glad."

Even Mrs. Highwood smiled. "I just knew it was the right decision. My friends always say my intuition is unparalleled. Why, just this morning two lords have arrived in the neighborhood. While we're here, Diana can get well *and* get married."

Hm. Susanna wasn't so sure about *that*.

"Now tell us everything about them," Sally insisted.

"There truly is not much to tell. Three gentlemen arrived in the neighborhood yesterday afternoon. They include a Lieutenant Colonel Bramwell, a Corporal Thorne, and Bramwell's cousin, Lord Payne. For his service to the Crown, Bramwell has been granted the title Earl of Rycliff. The castle is his." She turned to Sally. "May I see the lace now?"

"The castle is his?" asked Violet. "How can that be? A man just marches into town, and suddenly a centuries-old castle is his for the asking?"

Mrs. Lange harrumphed. "That's a man for you. Always taking, never asking."

"He was awarded the earldom in recognition of his valor, apparently," Susanna said. "He's been tasked with raising a local militia and providing a review. The field day will take the place of our usual midsummer fair."

"What?" Charlotte cried. "No midsummer fair? But I was so looking forward to it."

"I know, dear. We all looked forward to it. But we'll find other ways to amuse ourselves this summer, never fear."

"I'm sure you will." Sally gave her a knowing look.

"Cor. Two lords and an officer. No wonder you're taken with the lace this morning, Miss Finch. With the new gents in residence, all you ladies will want to look your best."

Several ladies pressed into a circle around her, investigating the wares with fresh interest.

Miss Kate Taylor didn't join them. Instead, she crossed the room to join Susanna. As Spindle Cove's music tutor, Kate was one of the rooming house's few year-round residents. She was also delightfully sensible, and among Susanna's closest friends.

"You look out of sorts," Kate said quietly.

"I'm not worried," she lied. "We've worked too hard to build this community, and our cause is too important. We won't let a few men divide us."

Kate looked around the room. "It seems to be starting already."

The group of young women had separated in two groups—those eagerly absorbing Sally Bright's beautification advice huddled on the left. On the right, the remainder stood in a defensive knot, casting worried glances at their gloves and slippers.

She'd feared precisely this reaction. A handful of the young ladies in Spindle Cove would fall victim to scarlet fever, eagerly chasing after the redcoats. The awkward, demure majority would crawl back into their protective shells, like hermit crabs.

"Diana must have a new ribbon," Mrs. Highwood decided. "Coral pink. She always looks her best in coral pink. And a deep green for Charlotte."

"And for Miss Minerva?" Sally asked.

Mrs. Highwood made a dismissive wave. "No ribbons for Minerva. She makes a knot of them, removing and donning those spectacles."

Susanna craned her neck for a glimpse of the bespectacled girl in question, anxious for her feelings. Fortunately,
Minerva had migrated to the shop's rear corner, where she
seemed to be examining some bottles of ink. The middle
Highwood sister was not what one could call a conven-
tional beauty, but a keen intellect lived behind those spectacles, and it didn't need a ribbon to adorn it.

"How do the men look?" Young Charlotte turned to Susanna. "Are they terribly handsome?"

"What has that to do with anything?"

Mrs. Highwood nodded sagely. "Charlotte, Miss Finch
is absolutely right. It makes no difference whether these
lords are handsome. So long as they possess a good fortune. Looks fade; gold doesn't."

"Mrs. Highwood, the young ladies needn't concern
themselves with the gentlemen's looks, fortunes, or favorite colors of ribbon. I don't believe they'll be mingling
socially."

"What? But they must, surely. They can't stay all the
way up there at that damp castle."

"They can't stay far away enough for me," Susanna
muttered. But no one heard her uncharacteristically un-
charitable remark, because at that moment Finn and
Rufus Bright appeared in the storeroom door.

"They're coming!" Finn shouted. "We spotted them
just—"

His twin finished, "Just down the lane. We're off to
mind their horses." The two disappeared as quickly as
they'd come.

Education was anywhere a person sought it, Susanna
believed. She learned something new every day. Today,
she learned what it felt like to be at the center of a wilde-
beest stampede.

Every person in the shop thundered past her, pushing

and pressing toward the diamond-paned windows for a look at the approaching men. She flattened herself against the door, holding her breath until the dust settled.

"Cor," Sally said. "They are handsome as anything."

"Oh!" said Mrs. Highwood, apparently too overset for multisyllabic words. "Oh."

"I can't see a thing," Charlotte whimpered, stamping her feet. "Minerva, your elbow is in my ear."

Susanna stood on tiptoe, stretching her neck for a glimpse. She didn't have to stretch far. There were times her freakish height came in handy.

There they were. All three of them, dismounting their horses on the village green. The Bright boys eagerly accepted the reins.

Pressed around her on all sides, the ladies cooed over Lord Payne's handsome features and debonair mien. Susanna couldn't spare the man a glance. Her attention was drawn immediately and unswervingly to the horrid Lord Rycliff, who was looking more dark and medieval than ever with his unshaven jaw and that impudently long hair tied in a thick queue at his nape. She couldn't stop looking at him. And she couldn't look at him without . . . *feeling* him. His solid warmth against her chest. His strong grip on her elbow. His hot kiss brushing over her lips.

"My goodness," Kate whispered in her ear. "They are rather . . . manly, aren't they?"

Yes, Susanna thought. God help her, he was.

"And that dark one is frightfully big."

"You should feel him up close."

Kate's eyes went wide, and a startled laugh burst from her lips. "What did you just say?"

"Er . . . I said, you should see him up close."

"No. You didn't. You said I should *feel* him up close." Her hazel eyes lit with a mischievous twinkle.

Ears hot with embarrassment, Susanna fluttered a hand in weak defense. "I'm a healer. We assess with our hands."

"If you say so." Kate turned back to the window.

Violet sighed loudly. "I suppose this means we'll have to cancel our afternoon salon."

"Of course not," Susanna countered. "There's no need to alter our plans. Most likely, the men won't trouble with us at all. But if the new Lord Rycliff and his party do see fit to take tea . . . We must do our best to welcome them."

This statement was met with a flurry of enthusiasm and a cyclone of alarm. Objections rose up all around her.

"Miss Finch, they won't understand. They'll mock us, just like the gentlemen in Town."

"To think, playing for an earl? I haven't anything fine enough to wear."

"I shall die of mortification. Positively *die*."

"*Ladies*." Susanna lifted her voice. "There is no cause for concern. We will go on as we always do. In a month's time, this militia business will be over and these men will have gone. Nothing in Spindle Cove will be the different for their visit."

For her friends' sake, she must maintain a brave front in the face of this invasion. But she knew, staring through the small window in the door, that her words were false. It was too late. Things were already changing in Spindle Cove.

Something had altered in *her*.

After dismounting from his gelding, Bram straightened his coat and had a look about the place. "A fair enough village," he mused. "Rather charming."

"I knew it," Colin said, adding a petulant curse.

The green was expansive, dotted with shade trees. Across the lane sat a neat row of buildings. He took the largest to be the inn. Narrow dirt lanes lined with cottages curved out from the village's center, following the contours of the valley. Toward the cove side of the village, he spied a cluster of humble cottages. Fishermen's abodes, no doubt. And in the center of the green loomed the church—a soaring cathedral, remarkably grand for a village of this size. He supposed it was a remnant of that medieval port city Sir Lewis had mentioned.

"This place is clean," Colin said carefully. "Too clean. And too quiet. It's unnatural. It's giving me the shudders."

Bram had to admit, the village was oddly immaculate and eerily empty of people. Each cobble sparkled in the street. The dirt lanes were swept clean of debris. Every shop front and cottage boasted neat window boxes overflowing with red geraniums.

A pair of lads rushed toward them. "Can we help with the horses, Lord Rycliff?"

Lord Rycliff? So, they knew him already. News traveled fast in a small village, he supposed.

Bram handed his reins to one of two eager, towheaded youths. "What are your names, lads?"

"Rufus Bright," the one on the left said. "And this is Finn."

"We're twins," Finn offered.

"You don't say." The Brights. A suitable name, what with those incandescent shocks of hair—so blond as to be nearly white. "See?" he said to Colin. "I told you the place couldn't be devoid of men."

"They're not men," Colin replied. "They're boys."

"They didn't germinate from the soil. If there are children, there must be men. What's more, men whose pegos aren't withered to twigs." He beckoned one of the youths. "Is your father about?"

A shock of lightning hair swiveled in the negative. "He's . . . uh, not here."

"When do you expect him back?"

The twins looked to each other, exchanging wary glances.

Finally, Rufus said, "Can't say, my lord. Errol—that's our older brother—he travels to and fro, bringing in wares for the shop. We own the All Things, across the way. As for Father . . . he hasn't been around for some time."

"Last time was almost two years ago," Finn said. "Came around just long enough to get another babe on Mum and dole out his knocks to the rest of us. He's fonder of his drink than his brats."

Rufus elbowed his twin. "That'll be enough airing of family business, then. What are you going to reveal next? The patches in your smallclothes?"

"He asked about our father. I told him the truth."

The truth was a damned shame. Not only because these boys had an absent sot for a father, but because Bram could have used a sober Mr. Bright in his militia. He sized up the twins before him. Fourteen, perhaps fifteen at the outside. A shade too young to be of any real use.

"Can you point us toward the smithy?" he asked.

"Has your horse thrown a shoe, my lord?"

"No. But I have other work for him." He needed to find the strongest, most capable men in the neighborhood. The smithy was as likely a place as any to start.

As the morning wore on, Bram began to comprehend why this Mr. Bright would have taken to drink.

This was supposed to be a simple task. As a lieutenant colonel, he'd been responsible for a thousand infantrymen. Here, he required only four-and-twenty men to form a volunteer force. After an hour spent scouring the village, he'd rounded up fewer likely prospects than he could count on one hand. Perhaps fewer than he could count on one thumb.

Discovering the absence of Mr. Bright was only the first disappointment, followed close on its heels by his visit to the smithy. The blacksmith, Aaron Dawes, was a strapping, solid fellow, as smiths usually were—and by appearances alone, Bram would have marked him an excellent candidate. What gave him pause, however, was entering the forge to find the man not shoeing an ox or hammering out an axe blade, but meticulously fashioning the hinge on a dainty locket.

Then there was the vicar. Bram had thought it prudent to stop in at the church and introduce himself. He hoped he could explain his military mission and have the cler-gyman's cooperation in recruiting local men. The vicar, one Mr. Keane, was young and clever enough from the looks of him—but all the excitable fellow could speak about was some Ladies' Auxiliary and new crewelwork cushions for the pews.

"Don't say I didn't warn you," Colin said, as they left their discouraging interview with Keane.

"What kind of vicar wears a pink waistcoat?"

"One in Spindle Cove. It's like I've been telling you, Bram. Shriveled twigs. Dried currants."

"There are other men. Real men. Somewhere."

There *had* to be others. The fishermen were all out to sea, of course, so the row of a half-dozen hovels and net huts by the cove had been emptied of men for the day. Surely there must be farmers out in the surrounding coun-tryside. But they'd likely traveled to the nearest market town, this being Saturday.

For the time being, Bram supposed there was only one

likely location to round up men. The long-favored haunt
of army recruiters and navy press gangs alike.

"Let's head for the tavern," he said. "I need a drink."

"I need a steak," Thorne said.

"And I need a wench," Colin put in. "Don't they have
those in little seaside villages? Tavern wenches?"

"That must be the place." He headed across the green,
toward a cheerful-looking establishment with a traditional tavern sign hanging above its entry. Thank God.
This was almost as good as a homecoming. Proper English pubs, at least, with their sticky floorboards and dark,
dank corners, were the true province of men.

Bram slowed as they approached the entrance. On
closer inspection, this didn't look like any tavern he'd ever
seen. There were lace curtains in the window. The delicate strains of pianoforte music wafted out to him. And
the sign hanging above the door read . . .

"Tell me that doesn't say what I think it says."

"The Blushing Pansy," his cousin read aloud, in a tone
of abject horror. "Tea shop and confectionery."

Bram swore. This was going to be ugly.

Correct that. As he opened the establishment's red-
painted door, he realized this scene was not going to be
ugly at all. It was going to be *pretty*, beyond all limits of
masculine tolerance.

──────── Chapter Six ────────

Sorry, cousin." Colin clapped a hand on Bram's shoulder as they entered the establishment. "I know you hate it when I'm right."

Bram surveyed the scene. No sticky floorboards. No dark, dank corners. No men.

What he found were several tables draped in white damask. Atop each surface sat a crockery vase of fresh wildflower blooms. And seated around each table were a handful of young ladies. Together, they must have numbered nearly a score. Befrocked, beribboned, and in some cases, bespectacled. To a one, bemused by the men's appearance.

The pianoforte music died a quick, mournful death. Then, as if on cue, the girls turned in unison to the center of the room, obviously looking to their leader for guidance.

Miss Susanna Finch.

Good God. Miss *Finch* was the spinster hive's queen bee? Her molten-bronze hair was a flash of wild beauty in the room's bland prettiness. And her scattered freckles did not fall in line with the otherwise ordered calm. Despite all his intentions to remain indifferent, Bram felt his blood heating to a quick, rebellious simmer.

"Why, Lord Rycliff. Lord Payne. Corporal Thorne.

What a surprise." She rose from her chair and dipped in a curtsy. "Won't you join us?"

"Go on. Let's at least eat," Colin muttered. "Where two or more ladies are gathered, there will be food. I'm fairly certain that's in the Scriptures."

"Do have a seat." Miss Finch waved them toward some vacant chairs at a table near the wall.

"You're the infantryman." Colin nudged him forward. "You first."

Bram eased and edged his way to an empty chair, dodging low ceiling beams as he went, feeling like the proverbial bull in the china shop. All around him, fragile females held highly breakable cups in their delicate grips. They followed him with saucer-wide eyes set in porcelain complexions. Bram suspected that with one sudden movement, he could shatter the whole scene.

"I'll fetch you some refreshments," she said.

Oh no. She wasn't leaving him alone with all this daintiness. He pulled the chair out, then held it for her. "My cousin will do it. Have a seat, Miss Finch."

A flicker of surprise crossed her features as she accepted. Bram took the adjacent chair for himself. Between the morning's observations and Colin's dire warnings . . . he knew something very strange was going on in this village. And whatever it was, Miss Finch would sit down and explain it to him.

Of course, once she did sit next to him, he found his powers of concentration immediately diminished. The dwarfish size of the table forced them so close, her shoulder rubbed his arm. From there, it was all too easy to imagine sweeter sources of friction. To recall the feel of her body under his.

The music resumed. A cup of tea appeared on the table.

She leaned close, bathing him in her hothouse scent. In a hushed murmur, she asked, "Milk or sugar?"

Bloody hell. She was offering him tea. His body responded as if she'd stood naked before him, balancing cream jug in one hand and sugar bowl in the other, asking him which substance he'd rather lick from her bare skin.

Both. Both, please.

"Neither." Bracing himself against temptation, Bram removed the flask from his breast pocket and added a generous splash of whiskey to the steaming cup. "What's going on here?"

"It's our weekly salon. As I told you yesterday, here in Spindle Cove we ladies have a schedule. Monday, country walks. Tuesday, sea bathing. We spend Wednesdays in the garden, and . . ."

"Yes, yes," he said, scratching his unshaven jaw. "I recall the schedule. On Thursday, I hope you foster orphaned lambs."

She went on, unruffled. "Aside from our group activities, each lady pursues her own interests. Art, music, science, poetry. On Saturdays, we celebrate our individual accomplishments. These salons help the young ladies develop their confidence before they return to wider society."

Bram couldn't imagine why the lady currently playing the pianoforte would ever lack for confidence in society. He had little musical ability himself, but he knew true talent when he heard it. This young woman coaxed sounds from the instrument he hadn't known a pianoforte could make—cascades of laughter and plaintive, heartfelt sighs. And the girl was pretty, too. Watching her in profile, he observed thick chestnut hair and delicate features. She wasn't Bram's usual sort, but she possessed the kind of beauty with which a man could pose no argument.

And while the girl played, Bram nearly managed to

stop lusting after Susanna Finch. Nothing short of musical genius could accomplish that.

"That's Miss Taylor," she whispered. "She's our music tutor."

Colin arrived, plunking a serving plate in the center of the table and helpfully dispelling the tension. "There," he said. "Food."

Bram eyed the refreshments. "Are you sure?"

The plate was lined with rows of tiny pastries and bite-sized cakes, each iced in a different pastel shade. Little piped rosettes and sugar pearls topped the dainty morsels.

"This isn't *food*." Bram picked up a lavender-iced cake between thumb and finger and stared at it. "This is . . . edible ornamentation."

"It's edible. That's all I care about." Colin shoved a bit of seedcake into his mouth.

"Oh, these lavender ones are Mr. Fosbury's specialty." She nodded toward the cake in Bram's hand and selected an identical morsel for herself. "They're filled with his own currant jelly. Divine."

"A *Mr.* Fosbury made these?" Bram lifted the lavender cake.

"Yes, of course. He's owned this place for a generation. It used to be a tavern."

So, this place *used* to be a tavern. With pints of proper ale, one would assume. And kidney pie. Steaks so rare, a man could still hear the cow lowing. Bram's stomach gave a despairing rumble.

"Why would a tavern keeper turn to baking teacakes?" He cast a look about the place, so cheerily furnished and refined. In the window, lace curtains fluttered gaily, mocking him *and* his lavender-iced petit four.

"Things change. Once the inn became a ladies' retreat, an alteration of business strategy only made sense."

"I see. So this place isn't a tavern any longer. It's a tea shop. Instead of real, hearty food we have this assortment of pastel absurdity. You've reduced a hardworking, decent man to piping rosettes to earn his keep."

"Nonsense. We haven't 'reduced' Mr. Fosbury to anything."

"Like the devil you haven't. You've . . . shriveled the man to currants." Bram threw away the cake in disgust, looking for somewhere to wipe the lavender icing from his fingers. In the end, he smeared violet streaks on the damask tablecloth, enjoying Miss Finch's gasp of dismay.

"That's a rather medieval view," she said, obviously affronted. "Here in Spindle Cove, we live in modern times. Why shouldn't a man make currant jam or pretty lockets, if such things please him? Why shouldn't a lady pursue geology or medicine, if she takes an interest?"

"The women aren't my concern." Bram looked around the place. "So where do all these 'modern' men congregate of an evening, since they're deprived of a tavern?"

She shrugged. "They go home, I suppose. What few remain."

"Fleeing the village, are they? Not hard to believe."

"Some joined the army or navy. Others left to seek work in larger towns. There simply aren't that many men in Spindle Cove." Her clear blue gaze met his. "I realize this makes your task more difficult, but to be perfectly frank . . . We have not felt it as a deprivation."

She took a sip of tea. He was surprised she could manage it through that coy little grin.

As she lowered the cup, her eyebrows arched. "I know what you're wanting, Lord Rycliff."

"Oh, I highly doubt that." Her imagination couldn't possibly be so vivid.

She reached for another cake, balancing it between her

thumb and forefinger. "You'd prefer we offer you a great, bloody slab of meat. Something you can pierce with your fork. Stab with your knife. *Conquer*, in brutish fashion. A man looks on his food as a conquest. But to a woman, it's rebellion. We are all ladies here, and Spindle Cove is our place to taste freedom, in small, sweet bites."

She lifted the iced morsel to her lips and took an arousing, unrepentant mouthful. Her nimble tongue darted out to rescue a stray bit of jam. She gave a little sigh of pleasure, and he nearly groaned aloud.

Bram forced his attention away, seeking refuge in the talented Miss Taylor's performance. She'd cast such a spell over the assembly, a goodly pause elapsed between the final strains of music and the first claps of enthusiastic applause. Bram clapped along with the rest. The only soul in the tavern not applauding was Thorne. But then, did Thorne count as a soul? The corporal stood impassive by the door, arms folded over his chest. Bram supposed that for Thorne, clapping strayed too close to emotional display . . . along with dancing, laughter, and any facial expression more communicative than a blink. The man was a damned rock. No, not merely a rock. A rock encased in iron. Then, for good measure, glazed with ice.

Therefore, Bram knew something truly shocking had occurred when he saw his corporal startle. No one else in the room would have noticed it—just a subtle tensing of the shoulders and a quick, fierce swallow. But for Thorne, this reaction might as well have been a bloodcurdling shriek.

Bram turned to see what had so taken his friend aback. Miss Taylor had risen from the pianoforte bench, smiling and dropping a gracious curtsy before returning to her seat. Now he was able to see what he couldn't have noticed, viewing her in profile. The other side of Miss Taylor's, fair, delicate face was marred by a port-wine birthmark. The heart-shaped splash of red pigment obscured a good portion of her right temple, before disappearing into her hairline.

A pity, that. Such a pretty girl.

As if reading his thoughts, Miss Finch gave him a pointed look. "Miss Taylor is one of my dearest friends. I'm sure I don't know a kinder person, or one more beautiful."

Her voice had honed to a blade-sharp edge, and she wielded it with precise intent.

Don't hurt my friend, it said.

Ah. So this explained matters. The strange state of affairs in this village, her resistance to the militia. Miss Finch styled herself the protector of this queer little clutch of female oddities. And in her eyes, that made Bram—or any red-blooded man, apparently—the enemy.

Interesting. Bram could respect her intent, even admire it. No doubt she fancied herself quite the problem solver. But her arithmetic needed fundamental correction. Men couldn't simply be removed from the equation. Protecting this place was a man's duty—Bram's duty, to be specific. And her brood of odd ducks complicated things.

Speaking of odd, a bespectacled young woman replaced Miss Taylor at the center of attention. This girl did not sit down to the pianoforte, or produce any musical instrument. Rather, she held a box of curiosities that she began circulating among the other ladies, whose lack of interest was plain. Bram tilted his head. From his view these treasures looked to be . . . lumps of earth. That would explain the general bemusement.

"What on earth is that girl doing?" Colin murmured around his third bite of seedcake. "She seems to be giving a lecture on dirt."

"That's Minerva Highwood." That blade-sharp tone again. "She's a geologist."

Colin made an amused sound. "Explains the six inches of mud at her hem."

"She's here for the summer with her mother and two sisters, Miss Diana and Miss Charlotte." Miss Finch indicated a group of fair-haired women at a nearby table.

"Well, well," Colin murmured. "Now *they* are interesting."

Another young lady rose to take her turn at the pianoforte. Colin drifted away from the table, taking the newly vacated seat—which just happened to be near Diana Highwood.

"What's he doing?" Miss Finch said. "Miss Highwood is convalescing. Surely your cousin doesn't mean to pursue—" She began to rise from her chair.

There she went, protecting again. He stayed her with a hand. "Never mind him. I'll manage my cousin. We're talking now. You and me."

As she sank back into her chair, he kicked the chair leg, turning it so that she'd be forced to face him. She glanced at his hand where he touched her gloved wrist. Just to vex them both, he kept it there. Satin heated beneath his fingertips. The row of buttons tempted.

Hell, everything about her tempted.

With effort, he let her go. "Let me be certain I understand you, Miss Finch. You've amassed a colony of unwed women, then driven away or gelded every red-blooded male in Spindle Cove. And yet you feel no deprivation."

"None whatsoever. In fact, I believe our situation to be ideal."

"You do realize, that sounds very . . ."

She tilted her head in empathy. "Threatening? I do understand how a man could perceive it that way."

"I was going to say, Sapphic."

Those lush, currant-stained lips parted in surprise.

Good. He was beginning to wonder what it would take

to get under her skin. And by tugging that chain of inquiry, he was dredging up far too many images of her skin. The softness of it, the heat . . . those delectable freckles, sprinkled like spice.

"Have I shocked you, Miss Finch?"

"I must own, you have. Not with your insinuations of romantic love between women, mind. But I would never have supposed you to be so versed in ancient Greek poetry. That is a shock indeed."

"I'll have you know, I attended Cambridge for three terms."

"Truly?" She stared at him in mock astonishment. "Three whole terms? Now that *is* impressive." Her voice was a low, seductive drawl that raised every last hair on his forearm.

At some point in this conversation, she'd ceased arguing with him and begun flirting with him. He doubted she even realized it—any more than she'd realized the danger yesterday, when her tattered frock had been one angry huff away from exposing her pale, supple breast. She lacked the experience to grasp the subtle distinction between antagonism and getting on very well indeed.

So Bram went perfectly still and held her gaze. Stared deeply, directly into her eyes until he made her aware of it, too—this scorching-hot cinder of attraction they juggled back and forth between them.

The air went warm with her effort not to breathe, and her gaze dipped—ever so briefly—to his mouth. The fleeting ghost of a kiss.

Oh yes, he told her with a subtle lift of his brow. *That's what we're doing here.*

She swallowed hard. But she didn't turn away.

Damn, they could be so good together. Just staring into her eyes, he saw it all. Those iris-hued irises held wit and passion, and . . . depths. Intriguing depths he very much wished to explore. A man could talk to a woman like this all night. At intervals, of course. There would need to be lengthy stretches of gasping and moaning, too.

She's Sir Lewis Finch's daughter, his conscience blared in his ear. The problem was, the rest of his body didn't bloody well care.

She cleared her throat, abruptly breaking the spell she'd cast on him. "Mrs. Lange, won't you favor us with a poem?"

Bram sat back in his chair. A slender, dark-haired young woman ascended to the dais, clutching a paper. She appeared meek and shrinking.

Until she opened her mouth, that was.

"O, vile betrayer! O, defiler of vows!"

Well. Now she had the room's attention.

"Hear my rage, like distant thunder. My heart, the beast doth ripped asunder. My cove, the wretched brute did plunder—though not thoroughly." She glanced up from her paper. "Small wonder."

Miss Finch leaned toward him and whispered, "Mrs. Lange is estranged from her husband."

"You don't say," he murmured back. He lifted his hands, readying some polite applause.

But the poem didn't stop there. Oh no. It went on.

For several minutes.

There were many, many verses of epic infamy to be chronicled, it would seem. And the longer the woman read aloud, the higher her voice pitched. Her hands even began to shake.

"All my trust he did betray, when to another he fain would stray. That cruel deed I did repay. With the help of a bronze tea tray. His blood had the temerity . . . to stain the drapes of dimity." She squeezed her eyes shut. "I recall it well, that rusty stain. It is my promise. Never . . . never . . . *never*—"

The room held its breath.

"—again."

Silence.

"Brava!" Colin shot to his feet, applauding wildly. "Well done, indeed. Let's have another."

Out of the corner of his eye, Bram saw Miss Finch's soft, lush lips twitching at the corners. She was struggling, mightily, not to laugh. And Bram was struggling, mightily, not to cover that mouth with his. To taste the sweetness of her laughter, the tart bite of her clever wit. To claim her, the way she needed to be claimed. In thorough, beastly, medieval fashion.

His only course of action was clear.

He pushed back from the table, screeching the chair legs against the floorboards. As every woman in the place turned to him in mute horror, he rose to his feet and muttered gruffly, "Afternoon."

Then he walked straight out the door.

Chapter Seven

usanna followed him.

Before she even knew what she was doing, she'd launched from her chair, swept out the door, and followed the impossible man into the lane. To be sure, she wanted him gone. But she couldn't allow him to leave like *that*.

"That was rather abrupt." Lifting her skirts, she hurried after him as he moved to reclaim his horse. "The young ladies were anxious, but they made every effort to welcome you. You might have at least taken proper leave."

For that matter, he might have accepted a dratted lavender teacake, or dinner last night at Summerfield. He might have refrained from needling her until she blushed and girlishly fidgeted with her hair, in front of all her protégées. He might have taken the trouble to *shave*.

What was wrong with this man, that he couldn't comport himself in polite society? His cousin was a viscount. Surely he'd been raised a gentleman, too.

She caught up to him on the green, only mildly winded. "Spindle Cove is a holiday village, Lord Rycliff. Visitors journey great distances to enjoy fine, sunny weather and a restorative atmosphere. If you take a deep breath and a good look around you, perhaps you'll find the place doing *you* some good. Because forgive me for saying it, but the presence of a dour, brooding lordship doesn't fit with the advertising."

"I'd imagine it doesn't." Rycliff took his horse's reins from Rufus Bright. He nodded toward the Blushing Pansy. "I didn't belong in that place. I knew it well. The question is, Miss Finch . . . what are *you* doing in this village?"

"I've been trying to explain it to you. We have a community of ladies here in Spindle Cove, and we support one another with friendship, intellectual stimulation, and healthful living."

"No, no. I can see how this might appeal to a mousy, awkward chit with no prospects for something better. But what are *you* doing here?"

Perplexed, she turned her gloved hands palms-up. "Living happily."

"Really," he said, giving her a skeptical look. Even his horse snorted in seeming disbelief. "A woman like you."

She bristled. Just what kind of woman did he think she was?

"If you think yourself content with no man in your life, Miss Finch, that only proves one thing." In a swift motion, he pulled himself into the saddle. His next words were spoken down at her, making her feel small and patronized. "You've been meeting all the wrong men."

He nudged his gelding into a canter and rode away, leaving her affronted and sputtering. She whirled on her heel, only to come nose-to-epaulet with Corporal Thorne.

She swallowed hard. From across a room, Thorne was an intimidating presence. Up close, he was terrifying. But Susanna's anger and curiosity were too greatly piqued. Together, they overrode all sense of etiquette or caution.

"What's the matter with that man?" she asked the corporal.

His eyes hardened.

"That man." She gestured down the lane. "Rycliff. Bramwell. Your superior."

His jaw hardened.

"You must know him quite well. You've probably worked alongside him for several years, his closest confidant. Tell me, then. Did it start in childhood? Was he neglected by his parents, mistreated by a governess? Locked away in an attic?"

Now the man's entire face turned to stone. A stone etched with unfriendly frown lines and a ruthless slash where the mouth should be.

"Or was it the war? He's haunted by memories of battle, perhaps. Was his regiment ambushed, at great loss of life? Was he captured and held prisoner behind enemy lines? I do hope he has *some* excuse."

She waited, watched. The corporal's face surrendered no clues whatsoever.

"He has a paralyzing fear of tea," she blurted out. "Or enclosed spaces. Spiders, that's my final guess. Blink once for yes, twice for no."

He didn't blink at all.

"Never mind," she said, exasperated. "I'll just have to drag it from him myself."

Some thirty huffing, panting minutes later, Susanna reached the top of the bluffs and the perimeter of Rycliff Castle. Naturally Lord Rycliff had arrived well ahead of her. She found his mount already unsaddled and grazing in the bailey.

"Lord Rycliff?" she called. Her shout echoed off the stones.

No answer.

She tried again, cupping her hands around her mouth. "Lord Rycliff, may I have a word?"

"Only one, Miss Finch?" The faint answer came from the direction of the keep. "I couldn't be that lucky."

She advanced toward the collection of stone towers, training her ears for his voice. "Where are you?"

"The armory."

The armory?

Following the sound of his reply, she made for the keep's arched entryway. Once inside, Susanna turned left and entered the hollow stone turret on the northeast corner. Now the armory, it would seem. She supposed it did make a suitable place to store powder and weaponry. Cool, dark, enclosed by stone. The crunch of dry gravel beneath her feet indicated the tower's roof was sufficiently intact to keep out the rain.

She stood in the entry, waiting for her eyes to adjust to the dim light. Slowly, the scene came into focus, and as it did, her heart sank.

She'd been half hoping—fully hoping, she supposed— that he would take this militia task lightly, limit his efforts to the bare minimum. The occasion required only a bit of show, she'd reasoned. Rycliff couldn't earnestly mean to scrape together a true fighting force in Spindle Cove.

But looking on this scene, she couldn't deny the truth. The man was serious about this militia. This was a serious amount of weaponry.

A row of Brown Bess muskets lined one side of the tower. To the other direction, cannonballs and grapeshot were stacked. A few newly constructed shelves on the far side held kegs of powder. And by them, with his back to her, stood Lord Rycliff.

He'd undressed on arrival and now wore only a loose shirt, breeches, and boots—no coat or cravat. The pale linen gleamed in the dim light, stretching over the muscled contours of his arms and back. Susanna wasn't a doctor, but she knew human anatomy well enough. Well enough to recognize what an excellent specimen of it he was. Without the hindrance of a coat, for example, she could appreciate that his backside was particularly well formed. Tight and muscled and . . .

And a completely inappropriate object of her attention. What was happening to her? She pulled her gaze upward, allowing a moment to compose herself before she called his attention. His hair was a long, dark queue, bound with twine. Its end hung just between his shoulder blades, where it curled like a fishhook, baiting her.

"Lord Rycliff?" she ventured. He did not turn. She took a deep breath and tried once again, putting some force into her voice. "*Lord—*"

"I know you're there, Miss Finch." His voice was quiet and controlled as he remained with his back to her, bending over something she could not see. "Hold your peace a moment. I'm measuring powder."

Susanna took a step into the room.

"There now," he murmured, low and seductive. "Yes. That's the way."

Good heavens. The sultry rasp in his voice had persuasive force. It moved her center of balance, rocking her from her toes to her heels. She took a step in reverse, and her back met the wall of ancient stone. A cool ridge calmed the place between her shoulder blades.

Without turning, he said, "Well, Miss Finch? What is it you're wanting?"

What a dangerous question.

She realized she was still hugging the wall. Pride propelled her two steps forward. As she advanced, something bleated at her, as though chastising her for trespassing. She stopped midstep and peered at it. "Did you know there's a lamb in here?"

"Never mind it. That's dinner."

She gave it a smile and a friendly pat. "Hullo, Dinner. Aren't you a sweet thing?"

"It's not his name, it's his . . . function." With an impatient oath, he turned, wiping his hands with a cloth. His palms were dusted with charcoal-colored powder, and his eyes, so dilated in the cool, dark stillness, glittered black as jet. "If there's something you mean to say, say it. Otherwise, be on your way."

She growled to herself. He was such a . . . Such a *man*. Crooning sweetly to his weaponry, then barking at her. As her father's daughter, Susanna understood that an ambitious man could seem married to his work. But this was ridiculous.

She squared her shoulders. "Lord Rycliff, I have an interest in maintaining village harmony, and I'm afraid we're not off to a neighborly start."

"And yet"—he crossed his arms over his chest—"here you are."

"Here I am. Because I won't be treated this way, do you see? And I won't let you terrorize my friends, either. Despite the awkwardness of our initial meeting, I have tried to be friendly. You, on the other hand, have been a perfect beast. The way you spoke to me last night. The way you behaved down in the tea shop. Even right now, this moment . . . I can tell by your gruff tone and that stern posture you mean to seem intimidating. But look." She gestured at the lamb. "Not even Dinner is frightened. I'm not, either."

"Then you're fools, the two of you. I could make a meal of you both."

She shook her head, stepping toward him. "I don't think so. I know you didn't expect to take up residence here, but people always come to Spindle Cove to get well. If I may say it, Lord Rycliff, I think you're hurting. You're like a great shaggy lion with a nettle in its paw. Once it's plucked, your good humor will be restored."

A prolonged pause ensued.

One dark brow quirked. "You mean to pluck my nettle?"

Flushing with heat, she bit her lip. "Not in so many words."

With a hollow chuckle, he stepped back, pushing a hand through his hair. "You need to leave. We can't have this discussion."

"Is it so very painful?" she asked, in a quiet voice. "Are you haunted by some tragedy? Did the ravages of war embitter you toward your fellow man?"

"*No.*" He wiped the powder measure clean and banged it on a shelf. "And no, and no. The only thing paining me right now"—he turned—"is you."

"Me?" Her breath caught. "That's ridiculous. I'm not a nettle."

"Oh no. You're something far, far worse."

"A burr?" she said helpfully. "A thistle perhaps? Roses have thorns, but I don't possess the right sort of beauty for that comparison." When he didn't laugh, she said, "Lord Rycliff, I fail to see how I'm causing you any problems."

"Let me explain for you, then." He spoke low and even. "I ought to be headed for Spain right now, on the way to rejoin my regiment. Instead, I have an earldom I didn't ask for, a castle I don't want, and a cousin determined to drive me mad, insolvent, or both. But your father's given me a chance to move on, leave it all behind. The only thing I need do is gather two dozen local men—equip them, arm them, and drill them into a respectable militia. Easy enough task, in a month's time. Almost insulting in its simplicity." He raised a single finger. "But there's a snag, isn't there? There *are* no local men. No real men, at any rate. Just spinsters and teacakes and poetry."

"There are men here. And if you need any help rounding them up, you only have to ask."

"Oh, I'm sure." He chuckled. " 'Ask Miss Finch.' Do you know how many times I heard those words this morning?"

She shook her head.

"More than I care to count." He began circling her with slow, heavy steps. "When I asked the Bright twins if there are seamstresses in the neighborhood, to sew uniforms . . . They said, 'Ask Miss Finch.' When I inquired with the smith where I might find stonemasons to do some work here at the castle . . . Well, Miss Finch would know that too. Ask her." He walked on. "Where do I find the parish register, for a list of all the local families? Well, your dandified vicar tells me, Miss Finch has been doing a study of the local birth records, and I will have to inquire with her. Ask. Miss. Finch. There's no escaping you. It's like you have the whole village playing some ceaseless round of Mother, May I."

Susanna squared her shoulders as he completed his circle and came to stand before her—a fraction too close. The intensity in his eyes told her he meant to draw closer still.

No, you may not, she silently willed. *You may not take two steps forward.*

He took them anyway.

"I try to be helpful," she said. "There's nothing wrong with that. And it's natural the villagers show me a certain deference, out of respect for my father. He is the local gentleman of rank."

"Your father is the local gentleman of rank?" He stood tall. "Well, now. I happen to be the local lord."

"Oh," she said, smiling with relief. "*Now* I understand. Your pride is wounded. That's your problem. Yes, I can see how that would be disappointing, to be given the title and feel so little influence with the local residents. But with time, I'm sure the villagers—"

He shook his head. "My pride's not wounded, for God's sake. And no, I'm not disappointed. Nor haunted, nor embittered, nor threatened. Stop trying to pin all these *emotions* on me like frilly pink ribbons. I'm not one of your delicate spinsters, Miss Finch. This isn't about my tender feelings. I have things to accomplish, and you"— he poked a single finger into her shoulder—"are hindering me."

"Lord Rycliff," she said carefully, "you are touching me."

"Yes, I am. And I didn't even ask. You see, I'm not going to *ask* Miss Finch anything. I'm going to *tell* her to stay far clear." The pressure of his fingertip bit into her shoulder. "You are my problem, Miss Finch. No, you're not a nettle, or a burr, or a delicate blossom of any kind. You're a goddamned powder keg, and every time I draw near you, we start throwing off sparks."

"I . . . I don't know what you mean."

"Oh yes, you do." He fingered the lacy edge of her cap sleeve, then slid a caress down her arm.

She was helpless to suppress a little shiver of pleasure.

He groaned deep in his chest. "See? You're full to bursting with passion. You may think you have it tightly capped and contained. Hidden from everyone, even yourself. Perhaps the pathetic souls who pass for men in that village are too cowed by your modern ideals to notice. But I only have to look at you, and I see it all. That core of dark, explosive potential, held together with just a bit of ribbon and lace." His voice deepened as his gaze wandered down her body. "I'm a damned fool to even be touching you, but I can't bring myself to stop."

His touch traced the edge of her elbow-length glove, skimming along the delicate border where satin met skin.

Sensation rushed through her entire body, lifting the hairs on the back of her neck. She thought of those creases in his palms, still limned with gunpowder. So perilous. His caresses made her feel shaken, rearranged.

Just a little dirty.

"Do you understand now?" he said, keeping up his bold caress. "This is dangerous. You'll leave straightaway, if you know what's best."

Leave? She couldn't move. Her body was so busy responding to his, it wouldn't spare a moment to heed her own commands. Her breath quickened. A strange ache grew in her breasts. Her heart thundered wildly, and a matching pulse beat at the juncture of her thighs.

"I know what you're doing." She lifted her chin. "You're just trying to change an unpleasant conversation. I said you're in pain, and I've piqued your pride. Why own up to possessing feelings, when it's much more manly to be loutish and crude? If you're hoping to push me away, it won't work."

"Won't it?" He propped a single finger under her chin. "This did the trick before."

He dipped his head, and his lips brushed hers.

Sparks. She could have sworn she saw them, swarming bright and orange. Pinprick heat branded her skin.

"What of this?" he asked. Another kiss. "Or this, perhaps."

His mouth moved over hers, teasing her with a series of brief, bruising kisses. There was meaning behind those kisses, so commanding and firm. They were like little words in . . . in German, or Dutch. One of those languages she really ought to know, but had never taken the trouble to learn. And now she was left frustrated, uncertain how to respond. Were they accusations? Warnings? Desperate pleas for something more?

Whatever sort of argument they were having, she knew one thing.

She could not let him win.

She made herself tall, pressed back at his aggressive mouth with little kisses of her own. In both hands, she gathered great fistfuls of his warm lawn shirt, as if she could shake some sense into the impossible man. Or maybe just to keep from falling, as the dizzying sensations rocketed through her body. Exhilaration lifted her stomach and set her heart floating loose in her chest.

When the kisses ended, she met his gaze, rather proud of herself for not dissolving on the spot. Despite the complete upheaval of her senses, she tried to appear worldly and composed. As if this sort of thing happened to her regularly, in the course of normal interaction. As if she often stood toe-to-toe with an enormous, virile, unshaven man in a room full of explosives, feeling these lethal sparks of attraction fly around and between them. And her breasts were just *always* grazing against a hard wall of muscled chest, her nipples drawing to taut, needy peaks out of mundane habit. Completely expected, regularly scheduled arousal.

"Well?" he asked. "Have I made my point? Are you leaving now?"

"I'm so sorry to disappoint you," she said, breathing hard. "But it would take far more than that to scare me."

A quick flex of his arms, and their bodies collided. And he whispered, just as his mouth fell on hers, "God, I was hoping you'd say that."

Chapter Eight

his kiss could be the end, Bram knew. He was foolishly, thoroughly kissing Miss Susanna Finch, clutching her slender body to his while he reveled in the faint currant spice of her lips, and this could be the end of everything. The end of all his plans, his military career. Perhaps the end of *him*, full stop.

And if that was the case, and he'd impulsively gambled his entire future on a forbidden kiss . . .

He might as well slow down and do the thing right.

He let his mouth linger over hers. She hadn't been kissed much. At least, not properly. He could tell in the way she was struggling to respond. She was unschooled, but she showed great natural aptitude.

He cradled her neck in one hand. "Softly, love. Let me show you."

He teased his lips over hers, brushing from bottom to top. Then again. And then once more, persuading her lips to part. She startled at the first touch of his tongue, but he held her tight until the instinct passed. And then he tasted her. The slow, sweet slide of his tongue against hers had him growling with satisfaction.

Yes, he told her without words. *Yes. Again.*

From their first meeting, he'd suspected this woman to be a temptress in a teapot, and she was proving him right with every tentative stroke of her tongue against his. Her inexperience only made the whole business sweeter. The way she clutched his shirt, chased his teasing tongue, slid her gloved finger along the edge of his unshaven jaw . . . She was inventing these small intimacies as she went, acting out of pure, untutored desire. These weren't practiced motions, honed on other men.

They were only for him.

He deepened the kiss, keeping his rhythm steady and sure. Each time taking just a little more, delving just a fraction deeper. The same way he would make love to her.

No sooner had the thought surfaced in his mind, than he seized on it. He *had* to make love to her. Someday. Not today. Today, she was only learning to kiss. She wasn't ready.

Bram, by contrast, was ready indeed. Ready, willing, and able. In a mindless, instinctive motion, he pulled her snug against his aching groin. If she could feel the abundant evidence of his arousal, she didn't shy away. Her breasts eased warm and soft against his chest as she leaned into the kiss.

Bending his head, he kissed her throat, her ear, losing himself in the scent of her. Her skin smelled of herbs, and she tasted . . . like a memory. A memory of a long-ago summer's day. Warm sun. Cool, crisp water. Tall grass and a gentle breeze. Everything good and real and fresh. Even her name was a whimsical song.

"Susanna," he whispered against her ear.

She sighed in his arms, as though she loved the sound of her name on his lips.

So he said it again, murmuring that light, stubborn

melody. "Susanna. Susanna fair." He nuzzled her earlobe, then drew it between his lips, suckling the delicate bud. Her little gasp stoked his desire.

She made him want so much. Too much. Damn, she made him *yearn*.

He kissed her again, taking time to savor each of her plump, lush lips before thrusting his tongue between them. This time, he delved deeper, took more. She made a mewling noise in the back of her throat, less a whimper than an erotic demand. There was urgency in her kiss now, and sweet frustration. He could taste how much she craved his touch, and the knowledge made him wild.

All this from a few simple kisses, with both of them fully clothed. Good Lord. He ran one hand down her arm and plucked at the topmost closure of her glove. They drove him mad with desire, these prim satin sheaths, with their endless stretches of buttons and arrow-straight seams. As matters stood, she could barely contain all that natural passion. What would happen when the gloves came off?

He loosed the top button with a flick of his thumb.

"Lord Rycliff," she said hoarsely.

"Bram," he corrected, undoing another. "After a kiss like that, you must call me Bram."

"Bram, please . . ."

"With pleasure." He kissed her lips again, sliding his fingers beneath the unbuttoned satin.

Her hands slid to his chest, and she pushed, hard.

"Lord Rycliff. *Please*."

The desperate catch in her voice surprised him. He glanced down to find her wearing an expression of distress, her bottom lip quivering. Her eyes were downcast.

Bram immediately found himself missing them. If he'd spent so much time thinking of her eyes, it must be because in their every interaction, she'd met his gaze directly. Unapologetic and undaunted. Until now.

Damn, and here he was certain she'd been enjoying this. He wasn't the sort to press himself on an unwilling woman.

"Susanna?" He reached to capture her chin, tilt her face to his. Her gaze was wide and pleading in the dark, and his heart gave a strange kick. Within him, lust and honor warred. He wanted her, yes. But he wanted to protect her, too. He wondered briefly if that meant he was a hypocrite.

No, he decided. It just meant he was a man.

"I . . ." Her lips parted, as though she would speak. Which would mean he needed to listen. He struggled to quell the bloodlust coursing through his veins, so he could make out her words over the mad pounding of his heart.

"My father," she breathed.

Her father.

His gut wrenched, and he released her at once. There it was, the instant cure for his lust. Somehow, for a solid, disastrous minute, he'd managed to forget Sir Lewis Finch entirely. His late father's good friend. A national hero. The man who held Bram's fate in his hands. How could he have possibly forgotten?

The answer was simple. Once he'd made the decision to kiss Susanna, *really* kiss her . . . He simply hadn't possessed the space in his brain or his arms or his heart to hold anything but her.

That kiss had been all-consuming. And it could not, would not happen again.

"Oh my God," she muttered, smoothing her upswept hair. "How did this happen?"

"I don't know. But it won't happen again."

She threw him a look, sharp as cut sapphires. "Of course it won't. It *can't.*"

"You need to stay far clear of me. Keep your distance."

"Goodness, yes." Her words were a fevered rush. "Plenty of distance. I'll stay far away from you. And you keep your men separate from my ladies, do you understand?"

"Perfectly. It's a bargain, then."

"Good." Her trembling fingers worked to refasten her gloves.

"Can I help with that?"

"No," she said sharply.

"Do you . . ." He cleared his throat. "Do you plan to tell your father?"

"About *this*?" She looked up at him, horrified. "Heavens, no. Are you mad? He must never hear of this."

A wave of emotion pushed through him, gone before he could name it. Profound relief, he supposed. "It's just, you mentioned him. Earlier."

"I did?" She frowned. "I did. Don't speak to my father, that's what I meant to say. Not about today, not about anything. When he proposed this militia scheme, I thought it just a bit of show, but seeing all this . . ." Her gaze turned to the rows of weaponry. "Please don't include him. He may want to be involved, but you mustn't allow it. He's aging, and his health isn't what it once was. I've no right to demand anything of you, but I must ask this."

He didn't know how to refuse. "Very well. You have my word."

"Then you have my thanks."

And that was all he had of her. For with those few words, she turned and fled.

That evening, as was the case most evenings, Susanna dined alone.

After dinner, she dressed for bed. Knowing she'd never be able to sleep, she chose a book—a weighty, soporific medical text. She tried to read, and failed miserably. After staring blankly at the same page for more than an hour, she rose from bed and made her way downstairs.

"Papa? Are you still up working?"

She folded an arm about her middle, wrapping her dressing gown close, and peered at the hallway clock by the light of her single candle. Already past midnight.

"Papa?" She hovered in the entrance of her father's workshop, situated on the ground floor of Summerfield. Until recent years, he'd used an outbuilding as his dabbling space, but she'd convinced him to move to the main house about the same time she'd convinced him to give up the field tests. She liked keeping him close. When he was working, he often remained secluded for hours, even days at a time. At least in the house, she knew whether he was eating.

And he wasn't eating. Not tonight, at least. His untouched dinner tray sat on a table by the door.

"Papa. You know, you really must take some food. Genius cannot subsist on air."

"Is that you, Susanna?" His silver-tufted head lifted, but he did not turn his gaze. The room was lined with worktables of different sorts. A woodworking table with planes and a lathe; a station for soldering lead. Tonight, he sat at his drafting table, amid rolls of paper and discarded stubs of charcoal.

"It's me."

He did not invite her in, and she knew better than to enter without an explicit invitation. It had always been this way, since she was a girl. When Papa was concentrating, he must not be disturbed. But if he was at work on a trifling matter, or frustrated to the point of throwing up his hands, he would invite her in and prop her on his knee. She would sit with him, marveling over his intricate drawings and calculations. They made as much sense to her as Greek. Less sense, truly, because she'd taught herself the Greek alphabet one rainy afternoon. But still, she'd loved sitting with him. Poring over the plans, feeling privy to arcane secrets and military history in the making.

"What do you need?" She recognized the absent quality in his voice. If she had something of importance to discuss, he would not turn her away. But neither did he wish to stop his work for trivialities.

"I don't want to interrupt. But I saw Lord Rycliff today. In the village. We talked." *And then I followed him up to his castle, where my lips collided with his. Repeatedly.*

God. She couldn't stop thinking of it. His whiskered jaw, his strong lips, his hands on her body. His taste. Susanna learned something new every day, but today was the first time she'd ever learned another person's *taste*. The secret of it was gnawing her from the inside, and there was no one she could tell. Not a soul. She was motherless, sisterless. The village was full of ladies, and she'd been on the listening end of their titillating confessions countless times. But if she confided in the wrong person and her moment of weakness became public knowledge . . . all those ladies would be called home. She would risk losing every friend she had.

She gave her head a slight knock against the doorframe. Stupid, stupid. "It seems Rycliff's plans for the militia are already proceeding apace. I just thought you'd like to know."

"Ah." He ripped a sheet of paper in half and drew a fresh one from the waiting stack. "That is good to hear."

"How do you know the man, Papa?"

"Who, Bramwell?"

Bram. After a kiss like that, you must call me Bram.

A shiver went through her. "Yes."

"His father was an old school friend. Went on to become a major general, highly decorated. Lived most of his commissioned years in India, but he died there not long ago."

A pang of sympathy pinched her heart. Was Bram still mourning his father? "When, exactly?"

Her father raised his head, squinting into some imaginary distance. "Must be over a year now."

Not so recently, then. But grief could easily outlast a year. Susanna hated to imagine how long she would mourn Papa, should he die unexpectedly.

"Did you know Mrs. Bramwell, too?"

With a penknife, he sharpened his stub of pencil and began to scribble again. "Met her a few times, the last when Victor was just an infant. Then they went to India, and that was the end of her. Dysentery, I believe."

"Oh dear. How tragic."

"Such things happen."

She bit her lip, knowing he meant her own mother. Though she'd died with her second stillborn child over a decade ago, Anna Rose Finch lived on in Susanna's memory: vividly beautiful, unfailingly patient and kind. But Papa found it hard to speak of her.

To change the subject, she said, "Shall I have Gertrude bring a fresh pot of tea? Coffee or chocolate, perhaps?"

"Yes, yes," he muttered, bending his head. "Whatever you think best."

Another sheet of paper hit the floor in a crumpled ball. Guilt pinched at the nape of her neck. She was distracting him from his work.

Susanna felt that she should leave, but something wouldn't let her go. Instead, she leaned against the doorjamb, watching him work. As a girl, she'd always been amused by the gargoyle-ish contortions of his features while he worked. If a perfect chevron of a frown could coax innovation from blank parchment, he ought to receive a divine bolt of brilliance just about . . .

Now.

"Aha." Out whisked a fresh sheet of paper. His hand danced back and forth, scribbling lines of text and calculations. There was a rhythm to genius, she'd often observed, and he'd caught its brisk cadence now. His shoulders hunched, walling out the world. Nothing she could say would draw his notice, save perhaps "Fire!" or "Elephants!"

"You see, Papa," she said casually, "he kissed me today. Lord Rycliff." She paused, and then wanting to test the name on her lips, she added, "Bram."

"Mm-hm."

There. Now she'd told someone. No matter that the information had sailed straight over her father's head like an errant musket volley. At least she was talking about it aloud.

"Papa?"

Her only answer was the sound of scribbling.

"I wasn't entirely truthful just now. In fact, Bram first kissed me yesterday." She bit her lip. "Today . . . today was something much more."

"Good," he muttered distractedly, running one hand through what remained of his hair. "Good, good."

"I don't know what to make of him. He's gruff and ill-mannered, and when he's not pushing me away, he's touching me places he shouldn't. I don't fear him, but when he's near me, I . . . I'm a little afraid of myself. I feel as though I'll explode."

She let a few moments pass. The sounds of scribbling continued.

"Oh, Papa." She turned her body, resting her forehead against the doorjamb. She twisted the end of her dressing gown sash. "I don't want you to worry. It won't happen again. I'm not one of those swooning, fanciful girls, run mad with scarlet fever when officers march by. I won't let him kiss me again, and I'm wise enough to know I can't allow a man like that anywhere near my heart."

"Yes," he mumbled, scribbling some more. "Just so."

Yes. Just so.

No matter how Lord Rycliff intrigued her, baited her . . . *kissed* her . . . she must keep the man at arm's length. Her inner peace and reputation depended on it, and the ladies of Spindle Cove depended on her.

She took a deep breath, feeling unburdened and resolved. "I'm so glad we had this talk, Papa."

Then she lifted the knife and fork from the dinner tray and carved the cooling hunk of roasted beef into thin slices. She split a roll and wedged the meat inside.

Breaking their unspoken agreement, she entered his workspace, walking on tiptoe around the edge of his desk. She balanced the sandwich by his inkwell, hoping he would notice it eventually.

"Good night." In an impulsive move, she leaned over the desk and kissed the top of his balding head. "Please remember to eat."

She made it all the way back to the door before he responded. And the words came in that same distant voice, as though he were speaking to her from the bottom of a fathomless well. "Good night, my dear. Good night."

Chapter Nine

hen she returned to her bed, Susanna told herself she needn't worry about Lord Rycliff. They'd agreed to keep the men and ladies separate. With any luck, they would both be so busy, she would scarcely see the man until the mid-summer fair.

She hadn't reckoned on church.

The very next morning, there he was. Seated directly across the aisle from her at a distance of four, perhaps five feet away.

And today, he'd shaved.

She noted that detail first. But he was stunning, generally. Resplendent in his dress uniform, bathed in a shaft of golden light from a clerestory window high above. The braid and buttons on his coat flashed with such polished luster, it almost hurt to look at him.

His eyes caught hers across the aisle.

With a gulp, Susanna buried her nose in her prayer book and resolved to think pure thoughts. It didn't work. Throughout the service, she was always a beat too late in standing or sitting. Whatever the topic of Mr. Keane's homily, it was utterly lost on her.

She couldn't help but steal glances whenever an excuse

presented itself—whether that excuse was an imaginary fly buzzing past, or the sudden, irresistible urge to stretch her neck. Of course, she was hardly alone. All the other parishioners were stealing looks, too. But Susanna felt reasonably certain she was the only one connecting those brief, forbidden glimpses with scandalous memories.

Those big, strong hands grasping the prayer book? Yesterday, they'd swept over her body with bold, irreverent intent.

That clean-shaven jaw, so well defined and masculine? Yesterday, she'd traced it with her gloved finger.

Those wide, sensual lips, currently mumbling their way through the litany? Yesterday, those lips had been kissing *her*. Passionately. Breathing her name in a hot, needy whisper. *Susanna. Susanna fair.*

When the call to prayer finally came, she clamped her eyes shut.

God preserve me. Deliver me from this most horrible affliction.

No mistake, she'd contracted a most virulent strain of infatuation.

Why him, of all men? Why couldn't she develop a silly *tendre* for the vicar, as so many of the innocent misses did? Mr. Keane was young and well-spoken, and he dressed very smart. Or if brute strength and heat were what enticed her, why didn't she dawdle around the blacksmith's forge?

She knew the answer, deep inside. Those other men never challenged her. If they had nothing else in common, she and Rycliff had a clash of strong wills. As a gunsmith's daughter, Susanna knew it took a good, hard strike of flint against metal to produce that many sparks.

When the service ended, she gathered her things and

made ready to escape home. Papa rarely came into the village for church, but sometimes he would join her for the Sunday meal. Especially if they had guests.

"Mr. Keane," she called, moving against the current of people as she made her way toward the pulpit. The crowd shifted, and she glimpsed his back to her. "My father and I would be delighted if you would join us for dinner today."

The vicar turned, revealing his conversation partner. Lord Rycliff.

Drat. Too late to change course now. The vicar bowed, and Susanna found it in herself to curtsy. "Can we count on you for dinner, Mr. Keane?" Sliding her gaze to the left, she said coolly, "Lord Rycliff, you would be welcome, too."

Mr. Keane smiled. "I thank you for the kind invitation, Miss Finch. But what with the call for volunteers today . . ."

"Today?" Susanna was taken aback. "I didn't realize Lord Rycliff meant to do that today."

Keane cleared his throat. "Er . . . I did announce it from the pulpit. Just now."

"You did?" Out of the corner of her eye, she saw Lord Rycliff's amused expression. "Oh. Oh, *that*. Yes, of course, Mr. Keane. I did hear you say that."

Rycliff spoke. "So you see, Miss Finch, the good vicar can't accept your kind invitation. He's going to volunteer."

"I am?" This seemed to be news to Mr. Keane. He flushed red. "Well, I . . . I am willing and able, of course. But I don't know that it's seemly for a clergyman to join a militia. I shall have to give it some reflection." He frowned and studied his linked hands. Then he brightened. "I know. Let's ask Miss Finch."

Rycliff's annoyance at hearing those three words could not have been more obvious. Or more satisfying.

Susanna smiled. "I believe Lord Rycliff has the right idea," she told the vicar truthfully. "In volunteering, you would make an excellent example. And indirectly you would be doing my father a favor. I would be most grateful."

"Then I'll volunteer," Keane said. "If you think it best, Miss Finch."

"I do." She turned to Rycliff. "Aren't you pleased to hear it, my lord?"

His eyes narrowed. "Ecstatic."

When they exited the church, Susanna was amazed. She hadn't seen this many people assembled on the green since last year's Feast of St. Ursula fair. As the church bell tolled, more and more villagers trickled out from the church. Yet more farming and herding folk funneled in from the countryside. She wasn't certain whether they were gathering to join the militia or simply to view the spectacle. She would imagine many of them didn't know yet, either.

She turned for home, but as she made her way across the green, Sally Bright gave a frantic tug on her sleeve. "Miss Finch, please. I need your help. Mother's beside herself."

"What is it? Has little Daisy taken ill?"

"No, no. It's Rufus and Finn, the scoundrels. They're determined to volunteer for Lord Rycliff's militia."

"But they're too young," Susanna said. "Not even fifteen."

"*I* know it. *You* know it. But they're planning to lie and say they meet the requirements, and who's going to stop them?" She shook her head, and her white-blond curls bounced with dismay. "Imagine Rufus and Finn, issued muskets. There's an omen of doomsday. But Mother doesn't know what to do."

"Never you worry, Sally. I'll have a word with Lord Rycliff."

She searched for him in the crowd. Big as he was, and

dressed in red, he couldn't be difficult to find. There he was—occupied, overseeing two men arranging tables. She recognized them as the wagon drivers from the other day. Leaving Sally at the edge of the green, Susanna approached.

"Lord Rycliff?"

Gathering a sheaf of papers, he drew her aside. "Miss Finch, don't you have someplace else to be? Isn't there a schedule to keep?"

"It's Sunday. We have no schedule on Sunday. But I'll be happy to let you be, just as soon as I have a word with you."

He pierced her with a look. "I thought we had an agreement. I keep my men away from your ladies, and you keep your distance from me. You're not holding your end of the bargain."

"It's but a momentary interruption. Just this once."

"Just this once?" He made a dismissive noise, rifling through papers. "What about just now in the church?"

"Very well, twice."

"Try again." He stacked his papers and looked up, devouring her with his intent green gaze. "You invaded my dreams at least a half-dozen times last night. When I'm awake, you keep traipsing through my thoughts. Sometimes you're barely clothed. What excuse can you make for that?"

She stammered to form a response, her tongue tripping against her teeth. "I . . . I would never *traipse*."

Idiotic reply.

"Hm." He tilted his head and regarded her thoughtfully. "Would you saunter?"

Susanna tempered a growl. Here he went again, trying to dismiss her with boorish innuendo. Caution would tell her to walk away, but her conscience wouldn't let her back down. The Bright women were depending on her.

"I need to speak to you about the Bright twins," she said. "Rufus and Finn. Their sister tells me they mean to volunteer, but you mustn't allow them."

One dark eyebrow lifted. "Oh, mustn't I?"

"They're too young. If they tell you different, they're lying."

"Why should I take your word over theirs? If I'm going to make up a sizable company, I need all the willing volunteers I can gather." He turned to her. "Miss Finch, my militia is precisely that. *My* militia. I gave you my word regarding your father, but beyond that I'll make my own decisions, without your contributions. Content yourself with managing all the women in this village, and I'll see to the men."

"Rufus and Finn are *boys*."

"If they join the militia, I'll make men of them." He looked around the crowd. "Miss Finch, I'm about to make the call for volunteers. Unless you mean to join the militia yourself, I suggest you remove yourself from the green and have a seat with the ladies. Where you belong."

Fuming, but seeing no immediate way to protest, she made a curtsy in retreat. "As you say, my lord."

"Well?" Sally asked, once she'd reached the edge of the green. "Did he see reason? Did he agree?"

"I don't know that that man will ever see reason." She straightened her gloves with angry tugs. "But don't you worry, Sally. I will make him agree. I'll just need to borrow a few things from the shop."

As Bram took the center of attention, he resolved to put the woman—*all* women—out of his mind. He turned his head slowly, scanning the crowd for men. He saw some males who were imprudently young, like the twins. He caught glimpses of a few who were impossibly old, grizzled and toothless. Here and there, he spied a man who ranged between. A handful of fishermen and farmers. The jewelry-making blacksmith stood near the dandified vicar. Fosbury emerged from the tea shop kitchen, dressed in an apron and covered in sugary dust.

Bram steeled his jaw. From this unlikely assortment of men, he would need to muster an elite, impeccably drilled fighting force. The alternative was the permanent end of his military career. He would remain in England a conquered, lamed, useless wretch. Defeated in every way.

Failure simply wasn't an option.

"Good morning," he announced, lifting his voice for all to hear. "Most of you will have heard, I'm Rycliff. The ancient title was revived and given me, and now I'm here to fortify and defend the castle. To that end, I'm calling for men to take up arms. I need able-bodied men, ages fifteen to five-and-forty."

He had their attention. He'd given the call. Now would be the ideal time to summon some motivational words, he supposed. "Let it be understood, England is at war. I want willing and able soldiers. Men of courage, prepared to fight and defend. If there are men among you who wish to be challenged, to become part of something larger than themselves . . . let them come. If there are men who desire to use their God-given strength in service of a noble cause . . . let them come. If there are men in this 'Spinster' Cove who want to be *real* men again . . . let them answer this call to arms."

He paused, expecting some sort of red-blooded, rallying cry in return.

He got silence. An interested, attentive silence, but silence nonetheless.

Well, if inspirational speeches weren't his strength, Bram still had one incontrovertible argument on his side.

He straightened his coat and said the rest. "Drill and training will last a month. Uniforms, firearms, and other supplies will be provided, and there will be wages. Eight shillings a day."

Now that caught their attention. Eight shillings was more than a full *week's* pay for most workingmen, and more than enough to overcome any reluctance. Murmurs of excitement swept the crowd, and several men began to move forward.

"Fall in line," he told them. "See Lord Payne for enrollment, then Corporal Thorne for outfitting."

There was a bit of a crush as the men made their way to the enrollment table, but Finn and Rufus Bright took the head of the line, no contest. Bram joined Colin behind the table.

"Names?" Colin asked.

"Rufus Ronald Bright."

"Phineas Philip Bright."

Colin dutifully inscribed the names. "Date of birth?"

"Eighth of August," Finn said, looking to his brother. "Seventeen ninety-ei—"

"Seven," Rufus finished. "We're over fifteen."

Bram interrupted, fixing the boys with a stern look. "Are you certain?"

"Yes, my lord." Finn stood tall and slapped a hand over his heart. "I'm over fifteen. May the devil take me if I'm telling you false, Lord Rycliff."

Bram sighed to himself. No doubt they'd stuffed scraps of papers with the number fifteen in their shoes. Oldest trick in the shiftless army recruiter's sack. With that scrap of paper beneath their heels, the lads could say with all honesty that they were "over" fifteen.

Susanna was right, the boys were obviously lying. And they *were* boys yet, not men. He regarded their matching, fresh-scrubbed faces that wouldn't know a razor's scrape for years. But if their birthdays truly were in August, that put their actual fifteenth birthday only a few months away. He surveyed the queue of men behind the twins, performing a quick mental tally. They numbered just under twenty, all in all. Not good. To form a company that would appear remotely impressive in formation, he needed twenty-four.

"Well?" Colin asked, looking up at Bram.

"You heard the lads. They're over fifteen."

The boys grinned as they completed the questions for Colin and proceeded to Thorne's table for measuring and firearms. Bram didn't even feel a twinge of guilt about putting muskets in the boys' hands. If they didn't already know how to handle a weapon and shoot, it was high time they learned.

One by one, the men worked through the line, giving Colin their names, ages, and other vital information before proceeding to Thorne to be measured for coats and issued firearms. As the morning progressed, Bram's knee began to ache. Then it started to throb. Before long, the damned joint was screaming with pain—so loud, he was surprised no one else could hear.

When Colin finished with the next recruit, Bram nudged his cousin aside. "You're too slow. Go help Thorne."

Lowering himself onto Colin's vacant campstool, Bram winced. He performed a surreptitious flex of his leg beneath the table, trying to ease the pain and focus on the enrollment list before him. He took his time dipping the quill.

"Now, then. Name?"

"Finch."

ram froze, quill poised above the paper, praying his ears deceived him.

"That's F-I-N-C-H," she spelled helpfully. "Finch. Like the bird."

He looked up. "Susanna, what the devil are you doing?"

"I don't know who Susanna is. But I, *Stuart* James Finch, am volunteering for your militia."

Gone was that frothy, leaf-green muslin frock he'd admired in church. In its place she'd donned a pair of nankeen breeches that fit her surprisingly well, a crisp linen shirt cuffed at the wrists, and a cobalt-blue topcoat that oddly enough did lovely things for her eyes.

And gloves, of course. Men's gloves. Heaven forbid Miss Finch appear in public without her gloves.

She went on, "My birth date is the fifth of November, 1788. And that's the God's honest truth, my lord."

Her hair was bound in a tight queue, and she was dressed in man's clothing, but there was absolutely nothing that wasn't feminine about her. Her voice, her bearing . . . God, even her scent. She couldn't fool a blind man.

Of course, she didn't mean to *fool* Bram. The interfering minx simply wanted to make a point. And she intended to make that point in front of scores of people. The entire village crowded around them, men and women alike, eager to see how this scene would unfold. They all wondered, who would emerge the victor?

He would. If he let her get the better of him today, he would never have the men's respect. What's more, he wouldn't deserve it.

"Write my name," she urged.

"You know I won't. Only men are eligible to serve."

"Well, I'm a man," she said.

He blinked at her.

"What?" Her voice dripped with mock innocence. "You took Rufus and Finn at their word. Why can't you take me at mine?"

He lowered his voice and leaned forward over the table. "Because in this case, I have firsthand knowledge that contradicts your word. Would you like me to tell all these people precisely *how* I know you're a woman?"

"Be my guest," she whispered through a tight smile. "If you'd rather be planning a wedding than a militia." She cast a glance to either side. "In a village *this* small, filled *this* chockablock with ladies, an announcement like that is sure to incite matrimonial panic."

They stared one another down for a long moment.

"If you accept Finn and Rufus," she said, "you have to accept me."

"Very well," he said, dipping the quill again. He would see just how far she was prepared to take this. "Stuart James Finch, born November fifth, 1788." He turned the paper and shoved it toward her. "Sign here."

She took the pen in her gloved hand and made a flowery signature, complete with flourish.

"Next," he said, rising from the table and gesturing toward Thorne, "we'll need to measure you for a uniform."

"But of course."

Bram walked her over to the second table and ripped

the measuring tape straight from Thorne's hand. "I believe I'll see to this recruit myself." He held up the tape for Susanna's inspection. "You have no objection, Finch?"

"None at all." She hiked her chin.

"Remove your coat, then."

She complied without argument.

He found himself without words.

Sweet heaven.

Bram wasn't fond of ladies' current fashions, with their high, empire waists and draped columns of skirt. While he approved of the way such designs served up the bosom for a man's appreciative view—what man didn't appreciate a nice view of plump breasts?—he didn't like the way they obscured the remainder of a woman's body. He liked shapely legs, trim ankles, generous hips. He had a particular fondness for a round, cuppable arse.

Who could have guessed that gentlemen's attire would perfectly hug Susanna Finch's every last feminine curve?

Her borrowed waistcoat wouldn't button at the top, due to the ample swell of her breasts. It did, however, fit snugly around her middle, emphasizing her slender waist and the sweet flare of her hips. Her breeches ended at the knee. Below them, white stockings clung to every contour of her long, lean calves and ankles.

"Turn around," he croaked.

She obeyed. And as she turned, she flipped her long queue of hair forward, giving him a clear view of her back . . . and backside. Those nankeen breeches stretched tight over a sweet, round arse. God, she was *made* for his hands. And stubborn, headstrong thing that she was, she'd given him the perfect excuse to touch her.

He began with her shoulders, placing the measuring tape at one shoulder and stretching it slowly across her back to the other. He took his time, allowing his touch to skim along the elegant slopes and ridges of her shoulder blades. As though he were touching her not for tailoring purposes, but for his pleasure and hers.

Her shoulder trembled under his touch. His heart kicked.

"Seventeen inches," he read aloud.

He measured her arm length next, beginning at the top of her shoulder and stretching the tape down the length of her arm, all the way to her wrist, before reading aloud the measurement.

"Stand tall, Finch."

As her shoulders squared, he fitted one end of the tape at the nape of her neck, just at the top of her collar. Then he stretched the narrow strip of marked fabric down the length of her spine, touching each individual vertebra. Then dipping lower, halfway down the delectable curve of her backside. He heard her sudden intake of breath, and it echoed in his groin.

"Twenty-six inches, for the coat length." As he stood, he pulled on the front of his own coat, hoping no one would notice he'd gained several inches in his personal measurements. This scene had him so aroused, he'd completely forgotten the pain in his knee.

"Face me, Finch."

She performed a slow, sensual about-face. Almost as though they were dancing.

"Arms up," he directed. "I'll measure your chest now." His blood heated at the mere thought of sliding his hands around the circumference of that lush bosom.

Her eyes flashed, and she crossed her arms, impeding him. "I believe I know that measurement. It's thirty-four inches."

He sighed gruffly. "Perfect." Damn, how he wanted to feel that body under his again. *Yearned* for it.

"Are we done?" she asked, shrugging back into her coat.

"Weapons next," he said, struggling to regain his composure. "I'll need to issue you a musket, Mr. Finch."

If she hadn't balked at the public measurements, perhaps forcing her to handle weaponry would do the trick. Even though her father invented the things, most gently bred ladies were reluctant to touch firearms, if not outright terrified of them.

He selected a musket and held it out to her.

"This is a flintlock," he said, ladling out his words in slow, patronizing increments. "The ball shoots from this barrel, see? Here is the trigger, in the middle. And the other end fits against your shoulder, like this."

"Is that so?" she said wonderingly. She reached for the weapon. "May I try?"

"Slowly there." He moved behind her. "I'll show you how to hold it."

"That won't be necessary." She smiled. "Your instructions were so lucid and crisp."

And then as he—and Thorne and Colin, and the entire population of Spindle Cove—looked on, Susanna Finch took a cartridge from the table, ripped it open with her neat, straight teeth, and spat both paper nub and ball to the ground. Setting the gun at half cock, she sprinkled a bit of powder in the pan and closed the frizzen. Then she poured the remainder of the powder charge down the barrel and tamped it down with the ramrod.

Bram had seen soldiers' wives clean and assemble their husbands' firearms. But he'd never witnessed anything like this. Susanna didn't just know the proper sequence, she *understood* the piece. Those gloved hands moved confidently, handling the weapon with ruthless, arousing grace. His desire, and his loins, had already been stirred by that measuring exercise. Now his arousal approached rifle-barrel proportions.

She shouldered the musket, cocked the hammer, and fired the blank charge. The weapon gave a violent kick against her shoulder, but she didn't even flinch.

"Have I caught the trick of it, do you think?" she asked coyly, lowering the musket.

Remarkable. Bram fought the urge to applaud. He hadn't been timing, but he would have guessed the elapsed time to be under twenty seconds. Perhaps as few as fifteen. There were elite riflemen who couldn't load and shoot in fifteen seconds.

"Where did you learn to do that?"

"My father, of course." She lifted one shoulder in a shrug. "Don't most men learn such things from their fathers?"

Yes. Most *men* did. Bram himself had learned everything about shooting from his father. He'd begged for his first fowling piece almost as soon as he'd been able to form the words. Not because he'd loved guns so very much, but because he'd worshipped his father. He'd always looked for any excuse to spend more time with the man. Those solemn, patient lessons on safety and cleaning and marksmanship . . . they were now some of Bram's most cherished memories. He wondered if it had been the same for her. If she'd sat through similar lessons at Sir Lewis's side. Mastered this weapon, learned its workings inside and out, drilled and practiced until she could fire by instinct—all as a way to feel closer to him.

And now Bram felt closer to *her*, in a way he'd never expected to feel. Strange. And damned inconvenient. He scrunched his shoulders together, trying to shake the feeling off.

"Did you want to see me fix a bayonet next?" she asked.

"That won't be necessary."

He stared at her—standing tall, musket propped against

her shoulder, braced in perfect position. He'd thought himself so clever, letting her proceed with this "I'm a man" charade. The joke was on him. Male or not, she was his most promising recruit. He was tempted to punish her by letting her enlist.

But she would be too great a distraction. For all the men, but for Bram most of all. Spending all day with her, while she wore those form-fitting breeches? He couldn't be leading drills with his staff at full, rigid attention.

And more importantly, he could not let her best him in front of the whole village. He would have to release her from duty somehow, without losing the Bright boys in the exchange.

His eye fell to the table. The answer gleamed up at him, polished and sharp.

"There's one more thing, Miss . . . *Mr.* Finch. One more requirement for volunteers."

"Really? And what's that?"

Bram turned to the row of ladies sitting at the edge of the green. "Ladies, I must prevail on you for your assistance. I need each one of you to locate a pair of scissors and bring it here, as soon as possible."

The women looked to one another. Then quite the scuffle ensued, as they ducked into the Queen's Ruby to raid their dressing tables and sewing boxes. In similar fashion, the storeroom of All Things was turned out like a pocket.

When every available pair of scissors and shears had apparently been unearthed, and all the ladies were armed and assembled on the green, Sally Bright stepped forward. "What would you like us to do with them, Lord Rycliff?"

"Put them to use," he answered. "In my militia, all volunteers must have short hair. Above the collar in back. At the sides, above the ear."

He looked to Susanna. She paled a shade, and those freckles fairly danced off her face.

Turning to the recruits, he made a sweep of his arm. "The ladies have chosen their weapons. Men, choose your lady."

The women exchanged surprised glances. Equally stunned, the men hung back. Some pairings were obvious, of course. A woman he reckoned to be Mrs. Fosbury already had her husband by the collar, tugging him over to sit on a stump and submit to the will of her shears. But the unmarried men and women of Spindle Cove stood about regarding one another in silence. Like Quakers at meeting, waiting on some signal from above. Good Lord, he needed to teach these men to take some initiative.

Bram turned to his cousin. "Aren't you always the one to start off the dance? Do the honors now."

Colin shot him a look. "I'm not a volunteer."

"No, you're not. You're indebted and compelled. You have no choice whatsoever."

Colin rose slowly, pulling down the front of his waistcoat. "Very well. As you say, I do like to have first pick of the ladies." He strode forward, doffing his hat with a broad, theatrical sweep and coming to kneel at Miss Diana Highwood's feet. "Miss Highwood, would you be so kind?"

The fair-haired lady blushed. "Er, yes. Certainly, Lord Payne. I would be honored."

The ladies tittered among themselves, surely interpreting this as partiality on Colin's part. Susanna was right about the matrimonial fervor. They'd be rumoring an engagement by noon. If only there were a bit of truth to it. Colin was welcome to enter an engagement, and then he wouldn't be Bram's problem anymore.

His current problem tilted her lovely, freckled head.

"You were supposed to keep your men *apart* from my ladies."

"Need I remind you who broke that agreement first?" He picked up the pair of scissors on the table—the ones Thorne had been using to cut the measuring tapes. "Well?" he asked loudly. "What will it be, Finch?"

She stared at the scissors, wide-eyed. "Above the collar, you say?"

"Oh yes."

"Every volunteer in the militia?"

"No exceptions."

Her eyes pleaded with him. She lowered her voice to a whisper. "They're boys. Finn and Rufus, I mean. Their mother is anxious for them. Try to understand."

"Oh, I understand." He understood that she was ostensibly trying to shield those boys from harm. But he also understood her other purpose—clinging to her position of power in this village. On that score, he could not let her win. "Perhaps neither you nor I wanted it, but I'm the lord now. My militia. My village. My rules." He held out the scissors. "Shear or be shorn."

After a long moment, she removed her borrowed hat and set it aside. Reaching both hands behind her neck, she unbound her long queue of hair, then shook out the locks with a sensual toss of her head. The newly freed hair tumbled about her shoulders in lush, golden-red waves that shimmered in the sunlight, dazzling him into a near stupor.

In that instant, Bram knew he'd made a grave tactical error.

With a resigned sigh, she met his gaze. "Very well. It's just hair."

It's just hair.

Good Lord. That molten bronze aura framing her face

was most definitely *not* "just hair." It was living, flow-ing beauty. It was a crown of glory. It was . . . like the righteous breath of angry angels. Some kind of religious experience, and he was probably damned just for daring to look upon it.

A faint, wistful noise scraped from his throat. He cov-ered it with a cough.

Let her cut it, he told himself. *You have no choice. If she wins this battle, it's all over. You're done for.*

"Let me have them," she said. "I'll do it myself." She reached for the shears.

He gripped them tight. "No."

"No?" Susanna repeated, trying not to betray her panic. A brave front was important here.

She truly didn't want to cut her hair—"that *hair*," as her cousins had less than affectionately cursed it. Wild and unfashionable as it might be, it suited her now, and it was one thing she had of her mother's. But Susanna would make the sacrifice, if it meant keeping Finn and Rufus safe.

If it meant besting *him*.

It would grow back, she told herself. It had all grown back once before, after that dreadful summer in Norfolk. Only she wanted to cut it herself this time. Quickly, and with as little thought as possible. She didn't think she could bear to stand still while another held the shears.

"Just give me them." Growing close to desperate, she tugged on the scissors handles. "I'll do it now."

He wouldn't let go.

"Finn and Rufus." He spoke low, only to her. "I'll make them drummer and fifer. They'll be in the militia, attend drill and draw wages. But they won't be armed. Will that suffice?"

She was stunned. He had her just where he wanted her—on the verge of public humiliation—and now he wished to compromise? "I . . . I suppose that will do. Yes."

"Very well, then. Does this mean you're a lady again?"

"I'll go change straightaway."

"Not so fast," he said, still clutching the scissors handles tight. He gave her a bold look. "Before you leave, you'll do a service for me. Just like the other ladies are doing."

Indeed, all around them the men and women of Spindle Cove were pairing off. As Diana busied herself with Lord Payne, the blacksmith made his way to the widowed Mrs. Watson and her shears. Finn and Rufus seemed to be arguing over which of them would be stuck with Sally.

"You want me to cut *your* hair?" Her mind's eye went to that long, overgrown tail of hair always dangling between his shoulders, taunting her.

"As I said, no exceptions." He pressed the shears into her hand. "Go on, then. I'm all yours."

Susanna cleared her throat. "I believe you'll have to kneel."

"Kneel?" He snorted. "Not a chance, Miss Finch. There's precisely one reason I will kneel before a woman, and this isn't it."

"Proposing marriage, I hope you mean."

A devilish spark lit his eyes. "No."

Awareness raced through her body. She glanced around them. All around the green, the business of clipping hair had occupied her friends and neighbors. This had become a private conversation. And a fortunate thing, too, considering what took place next.

"If you don't mean to kneel," she said, angling on tiptoe, "I don't know how you expect me to cut your hair. All the chairs are in use. I may be tall, but there's no way I can reach—oh!"

He framed her rib cage in both hands and lifted her into the air. The brute power in the motion thrilled her. This made two times in three days that he'd swept her off her feet. Three, if she counted yesterday's kiss.

Why was she counting? She shouldn't be counting.

He set her down atop the table, making her the taller of the two. "Steady?"

At her mute nod, he slid his hands from her waist. Now she was lost in memories of their embrace yesterday, the press of his body against hers . . . Their gazes clashed. The now-familiar sparks flew.

Susanna swallowed hard. "Turn around, if you will."

Thank God. For once, he obeyed.

She took it in her hand, that thick, dark hank at his nape, bound with a bit of leather cord. His hair was lush, soft. Probably the softest thing on this man, she mused. Once it was cut, he would be all angles and sinew, hard all over.

"Why the delay?" he taunted. "Are you afraid?"

"No." With a steady hand, she raised the shears. Grasping the queue of hair firmly in the other hand, she aimed . . . and snipped. "Oh dear." She dangled the lopped-off coil before his face, then dropped it to the ground without ceremony. "Pity."

He only chuckled, but she thought she caught a hint of bruised pride in his laughter. "I see you're enjoying your chance to play Delilah."

"You'd better hope I don't decide to play Judith. I'm holding shears at the moment, and I'd advise you to be still. I need to concentrate." Setting the scissors aside for a moment, she pulled back her own locks and wound them into a simple knot. Then she set about the work of clipping his hair, and they both went quiet.

And as she worked, the quiet deepened, grew profound.

The task was so intimate. In order to cut his hair evenly, she had to sift her fingers through the heavy locks, lifting and angling them for the shears. She touched his ear, his temple, his jaw.

"Wouldn't it be easier if you removed your gloves?" he asked.

"No." At the moment, those thin leather gloves were the only thing keeping her sane.

A palpable, sensual tension had thickened the air surrounding them. His breathing was audible, a husky sighing in and out. Her fingers faltered for a moment, and she scraped his ear with one blade of the shears. She was horrified, but he seemed to take no notice. Only the tiniest drop of blood welled at the site, but it took all she had not to press her lips to the wound.

After a few more snips, she laid the shears aside. To test the cut's evenness, she raised both hands to his hair and dragged her gloved fingertips over his scalp, slowly raking them from his hairline to his nape.

As her fingers made that long, gentle sweep, he made a sound. An involuntary moan. Or perhaps a groan. It originated not in his throat, but deep in his chest, somewhere in the region of his heart.

That rumbling sound was more than a sigh. It was a confession, a plea. With a simple brush of her fingertips, she'd called forth an expression of deep, hidden yearning. Her whole body ached with an instinctive response.

Oh goodness. Oh, Bram.

"Turn around," she whispered.

When he obeyed, his eyes were closed.

Hers were open. Open to a whole new man. This big, brutish soldier-turned-medieval lord, now shorn close as a yearling—looking vulnerable and lost, in need of care. *Her* care.

All his staunch denials of emotion echoed in her ears. Did he know how thoroughly he'd just betrayed them? She thought of those passionate kisses yesterday. How he used every excuse to touch her, in every interaction. Heavens, the way he'd taken her measurements . . . Sensation rippled down her spine, as though she could still feel the deliberate sweep of his thumb. She'd thought him merely trying to rattle her.

But now she saw his motives clear. Here it was, his secret. No childhood trauma, no ravages of war. Just a deep, unspoken desire for closeness. Oh, he'd rather die than admit it in such terms, but that low, yearning sound told all.

That was the sound a great shaggy beast made when the nettle in his paw was plucked.

Here was a man who needed touch, craved tenderness—and he was *starved* for them both. Just how much would he allow her to give? She teased her fingers through the clipped fringe at his temples. His Adam's apple bobbed in his throat. She let a single gloved fingertip skim the ridge of his cheekbone.

"That's enough." His eyes snapped open, cool and defiant.

Wounded by his sharp tone, she withdrew her touch.

"Well, Miss Finch." Stepping back, he ran a hand over his dark, now short hair. "Tell me, how do the men look?"

Susanna let her gaze wander the green. Everywhere she looked, she saw newly revealed, blinding-white scalp. "Like a flock of yearlings, freshly shorn."

"Wrong," he said. "They do not look like sheep. They look like soldiers. Men with a common purpose. A team. Soon I'll have them acting like one, too."

Taking her by the waist, he lifted her off the table and put her back on firm ground. Oddly enough, the world still felt unsteady.

"Have a good look at them. In a month's time, I'll have a militia. These will become men of duty, action. I'll have shown all your prim, sheltered spinsters precisely what *real* men can do." The corner of his mouth quirked. "Spindle Cove will be a much different place. And you, Miss Finch, will thank me."

She shook her head. He'd revealed too much. That brute male swagger couldn't intimidate her now, and she would not let such a challenge pass without a strong, confident response.

She calmly brushed stray snips of hair from his lapel. "In a month's time, this community I love, and this atmosphere we've worked so hard to foster, will be the same. Everything I see here today will remain unaltered, except for one thing. Spindle Cove will change *you*, Lord Rycliff.

"And if you threaten my ladies' health and happiness?" She laid a sweet touch to his cheek. "I will bring you to your knees."

Chapter Eleven

n Mondays, we always have country walks."

Susanna paced the Highwood sisters on the sloping footpath. Together, they trailed behind the larger group. The ladies made a rainbow-hued column of muslin, filing up the path.

"The Downlands are beautiful this time of year. When we reach the top of the ridge, you can see for miles. It feels like being on top of the world."

Thank heaven for scheduled activities. After yesterday's . . . excitement . . . on the green and yet another restless night, Susanna was grateful for the distraction. She walked with vigor and purpose, inhaling deep lungfuls of the green-scented air.

"The wildflowers are lovely." Charlotte plucked a stalk of lavender-tipped rampion from the hillside and twirled it between her fingertips.

Minerva tromped along at Susanna's side. "Miss Finch, you cannot know how much I hate to sound like my mother. But are you certain this exertion is good for Diana's health?"

"Absolutely. Exercise is the only way she'll grow stronger. We'll go slowly at first, and no farther than is comfortable." She touched Diana's arm. "Miss Highwood, you are to tell me if you feel the slightest hint of difficulty with your breathing. We'll stop and rest at once."

Her straw bonnet bobbed in agreement.

"And"—Susanna reached into her pocket and withdrew a small, capped bottle—"I have a special tincture for you. Keep it in your reticule at all times. It's too strong to be taken every day, mind. Only when you feel you truly need it. The cap measures the proper dose. Aaron Dawes fashioned it specially at his forge. He's so clever with these small things."

Miss Highwood accepted the small vial. "What's in it?"

"The layman's name is shrubby horsetail. Rather common-sounding, but its ability to open the lungs is unique indeed. The plant normally grows in warmer climes, but our coastal weather is mild enough that I'm able to cultivate it here."

"*You* made this?"

"Yes," Susanna answered. "I dabble in apothecary."

Minerva eyed the bottle warily. As they all continued their slow, steady climb, she drew Susanna aside. "Forgive me, Miss Finch, but my sister has suffered greatly. I don't like the idea of entrusting her health to a 'dabbler.'"

Susanna took her arm. "I knew I liked you, Minerva. You're absolutely right to protect your sister, and I should not have described my work that way. No more than you should say you 'dabble' in geology. Why is it that we women so often downplay our accomplishments?"

"I don't know. Men are always boasting of theirs."

"Too true. Let's boast to each other, then. I've made a careful, scientific study of apothecary for several years. I make remedies for many of the visitors and villagers, and I have solid, scientific reason to believe that in a breathing crisis, the contents of that vial can do your sister some good."

"In that case, I trust your expertise." Minerva smiled. "Now for *my* boasting." With a glance toward the other ladies, she slowed. They'd fallen well behind the main group now. "Can you keep a secret? I am the first—and only—female member of the Royal Geological Society."

Susanna gasped with delight. "How did you manage that?"

"By neglecting to tell them I'm female. I'm just M. R. Highwood to them, and all my contributions are made through written correspondence. Fossils are my area of specialty."

"Oh, then you are in exactly the right place. These chalk hills are filled with strange little nuggets, and the cove—wait until you see the cove tomorrow."

They went quiet for a while as the way grew steeper, and narrower—so that they were forced to walk single file.

"There's the castle." Up the path, Charlotte stood on her toes and waved her growing posy of wildflowers in the direction of the ruins. "It's so romantic, isn't it? With that backdrop of the sea."

"I suppose," Susanna said, keeping her own eyes on the ground. She knew very well what a picturesque sight it made, but she'd been trying to keep castles and romance in two distinctly different, tightly corked bottles on her mental shelf.

"Your turn, Miss Finch," Minerva whispered, following close behind. "Don't you have your own secret to tell?"

Susanna sighed. She did have a secret—a scandalous, explosive secret that involved Lord Rycliff and kisses in the armory and a great many emotions she couldn't sort out. She wished she could trust Minerva with it. But men and fossils were different things.

They rounded a bend in the path and nearly collided

with the other ladies. They'd all stopped in their tracks at the edge of an overlook, staring down in mute wonder at the valley below.

"Cor," said Violet Winterbottom. "Isn't that a sight?"

"Just look at them all," Kate Taylor breathed.

"For heaven's sake, what is it?" Susanna asked, pushing to the fore. "Did Mr. Yarborough's cows escape again?"

"No, no. These are beasts of a different sort." Kate grinned at her.

Sounds floated up to Susanna's ears. Halting, erratic drumbeats. The shrill squawk of a fife. The impatient whinny of a horse.

Finally, she got a look.

The men. There they were, down on the flat meadow just north of the castle bluffs. From this vantage, it was difficult to distinguish any of the men as individuals. She could not have singled out Mr. Fosbury or the smith. But Bram, as usual, stood out from the crowd. This time, not merely because he was the tallest and his coat the brightest, but because he rode on horseback, giving him the advantage of height to gauge the formation's precision. As they marched, he directed his mount to circle the group, giving direction from all sides.

He looked very capable and strong and active. Which was unfortunate, because those were all the qualities she found appealing in a man. She'd never grieved over her disastrous London season because the gentlemen had been such disappointments. So idle and useless. She found it so much easier to respect people who *did* something.

Violet shaded her brow with her hand. "It doesn't seem to be going very well, does it?"

Kate laughed. "They keep doing the same thing. Just a single line, marching back and forth. Over and over.

From this end of the meadow to that. Then they stop, turn around, and do it again." She looked to Violet. "How many times now?"

"I stopped counting at eight."

"We shouldn't be watching them," Susanna said.

"Why not?" Kate looked at her. "Aren't they meant to be preparing a field review? A public display?"

"Just the same, let's continue on our walk."

"Actually, Miss Finch," Diana said, "I'm feeling a bit winded. Perhaps a rest would do me good."

"Oh. But of course." Unable to argue, Susanna spread her shawl and took a seat on the hillside. All the other ladies did likewise, and no one even bothered to pretend that gathering wildflowers or spotting birds would be the purpose of the moment. They all stared, riveted to the meadow below and the new militia's halting, sorry drill.

Susanna worried. She'd agreed to keep her ladies apart from Bram's men. The physical distance separating them at the moment didn't allay her concerns. Being this far removed only made the ladies feel free to gawk and gossip.

"I recognize that bright green topcoat. That must be Mr. Keane."

"You would think his sense of rhythm would be better, what with all the singing in church."

An elbow dug into her side. "Lord Rycliff's dismounting, look."

Susanna resolved *not* to look.

"He's taking the musket from one of them. Perhaps he means to show them himself just how it's done."

Susanna renewed her resolution not to look. The blades of grass beneath her fingertips were more interesting by far. And lo, here was a *fascinating* ant.

A female sigh. "What's that small, fluffy thing trotting at his heels? Some kind of dog?"

Drat it, now she had to look. A broad smile stretched her cheeks. "No. That's His Lordship's pet lamb. The dear little thing follows him around. He's named it Dinner."

All the ladies laughed, and Susanna laughed with them, knowing how it would vex Bram to be teased. Odd—and a bit disconcerting—how she felt so confident predicting his reactions. For that matter, how she kept thinking of him as "Bram."

"Oh!" In a gesture that strongly recalled her mother, Charlotte pressed a hand to her heart. "They're removing their coats."

"Not only their coats."

As the ladies all sat gawping in silence, the men halted their exercise and removed first their coats, then their waistcoats and cravats.

"Why would they do that?" Charlotte asked.

"They're working hard," Diana replied. "Perhaps it's warm down there."

Kate laughed. "It's growing warm up here, too."

"It's not the heat," Susanna said, again surprised how easily she knew his mind. "Their coats are all different colors. Lord Rycliff wants them looking the same, so they'll act in unison, too."

Charlotte grabbed the spectacles from Minerva's hand and lifted them to her own eyes. "Drat. I can't make out anything."

"Goose," Minerva said, giving her little sister an affectionate shove. "I'm farsighted. Those only help with objects up close. And I don't know why you're making such a fuss over a few men in shirtsleeves, anyhow. From this distance, they're just pale, fleshy blurs."

Except for Bram. There was nothing undefined about *his* torso. Even from this distance, Susanna could clearly make out the linen-sheathed muscles of his shoulders and arms. She recalled their solid heat beneath her touch.

"We should be heading back to the village." She rose to her feet, brushing grass from her skirts and folding her Indian shawl into a neat rectangle.

Violet objected, "But Miss Finch, we haven't yet reached—"

"Miss Highwood is winded," she clipped, in a tone that would brook no argument. "This is far enough for today."

The ladies rose in silence, retying bonnet ribbons and preparing to walk home.

"What do you say, Miss Finch?" Kate smiled as the sound of feeble drumming resumed. "How many times do you suppose he'll make them march that same line?"

Susanna could not have given Kate a number, but she knew the answer just the same.

"Until they do it right."

"They'll never get this right," Thorne muttered. "Bloody hopeless, all of them."

Bram swore under his breath. For God's sake, he'd spent all day yesterday just trying to teach these men to march in a straight line. When they mustered on Tuesday morning, he'd decided to make the task even simpler. No strict formations—just marching in time across open land. Left, right, left.

But marching in time was easier with a drummer who could drum in time, and Finn Bright seemed to have been born without a sense of rhythm. Say nothing of Rufus's ear-stabbing squawks on the fife.

Despite all this, somehow they'd managed to cover the

crescent of high ground between Rycliff Castle and the steep cliffs marking the other end of the cove.

"Put them at ease," he directed Thorne. "See if they can manage to just . . . stand there for a while, without falling on their arses."

Bram would have fallen on his own saber before admitting it, but he was the one who needed a rest. He looked out across the cove. Perched on the arm of land opposite, sat the castle. So close, if one measured as the gulls flew, but a rather long march back. Blast it, he should have brought his horse.

"So that's the spindle, I take it?" Colin squinted at a column of rocks punctuating the inlet. The formation was tall and roundish, with a knobby sandstone top.

"I suppose."

Colin snorted. "Proof positive that this place was named by dried-up old maids. No man—hell, no woman with a lick of experience—would ever look at that and call it a *spindle*."

Bram released a slow breath. He had no patience for his cousin's adolescent humor today. The sun was warm on his back. The sky and sea were having a contest to out-blue each other. Wisps of white dotted both, sea foam mirroring the clouds. Watching the gulls soar on the wind, he felt his heart pulling against its tether, floating in his chest. The water looked cool and inviting, buoyant.

And his knee felt like a collection of glass shards, encased in flesh. Never in the eight months since his injury had he walked this far without his brace. He shouldn't *need* the brace anymore, damn it. What was a mile or three across the fields, anyhow?

Tell that to his ligaments. His whole leg throbbed with fiery pain, and he wasn't sure at all how he'd make it back to the castle. But he would. He would lead them all the way home, and never betray a wince.

The pain was good, Bram told himself. The pain would make him stronger. Next time, he would push himself a bit farther, and it would hurt a bit less.

A bright flutter down in the cove caught his eye. "What's that?"

"Well, I am growing dangerously out of practice," Colin answered. "But they look like ladies to me."

His cousin was right. The ladies—and Bram was certain he recognized Susanna Finch's tall, slender form among them—were picking their way along the shore. They paused as a group, removing their bonnets and wraps and draping them on the branches of a twisted, scrubby tree. As their headwear came off, Bram caught a glimpse of golden-red flame, and desire kindled to life inside him. He'd know that hair anywhere. It had played a rather vivid role in his dreams last night.

As they reached the shingle beach, the ladies disappeared from view. The curve of the inlet guarded them.

"What do you suppose they're doing?" Colin asked.

"It's Tuesday," Bram said. "They're sea bathing." *Mondays are country walks. Tuesday, sea bathing. Wednesday, we're in the garden . . .* That promise of gardening gave him hope. God, perhaps tomorrow he'd finally have a chance of escaping Susanna Finch and her maddening sensual distractions. As if it weren't bad enough watching her climb the hillside yesterday, now he had to suffer the knowledge that somewhere not too far below, she'd soon be wet to the skin.

The Bright twins set aside the drum and fife and joined them at the edge of the cliff.

"It's no use craning your necks from here," Rufus said.

"They're well hidden when they change into their bathing costumes."

"Bathing costumes?" Bram snorted. "Leave it to Englishwomen to civilize the ocean."

"If you want a better view, the best place to peek is down the ridge a bit," Finn said, gesturing toward the tapering point of land. When Bram raised an eyebrow, the boy's cheeks flushed red. "Or so I hear. From Rufus."

His twin gave him an elbow to the side.

By now the rest of the men had gathered, clustering around the edge of the bluff.

"Tell me about this path," Bram said.

"Just there." Finn pointed. "Steps, cut into the sandstone by pirates in our grandfather's day. Once was, at low tide you could climb all the way from sea to bluff. The path's eroded now. Breaks off halfway. But follow it down a bit, and you have the best view into the cove."

Bram frowned. "You're certain no one could climb up this way? If spies or smugglers learned of it, this path could present a true risk." He turned to the fishermen volunteers. "Are your boats available? I'd like to have a look at these bluffs from the water."

The vicar rushed to his side. "Oh, but my lord—"

"But what, Mr. Keane? It's a fine enough day. High tide."

"The ladies have their sea bathing, my lord." Keane wiped his reddened face with his sleeve. "Miss Finch wouldn't like the intrusion."

Bram huffed an impatient sigh. "Mr. Keane. The purpose of this militia is to protect Miss Finch—and all denizens of Spindle Cove—from unwanted intrusions. What if a French frigate sailed into view this moment, setting course for this cove? Or an American privateer? Do you think they'll hold off on invading merely because it's Tuesday? Are you going to postpone fighting them, simply because the ladies have their sea bathing?"

The blacksmith scratched his neck. "If any ship's stupid enough to set course for this cove, we'll all sit back and watch the rocks chew her up."

"There aren't so many rocks right here." Bram looked over the edge. In the patch of aquamarine water directly below them, very few boulders littered the surface. A decent-sized rowboat could make its way right up to the bluff's edge.

"Anyway," Fosbury said, "there's no French frigate on the horizon today. Nor any American privateers. We'll leave the ladies to their privacy."

"Privacy?" Bram echoed. "What privacy? You're all standing up here leering at them while they flip and float like mermaids."

Of course, he was no better than the rest. They all stood in silence for a long minute, as one by one the ladies took to the water, rapidly submerging themselves up to their chins in the sea. He counted them. One, two, three little spinsters . . . All the way up to eleven, and Miss Finch—with her unmistakable head of hair—made twelve.

By God, Bram would welcome a swim right now. He could all but feel the water surrounding him, cool and sensuous. He could all but see Susanna in his mind's eye, swimming alongside him. Stripped to a wet, translucent shift and wreathed with that glorious, unbound hair. She lay in the shallows, tracing lazy circles with her arms while foamy waves lapped at her breasts.

Focus, Bramwell.

Milk-white breasts, just the perfect size for his hands. Tipped with pert, rosy nipples.

Focus on something else, *you addled fool.*

Lowering his weight to a nearby boulder, he began

working loose his boots. Once he had them both off, he rolled his sleeves to the elbow. Clad only in breeches and shirt, Bram walked to the extreme end of the rocky ridge where it jutted out over the sea, gripping the sandstone surface with his bare toes.

"Wait," Colin said. "Just what are you doing? I know this militia isn't going how you'd planned, and the only thing this set of pathetic souls have in common is shriveled, pathetic sets of their own. But surely matters aren't that dire."

Bram rolled his eyes at his cousin. "I'm just having a look at this path for myself. Since the thought of a row-boat survey has everyone in such a tizzy."

"I'm not in a tizzy," Colin said. "But I'm not stupid enough to go walking that cliff's edge, either."

"Good. I think we could use some time apart." Bram walked out as far as he could and investigated. As Finn and Rufus had told him, the cut-stone steps descended a ways down the bluff before crumbling into nothingness. No one could ascend this cliff face without the help of ropes and pulleys. Maybe wings.

Having satisfied his curiosity, he turned on his boulder perch and faced the men. He wasn't wearing his officer's insignia, but he mustered the mien of authority and voice to match.

"Listen sharp, all of you. When I give an order, it will be followed. Today is the absolute last instance in which I will tolerate a moment's hesitation, on any man's part. Hemming, hawing, hedging, and fidgeting—and most especially 'ask-Miss-Finch-ing'—will heretofore be grounds for immediate discharge, without pay. Am I understood?"

A mumbled chorus of agreement rose up.

He jabbed a thumb into his chest. "I'm your lord and

commander now. When I say march, you march. When I say shoot, you shoot. And no matter what Miss Finch would think about it . . . if I tell you to take a flying leap off this cliff, you will damned well leap with a smile."

Before he alighted, he allowed himself one last glance down at the cove. All the ladies bobbing and floating in that cool, enticing, blue-crystal sea. One, two, three little spinsters . . .

He stopped. Frowned. Concentrated and looked again. And then his heart left his chest and tumbled straight off the cliff.

He counted only eleven.

Chapter Twelve

hat's Lord Rycliff doing up there?" Charlotte asked, pointing up at the bluff. "Peeping at us? Where are his clothes?"

"I don't know." Squinting as she continued to tread water, Susanna watched the barefooted Bram inching closer to the edge of the bluff.

"He looks very dire and serious."

"He always looks that way."

From high above, she heard Lord Payne call out. "Don't do it, Bram! You have so much to live for!"

The ladies shrieked as Rycliff, apparently ignoring his cousin, flexed his legs—and jumped.

"Oh God." Horrified, Susanna watched his long, perilous dive into the sea. "He's done it. He's seen how hopeless the men are, and it's driven him to suicide."

A mighty splash announced his impact with the water. She could only pray it wasn't the prelude to an impact with something else. That area was rocky. The entire cove was rocky. More likely than not, he'd struck his head on a boulder and would never surface.

"Go for help," she told Charlotte, hitching up the skirts of her bathing costume. "Call to the men up there and tell them to follow the path around to the beach."

"But . . . but I'm not dressed. Whatever would Mama say?"

"Charlotte, this is no time to be missish. This is life and death. Just do as I say."

Susanna propelled herself into the water, swimming toward the place he ought to have landed. She sliced through the waves with fast, confident strokes, but her progress was hampered by the dratted bathing costume they all wore for modesty's sake. The fabric dragged around her ankles, heavy and tangled.

"Lord Rycliff!" she called, nearing the bottom of the cliff. She pulled up and began to tread water, looking this way and that in vain. She saw a great number of rocks, but none of them resembled his stony lump of a head. "Lord Rycliff, are you well?"

No answer. Her skirt snagged on an obstacle, and the sudden tug pulled her under. She took a swallow of sea-water. As she surfaced, she sputtered and coughed.

"Bram!" she shouted, growing desperate now. "Bram, where are you? Are you hurt?"

He broke through the surface of the water, not two feet in front of her. Soaked to his skin and wearing a dark, dangerous look.

He was alive. The burst of relief was so visceral, so swift, she was nearly overwhelmed by it. "Bram, what on earth are you—"

He ignored her entirely, looking around the cove instead. "Where is she?"

"Who?"

"Number twelve." With a gulp of breath, he disappeared beneath the water's surface, leaving her treading water, utterly bewildered.

Number twelve? He wasn't making any sense. Heavens, this was like that ridiculous sheep-bombing all over again.

He broke the surface, pushing water off his face. "Have to find her. Dark-haired girl."

Minerva. Now it made sense. He was looking for Minerva Highwood. He'd dived off a cliff to save her. The brave, heroic, reckless, misguided idiot.

"I'll look over there." He took off swimming, stroking his way around a cluster of boulders.

"Wait," she called, swimming after him. "Bram, I can explain. She's not drowned, I promise."

"She was here. Now she's not."

"I know it looks that way. But if you'll—"

He gulped a deep breath and submerged himself again. It seemed an eternity before he surfaced. The man had the lung capacity of a whale.

When he finally came up for air, Susanna launched herself at him to keep him from going under again.

"Wait!"

She caught him from behind, like a child riding piggyback, wrapping her arms around his shoulders, and her legs—such as the bathing costume permitted—around his waist.

"She's fine!" she shouted in his ear, shaking him back and forth. "Listen to me. Number twelve. Minerva Highwood. She's alive and well."

"Where?" he managed, breathless. He shook himself, and seawater sprayed her in the eye.

"There's a cave." She sandwiched his head between her two hands and turned it. "That way. The entrance is under water at high tide, but I showed her how to swim into it. She's alive and well and looking for rocks. Geology. Remember?"

"Geology."

They were quiet for a time. She rose and fell in the water as he worked to catch his breath.

"It was good of you," she said, pressing her cheek to the back of his neck. "It was good of you to try to help her."

"But she's fine."

"Yes." *And so are you, thank the Lord.*

Several panting breaths later, he said, "I believe you're safe to release me. It's shallow enough to stand."

That was when she realized he hadn't moved once, for all her furious thrashing. She peered over his shoulder. The water hit him midtorso, matting his open shirt to his body. In the notch of his open collar, little droplets of spray clung to the dark hair on his chest, sparkling in the sunlight. Small waves licked at his dark male nipples, perfectly delineated by wet linen.

And she was plastered to his back, limbs clinging in every direction. Like a deranged octopus.

"Oh." Mortified, she slid off his back. She stretched her feet under her and found solid footing. "Well, that's rather embarrassing."

When she finally dragged her gaze up to his face, she realized he was staring at *her* nipples now. How predictable. Just like a man. Here she'd been worried he was dead, and he had the nerve to be alive. Outrageously, manifestly virile and strong and alive. How dare he. How *dare* he?

What with the excitement of that water rescue exercise, atop several days' worth of unspoken tension, a revealing haircut, and not least of all, that explosive kiss . . . There was too much emotion building inside her, and it had only two possible outlets. Irrational anger, or . . .

She wasn't going to contemplate "or." Irrational anger it would be.

"You reckless fool," she cried. "You mollusk-brained addlepate. What were you thinking, making a dive like that? Don't you see these rocks? You could have been killed!"

His chin jerked. "I might as well ask what *you're* doing, swimming out in that horrid getup. You could be dragged underwater like Ophelia and drown."

"I swam out here to rescue you, you beastly man. I'm a very strong swimmer."

"So am I. I don't need rescuing."

She turned her head and spat another mouthful of seawater. "Oh, you will when I'm through with you."

Beneath the water's surface, something brushed her waist. A fish? An eel? She batted at it, whirling.

"Easy. It's just me." His arm slid around her waist, and he pulled her close. They sank into the water, up to their necks. With a one-armed stroke, he tugged her between two boulders.

"What do you think you're doing?"

He glanced up at the bluff. "Giving us some privacy. We need to talk."

"Here? Now? We couldn't converse in some normal time and place?"

"That's the problem." He pushed a hand through his dark, wet hair. "I can't stop thinking about you. All the time. Everyplace. I have work to do up there. Men to drill. A watch to organize. A castle to defend. But I can't even concentrate, for thinking of you."

She stared at him. This? *This* was the conversation he wished to have. Well, she could see why he wouldn't come calling at the house to bring it up over tea.

"You tell me why that is, Susanna. Keep in mind, you're talking to a man who'll march a hundred miles out of his way, just to avoid a romantic attachment."

"Attachment?" She forced a casual laugh. An unconvincing string of ha-ha-has. "A barrel of warm pitch couldn't attach me to you."

He shook his head, looking perplexed. "I even like it when you snipe at me."

"You've seen me with a gun. If I were to snipe at you, I promise you'd feel it. And you wouldn't like it one bit." She had to extricate herself from this situation, and his big, brawny arms. She wrestled in his grip, but he only embraced her more tightly.

"You're not getting away. Not yet." His deep voice sent ripples through the water. "We're going to have this out, you and me. Right here. Right now. I'm going to tell you every wild, erotic, depraved thought you've inspired, and then you're going to run home scared. Lock your bedchamber door and stay there for the next month so I can concentrate and do my damned duty."

"That sounds like a very poorly thought-out plan."

"Thinking's not my strong point, of late."

This rush of sensual awareness . . . oh, it was dangerous. She could grow to enjoy it. To be honest, she already enjoyed it. But she could grow to *crave* it, and that would make for difficult, lonely times ahead. She knew he needed a bit of human closeness. Perhaps because of the war he'd gone without it for too long. But at most, he had in mind a frantic tangle of body parts, not a meshing of hearts and souls.

"I want you," he said simply. Starkly. Composure-destroyingly.

See? she told herself. *He couldn't be any more plain than that.*

"I want you. I dream about you. I am desperate to be near you," he said, sending a fresh shiver down her spine. "To touch you. All over." His hands roamed over her arms and back. "What is this hideous thing you're wearing?"

"It's a bathing costume."

"It feels like a shroud. And it's too damned opaque."

"Yes, well. That's rather the point. Opacity." Her breathing was quick; her words, stupid.

One of his hands slid down to capture her fingers. He raised them above the water's surface, shaking them as though they were some kind of damning evidence. "Who wears gloves in the ocean?"

She swallowed hard. "I do."

"These gloves of yours, they drive me mad. I want to strip them from your hands. Kiss those slender wrists, suck on each of those long, delicate fingers. And that would only be the beginning. I want to see the rest of you, too. Yours is a body made for a man's pleasure. It's a crime against nature to hide it."

This could not be happening. Not to *her*. She squeezed her eyes shut, then opened them again. "Lord Rycliff. You've forgotten yourself."

"No, I haven't." His green eyes held her captive. "I recall precisely who I am. I'm Lieutenant Colonel Victor St. George Bramwell, the Earl of Rycliff since a few days back. You're Susanna Jane Finch, and I want to see you bare. Bare, and pale, and soaked to the roots of your hair, glistening with moonlight and drops of seawater. I'd lick the salt from you."

His tongue swiped over her cheek, and she gasped. Her nipples peaked, straining against the rough, wet fabric.

"You're mad," she breathed.

His lips grazed her ear. "I'm perfectly clear of mind. Want to test my recollection? On Mondays, you have country walks. On Tuesdays, sea bathing. Tomorrow, perhaps I'll come find you in the garden and pull you into the shrubbery."

The suggestion made her weak. She imagined his body, atop hers. The heat of him, contrasting with the cool, damp ground. Her mind conjured the scents of grass and earth.

"And on Thursday . . ." He pulled back and gave her a wicked look. "That's interesting. We never did get to Thursday. Please tell me on Thursdays you oil yourselves up and wrestle Grecian-style."

She gasped. "You are horrid."

"And you love it. That's the worst of the matter. You want me every bit as badly as I want you. Because I'm exactly what you need. There's no one else in this village strong enough to take you on. You need a real man, to show you what to do with all that passion seething beneath your surface. You need to be challenged, mastered."

Mastered? "You need to be caged, you beast."

"A beast is just what you want. A big, dark medieval brute to throw you to the ground, tear the clothes from your body, and have his wicked way with you. I know I'm right. I haven't forgotten how *excited* you were in the aftermath of that blast."

The nerve of him!

How could he tell?

She lifted her chin. "Well, I haven't forgotten the sound you made when I first touched your brow. It wasn't even a moan, it was more like . . . like a whimper."

He made a dismissive sound.

"Oh yes. A plaintive, yearning whimper. Because you want an angel. A sweet, tender virgin to hold you and stroke you and whisper precious promises and make you feel human again."

"That's absurd," he scoffed. "You're just begging to be taught a hard, fast lesson in what it means to please a man."

"You're just longing to put your head in my lap and feel my fingers in your hair."

He backed her up against a rock. "You need a good ravaging."

"You," she breathed, "need a hug."

They stared at each other for long, tense moments. At first, looking each other in the eye. Then looking each other in the lips.

"You know what I think?" he said, coming closer. So close she could feel his breath wash warm against her cheek. "I think we're having one of those vexing arguments again."

"The kind where both sides are right?"

"Hell, yes."

And this time, when they kissed, they both made that sound. That deep, moaning, yearning, whimpering sound.

That sound that said *yes*.

And *at last*.

And *you are exactly what I need*.

She could feel the tension and urgency coiled in his muscles. But his kiss was patience itself. His mouth brushed hers, teasing her lips apart. Her pulse hammered as he made that first tantalizing pass with his tongue.

Oh dear. Oh dear oh dear oh dear.

There *was* passion, stockpiled inside her. He'd called her a powder keg, but that would be understating. She saw it all now, stretching in her mind's eye. Vast storehouses, whole magazines. Here were crates of kisses, never shared. Casks of sweet caresses kept sealed from the rain. Row upon row of breathy moans and sighs, all carefully bottled and tightly corked.

He uncapped one now, with a clever flick of his tongue. Pressed his thumb to the hinge of her jaw, unlocking yet more desire. He kissed her slow and deep, taking time to explore.

"Bram," she heard herself whisper. She pushed her hands through his cropped, sleek hair. "Oh, Bram."

The further he raided, the closer he came to the other rooms. Those unused, cobwebbed chambers of her heart. Would he dare to venture there? She doubted. Jumping off a cliff was a flashy sort of courage, but a man would need true strength and valor to break through those pad-locked doors. There were dark, uncharted spaces within her that had been built to house love, and even she was afraid to explore them. Terrified to learn just how vast and how achingly empty they truly were.

And her heart wasn't the only aching, empty place. Between her legs, she was both. As they kissed, he slid his hands to her backside and lifted her, bringing her pelvis flush against his. The prominent, hot ridge of his arousal rubbed against her sex. She moaned into his kiss, a word-less plea for something more. Surely he would know how to answer.

And answer he did.

He bit down on her lip. Hard.

"Ah!" He winced away from her, completely breaking their embrace.

Susanna opened her eyes to see him clutching his head and grimacing with pain.

"What the devil . . . ?" he said.

"Take that, you brute." Minerva Highwood moved be-tween them, soaked to the skin and clutching a weighted pouch in her hand.

"Minerva?" Reeling from the abrupt interruption, Su-sanna touched a finger to her lip, testing for blood.

"Don't worry, Miss Finch. I'm here now."

She must have swum out from the cave and . . . and *seen* them. Oh God.

"I'm fine, truly." Susanna's gaze snapped to the pouch dangling from Minerva's wrist. It looked like a reticule, fashioned from oilcloth. "What's in that?"

"Rocks. What else?"

Rocks. Good Lord. Susanna looked to Bram with fresh concern. The man had just taken a cudgel to the head. It was a wonder he hadn't fallen unconscious. She started toward him, but Minerva gave a little shriek and backed up, throwing her body in front of Susanna's.

"Brace yourself. Here he comes again, the . . . the rutting Zeus."

Bram was clearly still dazed, rubbing his head with one hand. With a growl of pain and a sudden, lurching motion, he stood tall—rising head, shoulders, and exquisitely chiseled torso out of the water. Water droplets sprayed everywhere, catching the sunlight and flashing like tiny sparks.

Rutting Zeus, indeed. He did rather look like a linen-draped Greek god, dripping with potency and a divine air of possession. The sight took Susanna's breath away. She briefly wondered if *she'd* been hit over the head with a sackful of rocks. He was beautiful. Dazzling in his masculine perfection.

"Don't worry." Minerva scrambled onto a nearby boulder, readying her stone-packed reticule. "I'll save you, Miss Finch."

Susanna reached for her. "Minerva, no! There's no need. He wasn't—"

Splash.

——Chapter Thirteen——

ram came to consciousness slowly, floating into awareness on a gentle, soothing wave. The world was dark, but he was warm all over. Delicious sensation lapped at his wounded leg, stroking away all the pain and soreness with a light, rhythmic touch.

As his eyes fluttered open, questions teased at the frayed edge of his mind. Where was he? Just who was touching him? And how did he make sure it never, ever stopped?

"Oh, Bram." Susanna's voice. "My goodness. Just look at this."

He struggled up on one elbow, wincing at the sudden lash of pain. He saw a tangle of white sheets. He saw his own dark, hairy legs. He saw her hands on his skin.

Her bare, ungloved hands.

He fell back against the mattress, seeking sleep again. Obviously, he was hallucinating. Or dead. Her touch felt like heaven.

"This explains so much," she said, clucking her tongue in mother-hen fashion. "You're compensating for this withered appendage."

Withered appendage? What the devil was she talking about? He shook his head, trying to clear it. Colin's dire predictions of shriveled twigs and dried currants rattled in his skull.

Wide awake now, he fought to sit up, wrestling the sheets. "Listen, you. I don't know what sort of liberties you've taken while I was insensible, or just what your spinster imagination prepared you to see. But I'll have you know, that water was damned cold."

She blinked at him. "I'm referring to your leg."

"Oh." His leg. *That* withered appendage.

How long had he been unconscious? An hour? More? She'd changed into a frock of striped muslin, but her hair was still wet, combed back from her face in dark amber furrows.

Her hands kept stroking. He saw that her fingers were glistening, coated with some sort of liniment. The herbal scent of it filled his head. Lust sent his blood rushing everywhere else. It had to be a sign of his prolonged celibacy that viewing her ungloved hands aroused him more than a woman's full nakedness had in the past.

Or maybe it was a sign that he wanted this woman more fiercely than he'd ever wanted another.

"Where are we?" he asked, looking about the room. A light, airy bedchamber, done up in chintz and hardwood. The mattress beneath him felt bowed like a hammock, strained and tested by his weight.

"Summerfield."

"How did we get here?"

"With great difficulty. You weigh as much as an ox. But you'll be glad to hear your men rallied to the challenge."

Deuce it. Damn it. Devil take it and fling it off a cliff. His second full day in command of new recruits, and he'd capped it by dropping unconscious, felled by a squinty bluestocking and her reticule. They'd carried his dead weight all the way here, likely passing through the village on the way and attracting a crowd of onlookers. Even the sheep had probably watched the processional, bleating with smug satisfaction. He was their lord and commander, and now they'd all seen him at his most feeble.

"Must have amused you, seeing me bludgeoned so soundly by a girl."

"Not at all," she said. "I was terrified."

She wasn't terrified at the moment. Just look at her leaning over him, giving him bold flashes of her pale, freckled bosom. Stroking his bared leg with talented, fearless fingers. Earlier, she'd called him a beast. Now she was treating him like a broken-winged bird.

He snarled down at his wounded leg. Withered appendage, indeed.

"Here." She pressed a cup into his hand. "Drink this."

He eyed it skeptically. "What is it?"

"Relief from pain, in liquid form. My own special preparation."

"You're a healer?" He frowned, and it hurt. "Should have figured you for one of those females with her little basket of herbs and sunshine."

"Herbs are good. They have their uses. For a wound like this, you need drugs."

He sipped. "Ugh. That is vile."

"Too much for you? If you like, I can add some honey. That's what I do for the village children."

He tossed back the rest of her potion without comment. He truly *couldn't* comment, what with the bitter taste scorching his throat.

After setting the drained cup aside, she returned her attention to his leg. "What happened to you?"

"A bullet happened to me."

"It's a miracle you didn't lose the leg."

"It wasn't a miracle, it was sheer force of will. Believe me, those bloodthirsty field surgeons tried to take it."

"Oh, I believe you. I've known my share of bloodthirsty surgeons. My youth was rife with them."

"Were you ill as a child?"

She shook her head. "No."

She dipped her fingers into the crock of liniment and moved her attentions up his leg, to his aching thigh muscles. Of course, by soothing the pain in those muscles, she was only creating new aches in his groin. Didn't she know how dangerous it could be to provoke a man this way?

He ought to tell her to stop. He couldn't.

Her touch was . . . God, it was just what he'd been needing. She was talented indeed.

"So how did you fend them off?" she asked. "The field surgeons."

"Thorne," he said. "Sat by my bedside with a pistol cocked, ready to fire at the first gleam of a bone saw."

"I imagine Thorne could have scared them off with a look." She traced a scar on the side of his knee, a thin line that stood out against the gnarled mess. "But someone operated here. Someone skilled."

He nodded. "Took three days, but we found a surgeon who promised not to amputate."

She traced a horizontal line across his thigh, above the bullet wound. There was no scar tissue there, but a leather strap had worn him bald in a telltale stripe of pale, baby-smooth skin. A matching band of hairless skin circled his upper calf. She touched that, too. He winced, not at the pain, but at the exposure. He hoped she wouldn't understand the significance of those bands.

"You've been wearing a brace," she said.

He didn't respond.

"Why did you remove it? Bram, you can't simply ignore an injury of this magnitude."

He had to ignore it. His purpose was not only training men, but leading them, inspiring them. How could he accomplish that with such an obvious weakness?

"I'm healed," he told her. "It scarcely pains me anymore."

She made a gruff, incredulous noise. "Liar. You're in great pain. And more than the usual amount today, I'd wager, after all that marching about the countryside. The water must have felt good."

"It did. But not as good as you." He reached for her, suddenly eager to take the aggressive role. He'd been lying here helplessly for much too long.

She batted his hand aside. "You should still be wearing the brace. Look at this swelling." Her fingertip traced his red, misshapen knee. "You're not ready to march without it."

Her pitying touch, those limiting words . . . Something in him snapped.

He seized her wrist in a grip so tight, she gasped. "Don't tell me what I'm ready to do." He squeezed harder still. "Do you hear me? Don't ever tell me what I can't do. Those surgeons told me I'd never walk again. I proved them wrong. My superiors think I can't command troops. I'll prove them wrong, too. If you mean to treat me like an invalid—a man you can coddle and nurse and stroke without any hint of danger . . ." He yanked on her wrist, pulling her atop him. He cinched his other arm around her waist. "I'll have to prove you wrong, as well."

Her eyes flashed. "Release me."

"Not a chance."

She struggled in his grip, and her short, quick breaths gave him a luscious display of her breasts.

"That won't work, love. My leg might be injured, but I'm strong as a bull everywhere else."

"Even bulls have their weaknesses." He felt her wriggling, insinuating one of her lithe, slender legs between his. The hot friction of their bodies, through just the thin layers of her frock and a linen sheet, had him aching. She made a quick strike, trying to knee him in the groin. Oh, she understood how to hurt a man. But he was one move ahead of her. He scissored his good leg over hers, trapping her lower body. Then he flipped them both, putting her on her back.

"There. I have you," he said, pinning one hand over her head. "And what will you do now?"

"I'll scream. There are two footmen just outside this room. My father's sleeping down the corridor."

"Go ahead, scream. Call the footmen and your father in. We'll be found in a very compromising position. My career will be over, you'll be ruined, and we'll be stuck together for life. We can't have that, now can we?"

"Lord, no."

Bram stared down at her. Odd. He'd spent his entire adulthood avoiding romantic entanglements. But here he was, completely tangled with this woman, and the idea of being forced to marry her didn't horrify him the way it ought. In fact, if he let himself envision spending a lifetime of nights in a graciously appointed bedchamber, atop a soft, clean mattress, with her lovely scent of herbs in the air and her pale body writhing under his . . .

It was the strangest, most foreign and unlikely image. But curiously, he didn't hate it.

She squirmed beneath him. "Brute. Beast."

Chuckling, he kissed her on the forehead. "That's more like it." He'd much rather have her scorn than her pity. Pity made him feel helpless. Provoking her ire made him feel alive. And she was so wonderfully easy to provoke.

"God, having you under me, in a bed . . ." He kissed

her, just at the corner of her lips. "You drive me mad with wanting, Susanna. We'd be so good together."

He gentled his grip on her wrist, but kept it pinned with just the weight of his arm atop hers. He slid one thumb along the line of her jaw, covering her racing pulse. Then dipping lower, caressing the tender slope of her throat. Her skin was so soft. Had she bathed? he wondered. Or would she still taste of the sea?

"Very well," she said. "You've made your point. You're a big, strong man, and I'm a helpless female. Now let me go."

"I'll release you, if that's truly what you want. But I don't think it is."

Flipping his hand, he slid the backs of his fingers down her chest, all the way to her bosom. He skimmed the exposed edge of her chemise. The sheer, lacy fabric rose and fell with her rhythmic breaths, like froth riding the edge of a wave.

If she wanted him to stop, she could stop him. Her arms were virtually unrestrained. He levered his weight onto one elbow. A quick dart to the side, and she'd be free.

She glanced in that very direction, obviously thinking the same.

But she didn't move. She wanted this, too.

In a slow, sure claiming, he fitted his palm over her breast. She bit back a gasp.

Bram struggled to contain his own groan of pleasure. The soft, round swell fit his hand so perfectly, warming under his touch. As he held her, her nipple tightened to a knot, pressing against the center of his palm. Just a small, concentrated dot of sensation, but unspeakably arousing. Her body was responding to his, *calling* to his. His cock answered, stiffening to a painful degree.

He bent his head and pressed his lips to her bared

throat, kneading the taut globe of her breast as he kissed a slow trail downward. She did taste of salt, and of sweet femininity. He licked her, sliding his tongue in a lazy, serpentine path over her collarbone. Then dipping down, to trace the border of her décolletage. There, her close-fitted bodice thwarted him. He slipped a single finger between fabric and skin, forcing the neckline to give, just a little. He needed to touch her there, feel that tight bead of her nipple press against the pad of his fingertip.

Working in tiny arcs, he skimmed his touch lower, exploring the warm satin of her skin. Learning the unique geography of the plump, delectable globe. His thumb finally grazed the textured edge of her areola, and triumph surged through him. He felt like a conquistador discovering a new territory. An enticing round island of promise, bordered by rippling dunes and capped with an upward-thrusting peak. He climbed it in increments, panting for breath. God, just a little further . . .

There.

She gave a startled, breathy cry, and her whole body bowed against his. Her passionate response nearly undid him. His thoughts unraveled, leaving him with just one thread of concentration.

More.

That was all he could think, all he could understand. More. He needed more of her. How could he stroke more, touch more, kiss more? He still had one of her arms pinned overhead. If he lowered it to her side, he reasoned, her neckline would have more give. He would make it yield to him, so he could take that delicious, straining peak into his mouth. But when he rose up a bit, meaning to draw her arm down to her side . . .

"Jesus."

He froze, staring. Struggling to make sense of what he beheld. From wrist to elbow, her delicate skin was a crosshatch of scars.

With a sharp mental tug, he reined in the arousal charging through his body. So here was the reason she always wore those enticing, buttoned gloves. She was hiding something, too.

Something much more serious than a nettle in her paw.

"Susanna fair," he said, skimming a touch over her marked skin. "What happened here?"

Susanna winced at his touch. Inside, she crumpled. She ought to have known she couldn't hide them forever. That she would never get this close to a man without those dratted scars ruining everything, one way or another.

"How old are these?" he asked, tracing a thin, healed line with his fingertip.

"Quite old," she said dismissively. "They're nothing. From gardening."

"Gardening? Did you pick a death match with a rose-bush?"

"No." She arched her back, rubbing her breasts against his chest. His touch had felt so good. So right. "Couldn't we just go back to where we left off?"

Apparently not.

As she wriggled beneath him, he used his weight and strength to keep her pinned. Not out of conquest, it seemed, but out of concern. "What happened? Tell me the truth."

"I . . ." She hesitated. Then she took a deep breath and decided to just be honest. He could make of the truth what he would. "They're from bloodletting."

"So many?" He cursed softly, running his fingertips over the ladder of scarred skin. "I thought you said you weren't ill as a child."

"I wasn't ill. That didn't stop the surgeons from trying to cure me."

"Tell me," he said.

Her gaze slanted to the corner. A wild pulse pounded in her ears, like a warning.

"You've seen *my* scars," he reminded her, easing aside to give her space. "I've told you everything."

"It was the year after my mother died." Her own voice sounded flat, remote. "Papa thought I needed feminine influence—someone to see that I grew into a young lady. So he sent me to Norfolk, to stay with relations."

"And you took ill there?"

"Only with homesickness. But my cousins didn't know what to do with me. They saw it their duty to make me ready for society, but they lamented that I would never fit in. I was tall and freckled, and my hair gave them the vapors. Not to mention, my behavior left much to be desired. I was . . . difficult."

"Of course you were."

She felt a stab of hurt at the flip comment. It must have been evident, for he quickly qualified his remark.

"I only mean," he said, "that was perfectly natural. You were sent to live with virtual strangers, and your mother had just died."

She nodded. "They understood that, at first. But when weeks went by and my comportment failed to improve . . . they thought something more must be wrong. That was when they called in the doctors."

"Who bled you."

"To begin with. They prescribed a variety of treatments, over time. I didn't respond as they hoped, you see. I do have an obstinate streak."

"I believe I've noticed that." He smiled a little. The warmth in his eyes gave her strength to continue.

"The doctors bled me more, dosed me with emetics and purgatives. After that, I refused my meals, took to hiding in the cupboards. They called the doctors back again, and again. When I fought them, they decided I suffered from hysteria. My treatments increased. Two footmen would restrain me, so the doctor could take yet more blood, dose me with more poison. They would bind me in blankets until I was drenched with sweat, and then force me to bathe in ice-cold water."

The painful memories rushed in on her, but they weren't as difficult to voice as she'd thought they'd be. After all this time, the words just flowed out of her, as if—

Oh, now *there* was an ironic thought.

As if she'd opened a vein.

"They . . ." She swallowed hard. "They shaved off all my hair and applied leeches to my scalp."

"Oh God." Guilt twisted his features. "The other day on the green, when I threatened to cut your hair . . ."

"No. Bram, please don't feel that way. You didn't know. How could you?"

He sighed. "Just tell me everything now."

"I've told the worst of it, truly. Just one vile, useless treatment after another. In the end, I was so weakened by it all, I truly took ill."

Frowning intently, he smoothed the hair from her brow. His eyes were the angry green of tempest-swept seas.

"You look so grieved," she said.

"I am."

Her heart pinched. Truly? Why would he care about the medical travails of a spinster, years upon years in the past? Surely war had shown him much worse. It had done far worse to him. And yet, something in his serious, battle-ready expression told her he did care. That if it were in any way humanly possible, he would go back in time and impale those surgeons on their own bloody lancets.

She could love him. God help her, she could love him for that alone.

"It's all right now. I did survive." She gave him a smile tipped with self-effacing humor, to keep the tale from growing too maudlin. Or perhaps to keep herself from bursting into grateful tears.

"That obstinate streak was to thank, I imagine. No doubt you simply refused to die."

"Something like that. I don't remember much of the illness, mercifully. I grew so weak, they sent an express to my father, thinking my time was near. He arrived, took one look at me, bundled me up in his cloak, and had me out of that house within the hour. He was furious."

"I can believe it. I'm furious now."

Blinking a moist sheen from her eyes, she cast a glance around the room. "That's when we moved here, to Summerfield. He bought the place so I could convalesce by the sea. Slowly, I recovered. I didn't need doctors or surgeons. Just nourishing food and fresh air. Once I was well enough, exercise."

"So," he said thoughtfully, running his thumb over her scars, "these are why . . ."

"Yes. They're why."

He didn't ask for further explanation, but she gave it anyway.

"You see, my father did eventually take me to London for my presentation at Court. And just as my cousins had predicted, I didn't fit in. But while I was standing at the edges of those elegant ballrooms, I realized there were others like me. Girls who, for one reason or another, didn't square with expectations. Who were in danger of being sent to some dreadful spa to take a 'cure' they didn't need. I began inviting them here for the summer. Just a few friends at first, but the number has grown each year. Mrs. Nichols is glad for the steady custom at the inn."

"And you turned your own talents to healing."

"I take after my father, I suppose. He's an inventor. All those surgeons' failed experiments made me curious to find better methods."

Again, he traced his fingertips over the crosshatch of scars. So many of them, from the razor-thin, superficial lines to the thick, gnarled evidence of a formidable fleam—a wooden implement nearly as thick as her wrist. She still shuddered to recall it.

"Damned butchers," he muttered. "I've seen veterinarians tap horses' arteries with less injury incurred."

"The marks would have been fainter if I'd struggled less. Do they . . ." She resisted the urge to look away. "Do they disgust you?"

In response, he pressed a kiss to her scarred wrist. Then another. Emotion swelled in her breast.

"Do you think me weaker for them?" she asked.

He cursed in denial. "These have nothing to do with weakness, Susanna. They're only proof of your strength."

"Well. I don't think you weaker for your scars, either." She stared deep into his eyes, willing him to absorb the meaning of her words. "No one would."

"It's not the same," he argued, shaking his head. "It's not the same. Your wounds can be hidden. They don't cause you to limp, or fall, or lag behind those you're meant to lead."

Perhaps not. But she was only just beginning to understand, her scars had held her back in different ways. She'd been afraid, for so long, to come this close to a man. To let the gloves come off, and take the chance of being hurt again.

"There are differences, to be sure," she whispered, drawing him down. "But I do know how it feels to fight a long, slow recovery. To feel confined in your own body, so frustrated with its limitations. And I know what it is to crave closeness, Bram. You don't have to attack me every time you wish to be touched. To be held."

She stretched her arms around him. He lay silent atop her, and she knew a moment of fear. She wanted to give him the same comfort he'd given her, but she was afraid of doing everything wrong. With trembling fingers, she stroked a light caress down his spine.

"Yes." He exhaled against her neck. "Yes, touch me. Just like that."

She caressed him with both hands now, covering his back with smooth, even strokes.

"Susanna?" he said, after minutes had passed.

"Yes."

"Feel strange. Can't lift my head."

"It's the drugs. They're taking you under now."

"Su-san-naa," he half whispered, half sang, in a slurred, drunken tone. "Susanna fair with brazen hair." As she laughed, he pressed his brow to her pounding pulse. "That's the perfect word for you, 'brazen.' Do you know why? Because your hair is like molten bronze. All gold and red and glowing. And you're bold and fearless, too."

"I have so many fears." Her heart was thumping like a hare's.

"You don't fear me. That first day, when we met. Those few seconds after the blast . . . you were under me, just like this. Soft. Warm. The perfect place to land. And you trusted me. I could see it in your eyes. You trusted me to guard you."

"You *kissed* me."

"Couldn't help myself. So pretty."

"Hush." She turned her head to kiss him quiet. Her heart couldn't take any more. The faint, drugging taste of laudanum lingered on his lips. "Just rest."

"Would have garroted those surgeons," he muttered. "Your relations, too. Never would have let them hurt you."

She couldn't help but smile at his sweet promises of violence, offered up like a posy of carnivorous blooms.

"I suppose they did mean to help," she said. "My relations, I mean. They just didn't know better. Looking back, I know I presented a challenge. I was so awkward and stubborn. Not a ladylike bone in my body. They used to set me at copying pages from this horrid, insipid book. *Mrs. Worthington's Wisdom for Young Ladies*. Oh, Bram. You would laugh at it so."

He was quiet for a long moment. Then his chest rumbled—not with a laugh, but with a loud, resonant snore.

She laughed at herself, and at the same time hot tears spilled from her eyes. In his sleep, he flexed a protective arm around her. His embrace felt so right.

Perhaps she could trust him to guard her. He was strong and principled, and she had no doubt he would risk his life to keep her safe, in body. But he couldn't make any promises to guard her heart.

And in her heart, she feared she was already falling. Tumbling headlong toward a world of pain.

Chapter Fourteen

uch."

Susanna released the rose blossom and stared at the tiny drop of welling blood on her finger. Reflexively, she stuck it in her mouth, soothing the hurt.

"Kate," she called across the garden, "would you finish the roses for me? I've forgotten my gloves this morning."

Incredible. She *never* forgot her gloves.

She left the roses and moved to the herbal bed, gathering great fistfuls of thorn-free lavender and snipping them free with shears. Soon her basket was heaped to overflowing with fragrant stalks. And still, she kept piling them higher.

Whenever she tried to still them, her hands began to tremble. Maybe because they were still heavy with the feel of his skin, his hair.

At this very moment, Bram remained asleep upstairs on the upper floor of Summerfield. Meanwhile, down here in the garden, Susanna was forced to keep up the Wednesday habit of hosting the Spindle Cove ladies. Gardening first, tea after. Normally, she appreciated both their company and their help. But today, she would have far rather been alone with her thoughts.

Because her thoughts were all of him. They made her

blush. They made her feel uncorseted, exposed. They made her sigh—*aloud*, for heaven's sake. Ladies clustered all around her, pulling weeds, cutting blooms, sketching bumblebees and blossoms. But when Susanna knelt beside the feverfew and let her gaze go unfocused, her thoughts climbed straight upstairs.

She saw him. Dark, powerful limbs, covered with even darker hair, all tangled among the white, crisp sheets. Her sleeping beast. In her mind's eye, she approached the bed, eased onto the mattress beside him. Stroked his cropped, velvet hair. Kissed the notch carved between his throat and clavicle. Heat raced along her skin, gathered between her thighs.

And then he woke, capturing her with his strong arms and that compassionate green gaze. His heavy weight atop her was a blessing, not a burden or a threat.

Susanna fair, he said. *You were the perfect place to land.*

"Miss Finch. Miss Finch!"

She shook herself, coming back into the present. "Yes, Mrs. Lange?" How long had the poor woman been trying to catch her attention?

"Did you want me to divide these lilies today? Or shall we leave them for another week?"

"Oh. Whatever you think best."

From beneath her straw bonnet, the other woman gave her an impatient look. "It is your garden, Miss Finch. And you always have an opinion."

"What's wrong, dear?" Mrs. Highwood asked. "It doesn't seem like you to be so distracted."

"I know. It's not. Forgive me."

"It's a lovely day," Kate said. "I can't imagine what has you so out of sorts."

"It's not a what." Minerva looked up from her sketchbook. "It's a who."

Susanna gave her a warning look. "Minerva, I'm sure you don't need—"

"Oh, I'm sure I do. And you mustn't be ashamed to talk about it, Miss Finch. You needn't suffer in silence, and the ladies ought to know. They may need to protect themselves." She closed her sketchbook and turned to the assembled ladies. "It's Lord Rycliff, the vile man. He did not hit his head when he made that dive yesterday. He survived the fall with no harm, and then he attacked Miss Finch in the cove."

"Minerva." Susanna put her hand to her temple. "He did not attack me."

"He did!" She turned to the others. "When I came upon them, they were both drenched to the skin. Poor Miss Finch was shaking like a leaf, and he had his hands . . . Well, let's just say he had his hands in places they oughtn't be. She tried to fend him off, but he wasn't having any of it."

I like it when you snipe at me. A thrill raced through her at the memory.

"It's fortunate I came along when I did," Minerva said. "And that I'd made such a good find of weighty specimens that morning."

Fortunate? Perhaps it was. Lord only knew what liberties Susanna would have allowed him without Minerva's interruption. And if those drugs hadn't carried him off to sleep last night . . .

She'd stayed an hour in his arms, unable to leave. Stroking his strong back and shoulders and listening to his gentle, rumbling snore. When she'd sensed herself drifting off to sleep too, she'd extricated herself from the bed and returned to her own room. Watching over a wounded man as he slept . . . that much was a healer's duty. Sleeping *with* him . . . now that was the privilege of a wife.

And she wasn't his wife, she reminded herself. She had

no business sharing a bed—or a cove, or an armory—with the man. No matter how passionate he proved her to be, or how exhilarated his caresses made her feel, or how sweetly he kissed her damaged wrists. If she gave into fleeting pleasure with him, she could lose everything she'd worked so hard to build.

She could lose everything *now*, if Minerva's "helpful" reports weren't contained.

"Minerva, you're mistaken," she said firmly. "You weren't wearing your spectacles, and you don't know what you saw." To the others, she declared, "I swam out to check on Lord Rycliff's health. We were discussing it when Minerva came along."

"That wasn't discussing, it was grappling," Minerva said. "And I'm not that blind. I know very well what I saw. He kissed you!"

Mrs. Lange made an outraged squawk. "I knew it. Men are such filthy invaders. I shall write a poem."

"He kissed you?" Kate's eyes flew wide. "Lord Rycliff kissed you? Yesterday?"

"Yes, he did," Minerva answered for her. "And it wasn't the first time, from the looks of things. Clearly he's been molesting her ever since he arrived in the neighborhood."

Susanna lowered herself onto the nearest bench. She felt her life unraveling at its seams.

"Oh, this is wonderful." Mrs. Highwood said, coming to sit at Susanna's side. "I knew you'd caught his eye, my dear. And Lord Payne has shown a marked preference for my Diana. Just think, the two of you could be cousins by marriage!"

"I am not marrying Lord Rycliff," Susanna insisted. "I don't know what would cause you to say such a thing." And she wished the older woman would stop saying it so loud. The man was still on the grounds of Summerfield, and there was no way of knowing when he might wake. He could be awake now.

He might be stretching, flexing those powerful limbs beyond the edges of the mattress and yawning like a grizzled lion.

"Lord Payne has not shown me any particular favor," Diana said. "Honestly, I don't wish him to."

"Pish. The man asked you to cut his hair! He's titled, handsome as the devil, and rich besides. Pretty as you are, he'll no doubt offer for you soon. See if you can't contrive to be trapped in a cove with him. A kiss would do the trick, I warrant."

"Mama!" Diana and Minerva spoke in unison.

"What is wrong with all of you?" Mrs. Highwood asked, looking from one to the other. "These men are lords. They are powerful, wealthy. You ought to encourage them."

"Believe me, encouragement is the last thing that's needed." Upon speaking the words, Susanna instantly worried. Would Bram take their encounter last night as encouragement? Did she wish him to? They understood each other now, on a level that went more than skin-deep. Assuming he retained some memory of the conversation when he woke.

"Lord Rycliff is not looking for a wife," she said firmly. "And neither is his cousin. If we were so foolish as to 'encourage' them, we would risk not only our own reputations, but the reputation of Spindle Cove." She looked from woman to woman around the group. "Do you all understand me? Nothing is going on here. *Nothing.*"

"But, Miss Finch—" Minerva objected.

"*Minerva.*" Susanna turned to her, hoping her new friend would someday understand and forgive her this harshness. "I am sorry to say it, but you are mistaken in what you saw, and your persistence is becoming wearisome. Lord Rycliff did not attack me yesterday, or any day. Nothing improper has transpired between us. In fact, he only made that jump from the cliff because he thought you had *drowned* and he hoped to save your life. To impugn his character after that brave, albeit misguided action seems most ungracious. My part in this conversation is concluded."

Minerva blinked at her, clearly hurt. Susanna felt horrible, but the future of their community was at stake. Where would Minerva hunt her fossils if word reached London of spinsters gone wild, and the Queen's Ruby was forced to close its doors?

"We'll be called to tea shortly." She picked up her basket and headed inside. "Until then, I'll be in the still-room, pounding herbs. I'm running low on liniment."

Kate followed her. "I'll help." As they neared the house, she whispered, "How was it? The kiss."

Susanna suppressed a little cry of frustration.

"You can tell me," Kate said, propping open the still-room door. When both had entered, she swiftly shut and locked it behind them. "Miss Finch, you know I won't tell a soul. I have nowhere else to live but here. Spindle Cove's fate is my fate, too."

Susanna leaned against the door and closed her eyes.

"Was it wonderful?"

"Wonderful" wasn't the word. There were no words to describe the wild, breathless flood of sensation.

And there was no way she could keep it a secret one instant longer. She gave a tiny nod and whispered, "Yes."

Kate clutched her arm. "I knew it. You must tell me everything."

"Oh, Kate. I can't. I shouldn't even have admitted that

much." She began taking bottles down from the shelves and snipped a bundle of dried St. John's wort from its string. "And it won't ever happen again."

"Don't you think he means to marry you?"

"Absolutely not. And I have no plans to marry him."

"I don't mean to pry," Kate said. "Truly, I don't. It's just my only chance to know. I mean . . . It won't ever be me, kissed in the cove by a lord."

Susanna let pestle drop against mortar. "Why wouldn't it be you? You're beautiful, and so talented."

"I'm an orphan of unknown family. A nobody. What's more, a nobody with this." She touched the birthmark at her temple.

Susanna set aside her work entirely and placed both hands on her friend's shoulders, looking her square in the eye. "Kate, if that little mark is your greatest imperfection, then you are surely the most lovely and lovable woman I know."

"Men don't seem to agree."

"Perhaps you've been meeting all the wrong men."

At the echo of Bram's words to her, Susanna bit back a rueful smile. No matter what happened, life would always be a bit different now. Because at last, Susanna knew what it was to feel *desired*, flaws and all. She felt the unexpected warmth of it lighting her from the inside, and she wanted Kate to experience the same.

"Your admirer will come along someday. I'm sure of it. But in the meantime . . ." She tugged one of her friend's chestnut curls. "This is Spindle Cove, Kate. We base our self-worth on our qualities and accomplishments, not just the opinions of gentlemen."

"Yes, I know. I know." A sheepish look stole into Kate's eyes. "But it's impossible to stop thinking about them, just the same."

Yes, Susanna silently agreed. It was. And with their leader indisposed upstairs, she suddenly worried what trouble the rest of the men were finding today.

In the shadow of Rycliff Castle, Colin Sandhurst regarded his troops.

They *were* his troops for the day, he presumed, since his fool cousin remained unconscious. Colin had warned him not to take that ridiculous dive off the cliff, but did Bram ever listen to him? Oh no. Of course not.

He'd half expected the whole militia business to be over after that show of absurdity. But apparently the lure of eight shillings and the promise of high entertainment had brought the recruits back for another day.

He clapped his hands together. "Right, then. Gather round, fellows. Over here."

Nothing happened.

Thorne shot him a smug look. "Fall in line!" he barked.

The men fell in line.

"Thank you, Corporal Thorne." Colin cleared his throat and addressed the men. "As you all know, our stalwart commander is currently flat on his back, nursing a head wound. A wound, I might add, given him by a little nothing of a girl. So today, as your first lieutenant, I am in charge. And we're going to have a different sort of drill today."

Keane, the vicar, raised a hand. "Are we going to learn a new formation?"

"No," Colin told him. "We're going to stage an invasion. Those little ladies down there in Spindle Cove have occupied what should be your village. *Our* village. Are we going to roll over and take that?"

The men looked from one to the other.

"No!" Colin supplied, exasperated. "No, we are not going to take that, not one evening more."

Bram had the right idea, at least. These men definitely needed some help reattaching their bollocks and reasserting their dominance in this village. But his cousin had the wrong tactic, appealing to some vague sense of honor and duty. There was a much better source of motivation—that primal, undeniable impulse that drove every man.

Sex.

"Tonight," he announced, "is the night we take back that village. And we're not going to do it by marching in lines or committing acts of brave idiocy. We're going to do it by being men. Manly men. The kind of men a woman wants to take control."

Brows wrinkled in confusion.

"But . . ." The blacksmith looked around the group. "We *are* men. Last I checked, anyhow."

"It's not just a matter of having the proper equipment. It's using the equipment properly." Leaping up on a crate, Colin spread his arms wide. "Look at me. Now look at yourselves. Now look back at me. I am the man you want to be like."

Dawes crossed his arms. "Why is that, precisely?"

"Do you know how many women I've bedded?" When Rufus and Finn perked, he waved at them. "Have a guess, boys."

"Seventeen," offered Finn.

"More."

"Eighteen."

"Still more."

"Er . . . nineteen?"

"Oh, for the love of God," he muttered. "We'll be here all day. Let's just call the number more than you can imagine. Because clearly, that is the case." Under his breath, he added, "Perhaps higher than you know how to count." He raised one arm over his head. "Tonight, we're going to march down to that village, and we're going to enjoy ourselves in our tavern."

"You mean the tea shop?" Fosbury asked. "But this is the ladies' card night."

"'But this is the ladies' card night,'" Colin mimicked in a high-pitched voice. "That right there is your problem. You've all let yourselves be henpecked. Gelded, by this gaggle of bluestockings. Tonight, the ladies are not going to play cards. They're going to dance."

Fosbury scratched the back of his neck. "Well, that is what they do sometimes on Fridays. Dancing. But just with each other. They don't ask us to join in."

With a heavy sigh, Colin massaged the bridge of his nose. "We're not going to wait for them to ask *us*, Fosbury." He dropped his hand and motioned to Dawes. "You, there. How do you ask a woman to dance?"

The blacksmith shrugged. "I don't. I don't dance."

Finn's hand shot up. "I know! I've heard Sally saying it to the mirror. 'May I have the pleasure of this dance?'" He affected a flourish and bow.

"Wrong," Colin said. "All wrong." He lifted his voice. "Every man, repeat after me. 'I believe this dance is mine.'"

The men mumbled the words back at him.

Pathetic.

Colin drew out his double-barreled pistol, cocked it carefully, raised it level with his shoulder, and shot it into the air. The resounding crack caught the group's attention. "Say it with conviction. 'I believe this dance is mine.'"

The men cleared their throats and shuffled their feet, saying, "I believe this dance is mine."

"Better. Try this. Your hair is a river of silk." When he got only puzzled stares in return, he explained, "The first line gets her in your arms. If you're going to woo a woman to your bed, you need a few more pretty words. Now repeat after me, damn it. 'Your hair is a river of silk.'"

"'Your hair is a river of silk,'" they echoed.

"Now we're getting somewhere." He paused, considering. "Now this one. 'Your eyes sparkle like diamonds.'"

They repeated, with a bit more spirit this time.

"'Your breasts are alabaster orbs.'"

"What?" Rufus objected. "That's stupid. I'm not saying that."

"Do you have some better suggestion?"

"Why can't you just say she's got a fair set of titties?"

Colin looked to Keane. "Vicar, cover your ears."

The man actually did it.

Colin groaned. Leaping down from the crate, he approached Rufus. "Now listen, lad. You don't go speaking of titties. It's crude. The ladies won't like it. Not unless you're well into the heat of things. Then, depending on the woman, she may like it well indeed. But when seduction is your aim, you can't go wrong with alabaster orbs."

"That's all sorts of wrong, that is." Thorne crossed his arms. "Alabaster's cold and hard. Don't know what kind of teats you've been suckling, but I like flesh-and-blood women myself. Don't you have something better than that?"

"Of course I do. But I'm not wasting my best lines on you lot." He raised the pistol and fired his second shot into the air. "Stand tall, snap those shoulders back, and say it loud and proud. 'Your breasts are alabaster orbs.'"

It took a half dozen more tries, but Colin finally heard the line roared back to his satisfaction.

"Well done," he said, pacing to and fro before them. "Now for the rewards. Ale." He thumped his fist on a sturdy barrel. With his boot, he rattled a nearby crate.

"Wine." Pausing for dramatic effect, he hefted a cask he'd raided from Bram's personal supply. "Whiskey."

"What are we going to do with all that?" Rufus asked.

"Use it for bootblack," Colin said dryly. "We'll *drink* it, of course. Tonight is the night we eat, drink, carouse, and make love to our women like we mean it. But wait. There's more."

He'd saved the sign for last. He'd spent all night working on the thing by torchlight. Not because he found any enjoyment in woodworking, but because the alternative was another sleepless night on his cold, uncomfortable pallet. After almost a week out of London, he was starved for a warm body and good sleep.

There was more than principle at stake tonight. He needed to find a woman, and soon.

"And with this, men"—he unveiled the painted sign with a swoosh of fabric—"I give you back your tavern."

ram woke to searing light, stabbing him straight through his eyelids. Someone placed a cool cup in his hand. He couldn't even bear to open his eyes and determine who it was, or investigate the contents of the cup. After a cautious sniff, he gulped it down. Water. Clear, crisp water. The most delicious thing he'd ever tasted. He would have muttered some words of thanks, but his tongue was too heavy. He couldn't coax it to move.

A beneficent hand closed the drapes. Darkness pulled on him, tugging him back to the pillows and back to sleep.

When he woke again, the harsh light was gone. Pushing back the bedclothes, he rose up on one elbow. He was alone in the bedchamber. A single flickering taper in a candlestick provided the room's only light.

Rubbing the sleep from his eyes, he sat up and swung his bare feet onto the floor. How much time had he lost? He peered at the clock on the bedside table. The clock read half-past seven. But if that were the case, the sun should be up. Unless . . .

Unless it was evening again. Wednesday evening. He massaged his aching temples. Damn it. He'd lost an entire day.

His officer's coat hung on a hook near the door. Draped

over a chair nearby were a shirt, trousers, and waist-coat. He recognized them as his own, but they weren't the ones he'd been wearing yesterday. Thorne must have come by and taken his sea-drenched clothes, replacing them with new.

Perched on the mattress edge, he tested his knee, flexing and straightening the joint. Remarkably, his leg pained him no worse for the long day of marching. In fact, it felt measurably better. Whether he could attribute that to Susanna's liniment, her noxious potion, her sooth-ing touch, or simply a full day's sound sleep, he couldn't guess. One way or another, he had her to thank.

With sudden, visceral force, a memory yanked him back some twenty hours. He was in this bed, and she was under him. He had her taut, plump breast in his hand, and her fingertips were soothing over his back, lulling him to sleep.

He'd been swamped by emotion, dragged underwater by its vicious undertow. Aroused by her touch, comforted by her whispered words, touched by the secrets she'd con-fessed. He'd simply felt *close* to her, in every possible way.

Out of habit, he pushed both hands through his hair, as if to smooth it back into a queue. Of course, his finger-tips only brushed the bandage wrapped about his head and whatever meager fringe had escaped her shears the other day.

This woman was changing him.

After draining a glass of water, he made good use of the washbasin and soap. He toweled himself dry, then dressed in the fresh clothes. After two days laid up in bed, he needed a shave, but that would have to wait. With a quick check of his cravat knot in the tiny mirror, he left the room.

Summerfield was well-appointed, but it wasn't a large

house. He easily located the back stairs and descended them with a brisk step, confident he'd find the kitchens nearby. Etiquette and simple decency demanded he search out Susanna and thank her for her care and hospitality—but he could better stomach that slice of humility after he'd found a morsel to eat. His stomach rumbled with hunger, and his head was light with it. Wouldn't do to reach the castle only to collapse in front of his men, yet again.

"Ho, there. Is that Rycliff?"

The question stopped him dead in the corridor. "Sir Lewis?"

The short, stoutish man emerged through a doorway, wearing a leather apron and wiping his hands on a rag. The few tenacious wisps of silver hair that still clung to his scalp were flying in all directions.

"Forgive me," he said, waving toward his disheveled state. "I've been working in my laboratory."

Bram nodded. The small action hurt.

Sir Lewis wadded the grease-stained rag into his apron pocket. "Susanna mentioned that she'd quarantined you in the house." The older man's blue eyes slid to Bram's bandaged crown. "Feeling better?"

"Yes." He tilted his head and looked past the man, into a large, lamp-lit space. "Your workshop?"

"Yes, yes." Sir Lewis's eyes gleamed as he jerked his head toward the room's interior. "Come have a look, if you like."

"I don't wish to disturb you."

"Not at all, not at all."

Bram followed him through the door, ducking to avoid bashing his head on the lintel. This room must have been a scullery at one point, or perhaps a laundry. The floor was ancient scoured slate, not wood parquet as in the corridor. Exposed brick covered the walls. A large, high window occupied much of the room's south side, admitting a purple gleam of fading daylight.

On the walls, all sorts of weapons were mounted on hooks. Not just the standard rifles and dueling pistols, but blunderbusses, crossbows . . . Above the door hung an ancient mace with spikes.

"If you'd like," Sir Lewis said, "I'll show you the medieval hall later. Shields, chain mail, and so forth. We don't get so many young men coming around to Summerfield, but those who do always take an interest."

"No doubt." Bram was beginning to understand why Susanna Finch remained unmarried. This house would frighten all but the most intrepid suitors away.

The thought of Susanna made him wince. He turned his gaze to a mahogany plaque above the hearth. On it were mounted a pair of gleaming, polished pistols. Pistols exactly like the one Bram, along with every commissioned officer in the British army, carried as his personal sidearm.

Finch pistols. Standard issue for decades now.

The diminutive, eccentric Sir Lewis Finch was, in his own way, one of England's greatest war heroes. Bram wouldn't be exaggerating to say he owed the man his life. He also owed Sir Lewis his newly bestowed title, the opportunity to raise a militia, and this one slim chance at regaining his command. And he'd spent yesterday tussling with the man's only daughter. Assaulting her in the cove. Pinning her to the bed with his naked limbs and groping her.

Blast it all. Susanna deserved better treatment. Sir Lewis deserved better treatment. And Bram probably deserved to be staring down the barrel of a Finch pistol just about now. Somehow he had to master his lust and refocus on his mission. If the menacing contents of this workshop didn't help him in those struggles, nothing would.

Scrubbing a hand over his face, he turned his gaze from

the weapons adorning the walls to the room's furnishings. Underneath the window lodged a long worktable, covered with soldering tools, measuring devices, rasps, and more. On a smaller desk, he found a disassembled flintlock mechanism. It was much like the standard firelock on most rifles, but the hammer was an unusual shape.

"May I?" he asked, reaching for it.

"Of course."

Bram picked up the firelock and turned it over in his hands, inspecting the intricate bit of machinery.

"It's meant to be an improved rifle lock," Sir Lewis said. "I almost have it perfected, I think. But I've left it alone for the moment, to work on the blasted cannon again. I've been agonizing over this one for years."

"A cannon?" He noticed the wooden scale model on the worktable. "Tell me about it."

Sir Lewis mussed his hair and made a sound of frustration. "I've been tinkering with this idea on and off for decades. It's a rifled cannon."

Bram whistled through his teeth, impressed. All cannons had smooth-bored barrels. They were the artillery equivalent of muskets—decent range and power, but only middling accuracy. But if a cannon could be grooved inside, like a rifle barrel, its projectiles would not only fly farther and faster, but their aim would be much more accurate. A rifled cannon would give the British army a keen advantage in any siege situation. It could be just the ace Wellington needed to boot Napoleon out of Spain.

"I must have tried a dozen variations on the design," Sir Lewis said, gesturing toward the miniature cannon on the tabletop. "And hundreds of concepts never left the drafting table. But I have a good feeling about this one." He patted the model. "This is it. I feel it in my old, creaky bones."

The older man smiled at Bram. "I understand you, Rycliff. Better than you know. We're both men of purpose and action, in our own separate ways. Neither of us is ready to retire the field just yet. I know it's difficult, being stuck in this quaint, tiny village while wars are being waged. Must be torture for you."

"Torture pretty well describes it." Sweet, freckled torture of the purest kind.

"Is my Susanna giving you trouble?"

Bram choked on his tongue. He felt his face heating as he coughed into his sleeve.

"Don't worry, you can be candid with me." Sir Lewis patted him on the back. "The dear girl means well, but I know she has a tendency to overreach. Clever as she is, she has the whole village hanging on her advice. She likes to help."

Yes, Bram thought. He was beginning to understand that Susanna Finch was driven to care for those around her. Whether it meant offering food, encouragement, healing salve . . . or the sweetest, most generous embrace a man could ever hope to know.

You don't have to attack me every time you wish to be touched. To be held.

He swallowed hard, trying to clear her taste from his mouth.

Sir Lewis went on, "But my daughter doesn't always understand a man's need to feel useful. To keep striving, working toward his goals." He spread his arms, indicating the workshop. "Susanna would rather I give this up entirely. But I can't do that, not a day before I give up breathing. I know you understand."

He nodded. "I do."

Bram did understand Sir Lewis perfectly. And it came as a great relief to finally feel *understood*. In the months since his injury, none of his peers—nor his superiors, for that matter—had sympathized with his unwavering determination to return to command. They all seemed to think Bram should be content, if not outright grateful, to retire and get on with the rest of his life. They couldn't comprehend that this *was* his life.

"For men like us, it's not enough to merely live. We need to leave a legacy behind." Sir Lewis touched a fingertip to the scale model cannon. "This cannon will be mine. I may be old and balding, but my greatest invention is yet to be unveiled."

His keen blue eyes met Bram's. "And you may be wounded, but I know your finest battles are yet to be fought. I want to give you every chance I can. I've written Generals Hardwick and Cummings and invited them to attend the militia's field review. I feel certain they'll see what I do. That you're your father's son. A man who won't remain hobbled. They'll doubtless agree England needs you back in command."

Emotion thickened his throat. "Sir Lewis . . . I don't know what to say. I don't how to thank you."

That was a lie. Bram knew exactly how to thank the man—and that was by keeping his head on straight, doing his duty, drilling a militia to pin-sharp precision, and staying the hell away from Susanna Finch.

A clock on the wall chimed eight.

"Can I interest you in dinner, Rycliff?"

Bram's stomach answered for him, loudly. "I appreciate the invitation, but . . . I'm not properly dressed."

"Neither am I." Sir Lewis laughed and indicated his own disheveled attire. "We don't stand on ceremony in this house, Rycliff."

"If that's the case, I wish you'd just call me Bram."

"Bram it is." The older man untied his apron and laid it

aside. Then he clapped Bram on the shoulder. "Let's go find something to eat, son."

The old man ushered him out of the workshop, down the corridor, and up a half flight of stairs.

As they wound through the house, rich, dark paneling welcomed Bram from room to room, and the collective warmth of dozens of candles seemed to seep into his bones. Not since his infancy had he resided in a house like this. For years now, he'd slung his campaign-weary bones in tents and barracks and officers' quarters. Then hospital beds and finally, in London, simple bachelor's rooms. He'd always avoided family residences such as Summerfield, purposely. Because they were more than houses. They were *homes*, and they weren't for him. They made him feel out of place, and strangely achy inside.

"Susanna will be pleased to see us, no matter what we're wearing," Sir Lewis said. "Most evenings I don't make it to the dining room at all. She's always after me to eat more, take care of myself."

Bram drew a deep breath and exhaled it slowly, trying to purge all improper thoughts of Susanna from his mind, body, heart and soul. Dinner was perfect. A completely civilized, chaperoned setting in which to see her, converse with her, and learn how to act like a normal human in her presence, rather than a slavering beast. His behavior over the last few days had been reprehensible. Beneath this warrior's coat, he was a gentleman by birth. He'd lost sight of it somehow in all those freckles, but unless he meant to throw away this chance at redemption and Sir Lewis's goodwill, it was time to start acting the part.

"Here we are." Sir Lewis led Bram around a turn in the corridor and through a set of paneled double doors, announcing loudly, "We have a guest tonight, Susanna. You may wish to order another table setting."

Here they went, Bram thought. He would eat dinner.
He would use the correct forks. He would engage her in
conversation that did not include the words "skin," "lick,"
or "powder keg." He would thank her for her kind hospitality and helpful ministrations. Then he would kiss her
hand, take his leave . . .

And never lay a finger on Susanna Finch again. On this
he was absolutely, irrevocably resolved.

Until he turned the corner.

Bram halted midstep. His vision blurred at the edges.
He felt certain he would faint. And his light-headedness
had nothing to do with his recent head injury or his fam-
ished state. It had everything to do with her.

Hideous bathing costume and men's breeches aside,
he'd yet to see her wearing anything besides a simple
muslin day dress. Tonight she was dressed for dinner,
clad in a sumptuous violet silk gown with beaded brocade
trim. The crystal wine goblets on the table took the can-
dlelight and honed it to luminous arrows, shooting brilliance in all directions. Picking out every seed pearl sewn
into her sash, every ribbon weaving through her shimmering, upswept hair. As she bent to smooth a wrinkle
in the tablecloth, artfully curled tendrils framed her face
and caressed the pale slope of her neck.

"Lord Rycliff." Straightening, she gave him a shy smile.

He couldn't speak. She looked . . .

Beautiful, he supposed he should say. But "beautiful"
wasn't a strong enough word. Neither was "dazzling,"
"breathtaking," or "devastating"—though that last came
a bit closer than the rest.

Her outward appearance was only part of the effect.
What called to him was the invitation implicit in her posture, her voice, her lovely blue eyes. She looked as though
she'd been waiting on him. Not just tonight, but every night.

She looked like home.

"I'm glad to see you awake," she said.

"Are you?"

"You brought my father to the dining table, only five minutes past eight. In this house, that's a small miracle."

Sir Lewis laughed. "And now that I'm here, I must beg you to excuse me for a moment." He raised work-streaked hands. "I'll just go wash before dinner."

The older man quit the room, and the two of them stood there, regarding each other.

She cleared her throat. "Are you feeling well?"

"I don't know," he answered. It was the truth. He wasn't sure of anything at the moment, except the fact that his boots were now carrying him forward. All his chaste resolutions and respect for Sir Lewis aside, he simply couldn't do otherwise. Whatever this was between them, it commanded his loyalty in a forceful, visceral way. To deny her pull would seem a dishonor all its own.

He watched her blush deepen as he drew near. It was some comfort to know that he affected her, too. He reached for her hand, where it rested atop the damask tablecloth.

"No gloves tonight?" he asked, running his thumb over her soft, protected skin, tracing each of her fingers and the delicate webs between.

She shook her head. "I haven't worn them all day. I mean to, but then I keep forgetting."

He tumbled into her gaze. Passed a small eternity wandering there.

"I . . ." he started.

"You . . ." she began.

To hell with words, he thought, sliding his hand around her waist. *To hell with it all.* If they had only moments together, he could not let them go to waste. Cool silk teased against his palm as he pulled her close. He drew a ragged breath, and his senses exploded with her unique, essential perfume.

"Bram," she whispered. "We can't."

"I know." And then he bent his head, seeking her kiss. Her mouth softened beneath his, lush and welcoming. Her kiss was tender and sweet, and in that quiet, stolen moment, worth any risk.

Light footsteps clattered down the corridor, jolting them apart.

A young woman tore into the room, followed by an apologetic footman.

"Miss Finch! Miss Finch, you must come at once." As the girl paused for breath, Bram recognized her as one of the young ladies from the Queen's Ruby. One of the quieter ones, whose name he hadn't yet learned.

"There's trouble in the village," she said.

Susanna crossed the room in a swift, determined ripple of silk. "What is it, Violet?"

"Oh, Miss Finch, you won't believe it. We've been *invaded*."

They'd been invaded.

Minerva touched a fingertip to her spectacles. She knew she had to be wearing them—she never went anywhere without her spectacles. But at the moment, nothing within her view was clear. The lines of reality had blurred, and the world simply didn't make sense.

A mere quarter hour ago, the ladies had been sitting down to cards in the Blushing Pansy. Seated at the window table with her mother and sisters, Minerva had begun to split and shuffle the deck of cards.

And then—before the first round could even be dealt—the men had come thundering in without warning, bringing with them what looked to be numerous bottles of liquor and the prelude to sheer chaos.

Down came the lace curtains and the Blushing Pansy's gilt-lettered sign. Up went an ancient broadsword and a set of steer horns mounted above the hearth. And outside, above the door, a new sign dangled.

"What does it say?" her mother asked, peering out the window.

Minerva looked over her spectacles. "The Rutting Bull."

"Oh dear," Diana muttered.

The ladies all froze in their seats, uncertain how to react. What was the proper etiquette, when civilization crumbled around a girl? Not even *Mrs. Worthington's Wisdom* covered this.

Leaping up a step to the small dais, Lord Payne took the center of attention. No surprise. Wherever the ladies were gathered, that man *always* took the center of attention. Minerva detested him. If Diana wished to marry, she deserved so much better than a proud, preening rake. Unfortunately, their mother seemed to have already embraced him as a future son-in-law.

"Fair ladies of Spindle Cove," Payne announced, "I regret to inform you that the Blushing Pansy tea shop has closed for the evening."

A murmur of confusion and dismay swept the ladies.

"However," Payne went on, "it is my great pleasure to announce that the Rutting Bull tavern is open for business."

A loud huzzah went up from the men.

"There will be drinking. There will be dancing. There will be dicing and debauchery of every pleasant sort. Ladies, you have been warned. Leave now or live high."

A man she didn't recognize—one of the farmers or fishermen, she supposed—produced a battered violin. He put bow to strings and began sawing away, producing a wild country dance.

The other men wasted no time clearing tables and chairs to the edges of the room. In some cases, with the mortified ladies still seated upon them. The blacksmith approached their table. With a curt nod and an intense, silent look, the big man reached under their table with one hand, lifting the entire piece of furniture by its pedestal and carrying it aside.

"Oh my," Diana said, as someone pressed a brimming flagon into her hand. She sniffed at its contents, then passed the drink to Minerva. "Is that ale, Min?"

She sipped at it. "Yes."

Miss Kate Taylor was urged to the pianoforte. A few of the younger girls grabbed hands and fled, trailing some vow to fetch Miss Finch.

"We should leave," Diana said.

"I don't understand," Charlotte said, raising her voice above the crescendo of music. "What's happening?"

"Opportunity, my dears." Their mother's face lit up like a bonfire. "*That's* what's happening. And don't think of leaving. We're staying right here. Smile, Diana. Here he comes."

Lord Payne cut a swath through the hubbub, making his way straight for their group. "Mrs. Highwood." He bowed deeply, gifting the fair-haired sisters with a brilliant, gleaming smile. "Miss Highwood. Miss Charlotte. How lovely you look this evening." Belatedly, he turned to Minerva and gave her a cool smile. "If it isn't our resident giant-slayer, Miss Miranda."

She narrowed her eyes at him. "It's Minerva."

"Right. Did you come armed this evening? With something other than those dagger-sharp looks, I mean."

"Unfortunately, no."

"In that case"—he extended a hand to Diana—"Miss Highwood, I believe this dance is mine."

When Diana didn't immediately accept, their mother intervened. "What are you waiting for, Diana? Permission? Of course you may dance with Lord Payne."

As the pair proceeded to the center of the floor, Minerva nudged her mother. "You cannot allow her to dance. Not like this. What of her asthma?"

"Pish. She hasn't suffered an attack in ages now. And Miss Finch is always saying healthful exercise will do her benefit. Dancing is good for her."

"I don't know about dancing, but Lord Payne is not good for her. Not in any way. I don't trust that man."

One of the Bright twins stepped into her line of vision, drawing her notice away. He made a nervous bow to Charlotte. "Miss Charlotte, your hair is a river of diamonds and your eyes are alabaster orbs."

Minerva couldn't help but laugh. "Charlotte, do you have cataracts?"

The poor youth flushed vermillion and stuck out his hand. "Care to dance?"

With a brief glance toward their mother for consent, Charlotte launched from her chair. "I'd be honored, Mr. . . . Er, which one are you?"

"It's Finn, miss. Unless I accidentally tread on your toes, in which case I'm Rufus." He grinned and offered a hand. The two joined the dancers.

Minerva stared at her mother. "You're letting Charlotte dance now? She's barely fourteen!"

"It's all in good fun. And it's just a local dance, not a London ball." Her mother clucked her tongue. "Be careful, Minerva. Your envy is showing."

She huffed a breath. She was *not* envious. Although,

as more and more couples paired off around her, she did begin to feel conspicuously alone. It wasn't an unfamiliar sensation.

"I keep telling you, Minerva. If only you'd give your cheeks a pinch and remove those spectacles, you'd be—"

"I'd be blind as a bat, Mother."

"But an *attractive* bat. They're only spectacles, you know. You do have a choice whether or not to wear them."

Minerva sighed. Perhaps she would like to catch a gentleman's attention someday, but not one whose entire opinion of her could be swayed by a minor alteration of appearance. If she married, she wanted a man with a brain in his head and some substance to his character. No vain aristocrats for her, no matter how slick their words or how devilishly handsome their smiles.

It just rankled, to always feel rejected by men like Lord Payne without ever having the chance to reject them first.

She lifted the flagon of ale in her hand and took a long, unladylike draught. Then she rose from her chair, determined not to sit and play the wallflower.

"Where are you going, Minerva?"

"As you say, Mother. I've decided to take this unplanned interruption as an opportunity."

Pushing through the increasingly raucous throng of dancers and drinkers, Minerva made her way to the exit. She'd left off in the middle of composing a most important letter that afternoon, and she might as well take this time to finish it. The members of the Royal Geological Society required adjustment in their thinking.

They were, after all, men.

─Chapter Sixteen─

usanna raced from the house, picking up her skirts and dashing down the lane.

"We could take a carriage," Bram said, catching her on the first turn. "Or ride."

"Not enough time," she said, gulping the cool night air. "This is faster."

Truth be told, she was glad of a chance to run. There were too many questions between them, so many emotions she felt unprepared to face. She slid a glance in his direction, wondering if his knee was paining him. She knew better than to ask. He would never admit to it, if it were.

But she slowed, just a little.

As they neared the center of the village, a dull roar reached her ears. There was no question about the source of the din. Together they raced the last distance past the church, and across the village green.

"I'll be damned." He halted beside her, panting for breath.

She clutched her side, staring up at the sign above the tea shop door. "The Rutting Bull? What's the meaning of this?"

"I know what it means. It means the men have taken back their tavern."

"*Our* tea shop, you mean."

"Not tonight." He grinned, shaking his head. "Ha. This scheme has Colin written all over it. But it's good to see them taking some initiative."

"This isn't amusing." Her hands flew to her hips. "Did you know they were planning this?"

At her accusing tone, his posture became defensive. "No, I didn't know they were planning this. I've spent the past thirty hours knocked cold. *Someone* dosed me with enough laudanum to drop a horse."

"No, Bram. *Someone* dosed you with the appropriate amount, and your battered body took the much-needed opportunity to rest. I was looking out for your well-being. And now I'm looking out for the well-being of my friends." She gestured toward the tea shop. "We have to put a stop to that scene. Those girls in there, they're unused to this sort of attention. They're going to make more of it than they ought."

"You're the one making too much of it. It's only a bit of dance and drink."

"Precisely. To a man like yourself, that's just harmless carousing. But these are delicate, sheltered young ladies. Their hearts and hopes are vulnerable. *Too* vulnerable. Not to mention their reputations. We have to intervene."

Together they looked to the tea-shop-turned-tavern. Loud music and laughter drifted out to them on the breeze, along with the sound of clinking glass.

"No." He shook his head. "I'm not going to put a stop to that scene, and neither are you. What's going on in there is important."

"Public drunkenness is important?"

"Yes, on occasion. More than that, fellowship. Brotherhood within a band of soldiers, and the duty those men are charged to carry out. It's *all* important. It's called pride, Susanna, and those men are getting their first taste of it in a long time."

"What do you mean, their first taste of it? They are decent, honorable men, all. Or at least they *were*."

"Come along. Before I arrived in this village, you and your muslin-clad minions had them reduced to mending lockets and piping icing on teacakes. You don't understand. Men need a purpose, Susanna. A worthy goal. One that we feel in our guts and our hearts, not just in our heads."

"*Men* need a purpose?" She sighed, exasperated. "Can't you understand women are the same? We crave our own goals and our own accomplishments, our own sisterhood as well. And there are precious few places we can find it, in a world ruled by the opposite sex. Everywhere else we are governed by men's rules, live at the mercy of male whims. But here, in this one tiny corner of the world, we are free to be our best and truest selves. Spindle Cove is *ours*, Bram. I will fight to my last breath before I let you destroy it. Women's needs are important, too."

He put both hands on her, tugging her away from the buildings and onto the green. Soon he had her ensconced beneath the canopy of an ancient willow tree. She'd always loved this tree, and the way its protective, low-hanging limbs made a sort of separate world. A green, fresh, gently tickling shelter that allowed just the right amount of sunlight through, yet kept out all but the heaviest rain. She'd always felt comfortable and safe under its branches.

Until now. The hungry glint in his eyes was danger itself. When he spoke, his voice had darkened. The whole night had darkened.

"I'll tell you what's most important of all. It's this." He

flexed those barrel-like biceps, drawing her body flush against a solid wall of muscle and heat. "Not women, not men, but what lies between two people who want each other more than air. You can argue with me all you want, but you can't fight this. I know you feel it."

Oh yes. She felt it. Hot, electric sensation hummed through her whole body, all the way to the beds of her toenails and the roots of her hair. Between her thighs, she was molten with it.

"*This* is important," he said. "It's the most vital, undeniable force in Creation. You can't deprive the whole village of it just because you're afraid of losing control."

Laughter burst from her throat. "*I'm* afraid to lose control? Oh, Bram. Please."

This, from the man so desperate to order someone—anyone—about, he was paying shepherds and fishermen exorbitant wages just to march at his command. Let it not be forgotten, he'd bombed a flock of sheep.

He was the one afraid of losing control. Terrified to his core. And she would happily remind him of all this—perhaps even admit she found it oddly endearing—if only he'd permit her the use of her lips and tongue.

But no. The impossible man had to conquer those, too.

He swept her into a kiss so wild and unrelenting, she had no choice but surrender.

Her mouth softened, and his tongue swept between her lips, probing deep. She accepted the challenge, parrying his thrusts with her own, enjoying the way they sparred so equally. He moaned with satisfaction, and she smiled against his lips. Apparently, she was good at this. She loved the way he brought out new strengths in her; talents she hadn't known she possessed.

He covered her neck with kisses, grinding his hips

against hers in a crude, delicious manner. "God, how I've been aching for you. Have you any idea what kind of dreams laudanum gives a man?"

"Did you dream of me?"

"Frequently." *Kiss.* "Vividly." *Kiss.* "Acrobatically."

Laughing softly, she pulled back to meet his gaze. "Oh, Bram. I had dreams of you, too. They all involved very high cliffs and very sharp rocks." She touched a hand to his cheek. "And sea monsters."

He smiled. "Little liar."

Perhaps she should have been offended, but she was too busy being stupidly thrilled. No one ever called her "little" anything.

"And just look at you," he said, stepping back and skimming his possessive hands over her waist and hips. "I don't even have words for how beautiful you are. You wore this for me, didn't you?"

"Predictable arrogance. I always dress for dinner."

"Ah, but you thought of me as you dressed. I know you did."

She had. Of course she had. And though she always dressed for dinner, she seldom wore anything this fine. Tonight she'd selected her best. Not because she planned for him to see it, but for a much simpler, more selfish reason. He'd made her feel beautiful inside, and it only seemed fitting that her outward appearance should match.

"And these bits of your hair, curling down . . . They're for me, too." He caught a stray lock and wound it about his fingers. "You can't know how I've been dying to touch your hair. Even softer than I dreamed." His touch dipped to her neckline, where he eased the violet silk aside to reveal a pale sliver of her white chemise. "Look at this," he said, fingering the neatly hemmed edge. "White and crisp and new. It's your best, isn't it? You wore your best for me."

She nodded, so entranced by his low, sensual whisper that she'd lost any capacity for denial.

"I want to see it," he said. "Let me see it."

"What?" Surely he couldn't be suggesting she remove her gown here, in the middle of the village green.

His hands slid to her back, and the closures of her gown. "You wore it for me, so let me see it. Just the shift, love. Just the shift. Do you know how long it's been since I've seen a girl in a plain white shift?"

Susanna didn't like speculating on the answer to that question. She only knew she hated all the girls who had come before.

His lips brushed her cheek, her neck. The scrape of his whiskers set her senses ablaze. "Let me see you. I only want to look."

"Only look?"

"Maybe touch, just a little. But only through your shift. I swear, nothing more. I'll remain clothed. If you tell me to stop, I'll stop." He tipped her chin. "You can trust me."

Could she? She felt herself nod.

His hands slid around her ribs and went to the closures at the back of her gown. "Are these false buttons?"

Without waiting for her answer, he eased the top hook free. Then another. And another. Her bodice began to gape in front. Cool night air rushed over her skin, drawing her nipples to tight peaks.

"Bram. We can't do this. Not here."

"Should we go somewhere else?" He loosened another closure at the back of her gown. Her left sleeve slipped from her shoulder in a ripple of violet, baring more of her crisp white chemise. Her ribs pressed against her stays as she struggled for breath.

Her gaze darted to the Blushing Pansy.

"No one can see," he murmured, pulling her close. His lips brushed the side of her neck. "They're all occupied in the tavern. Don't think of anyone else. It's just the two of us right now."

Another hook surrendered, and she felt her gown falling away. He drew the right sleeve down her shoulder, trailing kisses down the side of her neck. As if by instinct, she tilted her head to give him better access. His tongue slid lazily over her pulse, setting her senses aflame.

"Bram . . ."

"It's all right," he said. "It's all right to want this."

His words soothed her nerves. Still, her fingers trembled as she drew her arms out of her sleeves. Once she'd freed them, the violet silk bodice fell slack at her hips. From the waist up, she was clothed only in her corset and chemise.

His hands went to the small of her back, where her corset laces were secured in a tight knot. He fumbled a bit as he picked the tapes loose, as if his hands were unsteady. That subtle hint of uncertainty was comforting.

The laces slid free of their holes, and her corset fell away from her body. Air rushed into her lungs, dizzying and fresh. He let the garment fall softly to the grass. With it went all her confidence. She might as well have been stark naked, considering how vulnerable and exposed she felt.

"What shall I do?" Her voice shook.

His breath caressed her ear. "Just breathe." He pressed a kiss to her jaw. "Just be here with me. Just be you."

Warmth bloomed in her heart, suffusing her entire body.

Just be you, he said. He didn't want her to be different. He didn't wish she were someone else. He just wanted her to be herself.

She cupped his face in her hands and kissed him full on the lips. Because those precious words deserved a kiss. But most of all, because she was being herself—and kissing him was what she most wanted to do.

They sank into each other, deepening the kiss by slow, sensuous degrees. His tongue teased and coaxed, and she responded in kind. They kissed in an unhurried, almost playful fashion. For a minute. And then matters became serious indeed.

"I need to see you." His hands tugged at her gown, pushing it down over her hips. "All of you. Now."

She helped him, shimmying in place until the fabric gave way and slipped to the ground in a shimmering pool. He took both her hands and helped her step free. Then he stood back from her a pace, angling her to catch the best light. His gaze roamed over her. Every inch of her. Beneath the thin muslin, her nipples strained for his touch. The longer the silence stretched, the more impatient she grew. Then more uncertain. Her shift was thin, but it was so dark. Just how much could he see? Did he like what he saw? How did she compare with all those other girls he'd seen in plain white shifts, so very long ago?

"Lovely." A ragged sigh shook free of his chest. "So lovely. Thank you."

He drew a single fingertip up the inner slope of her arm. As his touch swept over her scars, she held her breath. But her wounds didn't give him a moment's pause.

"I don't know what it is," he said, tracing over her shoulder and dipping his fingers to the neckline of her shift. His touch blazed a fiery trail across the tops of her unbound breasts. "But there's nothing in the world more enticing than a shift like this. Sweet and pure, yet so revealing. Lace, ribbons, silks, furs . . . Nothing can compare."

His hand slid down, cupping her breast. She swallowed anxiously. But he stayed calm, kneading the soft globe with tantalizing pressure and rolling the taut nipple beneath his thumb.

With a thoughtful tilt of his head, he turned his attention toward her other breast. Now he cupped them both in his hands, plumping the left, then the right . . . as though he were testing and weighing them against each other. Men were so very strange. He pinched both her nipples at the same time, and she gasped with surprise and pleasure.

She covered the noise with a nervous laugh. "Couldn't you at least kiss me when you do that?"

"Gladly."

His lips brushed the hollow of her throat. Again, and then again. Light, feathery kisses that tore apart her resistance, shredded any resolve. His hands roamed her curves.

"Bram . . ."

"Just kisses," he murmured, his lips covering her racing pulse. "Just kisses. I swear, I'll press you no further. I'll stop the moment you say the word. Only let me kiss you, Susanna." He trailed his tongue down her neck.

And she sighed her approval, tilting her head to aid his descent. Just kisses. What harm could a few kisses be? It was no more than they'd already done. In her desire-drugged mind, he made so much sense.

His bent his head, and his tongue made a sure, deliberate pass over her nipple. Then he drew the linen-covered peak into his mouth.

She cried out, shocked by the sudden burst of pleasure.

"Hush," he murmured against her breast. "Just kisses. That's all. Just kisses."

Just kisses. Ha. Oh, certainly, these were just kisses. And the Great Pyramids of Egypt were merely little stacks of stone.

Sensation rocketed through her entire body. She'd never known anything so unbearably, exquisitely sweet. He licked and teased and pulled at her nipple, swirling his tongue in ever-widening circles until the fabric of her shift clung wet and heavy to her breast and the rosy flush of her skin showed through.

He gave her other breast the same careful attention, mouthing every curve. Pasting the linen to her aroused flesh.

"Yes," he breathed, drawing back to look at her. With his hands he framed her bosom, pulling the wet fabric tight until the dark buds of her nipples were thrust into relief. "Sweet heaven. Like rosebuds in a drift of fresh snow. And this"—he kissed his way down her belly, sinking lower and lower—"this, Susanna, is what will bring a man to his knees." He pressed his brow to her navel. His mouth settled in the cleft of her thighs, warm and dangerous.

"Bram," she whispered, frantic. "Bram, please get up. This can't be good for your injured leg."

He made a dismissive noise.

Well, now she'd botched matters. The stubborn fool would rather dive off a cliff than admit to a little pain. He certainly wasn't going to rise to his feet now.

He groaned a little, nuzzling her thigh. His big hand cupped her bottom. "You wanted this, remember? You said you'd bring me to my knees."

Of course she'd wanted him on his knees. Begging, pleading. Acknowledging her power over him. And now she had him doing exactly that—but something had gone all wrong. She was the one being conquered.

"Just kisses," he said, framing her waist in his hands and pulling the fabric of her shift taut. "Just kisses, I swear. Let me show you how good it can be. I know exactly what you need."

He pressed his open mouth to the linen covering her cleft. His tongue darted out, stroking her straight through the fabric, circling over that small, secret place that could bring her so much pleasure. Bliss forked through her, and her knees buckled.

Her breath caught, and she clutched wildly at his shoulders. "Bram, I can't . . ."

His hands tightened about her waist. Pausing briefly, he murmured, "I have you. You're safe with me. I won't let you fall."

"But—"

"Do you want me to stop?"

She couldn't make herself answer.

His husky laugh teased her in unbearable ways. "I didn't think so."

He applied himself with purpose now, stroking more firmly with his tongue. Waves of pleasure pushed through her, and she surrendered to them, going limp in his strong embrace. With his shoulder, he gently prodded her knee to the side, spreading her wide to his kiss. Exquisite sensation mounted higher and higher. The moist heat of his mouth mingled with the dew of her arousal. Dampness surged between her legs.

His attentions centered on that sensitive, swollen bud at the crest of her sex. He licked and stroked and nibbled until she was helpless with pleasure. The muscles in her thighs began to quiver. A whimper eased from her throat.

And the world began to constrict. The remote din of music and laughter faded. The wind ceased to blow. Everything was forgotten. Nothing existed but the two of them: his wicked, talented mouth and her intense, spiraling joy. He pushed her higher and higher, until she tumbled straight over the edge into a soul-shaking climax.

She cried out with it, rocked by waves of pleasure.

As she came back to herself, he held her tight, pressing his brow to her belly and whispering soothing words. His thumbs sketched comforting circles on the small of her back.

She sank to her knees, and he pulled her down to the ground. There they lay beneath the willow tree, their limbs tangled and knotted as tree roots. Their combined breath made a little cloud of fog—as if they had their own sky hanging over them, here in this world apart.

He flexed his strong arms, drawing her close. It wasn't until he had her molded against his chest, surrounded by his heat, that she realized she was trembling.

"Don't be afraid," he murmured, pressing kisses to her brow.

She wasn't afraid, just . . . overwhelmed. What did this mean to him? What did it mean to her? Just kisses, she reminded herself. To him, these were just kisses. He didn't want romantic attachments.

Don't get any ideas, she sternly told her heart.

"Don't be frightened," he told her. "You're so passionate. So beautiful. There's so much more I could show you. So much pleasure we could share."

"Tell me," she heard herself say.

She didn't know what possessed her to play innocent. Susanna certainly understood the concept of intercourse, if not from personal experience. She knew what the books said about coitus and human reproduction, and she'd worked alongside midwives, and she heard how the scullery maids giggled and gossiped among themselves. But she wanted to hear what it meant to him. What he thought it would mean between *them*.

He took her hand and brought it to his body, cupping her palm over the bulge tenting his breeches's fall. "Feel this?"

She nodded. How could she fail to feel it? It wasn't precisely a negligible size.

He kept her hand pressed snug, dragging her palm over his full length. His organ throbbed and strained beneath her touch. "It's for you, Susanna. For your pleasure."

"Good heavens. All of it?"

He chuckled low and kissed her neck. "Yes, all of it. It's made to fit inside you."

Leaving his manhood in her grasp, he let his own hand drop to the hem of her shift. He gathered the light, thin fabric and eased it up to her thigh, skimming his fingers along the sensitive hollow of her knee. Then his hand delved between her legs, spreading her thighs apart. His fingers found her warm, wet intimate flesh. As he traced the contours of her sex, gently exploring and teasing her apart, a low moan pulled from her chest.

"This"—he ground his erection against her hand—"belongs here." His finger slid inside her, giving her an exquisite sense of fullness and bliss. "It's as simple as that."

As simple as that.

So this was coupling, as he understood it. An uncomplicated, natural act. A mutual sating of needs and desires. They were made for this. His body *belonged* inside hers.

He pumped his finger in a slow rhythm, plunging a fraction deeper with every stroke. Though she'd just experienced a wrenching climax minutes ago, her arousal built at an astonishing pace. Soon she was arching her hips to meet his clever fingers, stroking her hand over his arousal in time with his thrusts. He kissed her thoroughly, forcing her jaw wide and delving deep with his tongue. She struggled to reciprocate, tasting and teasing him with voracious hunger. He growled his approval against her lips.

He slid his finger from her aching cleft, and she whimpered at the sudden loss. Her complaint was swiftly addressed, however, when he moved atop her, nestling between her thighs. She had to spread her legs wide to accommodate his hips—an act which drew her feminine mound snug against his hardness. He rocked against her in just the right place, and pure, bright pleasure shimmered through her veins.

He framed her face in his big hands. His gaze was dark and hungry as a wolf's. "Do you want me, Susanna?"

She couldn't dissemble. Her body made an answer of its own, as her hips tilted and arched, rubbing sinuously against his arousal. "Yes."

He didn't move. "Yes?"

Another man would have taken her at her first answer, if he'd bothered to ask at all. But he wanted to be absolutely certain she wanted this, too. If she'd harbored any lingering reluctance, his thoughtful concern dissolved it.

Yes, she wanted this. Not just *this*. She wanted *him*. Perhaps she would never marry. Perhaps she would never know true, lasting love with a man. But she wanted to explore passion and pleasure, and she wanted it to be with Bram. In all her five-and-twenty years, no man had ever made her feel this way. She might be waiting another five-and-twenty to experience this wonderful yearning again.

"Yes," she said again.

Still, he hesitated. "We shouldn't. Not tonight. Your first time really should be in a bed. What's more, that bed should be a marriage bed, for a girl like you."

"I never planned to marry at all. And as for beds . . ." She looked up at the willow branches sheltering them, and the scattered stars twinkling through. A more romantic setting couldn't exist. "Everyone has beds. I'll take this. So long as—" She cleared her throat. "You will be careful, won't you? At the end. I shouldn't want to get with child."

"I can be careful. But you should know, there's always a chance."

"I know. I'm willing to take the risk, if you are."

"To be with you?" He kissed her lips. "I'd risk a firing squad."

Her heart turned over in her chest. "Then yes. To all of it."

This time, he took her at her word. With one hand he impatiently pushed her shift higher, baring her abdomen and her left breast. He paused a moment, just looking.

"So beautiful."

The words rushed over her skin on a hot, ragged breath, drawing her nipple to a tight pucker. He bent his head and suckled her, drawing the aroused peak deep into his mouth and swirling his tongue around the sensitive tip. As he sucked and licked, the rough fringe of his whiskers scraped over her tender skin. Her every nerve attenuated, drawing tense and thin with the mounting pleasure.

"Touch me," he urged, between swipes of his tongue. "I want to feel your hands on me."

Susanna had never been happier to take his direction. She reached down, yanking his shirt free of his waistband and sliding both palms beneath it, exploring the smooth, muscled planes of his back. Then she wiggled a hand between their bodies, searching for the closures of his trousers. With an eager tilt of his hips, he aided her search. She undid the buttons on one side of the flap, working her fingers inside.

Oh. My.

Her senses were overwhelmed. The heat and weight of him, filling her grip. His needy groan of encouragement, buzzing around her nipple.

She stroked gently, as much as the cramped circumstances would allow, skimming her palm along his length and marveling at the texture. Like ridged velvet over heated iron. So smooth and so strong.

This belongs *inside me.* Her intimate muscles clenched at the thought.

"I can't wait," he said, abandoning her breast. "I can't wait any longer."

She released her grip on him as he pushed her shift higher, bunching the fabric under her arms. His erection wedged hot and eager between their bodies. He thrust against her bared sex, teasing up and down her cleft. The intense pleasure left her breathless, mindless.

"Last chance," he said through gritted teeth, changing his angle and tilting her hips. "If you don't want this, Susanna . . ."

The feral snarl of his lips gave her a heartbeat's pause. He was right, this was the most vital, undeniable force in nature. Her whole body craved release, possession. The power of the moment was almost too much.

"I want this," she managed. "I want you."

──Chapter Seventeen──

hen I'm yours," Bram whispered, nudging into her heat, just an inch. Rapture chased along the surface of his skin. "Take me. Take me in."

He worked into her slowly, in steady, deepening thrusts, putting most of his weight on his good knee and forcing himself to be patient as her body learned to accommodate his. She looked up at him with eyes so wide and unguarded, he could read her every emotion. He saw anxiety, trepidation. Understandable, as this was her first time. But there was trust as well, overwhelming her fear.

Overwhelming *him*.

With each exquisite, incremental advance, he offered words of encouragement and praise. "Yes, love . . . You feel so good . . . So good . . . Just like that . . . Just a bit more . . ."

As he sheathed himself fully with one last, unfettered thrust, she gave a pained gasp. His heart twisted in his chest. He hated to hurt her.

"Is the pain too much?"

She bit her lip bravely and shook her head no.

"Can—" Her body clenched around his, and he released a helpless groan of pleasure. "Can you bear it if I move?"

"Is moving necessary?"

He struggled valiantly not to laugh. "I think so, love. I . . . I have to move, or I'll go mad."

He slid out of her just a bit before plunging back in, even deeper than before. She was so warm and soft, and so damned tight. The pleasure had a keen, sweet edge. Balancing his weight on his elbows to keep from crushing her flat, he worked his hips back and forth, gently. For what seemed like ages, he restrained himself to only the most easy, gliding, undemanding of motions. All the while, the need for fast, furious, pumping release clamored in his veins. He fought it back through sheer force of will. She deserved better than an animalistic humping. This was a precious gift she'd bestowed on him, and he didn't want her to regret it. Not tonight. Not forty years from now.

"Is it better?" he asked.

"A little."

A little. A little wasn't enough. With a silent curse, he lowered his body to cover hers. "I want to make this good for you."

"It is good," she breathed. Her hands slid over his back, and her breasts molded beneath his chest, soft and warm. "I like this. I like having you so close to me."

"So do I."

As he slid into her the next time, her hips canted to meet his. She gave an encouraging moan. So he did it again. And again.

"That's . . ." She arched again, riding his thrusts like a wave. "Oh, Bram. It's so good now."

Holy God, it *was*. It was so damned good now. The angle, the rhythm, the way her body fit and moved with his. They'd achieved true unison of bodies and purpose, and it was like nothing he'd ever felt before. He'd never known he could so completely lose himself in a woman, and at the same time, feel he'd come home.

There was a world out there, somewhere beyond these willow branches. Oceans, mountains, glaciers, dunes. Somewhere, far away, wars were being waged. Bram could not have cared less. He didn't want to be anywhere else but inside this woman, as deep as he could go. He had no purpose, no duty in this life other than to fill her and please her and make her gasp and moan and scream.

She was where he belonged.

He reached down to lift her leg and wrap it over his hip, and her body drew him deeper still. They kissed deeply, too. He took his time exploring her lush, generous mouth, marveling at how good it felt to claim her both ways at once. Tall as he was, with other women he couldn't always kiss and thrust deep at the same time. But Susanna was his perfect match.

What their kisses lost in finesse, they gained in sensual urgency. Her fingernails bit into his shoulders, and the effect was that of a bee sting to a grazing bull. It drove him into a frenzy. His hips bucked as he pushed into her again and again, abandoning all gentleness, single-minded in his pursuit of her climax.

She *had* to come. She had to come *first*.

Which meant she had to come *soon*.

Please, Susanna. Please.

Her eyes fluttered closed, and her head rolled back. Her pale swan's neck stretched into an elegant, erotic curve, gleaming like quicksilver in the dark. So lovely, it made his heart ache.

"God, you're beautiful. You're so beautiful."

Her body tightened around his, and she cried out. He rode the exquisite wave of her climax as long as he dared. And when he knew he couldn't last another thrust without spilling, he pulled free of her tight, clasping embrace and took himself in hand. He spent his seed all over the sweet, rounded slope of her belly—not into a fold of his shirt or her shift, as might have been the more gentlemanly manner. In some primitive way, it satisfied him to mark her.

You're mine now.

He lowered himself beside her, curling his body around hers and caging her with his limbs. The protective impulses swelling inside him were almost more than he could bear. They choked his speech for a moment.

"Are you well?" he asked, once he could manage words.

"Yes." She nestled into his chest, and he tightened an arm around her, drawing her close. "Oh, Bram. I never dreamed it could be that way."

Neither did I, he felt like saying. *Neither did I.*

He'd had his share of tumbles, and he'd always enjoyed them thoroughly. But it had never been like this. It seemed impossible that they'd grown so close, so fast. But here they were, and he wouldn't wish to be anywhere else. He pressed a kiss to her hair and held it, inhaling deep of her sweet, fresh scent.

"We shouldn't have done this," he said, failing to muster any hint of regret.

"I know." She sighed, sounding equally uncontrite. "But I'm so glad we did. It was lovely."

"It was more than lovely. It was . . ." He grasped for another word and came up empty.

"Indescribable?" He heard the smile in her voice. "Yes. It was."

A sudden noise made him freeze. Angry shouting, originating from somewhere a fair distance away . . . but even so, all too near.

"Did you hear that?" she asked, clutching him tight.

And then the crash of breaking glass jolted them apart. Bram hurried to gain his feet, then extended a hand to help her do the same. Individually, they began reassembling garments without further discussion. Ignoring the noise was never an option. Whatever disturbance had occurred, it would no doubt require one—or both—of them to sort it out. Their idyllic interlude was over. Duty called.

Bram had his breeches refastened in a matter of moments. He turned to help Susanna with her gown.

"I can manage," she said, tilting her head toward the unknown source of the commotion. "Go on ahead."

He took her at her word, dashing out from beneath the willow's canopy and making his way across the green.

There, in the lane between the All Things shop and the Blushing Bull, or the Rutting Pansy, or whatever it was called tonight—a small crowd had formed. The way the men bunched and jostled in a ring, Bram suspected fisticuffs had broken out.

He pushed his way to the center, eager to break up the fight before any more damage could be done, to bodies, property, or morale. Much as he'd hoped to imbue his men with a bit of red-blooded combative spirit, it wasn't meant to be directed within the ranks.

However, he didn't find any of his men at the center of the circle.

He found the boys. Rufus and Finn, rolling around on the ground. Scrapping but good, with fists swinging—and teeth and knees involved, too. By the looks of the scene, they'd tumbled straight through the tea shop's front window. Shards of broken glass and bits of window leading covered the ground.

"Dodgy bastard," one of the twins spat. A trickle of blood from his temple made it hard to tell which one.

"Shite for brains," the other replied, reversing their positions and landing a punch to the gut. "We're twins. If I'm a bastard, you're one too."

"You're the only one what's a lying scum."

As they rolled, glass crunched beneath them. Time to put a stop to this, Bram decided. He reached out and plucked the topmost Bright twin—he still didn't know which—off the other. "That'll be enough, you two. What's going on here?"

"Rufus started it," one said, pointing.

"Aye, but it's Finn's fault," the other shot back, dabbing the blood at his temple.

Well, at least now Bram had their identities sorted out. He turned to Rufus. "What happened?"

Rufus glared at his brother. "He lied to Miss Charlotte, he did. Danced with her twice. First, as himself. Then once again, saying he was me."

Finn just tugged his ear and grinned. "You're just sorry you didn't think of it."

"I'll pound you, you little—" Rufus lunged, but Bram held him back.

"Hold there," he said. "Both of you." Once he had both boys by the collar, he cast a glance at Charlotte Highwood, who looked as excited as any fourteen-year-old girl could be about having two boys fight over her attentions. She surely wasn't going to be of any help in calming them. The crowd of onlookers appeared more amused than anything.

Bram knew he had to make it clear that boys or no, brothers or no, such fighting wouldn't be tolerated. "Now, listen," he said sternly, giving each boy a rough shake. "This isn't seemly behavior for two—"

"Help! Oh, help!"

They all turned toward the frantic female voice.

The ladies clustered in the entry of the tea shop-turned-tavern. Miss Diana Highwood sat slumped in the doorway, struggling for breath. Her complexion was pale and clammy, and her fingers were curled into misshapen fists.

"It's her asthma again," Mrs. Highwood said, her hands fluttering. "Oh dear. Oh dear. This wasn't supposed to happen here. Miss Finch promised Spindle Cove would be her cure."

Susanna was already there, one hand soothing the gasping woman's shoulder. "Her tincture," she said calmly. "Where is her tincture? She keeps it in her reticule."

"I . . . I don't know. It might be inside, or at the inn, or . . ." Charlotte paled. "I don't know."

"Search inside," Susanna told Fosbury. "The tables, the floor, the pianoforte." To a few of the other ladies, she said, "Go search the Highwoods' rooms at the inn."

Once these runners had been dispatched, she caught Rufus's eye. "I have a spare batch in my stillroom. A blue bottle, right side of the top shelf. You and Finn run as fast as you can to Summerfield and bring it back."

The twins nodded and dashed off down the lane.

"Let me go instead," Bram said.

She shook her head. "They need the distraction." Her gaze flicked to Bram's knee. "And they're faster."

Right. And Bram was just a lamed, useless lump. "Shall I go for a doctor?"

"No," she answered firmly. "She's been subjected to enough doctors. And there's no proper physician for miles, at any rate."

He nodded and stepped back. Damn it. He would never shy from a battle. He'd accept any risk to his own life, if it meant saving another's. But there was nothing he could do to help Susanna right now, and the feeling ate him raw. If he'd learned one thing in his eight months of convalescence, it was that he didn't cope well with helplessness.

But Susanna had this entire scene under control. Turning her attention to Diana, she spoke calmly, stroking the young woman's back in slow, soothing circles. "Just relax, dear. Remain calm, and you'll come through this."

"It's here. The tincture. It's here." The blacksmith emerged from the tea shop, his face stark and pale. He pressed a tiny bottle into Susanna's hand and stepped back immediately.

"Thank you." With sure fingers, Susanna unscrewed the bottle's top and measured a capful of dark liquid. She looked to Bram. "Will you hold her? If she trembles, the medicine might spill."

"Of course." Finally, something he could do. He knelt beside the gasping woman and wrapped her slender body in his arms. Her tremors shook through him.

"Don't be afraid to hold her tight," Susanna said. "Just keep her immobile." She tilted Diana's head back to rest against his shoulder, then poured the capful of tincture between her quivering, blue-tinged lips. "Swallow, dear. I know it's difficult, but you can do it."

Miss Highwood nodded a bit and managed a choking, harsh swallow. Then her gasping resumed.

"What now?" Bram asked, looking to Susanna.

"Now we wait."

They waited, in tense, painful silence, listening to the sounds of Miss Highwood struggling for breath. After a few minutes, her rasping softened to a gentler wheeze, and a faint wash of pink returned to her cheeks. No matter what ribbing he might take for it later, Bram decided right there—pink was his new favorite color.

As Diana's struggles eased, everyone watching drew a deep, grateful breath.

"That's it," Susanna murmured to her friend. "That's it. Take deep, slow breaths. The worst is behind you now."

Bram released the young woman and left her in Susanna's care.

"It's all right, dear," she mumbled, stroking Diana's damp brow. "It's over now. All's well." Then Susanna glanced up, and her face went blank with dismay. "Heavens. Just look at this place."

Bram watched as she made a slow, heartrending survey of the scene. Her gaze traveled from the shambles of the tea shop, to the broken glass in the lane, to the trembling woman in her arms. Miss Highwood might have survived this episode, but Spindle Cove's peaceful atmosphere had not.

Minerva Highwood came dashing out from the Queen's Ruby. She flew straight to her sister's side, taking her hand. "Diana. My God, what's happened?"

"She had a breathing crisis," Susanna answered. "But she's better now."

Minerva kissed her sister's pale brow. "Oh, Diana. I'm so sorry. I should never have left you in that place. I knew the dancing was a bad idea."

"It was hardly your fault, Minerva."

Minerva's head whipped up. "Oh, I know very well whose fault it was." Her gaze focused on a distant target. "This is all your doing."

To a one, every head in the crowd swiveled to face Colin. But Bram felt the guilt landing squarely on him. To be sure, his cousin was responsible for this mess. But Bram was responsible for his cousin.

Susanna knew it, too. While everyone else was glaring daggers at Colin, her eyes met Bram's. And her gaze couldn't have said any more plainly, *I warned you this would happen.*

"We never should have stayed in this wretched place," Mrs. Highwood wailed, clutching a handkerchief to her mouth. "Lords or no lords. I *knew* that spa in Kent would have been the better choice."

"Mama, please. Let's discuss this inside." Minerva took her mother by the arm.

Slowly, Susanna helped Diana Highwood to her feet. "Come along, ladies. Let's take her back to the rooming house where she can rest."

"Can we help you move her?" Bram asked, putting a hand under Miss Highwood's elbow to help.

"No, thank you, my lord." Susanna gave him a sad half smile. "You and your friends have done quite enough this evening."

"I'll wait for you," he murmured. "See you back to Summerfield later."

She shook her head. "Please don't."

"I want to help. Give me something to do."

"Just leave me be," she whispered. Her eyes darted to the side, and he could tell she was conscious of how everyone stared at the two of them. "*Please.*"

To leave her be, when she was so clearly upset and vulnerable, went against every protective impulse in his body. But he'd asked her what he could do, and she'd answered him. Honor bade him to comply. For now.

With a reluctant nod, he stepped back. Young ladies clustered around her as they all retreated to the Queen's Ruby.

He'd let her down. She'd asked him to put a stop to this madness, and he'd refused. Now Miss Highwood was taken ill, the tea shop was in shambles, and he'd put both her reputation and her cherished community at risk. After all their confessions last night, he understood what this place meant to her, how much effort and care she'd devoted to its success.

She'd given him her virginity under the willow tree. And he'd let her down. Bloody hell.

Tomorrow, he'd see about making it up to her.

Tonight, his cousin would have hell to pay.

"Go home, all of you," he told the men milling about the lane. "Sleep off your drink and return to this spot at sunrise. There'll be no drill tomorrow until we put this place to rights."

One by one, the men dispersed, leaving him and Colin alone.

Colin shook his head, regarding the scene. "Well, I've certainly left my mark on this place. There isn't a tavern or ballroom or woman in England I can't leave ruined and panting for more."

Bram glared at him, enraged. "You think this is amusing? Fosbury's establishment is in splinters, and a young lady almost died here tonight. In my arms."

"I know, I know." Looking grieved, Colin pushed both hands through his hair. "It's not amusing at all. But how was I to know she would suffer such an attack? I never meant any harm, you must know. We only meant to have a bit of fun."

"*Fun.*" Bram fired the word back at him. "Did you ever stop to think that perhaps the ladies have a reason for keeping this a peaceful village? Or that perhaps the mission we're here to accomplish is more important than an evening's debauchery?" When Colin didn't immediately reply, he said, "No. Of course you didn't consider it. You never consider anyone else, except to see them standing in the way of your *fun.*"

"Please. You never consider the feelings of others, either. We're all just obstacles to your military glory." Colin threw up his hands. "I don't even want to be in this godforsaken, disgustingly charming place."

"Then leave. Go find one of your many dissolute friends and leech off him for the next few months."

"Do you really think that idea hasn't occurred to me,

on a damned near hourly basis since we arrived? Good Lord, as if I couldn't find better accommodations than that ghastly castle."

"Then why are you still here?"

"Because you're my cousin, Bram!"

For a well-established fact, this sudden outburst rather surprised them both.

Colin made a fist. "You've been my closest kin since my parents . . . since I was a boy. And since your father died, I'm all you've got, too. We've barely spoken to each other in over a decade. I thought it might be nice to try this 'family' thing the rest of the world seems so keen on. An idiotic notion, clearly."

"Clearly."

Bram paced in a slow circle, swinging his arms in frustration. This was brilliant. Just exactly what he needed to hear right now—that atop betraying Sir Lewis, deflowering Susanna, and contributing to the village's destruction tonight, he was somehow failing Colin, too. *This* was why he needed to return to his regiment. In the army, he had a routine, a drill book, marching orders. There, he always knew what to do. If he never resumed his command, this would be his life, it seemed. A string of disappointments and failures.

The futility of it all incited him to unreasoned anger.

Colin scratched behind his ear. "Just think, and all those years growing up alone, I thought I was missing out on something."

"Guess you learned your lesson there."

"What does either of us know about family, anyhow?"

"I know something about it," Bram returned. "I know we're doing it wrong. I don't respect you. You don't respect me. We've only been at each other's throats this whole time."

"You're such a principled, arrogant ass. If you respected me, I'd have your sanity challenged. And so far as filial affection is concerned . . ." Colin gestured angrily toward the spot where the Bright twins had grappled. "It seems clawing at one another's throats is the standard practice."

"Well, in that case." With his left hand, Bram grabbed Colin by the shirtfront. His right fist made an impulsive swing at his cousin's jaw. He checked the strength of the blow somewhat, but it still landed with enough force to send Colin's head whipping left. "That's for Miss Highwood." He drove a halfhearted, joyless punch into his cousin's gut. "And that's for . . . for *fun*."

He waited, breathing hard, holding his cousin by the collar and bracing himself for retaliation. Longing for it, truly. Bram knew he had blows coming to him—for Susanna, for Sir Lewis, for everything. The impact could only come as a relief.

But his cousin wouldn't do him even that favor. He simply touched his tongue to his bruised lip and said, "I'll be off in the morning, Bram. I'd let you be rid of me sooner, but I don't travel at night."

"Oh no, you don't." Bram gave him a shake.

Damn it, what was he going to do with this man? If he left here, nothing good could come of it. Of him. As a young, unattached, soon-to-be-wealthy peer, Colin had no checks on his behavior. Since a tragically young age, he'd been lacking both a father's example and a mother's understanding.

Susanna, he thought with a bittersweet twinge, would probably argue Colin needed a hug.

Well, Bram didn't know how to offer his cousin any of those things—not with a straight face, at any rate. But he knew how to be an officer, and experience had taught him that duty and discipline could patch a good many holes in a man's life.

He might be the only person in the world who could offer Colin this: the chance to rise to expectations, rather than sink to them.

"You're not leaving," he told him. "Not now, and not tomorrow, either." He released his cousin, then gestured at the scene of destruction and chaos. "You broke this, and you're damned well going to mend it."

Spindle Cove was falling to pieces.

Once she'd seen that Diana was safely upstairs and resting in her bed, Susanna descended to the drawing room of the Queen's Ruby. There she found her whole world breaking apart. Complaints and confessions detonated in every corner of the room.

"Oh Lord. Oh Lord," a voice pitched above frantic flapping. A gull's wing couldn't have worked harder than that fan. "I feel an attack of nerves coming on."

"I can't believe I drank *whiskey*," mourned another. "And danced with a *fisherman*. If my uncle hears of this, I'll be called home in such disgrace."

"Perhaps I ought to go upstairs. Start packing my things now."

And then came the observation that froze Susanna's blood.

"Miss Finch, what's happened to your gown? The buttons are all askew. And look at your hair."

"I . . ." Susanna strove to keep calm. "I suppose I dressed too hurriedly tonight."

"But it wasn't like that at Summerfield," Violet Winterbottom said. "And I thought for certain you would have arrived in the village long before me—I was forced to rest for so long—but you didn't. Did you meet with some accident on the way?"

"Something like that." As she melted into a nearby chair, Susanna's conscience stabbed at her. Then she knew the piercing quality of Kate Taylor's curious gaze. Then Minerva's.

They all turned to her, every lady in the room. Staring. Noticing. Then *wondering*.

She'd been so foolish. What she'd shared with Bram had been . . . indescribable, and she couldn't bring herself to regret it. But to engage in it on the village green, where they had every chance of discovery? While complete pandemonium broke out nearby, putting a woman's life at risk?

And Miss Highwood wasn't the only one in danger. Women like Kate and Minerva . . . If Spindle Cove ceased to be a reputable place, what chance would they have to pursue their talents and enjoy the freedom of independent thought?

"Miss Finch?" Kate asked quietly, coming to sit beside her and take her hand. "Is there anything you wish to tell us? Anything at all?"

Susanna squeezed her friend's hand and looked around the room. She was not a resentful person as a matter of course. But in that brief moment, she rather hated the world. She hated that all these bright, unconventional women were here because they'd been made to think there was something wrong with them. That they had to escape from society, just to be themselves. She hated that the slightest hint of her behavior tonight could put their safe haven at risk—assuming that tavern debacle hadn't ruined everything anyway.

And most of all, she hated that she could not sit here with her only friends and confess to them that she'd just given her virginity to the strongest, most sensual, wonderfully tender man. That beneath her rumpled clothing, she was still flushed and damp and . . . pleasantly sticky from his attentions. That she was changed inside, still reeling from the pleasure and profundity of it all. Little echoes of bliss cinched tight in her belly, and her heart brimmed with emotion. And did they *know* the wicked things a man could do with his tongue?

It was so wrong, that the world forced her to keep quiet. But Susanna had long ago resigned herself to the fact that she could not single-handedly change the world. At best, she could protect her small corner of it.

Tonight, she'd failed at even that.

"On my way into the village, I had a tumble," she said, "and my gown took the brunt of it. That's all." She rose from her chair, preparing to leave. "I'm going home to rest. I suggest you all do the same. I know it's been an unusual evening, but I hope to see you all in the morning. It's Thursday, and we do have our schedule."

Chapter Eighteen

 ondays are country walks. Tuesdays, sea bathing. Wednesdays, you'd find us in the garden.

"And on Thursdays . . ." Bram said aloud, "they shoot."

Of course they did.

He stood with Colin on the edge of a green, level meadow near Summerfield. The two of them watched as the assembled fragile-flower ladies of Spindle Cove donned doeskin gloves and arranged themselves in a rail-straight line, facing down a distant row of targets. Behind the women sat a long wooden table, atop which lay bows, arrows, pistols, flintlock rifles. Quite the buffet of weaponry.

At the head of the line, Susanna announced the first course. "Bows up, ladies." She herself fitted an arrow to her bowstring and drew it back. "On three. One . . . Two . . ."

Thwack.

In unison, the ladies released arrows that flew true to their targets.

Bram craned his neck to see how Susanna's had landed. Dead center, of course. He wasn't surprised. At this point, very little would surprise him, where Susanna Finch was concerned. She could tell him she ran an elite espionage ring out of her morning room, and he would believe it.

The ladies walked briskly across the meadow to retrieve their arrows. Bram's eyes were fixed on Susanna as she crossed the ground in smooth, confident strides. She moved through the tallish grass like an African gazelle, all long legs and graceful strength.

"Pistols, please," she said, once they'd all returned. She traded her bow and arrow for a single-barreled weapon.

Each lady in line lifted a similar firearm and held it in braced, outstretched arms, staring down her respective bull's-eye. When Susanna cocked her pistol, the others followed suit. The chorus of clicks raced down Bram's spine.

"I find this scene wildly arousing," Colin murmured, echoing Bram's own thoughts. "Is that wrong?"

"If it is, I can promise you company in hell."

His cousin made an amused sound. "And you thought we have nothing in common."

Susanna leveled her pistol and took aim. "One . . . Two . . ."

Crack.

Neat, smoking holes appeared on each of the targets. In unison, the girls lowered their pistols and set them aside. Bram whistled low, admiring the accuracy of the ladies' marksmanship.

"Rifles next," Susanna called out, shouldering her own firearm. "One . . . Two . . ."

Bang.

Once again, true shots, all. One of the targets exploded with a little burst of paper, rather than the usual batting and straw. A breeze carried a scrap of it to land at Bram's boots.

"What's this?" Colin asked. He bent to retrieve it. "A page from some book. By a Mrs. Worthington?"

The name was oddly familiar to Bram, but he couldn't think why.

Colin shook his head. "I've no idea why this place is called Spinster Cove. It ought to be Amazon Inlet. Or Valkyrie Bay."

"No doubt." Here Bram had been straining and sweating through his effort to round up the local men and train them into a fighting force. Meanwhile, Susanna had already organized her own army. An army of females, no less.

She was, quite simply, the most amazing woman he'd ever known. More the pity that this morning, as she stared down that target, she was probably envisioning Bram's face on it—if not his nether regions.

Steeling his nerve, he strode forward into the breach. As he walked the line of markswomen, he had the distinct sensation of being a moving target. Susanna caught sight of him and stopped short.

As he neared her, he held up his open hands in a gesture of peace. "I told you I'd risk a firing squad."

She wasn't amused. "What are you doing here?"

"Watching. Admiring." He flicked a glance toward the women. "You've trained your ladies well. I'm impressed. Impressed, but not surprised."

A blush climbed her throat. "I've always believed a woman should know how to protect herself." She reached for the powder horn and a gleaming, polished example of the pistol with which she shared a name.

"The men have been working since sunup to put the tea shop back to rights," he said. He nodded toward his cousin. "And I've brought Payne along to apologize. If he doesn't do a fair job of it, you can use him for target practice."

She didn't smile. "Unfortunately, the tea shop is the least of the damage incurred. And it's not me who deserves his apology."

Concerned, he looked around the shooting party. "Is Miss Highwood still feeling poorly?"

She poured a measure of powder into the pistol, following the charge with a patch-wrapped ball. "I stopped by early this morning. She's resting for caution's sake, but I don't think she'll suffer any lasting effects from the incident."

"I'm glad to hear it."

"However"—she cocked her weapon—"her mother is now set on removing her daughters from Spindle Cove. There's a new spa in Kent, you see. She's heard they do remarkable things with leeches and mercury."

Susanna turned, leveled her pistol at the distant target, and shot. A whisper of smoke wafted from the gun barrel. He could have sworn he glimpsed smoke emanating from her ears, as well.

Bram muttered an oath. "I'll send my cousin to call on them, too. I'm told he can be very charming and persuasive with the ladies."

"In all honesty, my lord, I'm not sure which has the greater toxic potential. Your cousin's charm, or the mercury." She lowered her weapon and her voice. "Mrs. Highwood is all but packing her trunks. Miss Winterbottom and Mrs. Lange are speaking of leaving, too. If *they* leave, others will doubtless follow. If the general concern reaches Society at large, our reputation as a safe haven will be destroyed. All the families will call their daughters and wards home. Everything will come to an end. And for what? This absurd militia is doomed to fail. The men are hopeless."

Never mind the weapons, or the dozen ladies looking

on. Bram longed to pull her into his arms, hold her just as close and tight as he had beneath that willow tree.

"Susanna, look at me."

He waited until those clear, iris-blue eyes met his.

"I will mend this," he said. "I know I let you down last night, but it won't happen again. My cousin and I *will* convince the ladies it's safe to stay. Until the midsummer fair, I *will* keep the men tightly reined and out of your way. And someway, somehow, over the course of the next fortnight, I *will* drill them into an elite, precise militia to impress your father's guests."

She made a sound of disbelief.

"I will," he repeated. "Because that's an officer's duty. To make unlikely men into soldiers, and to ensure they turn up trained and prepared, wherever and whenever they're needed. It's what I do, and I'm good at it."

She released a breath. "I know. I'm sure you're a very capable commander, when you don't have to contend with teacakes and poetry and cudgel-wielding bluestockings."

"I have been distracted. But that's all to do with you, Miss Finch."

Her lips curved a little. A tiny fishhook of a smile that had his heart instantly snagged.

But then it faded, and she turned from him, looking off to the distance, toward the village. Her spine was straight; her shoulders, bravely squared. But the fear was there, in the tiny quiver of her bottom lip and the gooseflesh dotting the graceful curve of her shoulder. She felt responsible for the place, and she was scared.

He couldn't let her feel that way. Not when he had the perfect opportunity and every honorable reason to make her problems his own. To make *Susanna* his own. Right now, this very morning. He'd been thinking on the possibility all night, but now the decision simply clicked within him. Crisp and clear as the sound of a pistol being cocked.

"Don't worry. About anything." He stepped back a pace, heading in the direction of the house. "I'm going to leave my cousin here to grovel before your ladies. Make him fall on his knees, if you would. I'm off to have a talk with your father."

"Wait," she said, turning back to him. "You promised not to involve my father. You gave me your word."

"Oh, don't worry." He turned away. "I'm not talking to him about the militia. This is strictly to do with you and me."

Susanna watched him as he walked toward the house, wondering if she'd understood him correctly. Did he just say he meant to speak with her father? About the two of them?

If he intended that the way it sounded . . .

"Oh drat." She picked up her skirts and gave chase.

She caught up to him just as he reached the house's side entrance. "What do you mean," she asked, panting, "that you're going to speak to my father? About *us*? Surely you can't mean that the way it sounds."

"Certainly I can."

A footman opened the door for him, and he walked through. Leaving her on the threshold with no further explanation. Teasing, cryptic man.

"Wait just a minute," she called, chasing him down the corridor. "Are you referring to"—she dropped her voice to a scandalized whisper—"*marriage*? And if that's the case, shouldn't you be talking to me first?"

"What we did last night renders that conversation rather irrelevant, don't you agree?"

"No. No, I don't agree." Panic struck her in the breastbone. She put a hand on his arm, arresting his progress. "You're going to tell my *father*. About last night."

"Not in so many words. But when I offer for you so abruptly, I wager he's going to gather the reason why."

"Precisely. And if my father gathers the reason why, *everyone* will. All the ladies. The whole village. Bram, you can't."

"Susanna, I must." His jade-green gaze captured hers. "It's the only decent thing to do."

She threw up her hands. "Since when do you care about decent behavior?"

He didn't answer, only turned and walked on. This time, there was no stopping him until he'd turned down the rear corridor and halted in the entry of her father's workshop.

"Sir Lewis?" He rapped smartly on the doorjamb.

"Not now, please," her father replied, his voice hazy.

"He's working," Susanna whispered. "No one disturbs him when he's working."

Bram only raised his voice. "Sir Lewis, it's Bramwell. I need to speak with you on a matter of some urgency."

Good God. Susanna *urgently* needed to knock some sense into this man.

Her father sighed. "Very well, then. Go on to my library. I'll meet you there in a moment."

"Thank you, sir."

Bram turned on his heel without further comment, making his way toward Sir Lewis's library. Susanna stood there for a moment, dumbstruck, wondering whether her best hopes lay in reasoning with Bram or distracting her father. Perhaps she ought to simply run upstairs, pack a valise, and abscond to a small, uncharted territory. She'd heard the Sandwich Islands were lovely this time of year.

The idea was tempting, but she took her chances with

the library. Bram stood grim and monolithic in the center of the Egyptian-themed room, looking like a man awaiting his own funeral.

"Why on earth are you doing this?" she asked, shutting the door. Obviously, not because he wished to.

"Because it's the honorable thing. The only thing I can do." He released a curt sigh. "I should not have done what I did last night if I weren't prepared to do this today."

"But don't I enter this question at all? Don't you have the slightest regard for my feelings in the matter?"

"I have every regard for you and your feelings. That's the point. You're a gentlewoman, and last night I took your virtue."

"You didn't *take* it. I *gave* it. Freely, and with no expectations."

He shook his head. "Listen, I know you're full of modern ideas. But my own views on marriage are more traditional. Or medieval, as you're so fond of saying. If a man deflowers a gently bred virgin in a public square, he ought to marry her. End of story."

End of story. That was the problem, wasn't it? She might not be so panicked at the idea of marrying him—in fact, the prospect might make her dizzyingly happy—if he saw their wedding as the *beginning* of a story. A story that included love and a home and a family, and ended with the words "happily ever after."

But he didn't, as his next words made clear.

"It will come out to your advantage, you'll see. We'll marry before I go back to war, and then you'll be free to do as you please. You'll be Lady Rycliff. You can continue your work, but as a countess. It can only help the village's reputation." As an offhand addition, he told the desk blotter, "I have money. A good deal of it. You'll be well provided for."

"How very practical," she muttered. It had been many years since Susanna had daydreamed about receiving marriage offers, but she was certain none of those imagined proposals had sounded quite like *this*.

She moved into his line of sight, standing in front of her father's desk. She placed both hands on the desk's carved wood edge and hoisted herself up so that she sat on the desktop, legs dangling.

"I don't lack money. Nor do I lack social influence. If you go through with this fool plan this morning, however, *you* may find yourself lacking a pulse." She raised her hands to shoulder height. "Every room of this house holds lethal weaponry. You do realize, there's a solid chance my father could kill you."

If he doesn't collapse of an apoplexy first.

He shrugged. "If I were him, I'd want to kill me, too."

"And even if he doesn't," she went on, "he could ruin you. Strip you of all your honors and insignia. Have you demoted to the lowest rank of foot soldier."

He didn't reply right away. Aha. So that argument made some impression.

"Think of your commission, Bram. And *please* stop being so dratted chivalrous, or I'll . . ." She gestured wildly toward the alabaster sarcophagus. "Or I'll stuff you in that coffin and close the lid."

His brow quirked. "When you talk like that, you know you only make me want you more."

He took a step forward, drawing close. Too close.

"This isn't just chivalry." His voice was a low, arousing rumble. His hand brushed her calf, and desire forked through her like lightning. "You must know that. What we shared last night? I want to do it again. And again. And again. Hard and fast. Slow and sweet. Every way in between."

A long, languid sigh escaped her lips. Just those words had her warm and pink all over. How stupid she'd been, to think one taste of passion would satisfy her for a lifetime. She would hunger for this man as long as she lived.

He leaned in for a kiss, but she put a hand to his chest. Keeping some distance between them, but also maintaining contact. Enjoying the strong, male feel of him under her touch.

"Bram," she said, swallowing hard, "lust isn't a good reason to marry."

He paused to reflect. "I think it's the reason most people marry."

"We're not most people." She felt herself frowning as she searched for a way to make him understand. "This may be silly to say now, after all that's happened between us, but I . . . I like you."

His chin ducked in surprise. "You . . . like me."

"Yes. I do. I've come to like you. A great deal, you see. And I respect your deep commitment to your work. Because I feel the same. I wouldn't want you to destroy your career and reputation. And I hope you wouldn't want to see mine destroyed. But that's what could happen, for both of us, if you insist on talking to my father today."

He stood tall and rubbed the back of his neck. "I have to offer for you. I have to offer for you, or I can't live with myself."

"You *have* offered." Tilting her head, she gestured loosely between them. "In some way that involves no declarations of sentiment or actual posing of questions, you've offered to wed me in haste, bed me with enthusiasm, and then leave me alone to deal with speculation and scandal, all so you can go throw yourself in front of another bullet with a clear conscience. Please accept my polite refusal. My lord."

He shook his head. "It's the deceit, Susanna. I can't stomach the lies. Your father has done a great deal for me. He at least deserves my honesty."

"Hullo. What's going on here?"

Her father stood in the doorway, still dressed in his work apron.

Susanna smiled, sat tall on the desk, and chirped, "Oh, nothing. Lord Rycliff and I were just having a scandalous, clandestine affair."

Her father froze.

Susanna kept that smile pasted on her face.

And finally, with the same palpable, atmospheric relief that accompanied a storm breaking, Papa finally burst into wry, disbelieving laughter.

"*There*," she whispered, brushing past a stunned Bram as she dismounted the desk. "No more deceit."

She tapped her chin meaningfully. Taking the hint, he shut his gaping mouth. He shot her a fierce green look, equal parts admiration and annoyance.

Rubbing his hands on his apron, Papa said, still chuckling, "I did wonder why I found myself dining alone last night. Rycliff is lucky I heard about that hubbub in the village last night. If not, I might be testing the new rifle lock on him this morning." He crossed to the bar and unstoppered a decanter of whiskey. "Well, Bram? Out with it. Let's keep this brief."

"Absolutely," Bram said. "Sir Lewis, I came to discuss an important matter with you. It involves Miss Finch. And a proposal."

Her stomach plummeted to the floor. Still? He meant to pursue this *still*? Oh, he was so wretchedly honorable and good.

"What kind of proposal?" her father asked.

Bram cleared his throat. "The usual kind. You see, sir
. . . Last night, Miss Finch and I—"

"Were talking," Susanna interjected. "About the militia
review."

"Oh really?" Papa turned and handed Bram a tumbler
of whiskey.

Bram lifted the glass, sipped—then seemed to think
better of the gradual approach and drained the rest in a
single swallow. "As you know, we were called away from
the dining room to deal with some disturbance in the village. But when we arrived there, one thing led to another,
and . . ." He cleared his throat. "Sir Lewis, we engaged in—"

"Intense debate," Susanna finished. "We argued.
Most"—she flicked a glance at Bram—"passionately."

"Whatever about?" Sir Lewis frowned as he lifted his
own glass.

"Sex."

Bram, curse him, just *thrust* that word into conversation. It was bold, bald, and unfortunately for her, impossible to cut short. In the ensuing tense silence, he slid her
a look that said, *Take that.*

She hoisted her chin. "Yes. Just so. The sexes. Male and
female. In our village. You see, Papa, the militia endeavor
has been disrupting the ladies' restorative atmosphere. It
seems the needs of men and women in this village are
at odds, and Lord Rycliff and I exchanged some rather
heated words."

"Oh yes," he said dryly. "I'm afraid I gave Miss Finch
quite the tongue-lashing."

A violent coughing fit seized Susanna.

"However," Bram continued, "when we concluded that
argument, we adjourned to the village green. And *that*
was where we joined—"

"Forces," Susanna supplied, fairly shouting the word. An echo bounced back at her from the ancient sarcophagus.

Her father blinked at her. "Forces."

"Yes." She smoothed her damp palms on her skirts. "We decided to put aside our differences and work together for the good of the whole."

She slid a glance toward Bram. He leaned one hand against a papyrus-shaped column and made a magnanimous wave with his empty glass. "Oh, do go on. You tell him everything. I'll wait and have my say at the end."

They exchanged looks of challenge and amusement. It must be wrong, she thought—very wrong indeed, that this conversation was fraught with imminent peril, and yet they were having so much fun.

"I understand," she said, trying for a more serious tone, "that this militia review is important. Important to you, Papa." She turned to her father. "And important to Lord Rycliff, as well. But if I may say it . . . much as I know this is difficult for Lord Rycliff to admit . . . initial prospects do not look encouraging. Quite frankly, his recruits are hopeless. The review could prove a disaster, embarrassing us all."

"Now, wait," Bram said, pushing off the column. "That's premature. We've only had a few days. I will train those men into a—"

Susanna raised an open palm. "You did tell me I could have my say." Turning back to her father, she continued, "At the same time, Papa, the ladies at the Queen's Ruby are growing concerned. The militia exercises have disrupted their schedule, and they've lost the highlight of their summer—planning the midsummer fair. Some are thinking of leaving Spindle Cove entirely, which could prove disastrous in its own, albeit different way."

She drew a deep breath. "So Lord Rycliff and I have

decided to join forces and work together, to protect what's most dear to us both. The militia drills and preparations will become the joint project of all village residents. Men and ladies, together. There's so much to be done, and Lord Rycliff has admitted he can't do it without my help." She gave Bram a cautious glance. "But together, we can plan a display to do you proud. What do you think, Papa?"

Her father sighed. "It all sounds eminently logical. And entirely unworthy of this urgent conference that disrupted my work."

"There is something else," Bram said. "A question that requires your answer."

Susanna gulped. "Can we have a ball?"

"A ball?" Bram and her father echoed in unison.

"Yes, a ball." She'd blurted out the idea without thinking, but upon reflection, Susanna saw that it was perfect. "That's the proposal. We'd like to hold a ball here, at Summerfield. An officers' ball, directly following the field review. I know you will have esteemed guests for the occasion, Papa. A ball is the perfect way to honor and entertain them. It will also serve as a reward for the militia volunteers, after all their hard work. And it will give the young ladies something to look forward to. A reason to stay. It's perfect."

"Very well, Susanna. You may have a ball." Her father plunked his glass on the desk.

And then his manner changed, somehow. His gaze roamed the blotter absently, as though he'd misplaced his chain of thought. And Susanna felt dropped, without warning, into one of those awful, terrifying moments. Those moments where the filter of daughterly affection slipped, and suddenly she wasn't looking at her dear familiar papa, the charismatic, eccentric hero of her childhood—but simply at a stranger named Lewis Finch. And that man looked so old and so tired.

He rubbed his eyes. "I know this militia business seems rather silly on the face of things. But there's a great deal hanging in the balance—for us all, in one way or another. I'm gratified to see the two of you working together to ensure its success. Thank you. Now, if you'll both excuse me."

And he was gone, exiting through the side door.

Bram turned to her. His expression was blank. "I can't believe you just did that."

"You can't believe I did what? Save your life and your career? Not that you seem to make a distinction between the two."

He stared out the window. "Susanna, you just gave him reason to doubt me. He assigned me a duty, and you told him I can't do it."

She winced. How was it that men could be so big and strong in body, and yet so fragile when it came to pride?

"I told him you can't do it *alone*. And there's no shame in that." She moved to stand at his side. She began to reach for him, but thought better of it, crossing her arms instead. "As my father just said, a great deal hangs in the balance. I know what this means to you, truly. You need to prove yourself after your injury, and this is your one chance."

A flicker of denial crossed his features, like a knee-jerk reflex. But then he nodded. "Yes."

She wanted so badly to hug him. Perhaps, once this militia was a success and he *had* proved himself, he could turn his attention to all those other, less easily admitted needs. Like his palpable yearning for closeness and affection. Or his obvious, unspoken desire for a true home. Perhaps he'd even change his mind, and decide to stay. But she knew he couldn't consider any of those things until he felt strong and whole again, in command of himself and others.

"Then let me help." She said honestly, "For both your sake and my father's, I want to see you succeed. But we must face facts. You have a little more than a fortnight to get those men uniformed, drilled, and trained to perfection. Not to mention all the preparations for the day itself. There's so much work to be done. I know this village, inside and out. You can't do it without me."

He pushed a hand through his hair. "Now that you've thrown an officers' ball into the mix, I suppose I can't."

"It was a spur-of-the-moment idea," she admitted. "But a good one. If anything can convince Mrs. Highwood and the others to stay, it's the prospect of planning a ball. We'll need everyone working together, men and ladies. If we're going to keep both our dreams from disintegrating, we have to make this day a grand success."

"Something tells me Miss Finch has a plan."

"Not a plan," she said, smiling a little. "A schedule. As you know, Mondays are country walks. Tuesdays, sea bathing. On Wednesdays we're in the garden, and Thursdays we shoot. On Fridays, we've always climbed up to the castle. To picnic, sketch, stage our little theatricals. Or sometimes just to plot and scheme."

"Well," he said. "We can't disrupt the ladies' schedule, now can we? Bring them all up, then. It'll be a good way for the men to patch things over, after last night's mayhem."

"We'll plot and scheme together, Bram. You'll see, it will all come out right."

She stared up at him, so handsome and strong. Along with all the other firsts he'd given her, he'd now made her first offer of marriage. A forced and unromantic one, but still. She rather treasured the sentiment, and she wanted to repay it somehow.

On impulse, she leaned forward and kissed his cheek. "Thank you. For everything."

He grasped her elbow, forbidding her to retreat. "What about us?" His words were hot against her ear. "How do matters stand between us?"

"Why, I . . . I still like you." Nerves fluttered in her chest, but she kept her tone light. "Do you like me?"

A few moments passed in silence. She would have counted them in heartbeats, but her foolish heart had become a most unreliable timepiece. It gave three pounding beats in a flurry, then none at all.

Just when she'd begun to despair, he turned his head, catching her in a passionate, openmouthed kiss. He put both arms around her, fisting his hands in the fabric of her dress, lifting her up and against his chest. So that her body recalled every inch of his, every second of their blissful lovemaking. The now-familiar ache returned— that sweet, hollow pang of desire that only deepened as his tongue flickered over hers. In a matter of seconds, he had her gasping. Needing. Damp.

Then he set her back on her toes. Pressed his brow to hers and released a deep, resonant sigh. And just before turning to leave, he spoke a single word.

He said, "No."

Chapter Nineteen

e did not "like" Susanna Finch. Of this much, Bram was certain.

"Like" was . . . the verbal equivalent of blancmange. Pleasant enough, blandly sweet. Always on the table. Not something a man turned down, but not something he asked for second helpings of, either. The word "like" did not communicate an unspoken connection of similar minds, or an obsessive attention to freckles. It certainly didn't encompass the sort of wild, reckless, unreasoned lust that had driven him to deflower a virgin on the village green.

No, he did not "like" her. Beyond that, Bram was at a loss to describe his emotional state. Putting labels on feelings was Susanna's hobby, not his.

And at the moment, she was occupied.

"Mrs. Lange has excellent penmanship," she muttered, scratching with a pencil on paper as she did. "I'll put her on invitations."

She had arrived at the castle early that morning, well in advance of the picnicking girls. Together, they'd convened their council atop the southwest turret of Rycliff Castle's keep. They'd been sitting here on campstools for hours now, with a backdrop of gulls swooping over the brilliant aquamarine sea, sorting out all the tasks to be accomplished in the next fortnight.

Well, *she* had been sorting out the tasks. Bram had mostly been staring at her, occasionally stealing sips of whiskey, and trying to sort out the tangle of feelings and impulses churning in his chest.

"Patches will be Charlotte's task. As well as . . . rolling . . . cartridges." She scribbled as she spoke, adding to the bottom of a very long list. She kept her gaze stubbornly trained on the paper.

His gaze was riveted to her. He was fascinated. Just when he'd started to think he knew Susanna Finch, the morning light introduced her all over again. Every hour—every minute, perhaps—announced another facet of her beauty. Each tilt of her head invented new alloys of copper and gold. And now—just this second—the advancing veil of sunlight made its way over the crest of her shoulder, and he could see how the skin of her décolletage was so delicate and fair . . . nearly translucent.

And bloody hell. This journeyed far beyond "like," rocketed straight past "fondness," and pushed all the way to the brink of absurdity.

He knew all her objections to marriage were logical. She'd built her life and village around happy spinsterhood, and the demands of his military career left no room for a wife. A hasty wedding could mean grief for Sir Lewis, scandal for Susanna, and God knew what for Bram. But he *was* going to marry her, despite it. Because when he looked at Susanna, all he could think was one word. It wasn't a particularly elegant or poetic word, any more so than "like." But it had a straightforward eloquence all its own.

Mine.

No matter what it cost him, he simply had to make her his.

"There," she said. "I think that's everything." She let the list fall to her lap. "It's so much work. But I think we can do it."

"I know we can." He took the list from her and read through it. It was every bit as thorough and well planned as he'd known it would be. He forced himself to focus, setting aside all his lustful desires and marital plans. For the next fortnight or so, these tasks required his full attention. He didn't want to let Susanna and her father down. Nor the rest of the village, which he was suddenly—and unexpectedly—beginning to care about.

"I think everyone's arrived by now." She peered down over the crenellated edge of the turret. Below, the assembled men and women of Spindle Cove were picnicking on the grassy, even ground of the bailey.

"I suppose that means my cousin groveled prettily enough."

She smiled. "I suppose it does. And what an occasion the rest of your men have made it. You've outdone yourselves."

"Hardly." But Bram had taken the picnic invitation in earnest. In anticipation of their guests, his militia volunteers had set out canopies and blankets and heaped a table with refreshments, courtesy of the Blushing Pansy. At least, he assumed the Fosburys' establishment was back to being the Blushing Pansy. The building was returned to rights, but last he'd been in the village, no sign at all had swung above the red-painted door.

"Rufus and Finn seem to have mended their differences," she observed.

"They've learned their lesson. That they'll catch more female attention united in mischief than divided by rancor."

The twins had tied a scarf to that dratted lamb, and offered a prize to the first girl to remove it. Giving chase, Charlotte dashed after Dinner for the full length of the keep, only to catch her toe on a rock and sprawl to the ground.

Beside him, Susanna gave a sharp gasp. She clutched Bram's hand. Even through her gloves, her fingernails bit into his flesh.

"It's all right," he told her. "They're made of India rubber at that age. She'll bounce back up."

He understood, in that moment, how keenly she felt it when any of her young ladies suffered the smallest humiliation or pain. When the situation demanded it, as was the case during Diana's attack, she could be strong and collected and brave. But here with him, she didn't hide her concern. She would allow him to comfort her. And perhaps, someday, she would listen patiently if a dark, dreary night found him well in his cups and he drunkenly confessed to still feeling scores of wounds that weren't his own, but those of men under his command.

As they looked on, Mr. Keane helped Charlotte to her feet. The girl gamely brushed out her skirts. Fosbury offered a consolatory teacake, and everyone watching had a good-natured laugh.

"She's unharmed." He squeezed her fingers, only too glad for the excuse. "See?"

"Poor dear." She didn't withdraw her hand. Instead, she leaned into him, just a little. "But after that disaster with the tea shop, it's good to see them all like this. The ladies and men together, enjoying each other's company."

"They'd best enjoy themselves now," he said. "After this morning, there'll be no time for amusement. Every soul in Spindle Cove will have a great deal of work ahead of him."

"Or her," she finished pointedly. "Right. We should go

down and make the announcement. If we're asking them to work together, I think it's important we present a united front."

"I couldn't agree more," he said, as they descended the circling stone staircase. He paused, just before they stepped onto the green. "Here's an idea. Why don't I introduce you as the future Lady Rycliff?"

Her eyes flew wide with panic. "Because I'm *not*?"

"Not yet." *But you will be.* She ought to know he had no idea of abandoning his suit, only postponing it. He considered. "The *future* future Lady Rycliff, perhaps? Or I could just call you my mistress."

"Bram!" She nudged him in the ribs.

"My illicit lover, then." At her pained look, he said, "What? So long as you refuse to marry me, that's exactly what you are."

"You're horrid."

"You love it."

"God help me," she whimpered, as he tugged her out of the keep and onto the bailey green.

"Gather round," Bram called as they came to stand in the center of the grassy expanse. "Miss Finch and I have some announcements to make."

At his use of her proper name, Susanna exhaled with relief. She hoped Bram wouldn't be so bold as to announce their tryst as a matter of public business . . . but after that narrow escape with Papa yesterday, she wasn't sure she could put it past him.

All around the green, the ladies and men exchanged intrigued glances as they set aside their teacakes and lemonade to listen.

"As you all know," Bram began, "I've given my word to Sir Lewis Finch, and by proxy, the Duke of Tunbridge, that Spindle Cove will present a field review. A precise, choreographed display of our military might and readiness on the date of the midsummer fair, scarcely more than a fortnight away."

The men looked to one another.

Aaron Dawes shook his head. "Rather a daunting task, my lord."

"A daunting task?" Fosbury said. "Try 'hopeless.' We can't march in a straight line."

"We don't even have proper uniforms," Keane added.

A murmur of general agreement rippled through the crowd.

"We're not hopeless," Bram said, in an authoritative voice that made everyone present snap to attention, Susanna included. "Nor even daunted. We have manpower. We have supplies. And we have a plan." He waved to her. "Miss Finch will explain."

Susanna held up the list in her gloved hand. "We're all going to work together. The ladies and the men."

"The ladies?" Mrs. Highwood exclaimed. "What place have ladies in planning a militia review?"

Susanna replied calmly, "In Spindle Cove, ladies can do anything. I know it's outside the realm of our usual activities, but on this short notice, everyone must contribute according to his or her strongest talents. The men need our help, and we need the men to succeed. If the militia is found lacking, do you think the duke will leave the castle unprotected? No. He will surely send other troops to encamp here. And needless to say, if a company of strange soldiers encamp on these bluffs, Spindle Cove as we know it"—she turned her gaze from lady to lady—"as we love and *need* it, will cease to exist."

Dismay rumbled through the group.

"She's right, the village would be overrun."

"We'd all have to go home."

"And here we've just fixed up the tea shop."

Charlotte leaped to her feet. "We can't let it happen, Miss Finch!"

"It *won't* happen, Charlotte. We just have to show the duke and a few visiting generals that Lord Rycliff's militia is ready and able to defend Spindle Cove."

Bram took over. "All volunteers will encamp here, at the castle. Your time and full efforts, sunup to sundown, will be required. We've worked out a schedule. Corporal Thorne will take charge of drilling you through the formations. Prepare to march your feet to stumps. The lines must be crisp; the formations, exact. Lord Payne"—he shot a look at his surprised cousin—"with his natural talent for explosions, will be in charge of artillery. As for firearms . . ." He motioned in Susanna's direction. "Miss Finch will lead daily practice in marksmanship."

A murmur of surprise swept the assembled ladies and men.

"What?" Mrs. Highwood cried. "A lady, teaching men to shoot?"

"Didn't you know?" Bram asked, sliding her a knowing look. "She's a thing of beauty with a gun."

Fighting a blush, Susanna returned her attention to the list. "Miss Taylor will suspend her regular music lessons to give Finn and Rufus Bright intensive tutoring. Mrs. Montgomery and Mrs. Fosbury will jointly lead the uniforms committee. All available ladies will assist with the sewing in the evenings." She lowered the paper. "It's vital that the men look their polished and tailored best, to make a good impression."

Bram added, "It's also vital that the visitors be entertained. They'll be guests at—"

"Summerfield," Susanna finished, growing a touch excited despite herself. "We'll be hosting an officers' ball, to follow the field review."

"A ball?" Mrs. Highwood said. "Oh, that *is* good news. At long last, my Diana will have her chance to shine. She'll have recovered her health by then, don't you think?"

"I'm certain of it."

"And Lord Payne, you devil . . ." The matron's face creased with a smile as she waved her handkerchief at Colin. "You must promise her a nice, slow quadrille this time. None of that wild country dancing."

Colin bowed. "As you like, ma'am."

Hoping to redirect the conversation, Susanna cleared her throat. "Now, for preparations. I will ask Miss Winterbottom and Mrs. Montgomery to assist with the menus. Sally Bright and Mr. Keane—you two possess the best eye for color, so decorations are yours. Miss Taylor is the natural choice for music, and Mr. Fosbury, I do hope you'll bake us some cakes. Our chef at Summerfield can't match your confections." She smiled at him over the paper. "Now, Mrs. Lange—"

The woman in question sat tall. "You don't have to ask. I'd be glad to compose a poem for the occasion."

"That would be very . . ." Susanna paused. "Special," she finished. "Thank you, Mrs. Lange."

"What about me?" Charlotte waved her hand. "Everyone else has a task. I want one, too."

She smiled. "I have a very important job for you, Charlotte. And I'll explain it to you later, back at the rooming house." She lowered the paper. "It goes without saying, our usual activity schedule is suspended."

"We have a lot of work ahead of us," Bram said. "And it starts this afternoon. Finish your refreshments. Pack away the blankets and canopies. Take the scarf off the sheep. All men should assemble for drill in a quarter hour's time."

"Ladies," Susanna called out, before the entire group dispersed, "we will adjourn to the inn to begin cutting pieces for uniforms."

As the men and women rose from their blankets and began to remove all evidence of merriment, she turned to Bram. "I think that went as well as could be expected."

He nodded. "It went well indeed."

To be truthful, she'd enjoyed the past quarter hour immensely. Standing *next* to Bram as an equal, rather than squaring off against him. Speaking together, instead of over each other's words. As they'd addressed their friends and neighbors, the air had hummed with a pleasant chord of harmony, and she'd almost felt as if . . .

She dropped a step back, cocked her head, and peered at him.

"What is it?" he asked, looking self-conscious.

"It's just . . . You look very lordly, all of a sudden. Standing there in front of the keep, addressing all the villagers. It's as though you were born to the Rycliff title, instead of gifted it a week ago."

"Well, I wasn't." His brows drew together. "My father was a major general, not an earl of any sort. I don't mean to forget that, ever."

"Of course not. I didn't mean it that way. Your father was a great man, and naturally you'll always be proud to be his son. But that doesn't mean he couldn't be proud of *you* today, does it?"

He had no reply to that. After a prolonged pause, he said, "I'd best go ready myself for drill."

"Yes. I suppose I should be going, too."

As he began to walk past her toward the keep, she once

again noted the slight hitch in his gait. An impulse seized her. "Wait."

She could have reached out to catch his arm or his shoulder. But no. She had to go pressing her hand flat against his strong, solid chest. Realizing her mistake, she snatched it back—but the thumping echo of his heartbeat lingered on her palm.

A furtive glance around her indicated that no one had observed the bold gesture. Not this time, at least. But judging by the hot blush scalding her cheeks, Susanna knew she was going to have to work very hard to keep her attraction to Bram below notice.

Which made her next words imprudent as anything.

"There's one other task we need to address. One not on the list." She still clutched the paper in her hand and spoke low. "Something that requires the two of us to work together. Alone."

"Is that so?" Surprise—and desire—flared in his jade-green eyes. "I can't deny that I'm intrigued. Name the place and time. I'll be there."

"The cove," she murmured, sending up a prayer that she wasn't making an enormous mistake. "After dark. Tonight."

tars blanketed the clear night, and the moon hung large and yellow in the sky. A fortunate thing, or Bram would have had no light by which to pick his way down to the cove. He kept his eyes trained on the path, careful not to misstep. As a result, he reached the pebbled shore without any idea where—or even *if*—he would find Susanna. He didn't see her anywhere along the beach.

Perhaps she hadn't been able to slip away. Perhaps she'd changed her mind about meeting him. Perhaps she'd never intended to meet him at all, but only meant to play him a clever trick.

A soft splash drew his attention.

"Over here," he heard her call.

He approached the water's edge. "Susanna?"

"I'm here. In the water."

"In the water?" His eyes adjusted to the darkness. There she was, his alluring mermaid, submerged to her neck in the sea. "What are you wearing under there?"

"Come join me if you want to find out."

Bram had never shucked his clothes faster. He stripped straight down to his skin. This wasn't one of Spindle Cove's warm, sunny afternoons. He would have a long walk back to the castle, and he didn't want to make it in sopping wet clothes.

"Damn, this water is cold," he said, testing it with his toes.

"It's not so bad tonight, truly. You'll grow accustomed to it."

He dashed into the sea, knowing it was better to douse himself all at once than to draw out the torture by slow degrees. He met her some distance out from shore, in a place where the water line hit him mid-abdomen. Unable to get a good look in the dark, he gave her shoulder an exploratory grope.

When he caught a handful of rough fabric, he groaned. "Not the wretched bathing costume."

She laughed, a husky, arousing laugh.

Blast it, he knew he shouldn't press matters too far. But she was so close, and they were finally alone again. He couldn't resist doing what he'd been wanting to do all day. In a quick move, he pulled her close, wrapping arms and legs about her slender form. Holding her tight.

In his arms, she went utterly still. He felt her every muscle go rigid as steel.

"Bram. What are you doing?"

"I'm embracing you. It's cold."

"You're . . ." She lowered her voice to a whisper. "*You're naked.*"

"Sorry, I forgot my bathing costume." He chuckled. "You've seen all there is to see of me already. And there's no one here but the two of us."

"*Precisely.*"

"*Then why is it we're whispering?*"

Peeved, she said aloud, "I don't know."

He teased her ear with his breath. "We could warm each other."

She made a frustrated noise and pushed away. "Be serious, please. We're here for a reason."

"Believe me, I know I'm here for a reason. The reason is you."

"No. The reason is your knee."

"My knee?"

"Yes. I know it's been paining you. If you're going to make it through these next few weeks, you need to care for it properly. And if you're determined to return to field command after that . . . Well, I'm equally determined to send you back with as much strength and stamina as possible."

"I *am* strong." His pride was piqued. "And you should know, I have abundant stamina."

With a dismissive noise, she moved away. She swam a few strokes to a nearby boulder, reaching for something. The way the mysterious object rattled, he imagined it to be some sort of chain. When she returned carrying it just at the water's surface, he caught the gleam of metal in the moonlight.

"What is that?" he asked, peering at it. "Some sort of medieval torture device?"

"Yes. That's exactly what it is."

"God. I was joking. But you aren't, are you?"

"No. I borrowed it from my father's collection. There's an ankle cuff, and this ball is attached. It's deuced heavy. Here." She dumped the ball into his hands.

"You're right," he said, his voice suddenly strained. "It is deuced heavy."

From a cord tied about her neck, she produced a thick key. With a bit of trial and error, she managed to fit the key into a hole in the iron cuff. The two halves opened like a clamshell.

"This fits around your ankle, see?" she said. "Stand on your good leg, lift the bad, and I'll secure the thing."

"Now wait just a minute. Let me be certain I understand this. You have me out here in the freezing ocean, naked—"

"I didn't ask you to be naked."

"And now you propose to leg-shackle me."

"Only in the literal sense."

"Yes. It's the literal sense that concerns me. Being literally leg-shackled is bad enough, no need of metaphors. So once you have me bound and chained, how am I to know you won't just leave me here to freeze all night and be picked apart by gulls tomorrow morning?"

She unlooped the key from her own neck and transferred the necklace to him. "There. You may hold the key. Does that make you feel better?"

"Not really. I still don't understand what your purpose is."

"You'll understand soon enough. Just lift your leg."

He obeyed, tilting his head back to stare up at the night. There was nothing like a sky full of stars to make a man reckon with his own humility. How, precisely, had he arrived at this? He was taking orders from a spinster, willingly submitting himself to her medieval torture devices. And she wasn't even naked.

"You can never tell a soul about this," he said. "I mean it, Susanna. I'll deny it to my grave. My reputation would never recover."

"*Your* reputation? Do you think I'm eager to spread tales of this scene?" She fixed the cuff around his leg, and it snapped into place. "Now slowly lower your foot, and drop the ball into the water."

Once again, he did as directed. The ball sank quickly to the pebbled bottom, dragging his foot down with it.

"There. Now you have resistance."

"I didn't realize I was short on resistance. I rather thought you'd been giving me ample supply."

"Physical resistance." She retreated soundlessly, slicing back through the calm water to put space between them. "Walk toward me, slowly. You'll see."

He stepped forward onto his good leg. When he tried to take a step with his injured leg, the ball and shackle dragged behind him. Heavy, but with the water's help, not impossible to move.

"That's good," she said, backing up another pace. "Keep moving. Be certain to lift your leg, not drag it. As if you're marching."

He took several lunging paces more, chasing her through the chest-deep water. "Tell me why I'm doing this?" He backed her against a boulder, but she darted to the side, swimming away.

"Come this way now," she directed, shaking her hair free of salty spray. "And I'll explain."

He moved forward again. "Explain."

"It's like this, Bram. You're a large man."

"I'm so glad you've noticed."

"What I mean is, you're heavy. You're absolutely right that you need to use your leg in order to recover your full strength. Once your wound healed, staying abed was of no further benefit. But when you walk—or run, or march—on solid ground, you're adding your entire body weight to every step. And you're so big, it's too much strain. Here in the sea, the buoyancy relieves the pressure on your knee. And the shackle gives you a weight to work against."

He almost reached her, but again she swam out of his reach. He received only a splash of seawater for his pains.

"If you do this regularly," she called out to him, surfacing some distance away, "you'll be able to rebuild your strength without heaping more damage on your knee."

He had to admit, the theory of it made some sense. "Who taught you all this?"

"No one. Two summers ago, we had a girl here recovering from a nasty fall from a horse. She'd broken her leg and hip. Even months later, she could barely hobble around. Her physician at home had told her she would be an invalid. The poor thing was devastated. Only sixteen, you know. She thought she would never have a season, never marry. Fortunately, her father decided to send her here."

"For a cure?" Bram lunged in her direction. He was catching the rhythm of this exercise now, and this time she barely escaped him.

"I doubt he had any hope of a cure. He was probably hoping she would acclimate to life as an invalid spinster. But the sea bathing helped her tremendously. We did exercises like these several times a week. By the time she left at the end of the summer, she was walking unaided. Even dancing." He could hear the pride in her voice. "I received a letter from her just a month ago. She's engaged. Her new betrothed is the heir to a barony. He's very handsome, I'm given to understand."

"Good for her. But what about you?"

"What about me?"

"How is it you've never married?"

A soft splash. "It's an easy enough thing. Every morning I wake up, go about my day, and return to bed at night without having recited marriage vows. After several years, I have the trick of it down."

The tone of her remark was easy, light—but he could tell there was a deeper emotion beneath it. "You can't tell me no one ever asked."

She didn't tell him that.

"I never had any reason to marry," she said. "I am my father's only child, and there is no entail. His fortune and Summerfield will come to me, eventually. Though hopefully no time soon."

"But security isn't the only reason you might wish to marry. Don't you want a husband and children? Or are you too modern for that?"

She was silent for a while. When she finally spoke, she said, "Turn around. Walk to that boulder, and then double back to this spot."

He didn't move, just crossed his arms over his chest. "Oh no. You can't pull that trick with me."

"What trick?"

"Deflecting an uncomfortable question by giving an order. It won't work, not with me."

"I don't know what you mean." She tried to sound bored.

He wasn't fooled. "Of course you do. Because you once accused me of doing the exact same thing." He shook his head. "I've never met a woman like you. You're so much like *me*. It's as though we're two examples of some rare, exotic breed. Only I'm the male specimen, and you're the female. Clever as you are, you must know what that means."

"Enlighten me."

"It means we should mate. We have a responsibility to Nature."

Laughing, she pushed a wave of spray in his direction. "You must have learned that line from your cousin. Does it work on other women?"

"What other women?" He barely remembered that other women existed. Tonight, they were like a waterlogged rendition of Adam and Eve, and this cove was their isolated Eden. For him, she was the only woman in the world.

God, he wanted her so fiercely. She could have no idea. With every erotic splash of her lithe body undulating in the water, his imagination ran wild. He pictured the two of them, linked in all manner of strange, salty embraces. His cock stiffened to a painful degree, jutting out in front of him despite the cold, carving his way through the water like the prow of a ship. The HMS *Priapism*.

"The boulder," she reminded him. "March to the boulder and back."

"Here's what I'll do. I'll turn around, walk all the way to *that* boulder"—he pointed to one much farther distant, near the spindle—"and double back in under a minute's time. But you must remain in that exact spot. And when I reach you, I want a reward for my pains."

"Oh really? And what sort of reward would that be?"

"A kiss."

"No. Absolutely not."

"Come along." He stood tall, shoulders and torso emerging from the water. Seawater traced cold rivulets down his chest and back. "You've been leading me a merry chase, weaving circles in the shingle as if we're playing some foolish parlor game. I deserve a forfeit. A kiss."

She shook her head. "After the other night? I know there's no such thing as 'just a kiss' with you. We're here to work on your knee."

"Well, I'm not moving until I'm promised a kiss."

She was silent for a moment. "Very well. A kiss. But you don't get to kiss me. I will be the one to kiss you. Do you understand?"

Oh, he understood. He understood this little exercise of hers was about to become very interesting.

Energized with a new sense of motivation, he did just as he'd promised. He turned, covered the distance to the far boulder in large, powerful strides, and then he worked his way back to her. By the time he'd completed the circuit, his breath was a loud, painful rasp.

"Now," he said, taking her by the waist and pulling her close. "Kiss me."

The moon had emerged from behind a cloud, bathing her in silvery light. So beautiful. She could have been a water nymph, or a fierce, avenging angel. She framed his face in both her hands. Those elegant, yet so capable hands. He moved with her as she tugged his head down, reflexively wetting his lips in preparation.

And then she kissed him—square on the forehead. Her lips pressed to his brow and lingered, blessing him with warmth and sweetness.

"There," she whispered, pulling away.

He stared at her, his throat working. He didn't know whether to rage or laugh or weep. No, that kiss hadn't been the openmouthed, passionate tangle of tongues his body craved. It had been exactly what his soul needed. He wouldn't have known to ask for a kiss like that. The warmth of it sank straight through him, coming to rest in his heart.

She still held his face in her hands. Her thumb dabbed a salty drop from his cheek. "I know what you need, Bram."

Sweet heaven. Perhaps she did. And what else did he need, that he couldn't have known to put into words? He was desperate to find out. Wordlessly, he slipped away from her. Covered the distance to the boulder in strong, purposeful strides. Returned to her, splashing his way through wave and foam, to stand breathless with need and longing.

"Again."

This time she reached for his hand. She lifted it to her face, curling his wet fingers over the curve of her cheek. Then she turned her face, nuzzling into his caress. Her breath rushed over his chilled flesh, rousing his every nerve to attention. And then she pressed a kiss to the exact center of his palm.

A bolt of bliss streaked from the spot, rushing straight for his core. Bloody hell. A tiny kiss on his palm. He felt it everywhere. His knees went weak. He wanted to fall at her feet, lay his head in her lap for hours. *I am your slave.*

He withdrew his hand, flexing it to disperse the sensation and get a grip on himself. Who could have guessed a fully grown man could be utterly felled by such a tiny, precise assault? Did the army know this? Maybe they ought to issue plate armor to protect soldiers' vulnerable palms.

"Susanna." He reached for her.

Quick as a fish, she wriggled away. "If you want more, you must work for them."

He retreated again, making his way to the boulder more slowly this time. Partly out of fatigue, but mostly because he needed time to calm himself. His heart thudded loudly in his chest, battering his ribs. He couldn't let her see, didn't dare let her know that with those two tiny kisses, she'd shaken him to his soul.

On his way back to her, he tried to shrug off the sensation and find a way to regain control. He was a soldier, he told himself. Not a supplicant. As he slashed his way through the water, his blood rushed through his limbs, hot and powerful.

But just as he neared her, he misjudged his step. The chain caught on a rock, and his ankle turned. He lunged forward, loosing an involuntary growl of pain.

She dashed to him, fighting her way through the water. "Are you all right? Are you hurt?"

"I'm fine," he said, denying the fresh stab of agony. It wasn't his knee that hurt so fiercely, but his pride. "I'm perfectly fine."

"You've done enough for tonight." She unlooped the ribbon and key from his neck and disappeared beneath the water. After a bit of tugging, he felt the cuff release.

"Put it back," he said, once she'd surfaced. "I can do more. I'm not even fatigued."

"Be patient with yourself." She pushed the water from her face. "You've made a remarkable recovery, and you'll get stronger still. But you were shot, Bram. You have to accept that your leg will never be quite the same."

"It will be the same. It has to be. I can't accept anything less than a complete recovery."

"Why?"

"Because I need to lead."

She choked on a laugh. "You don't need a perfect knee for that. You have more leadership in your great toe than most men have in their whole bodies."

He made a pained face that was meant to indicate modesty.

She took it as *Do go on, please.* "Truly. People just naturally want to please you. Take Rufus and Finn. You don't know them well enough to see it yet. But I do, and those boys worship the ground you limp on."

"Those boys just need a man to look up to."

"Well, they couldn't have chosen a better one." She wreathed her arms around his neck.

Cool water swirled around them, emphasizing the heat where their bodies met. Right now, he felt closer to her than ever, and still he wanted more. Every cell in his body craved that perfect union of bodies they'd achieved under the willow tree. But if he ignored the frantic clamor in his loins and took time to hear the insistent, steady message of his heart . . . simply holding her was lovely. Peaceful. Right.

"If I'm such a remarkable leader," he said, "why is it I can't bring you in line?"

"Because you don't want to. You like me this way." She smiled the smug little smile of a woman who was utterly convinced she was right.

But she was wrong. He didn't like her this way.

He thought he might *love* her this way.

Damn. *Love*. It wasn't something Bram had much experience handling. The very idea of it seemed dangerous, unsafe. So he dealt with it the same way he treated other hazardous, explosive things. He tucked it away in a cool, dark place inside him—to be examined and measured at some later time. When his hands weren't trembling, and his loins weren't aching with unspent lust. And his heart wasn't pounding so damned loud.

"I'm going to marry you," he said.

"Oh, Bram." Her features screwed into an expression of dismay.

"No, no. Don't make that face. Every time I propose to you, you make that twisty, unhappy face. It wears on a man's confidence."

"I might be making a different, much more pleasant face—if only you were planning to stay. Not just marry me before you leave and get on with the rest of your life." She glanced out toward the open sea. "There's a peculiar curse to residing in a holiday locale. Friendships are abundant, but brief. Ladies stay for a month or two, then they go home. Just when I've grown close to people, they leave. It's bearable, for a friendship." She eyed him. "Perhaps even for a scandalous, clandestine affair. But a marriage?"

"I can't offer to bring you with me. The way you describe your life here sounds rather like life on campaign. With one notable difference. Just when I've grown close to people, they die." His own mother had been the first in that succession, but far from the last. He could never put Susanna at risk.

"Perhaps," she said slowly, teasing her fingers through the hair at his nape, "you and I could grow very, very close. You could promise not to leave. And I could promise not to die. Wouldn't that be a welcome change for us both?"

He sighed. "I can promise to come back. Eventually."

"From war? Bram, no one can make such a promise. I wish I understood why returning to field command is so important to you. Is it just a matter of proving you can?"

"Partly."

"But not entirely."

She looked up at him, those patient blue eyes sparkling in the night. If he couldn't talk to her, he couldn't talk to anyone.

"I just don't have anything else. I'm an infantry officer, Susanna. It's all I've ever been, all I've ever wanted since I was a boy. I wanted it so badly, I left Cambridge the month I turned twenty-one. That was when I could finally access the small legacy my grandfather left me, and I used it to purchase my first commission. My father made a show of being angry, but I know he was secretly pleased that I'd done it on my own. I never relied on his influence. I paid my dues, rose up through the ranks. I made him proud. When news reached me of his death—" He broke off, unsure how to continue.

Beneath the water's surface, her hand found his. "I'm

so sorry, Bram. I can't even imagine how devastating it must have been."

She couldn't imagine, and he didn't know how to explain. Bram thought of his father's last letter. He'd received it through the usual mail, a full week after the express informing him of the major general's death. The letter's contents were nothing out of the ordinary. But Bram would never forget the closing. *Don't feel rushed in writing back,* his father had written. *I know you've been writing too many letters, of late.*

His father had obviously learned of Badajoz, where the allied forces had taken the garrison at human costs so great, Wellington himself wept over the carnage. And therefore he'd known Bram was writing condolence letters by the dozen, to the surviving families of his fallen men—to the point where his hand cramped up and his vocabulary went dry as the inkwell. There were only so many words for "regret."

His father hadn't offered any hollow words of comfort or tried to impose meaning on senseless death. He'd simply let Bram know he understood.

Bram couldn't voice what it meant, to know they'd reached a place where they understood each other as men, as fellow officers. As equals. If he retired from command and became just another privileged lord loafing around England . . . He wasn't sure his father would still understand that man. Bram wasn't sure he would understand *himself.*

"Losing my father was hard," he said. "Damned hard. But what it made it a little easier was telling myself I'd continue making him proud. Carry the family banner forward. Keep his legacy alive." He released a breath. "That lasted all of a few months, and then I was shot. Couldn't be so lucky as to have a glorious, noble death on the battlefield. Now I'm just another lamed soldier with no prospects of returning to command."

"Oh, Bram." She brushed his face with her free hand, pushing aside drops of salt water on either cheek. He feared they weren't all from the sea.

"Sir Lewis was my very last chance. I've written to every retired general I could imagine, asking for a good word. I've felt out every colonel who might be in need of a lieutenant, hoping one of them would put in a request. Nothing. No one wants me like this."

The night's silence was profound.

"Well, I do."

At her words, his heart seized. He clutched her tight with both arms, as if this tiny cove were a bottomless ocean, and she a life preserver.

"*I* want you like this," she said again. Bending her head, she kissed the underside of his jaw. Her lips lingered there for a hot, sensuous moment. Then she ran her tongue down his neck and brought her body flush with his. "Just as you are. Right here, right now."

ight *here*?" he echoed, his voice breaking with surprise. "Right *now*?"

Susanna couldn't help but laugh a little. It felt good to catch him off guard, lighten the sadness in his voice. "It can be accomplished in the water, can't it?"

He nodded numbly. "It can."

"Unless you have some objection."

He shook his head, just as numbly. "I don't."

"Good."

Her hands went to the buttons down the front of her bathing costume. His throat worked as she loosened them one by one. She wriggled her arms free and pushed the garment down into the water so she could step out. Then she tossed the whole sodden heap over a nearby rock.

"Wait, Susanna—" He took her by the waist. "You don't have to do this just because . . ."

"I'm not." She put her fingers to his lips. "I'm not."

When she dropped her hand, placing it flat against his chest, his heartbeat *whomp*ed beneath her touch. His palpably anxious response made her own heart flutter.

He needed her right now. He needed to know that someone could see all his weaknesses, all his flaws—and still find him not only desirable, but worthy and strong.

Vulnerable as she felt, she couldn't bring herself to deny him that reassurance. Not when it was the simple truth.

What was more, she needed him, too.

"Don't look so stunned," she teased. "I want you, Bram. So much. All the time. When it comes to you, this buttoned-up spinster is just seething with wild, insatiable passion." She kissed him, teasing her tongue over his lips. "It should hardly come as any surprise. You've been telling me so since the very beginning."

"I know," he said wonderingly. "I know. The surprise is that you listened." He cradled her neck in one hand and claimed her mouth in a deep, masterful kiss.

She reveled in the sensual surrender for a few moments. Then she gently pushed away. "Wait," she said, panting. "This is my turn tonight. I want to touch you, everywhere."

He spread his arms in invitation. "I won't stop you."

She began by running her hands over those massive, muscled arms, tracing every cord and sinew. Then skimming up to his shoulders and down his chest—rock-hard and lightly covered with damp, dark whorls of hair. She trailed her fingers down his tensed, ridged abdomen and through a rougher thicket of hair before finally claiming her prize.

With a single fingertip, she traced the smooth, flared crown of his erection. When she slid her palm along the underside, skimming down the thick, ridged column, he jerked and bobbed away from her touch.

Come back here, you. She wrapped both hands around him, stacking her grips in an attempt to envelop his full length. She couldn't, not quite—so she treated them both to a long, luxuriant stroke, dragging her touch from his base to his tip.

"God." He gave a strangled groan. "Couldn't you kiss me when you do that?"

Her mouth watered at the mere suggestion. She moved forward, angling to kiss his jaw, his throat. With her tongue, she traced the ridge of his collarbone before dipping just beneath the water's surface to graze his nipple. The salty tang of the seawater mingled with the earthy musk of his skin.

Arousal built within her, and she could feel his erection swelling even larger in her hands. But they made the unspoken decision not to rush. To continue exploring each other as long as they could resist the temptation for more.

As she caressed him below the water, he fondled her breasts. First kneading them separately, then pushing them together so he could bend his head and nuzzle both tips. He mouthed each peak thoroughly, teasing her with the alternating hot and cold sensations.

Then he pulled back, studying her in the dark. "Have you noticed," he said conversationally, "that your right breast is a bit larger than the left?"

Susanna was sure her cheeks must be glowing in the dark, her blush came so fast and fierce. "They're *my* breasts. Of course I've noticed." *And I've only been self-conscious about it all my adult life, thank you very much.*

"It's like they have two different personalities. One's generous and nurturing." He lifted the other. "And the other . . . it's saucy, isn't it? It wants a tweak." He gave her left nipple a pinch.

"*Bram.*" What a conversation. Hoping to distract him, she slid her hand down his shaft and teased her fingers lower, until she cupped the soft, vulnerable sac beneath. He groaned and shivered, encouraging her as she explored, rolling the two pendulous weights in her palm.

Interesting. He wasn't symmetrical everywhere, either.

"Don't be vexed," he said, still fondling her breasts. "I meant it as a compliment. I quite adore them both."

That was some comfort, she supposed. "I didn't know there were men with penchants for mismatched breasts."

"I adore them because they're yours, Susanna. I adore every bit of you." His hands roamed lower. "These hips make me wild. This round, cuppable arse was made for my hands. And your long, shapely legs . . ." He kissed her deeply, skimming a hand down her leg and lifting it to drape over his hip, pulling their bodies into intimate contact. "God, I love that you're tall."

"Truly?" She'd been in the habit of thinking it her greatest detraction where suitors were concerned. Well, aside from the freckles. And the hair. And her habit of voicing contrary opinions when she ought to dispense demure nods. "Why would you say that?"

"Because *I'm* tall," he said, nuzzling her throat. "With a short woman, it's always deuced awkward. Bits don't align the way they should."

Lord. That would teach her to ask. How she hated the idea of him "aligning bits" with petite, delicate beauties. The very thought made her ill.

"And I love this." His fingers found her cleft, parting her to slip deep inside. "I love feeling how tight you are. Knowing that there haven't been others."

She laughed a little, still feeling the stab of jealousy. "Of course there haven't been others. Could you tell me the same?"

Pulling back, he stared deep into her eyes with a bone-melting, erotic sincerity. "I can tell you this. There's never been anyone like you."

"Oh," she sighed, as his fingers plunged deep.

"Say it." His teasing tone took on a rougher undercurrent. "Say the words. Say you're mine."

Alarms clanged in her heart. She knew he needed to feel strong and powerful right now, but truly. There was

possessive, and then there was . . . medieval. "It's so belit-
tling, Bram. I wish you wouldn't say that."

"You just wish you didn't like it so much." He added a
second finger to the first. "Mine. Mine. Mine." He thrust
his fingers deeper with each repetition. Her intimate muscles clenched around them, and she gasped with pleasant
shock.

"See?" he gloated.

Drat it. For a man, he was right entirely too often. It did
feel so good. But ever since her illness and those horrid
treatments, she'd set a great of deal of comfort in the idea
that her body was *hers*. No one else's.

"Say it," he whispered, nuzzling her ear. His thumb circled her pearl. "Susanna fair. I want to hear you say you're
mine."

She framed his face in her hands and looked him in the
eye. "I'll say this. I claim sole possession of my body, my
heart, and my soul. And tonight, I choose to share them
all with you."

His fingers slid from her body, leaving her feeling
hollow inside. "God. That's . . ."

"Disappointing? Intimidating? Too much, too soon?"

He shook his head, moving in for a kiss. "I was going
to say, it's even better." His tongue traced her bottom lip.
"So much better."

Her heart ballooned in her chest. She'd never dreamed
it could hold so much joy.

As they kissed, he grasped her hips, lifting her in the
water.

"It's time, love." His breath was labored. "Wrap your
legs around my waist."

She did as he asked, locking her ankles at the small of
his back. As he supported her weight, she reached be-

tween them to guide his erection. They came together in a slow, sensuous joining.

She gasped as he filled her, stretching her wide. It didn't hurt anymore, but just like the first time, she doubted she could take him all. He was patient, however, working into her by delicious degrees until they were one.

As isolated and alone as they were in this cove, they could have been loud, loosing wild cries and urgent groans into the dark of night. Instead, they moved in swift, rhythmic silence. The only sounds were the soft splashes of the water and their increasingly ragged breath.

She clung to his neck. The rest of her went boneless in the buoyant water. For the moment, she was only too happy to give him complete control. With strong, purposeful motions, he lifted her hips again and again, sliding her up and down his hard length. With every stroke, pushing her closer and closer to bliss. The tendons of his neck and shoulders stood out like ropes, and his jaw was tensed with effort.

She'd never felt so powerful, so desirable. So safe to release all her inhibitions and cares. To surrender to the strong, guiding force of his thrusts as he prodded her higher. And higher still. So close to that teasing, elusive peak.

"Here," he panted, taking one of her hands and wedging it between them, right where their bodies joined. "Touch yourself here."

His hands took her hips again, and he thrust even deeper. As he moved within her, her trapped fingertips rubbed back and forth over the swollen nub at the crest of her sex, giving her just the friction she needed. Her climax built in the distance, gathering strength. In her mind's eye, she saw it coming, as if she were viewing a wave from the shore. An imminent, devastating swell of pleasure. It awed her—frightened her, even—as it loomed near, inescapable and intense. Then the wave broke, crashing over and through her body as he kept up his steady, powerful rhythm.

She cried his name. She might have cried a few joyous tears, as well.

He cursed.

With an urgent gasp, he pulled free of her body. She reached for him, tangling her grip with his as he stroked himself the remaining distance to release. His seed jetted against her belly, a burst of welcome heat in the cooling cove.

His temple pressed against hers as he brought her close. His labored breath crashed hot against her ear. "Hold me."

Oh, Bram.

She lashed her bare arms and legs around his body, clutching him as close as she could. Kissing his shoulders, his throat, his jaw, his ear. Running her fingers through his damp, clipped hair. Rocking him, just a little. Back and forth, in time with the waves.

A flood of tenderness rushed from her heart and spread through her entire body, suffusing even her fingers and toes with warmth. She brought him closer still, wanting him to feel it. As if she could wrap him in a blanket of affection and hold him there forever. He had so much pride, and so much family honor, wrapped up in returning to war. How could she possibly entice him to stay? She was going to try her damnedest, but the day might come quite soon when she would have to let him go.

But for tonight, he'd asked her to hold him, and Susanna was going to do just that. Hold on to this passionate connection they shared. Hold on to this transcendent, if all too fleeting, joy.

Hold on to *him*. Just as long as she possibly could.

—Chapter Twenty-two—

eally. The man was impossible. When Susanna managed to get her hands on him, she was going to fling him off the bluffs herself.

It was late afternoon, almost evening. After a long day overseeing progress in the village, she ought to be heading home, making sure her father had eaten something today. Instead, she huffed all the way up to the castle ruins. On the way, she passed Corporal Thorne drilling the majority of the militiamen on the flat. Straight lines, straighter posture, a respectable unity of rhythm. Not perfect yet, but they'd made formidable progress in the past week. At marksmanship, she had all but a few of them loading and shooting in under twenty seconds now.

A few minutes' more walking, and she reached the castle.

"Where is your lord?" she asked a lone volunteer standing sentry at the ancient, crumbling gatehouse. She recognized him as one of Bram's farm recruits.

"Beg pardon, miss. I . . . I don't believe he's available."

"What do you mean, he's not available? He's found time to devil me with these ridiculous orders all day." In her fist, she clutched his latest handwritten missive. "This is the third one he's sent this afternoon alone. I know he's here."

"He's here," the man hedged, "but . . ."

"Lord Rycliff!" she called, striding past the soldier.

Dinner greeted her as she crossed the bailey, with a friendly bleat and a questing nudge at her pocket.

"Someone's been spoiling you." Pausing to spare the lamb a brief pat, she passed into the grassy, open center of the castle grounds, drew to a halt, and lifted her voice. "Lord Rycliff, I need a word."

"Up here, Miss Finch."

She tilted her head to view the keep.

"On the parapet," he called.

Shading her eyes, she let her gaze climb higher still. From atop the southwest turret, between the crenellated notches of the battlement, he lifted a hand in salutation. The sinking, amber sun lit him from the back, bathing him in a glowing corona of light. Like a halo of fire—perfectly befitting the handsome, tormenting devil.

"I'd appreciate if you'd come down, my lord," she called. "We need to talk."

"It's my turn on watch."

"You're the commander. Can't you make it someone else's turn?"

"I don't shirk my duty that way, Miss Finch."

Susanna marched through the keep's open door, crossed the roofless, ancient hall, and went straight for the spiral staircase of the southwest tower. If he refused to come down and talk to her, she would simply climb up to confront him.

As she ascended the stone risers, she called out, "What's the meaning of all these missives? The seamstresses are tying their fingers in knots, trying to appease your absurd demands with the uniforms. First, you send a note demanding the coat lining should be bronze silk. We're twelve pieces into the cutting, and now another note: Not bronze anymore, but blue. Not just any blue, mind. *Iris* blue. Well, no sooner do we have the blue laid out, than the next missive arrives. 'I want pink,' it says. Pink, of all colors! Are you serious?"

Lord, there were a great many stairs. Her brain whirled with the constant circling. She paused a moment, leaning a hand on the stone wall and gathering breath for the remainder of the climb. As well as for the remainder of her complaints.

"It's my militia, Miss Finch," he called down to her. "I want what I want."

"It's not as though we have nothing else to do, you realize," she went on. "It's not only the uniforms. We've only a matter of days before the field review. I have the ladies rolling cartridges. Miss Taylor is struggling valiantly to repair Finn and Rufus's sense of rhythm. With marksmanship practice scheduled to last all tomorrow morning, we simply don't have time for your capricious whims regarding coat lining and—"

No sooner had she gained the top of the stairs than he had her wrapped in his arms. He swept her straight off her feet.

In a swift motion, he carried her to the opposite side of the tower and pressed her against the parapet of cool, hard stone. At her back, the top edge of the wall caught her just beneath the shoulder blades. From the front, his solid heat and brute strength trapped her. Excited her. She'd already been short of breath, but this . . . ? This was dizzying.

"I told you," he said in a low, possessive growl, "I want what I want. And what I want right now, so fiercely I can scarcely see straight, is you." His kiss bruised her mouth. "I can't believe it took three of those ridiculous notes to get you up here. Stubborn girl."

"*That* was your purpose? Bram, you might have just said so."

"I did say so." His lips traced the curves of her neck. "Those notes were all about you. This shimmering bronze hair. Your iris-blue eyes." He licked the underside of her jaw. "All your many, many, luscious shades of pink."

A sigh of pleasure eased past her lips. "*Bram.*"

She should have been angry, but his embrace felt so good. So necessary. In the week since their tryst in the cove, they'd managed to steal a few hours together nearly every evening, making love beneath the night sky and then conversing on every topic under the stars. Still, she couldn't be parted from him for a minute without missing him. These big, grasping hands and these hot, hungry kisses.

"What about the uniforms?" she asked.

"To the devil with the uniforms. Make the coat linings any color you wish. I don't give a damn about any of it."

He slid his hands to her bottom and pulled her flush against him, bringing her belly in contact with his prominent arousal. The evident, intense hunger in his eyes sent desire racing through her.

"I want you," he said. Rather redundantly.

She wet her lips. "Perhaps tonight I can slip away from Summerfield."

"No. Not tonight." He kneaded her backside with both hands, lifting and molding her body to his. "Here. Now."

The idea made her heart race, and made her intimate places go soft with longing. She glanced to either side. "We couldn't possibly."

"No one can see us," he said, guessing her question. "Not on this side of the tower. There's only rocks and sea below us here."

The other three parapets were unoccupied. All the men

were down the slope, at drill. He was right, there was no one to see. A mild breeze whipped around and between them. The purpling sky hung so close overhead, she felt as though she could brush it with her fingertips. They stood on top of the world, alone.

His teeth caught lightly on her earlobe. "I swam alone last night, you know. Worked my way back and forth across that cove until my muscles were jelly. You owe me more kisses than I can count."

She had a vision of the two of them, tangled in a warm, pillow-heaped bed. He was outstretched on the mattress, utterly naked, and her hair was unbound, dragging over them both as she repaid those kisses she owed. Ran her lips and tongue over his every last hot, needy inch.

"I . . ." She gasped as his palm slid to cup her breast. "I thought you were meant to be on watch."

"So I am." He kneaded the taut globe thoughtfully, rolling her hardened nipple beneath his thumb. "Very well. Keep watch with me."

Stepping back, he grasped her by the waist and spun her about, so that she faced the stone parapet. He moved her sideways, positioning her before one of the crenels—a gap in the battlement designed for an archer to shoot through.

"Can you see?" he asked roughly, bending her forward so that her elbows rested in the crenel notch and pulling up her skirts. "See the cove clear, and the Channel beyond?"

"Yes." Below them, she could clearly survey the rocky inlet and expansive waters. In the distance, a few white sails puffed. To the west, the orange-yellow sun was slinking toward the horizon.

"Good. Keep your eyes open. The watch is yours."

With firm, insistent tugs, he gathered her skirts and petticoats, lifting them to her waist. He found the slit in her drawers and widened it with a loud rent of fabric, baring her delicate flesh to the cooling breeze and his warm, rough touch.

He petted her, parted her, spread her wide to his view. His fingertips traced every contour of her intimate flesh. She'd never felt so exposed. If she'd paused to think too hard about what he was seeing and doing, Susanna would have lost her nerve altogether. So she did as he said. She kept the watch, training her eyes on the sparkling blue water and the silver-kissed horizon.

A muted rustle told her he was freeing the closures of his breeches. She grew restless with need, damp with anticipation. A little cry of relief escaped her when his hot, aroused length sprang up to lodge snug against her cleft.

His hands caressed her bared bottom and thighs. "God, I think I'm going mad. You can't imagine how much I think of this. All the time, everywhere. Yesterday, I stopped in the shop for ink, and all I could think of was you, spreading your legs for me on the countertop. Or bent over the display case. Then slammed against the storeroom shelves, skirts hiked to your waist and one leg propped on a crate. Every waking moment, I'm thinking of this. Every night, I'm aching for it." He worked his hard, thick shaft against her, sliding back and forth over her sensitized flesh. "Tell me you want it, too."

Wasn't showing enough? She wriggled her hips, increasingly desperate for him.

"Tell me, love. I need to hear it. I need to know this madness isn't mine alone."

"I . . ." She swallowed. "I want you." Excitement raced along her skin. Just uttering those syllables pushed her to a new, wanton degree of arousal. The madness was definitely shared.

"You want *this*." He nudged her opening with the smooth, blunt crown of his erection. "In you, hard and deep. Isn't that right?"

Those words . . . so indecent. So crude. So utterly arousing.

"Y-yes."

He licked her ear. "Did you say something?"

Decency be damned. She had to have him, soon, or she would die of wanting. "Yes," she said. "I want it. All of it. In me. Now. Please."

Yes.

Yes. He entered her on a slow, gliding stroke. Stretching her. Filling her. Then retreating for a brief, agonizing pause before thrusting deeper still.

He set a rhythm, rocking her against the ancient parapet, and as they moved together, he lavished kisses over her bared neck and shoulders. The tight knots of her nipples chafed against her corset seams. Bliss curled and coiled from her center, spreading through every inch of her body.

He slid one hand around her hips, sifting through the folds of petticoat. His talented fingers knew just how to please her, circling gently over that needy bud as he kept up his strong, steady thrusts.

"Bram," she gasped. "Hold me. Tight."

"I have you." His arms tightened around her middle. His pace did not relent. "I have you."

She stared, eyes wide and unfocused, at that thin, indigo line of horizon. And then he pushed her beyond it. Flinging her off the map of charted sensation and into unknown, unimagined bliss. It went on, and on. She rode the crest of pleasure as far as it would take her. Startled sounds of pleasure pushed from her throat, mingling with the cries of gulls. She was helpless to stop them.

"Holy God." With a profane growl, he pulled her hips tight to his, burying his full length inside her. Her intimate muscles clamped around his thickness. They moaned in unison. After a few thumping heartbeats' pause, he began to move again.

He was close to his peak. She could sense it in the acceleration of his rhythm and the new, deeper angle of his thrusts. His guttural noises of satisfaction. If he wasn't careful . . .

"Bram. Take care."

"I don't want to take care." He bent close, breathing in her ear. "I want to take *you*. Mark you. Spend inside you, and feel you holding me tight while I fill you with my seed. I want the world to know you're mine."

Oh God. Those words . . . they both frightened and aroused her. She opened her mouth to object, to plead with him. *Take care, take care. Take care with my heart when you say such things.* But then he shifted, thrusting deeper still, and his thumb grazed her flesh just where she needed it. Pleasure racked her body for a second time, and the only sounds from her mouth were primal, desperate moans.

She hadn't known, hadn't dreamed she could feel so exposed. With each one of these hasty, stolen couplings, he stripped yet more layers from the woman she'd always believed herself to be. He denuded her of witty banter, of polite virtue, of all the trappings of a gently bred, overly educated spinster. Reducing her to nothing but raw, wild sensation and a fiercely thumping, wholly unguarded heart.

While the last pulses of her climax were still shuddering through her, he withdrew from her body. She felt the hot splash of his seed against her thigh. In the aftermath, he held her, brushing sweet kisses to her temple and cheek.

His breath came in ragged huffs. He pressed his brow to her shoulder and gathered her close. "That gets more difficult every time."

"I know." Tugging down her petticoats, she slid free. When she had her clothing rearranged, she slowly turned to face him. The words stuck in her throat, but she forced them out. "Perhaps this time should be the last."

"Susanna. You know I didn't mean it that way." He hiked his breeches from where they hung tangled about his knees. With impatient motions, he began to straighten the falls and fasten the buttons.

She smoothed her hair. "I should go."

"Wait." He grasped her wrist, forbidding her to leave. "What do you mean? You can't mean to run away from me. From this."

"I'm not running away. You're the one who's leaving. And we can't keep doing this. We're going to be caught."

"So what if we are caught?" he said. "You know I plan to marry you. I'd marry you tomorrow."

"Yes. And then you'd leave me a few days after that."

With the hint of an ironic smile, he gestured out over the castle ruins. "If I'm not inducement enough, this great, moldering heap of stone could be all yours."

She sniffed, looking around the jumble of walls and turrets that had once housed all her dreams. "You have no idea the affection I hold for this great, moldering heap of stone. I just wish a resident Lord Rycliff came with it."

He *belonged* here in Spindle Cove. Ever since he'd addressed the village the day of the picnic, Susanna had felt certain of it. Bram was strong and capable. A good leader, with an innate sense of loyalty and honor. This place could use a man like him. If he would only trade his military life for a calmer, more peaceful existence, she could see him being so happy, living here as Lord Rycliff.

And she could be so happy—so blissfully, completely happy—as his wife.

"Don't you want a real home, Bram? You know, a place with a roof and . . . and walls, and those rare luxuries called windows? Upholstery, even. Carpets, drapes. Proper meals and a nice, warm bed."

"I've never been one for homely comforts. Five-course meals on fine china, wallpapered parlors . . . That life just isn't for me. But I could grow to appreciate a bed, if you're the one warming it." He tugged on her wrist, attempting to draw her close.

She resisted. She would never have the strength to say this without the benefit of some distance between them. "A home isn't only defined by what *you* need, Bram. It's also about the people who need you. What am I to do when you're gone? What about your cousin? What about all the men and women in Spindle Cove who are working so hard for you right now, even as we speak? You're their lord. Doesn't that mean anything to you?"

"Yes. It does." His gaze firmed, and so did his grip. "It means a great deal. And the best way I know how to repay them is by finishing this war. Protecting the freedoms they enjoy and the sovereignty of the land they call home. Susanna, this isn't a matter of England clinging to some island it probably should have never seized. You know Bonaparte must be defeated."

"And he can't possibly be defeated without your personal presence in Spain? That's a bit arrogant, don't you think? My father has done more to combat Napoleon's forces than you ever will, and he hasn't left Sussex in a decade."

"Well, I'm not like your father."

"No, you're not." She lifted one shoulder. "And once

Napoleon is defeated, what then? There will always be another conflict, another campaign. An outpost somewhere that requires defense. Where does it end?"

"That's the thing about duty," he bit out. "It doesn't."

She stared at him, slowly shaking her head. "You're afraid."

He made a dismissive noise.

"You are. You are a big, strong man with a wounded leg, who feels useless and terrified. You say you don't need a home or a family or a community or love?" She gave a disbelieving laugh. "Please. You want those things so badly, the yearning just wafts from you like steam. But you're afraid to truly reach for them. Afraid you'll fail. You'd rather die chasing your old life than screw up the courage to forge a new one."

His hand clenched her wrist, tight as a manacle. "Who said anything about dying or failing? Christ, you're always limiting people, holding them back. Your father's too old to work. Your friends are too delicate to dance."

"Limiting people? After all you've learned of me and this place, you would accuse me of holding these young women back?" A lump formed in her throat. "How can you say such a thing?"

"After all you've learned of me, you still can't trust me? Marry me, and trust that I'll finish this war and come back to you. For God's sake, Susanna—" His voice broke, and he looked away briefly before continuing. "I'm no stranger to doubt, this past year. But of all people, I thought you believed in me."

"I do." A tear trickled down her cheek, and she dabbed it with the heel of her free hand. "I do believe in you, Bram. I believe in you more than you believe in yourself. Do I believe you can be a capable field commander? Of course I do. But I also believe you could be so much more.

A leader off the battlefield, as well as on. A respected lord, essential to his community . . . perhaps even a voice for your soldiers in Parliament." She pressed a fist to her belly. "I believe you'd make a wonderful husband and father."

His grip on her arm gentled. "Then why—"

"I just can't marry you, not like this." She tugged her wrist from his clasp. With her other hand, she cradled it, rubbing away the red marks of his grip and cursing the scars that would never, ever fade. She stumbled a pace in retreat. "Can't you understand? I won't be abandoned again."

The world was suddenly so quiet. No crashing waves, no gusting breeze. No calling gulls.

When she finally gathered the strength to look at him, his eyes were intense, searching. And his question pierced her straight through the heart.

"Who's afraid now?"

She let action be her answer. She turned and fled.

—Chapter Twenty-three—

 few evenings later, Bram stood watch on the very same turret. It was a dark, cloudy night, and there was nothing but shifting mist to see. With so little to occupy his thoughts, he once again found himself reliving that last encounter with Susanna. Again and again, the night brought her words back to him.

I won't be abandoned again.

God above, he did not intend to abandon her. All he wanted was to marry the woman, so that no matter how far apart the world flung them, there would always be a tether connecting her life to his.

She *needed* a man like him. A man sure enough of himself to enjoy her cleverness, rather than be cowed by it. A man brave enough to challenge her, to push her beyond the boundaries she'd set for herself. A man strong enough to protect her, if she ventured a little too far. Those were all the things she needed, as the remarkable woman she'd become.

But somewhere inside that woman huddled an awkward, frightened, wounded girl, who desperately craved something else: a man who would tuck neatly into her safe, scheduled life and promise to never, ever leave her alone. Bram just didn't think he could—or even *should*—be that man for her.

When Thorne came to relieve him at the pitch-black hour of two, Bram accepted the torch his corporal silently offered and made his way down the winding stairs. Moths fluttered around him, drawn to the heat and flame.

He emerged onto the bailey and surveyed the neat rows of tents. The sounds of snoring and the occasional cough kept the night from growing too still. A fluffy ghost of a creature wandered toward him, emerging from the shadows.

Bram stared down at the lamb.

The lamb stared up at him.

He gave in and withdrew a handful of corn from his pocket, strewing it on the ground. "Why can't I eat you?" he asked irritably. Though he knew the answer well enough. "Because she named you, you miserable thing. And now I'm stuck with a pet."

Ever since he'd arrived here, Susanna had been busy as a spider, spinning little wisps of sentiment, connecting him to this place in ways he had no wish to be connected. If he didn't leave soon, he'd begin to feel trapped.

He approached the tent he knew to be Colin's and softly cleared his throat. A rustle moved through the tent. There was a muffled banging noise, and one of the tent poles shivered. Good, he was awake.

"It's Bram," he whispered. "I need to speak with you about the artillery demonstration."

No reply. No further movement.

Bram crouched and held his torch near the canvas flap, knowing the light would shine through. "Colin." He nudged the canvas with his elbow. "*Colin*. We need to discuss the artillery demonstration. Sir Lewis has a new—"

Someone standing behind him tapped his shoulder. "What do you want?"

Bram jumped in his skin, nearly dropping his torch. "Jesus." He rose to a standing position, turned, and lifted his torch to illuminate . . .

Colin.

His cousin stood next to him, the picture of nonchalance, dressed in an unbuttoned, uncuffed shirt and loose trousers. In one hand, he clutched a bottle of wine by its slender neck. "Yes, Bram? What can I do for you?"

Bram looked at Colin. Then he looked at the tent. "If you're out here with me," he said, waving his torch at his cousin, "then . . . who's in your tent?"

"A friend. And I'd like to get back to entertaining her, if you don't mind." Colin uncorked the wine bottle with his teeth and spat the cork aside. "What is it that can't wait for morning?"

"What the devil are you doing with a woman in your tent?"

He cocked his head. "Hm. Just how detailed would you like my answer to be?"

"Whoever she is, you're marrying her."

"I don't think so." Colin took a few steps away from the tent, motioning Bram to follow. Once they were some paces away, he lowered his voice and said, "It's the only way I can sleep, Bram. It's either a woman's embrace or an interminable night awake. When I told you I don't sleep alone, it wasn't an expression of preference. It's a statement of fact."

"After all these years?" Bram lifted the torch to make out his cousin's expression. "Still?"

Colin shrugged. "Still." He lifted the bottle of wine to his lips and drew a long pull.

A pang of sympathy took Bram by surprise. He knew Colin had suffered nightmares and sleeplessness in his youth, after the tragic accident that took his parents' lives. During Colin's first year at school, a few boys in his dormitory had taken to teasing him over the nighttime shouts and tears. Bram—then the biggest boy in fourth form—had pummeled some sense into the bullies, and that had been the end of that. None of them had dared to tease Colin again, and Bram had assumed his cousin's dreams eventually ceased.

Evidently, they hadn't ceased. They'd persisted. For decades. Damn.

"So who's in the tent?" Bram asked. A bat swooshed by his ear, and they both ducked. "Not Miss Highwood, I hope."

"God, no." Colin laughed a bit. "Miss Highwood is a lovely girl, no mistake, but she's refined, innocent. And too delicate by far for my needs. Fiona and I . . . well, we understand each other on a more basic level."

"Fiona?" Bram frowned. He didn't even recall a woman named Fiona.

"Mrs. Lange," Colin clarified, brushing past him. "You'll thank me when her poetry improves."

Bram caught him by the arm. "But she's married."

"Only in name." He cast a peeved glance at Bram's grip. "I hope you're not planning to give me some sermon on morals. As many times as you've been skulking off to meet Miss Finch?"

Bram could only stare at him. Here he'd thought he and Susanna had been so careful, remaining beneath everyone's notice. But evidently Colin had been awake. And paying attention.

"So don't judge me," his cousin said. "Fiona and I have a mature understanding. I may be a rake, but I'm not a total cad. I've yet to ruin an innocent girl. And I've never come close to breaking a woman's heart."

"I don't mean to ruin Susanna," Bram insisted. *And hers isn't the only heart involved.*

"Oh, so you're marrying her?"

He sighed heavily. "I don't know."

"Why not? Holding out for better?"

"What? God, no." *Better?* Bram didn't know a soul alive who could best Susanna for cleverness, courage, beauty, passion, or generosity of spirit. A better woman didn't exist.

"Ah, so you're scared."

"I'm not scared."

"Of course you are. You're human. We're all scared, every last one of us. Afraid of life, of love, of dying. Maybe marching in neat rows all day distracts you from the truth of it. But when the sun goes down? We're all just stumbling through the darkness, trying to outlast another night." Colin downed another swig of wine, then stared at the bottle. "Excellent vintage. Makes me sound almost intelligent."

"You *are* intelligent. You could be making something of your life, you know. If you weren't so determined to waste all your talents, along with your fortune."

"Don't speak to me of wasting gifts, Bram. If that woman loves you, and you toss that away . . . I don't ever want to hear another 'life lesson' from your lips."

"Believe me, I'm not tossing anything away. But I don't know that she loves me."

"Please." Colin waved the wine bottle at him. "You're rich, and now titled as well. Granted, there's that stiff knee to contend with, but you do have all your own teeth." He raised an impish brow. "And assuming handsomely sized male equipment runs in our family line . . ."

Bram shook his head.

"Oh," Colin said pityingly. "It doesn't?"

"It *does*"—Bram made a fist—"not matter."

This was absurd. Since when did his cousin dispense witty aphorisms and advice? Damn it, Bram was supposed to be the voice of wisdom in this relationship. "No matter how many inches are in a man's trousers, no matter how many pounds are in his bank account . . . those numbers don't add up to love."

"I suppose you're right. And more's the pity for me." Colin nodded thoughtfully. "Well, Lord Elevated-to-the-Peerage-for-Valor, here's a wild notion. If you want to know if Miss Finch loves you, have you considered taking a firm grip on your bollocks, and . . . I don't know . . . asking her?"

Bram just stared at him.

"Good. You stand there and think about that." Backing away in the direction of his tent, Colin waved a dismissal. "If you'll excuse me, a warm bed awaits."

"There's a faster way, Charlotte," Susanna said, tugging off her gloves and gently nudging the girl aside. "At this pace, you'll be here all day."

Charlotte and a few of the other ladies had been spending every afternoon rolling black powder cartridges. However, the men had been using so many during their daily marksmanship drills, the women had scarcely been able to keep pace. With the review scheduled for tomorrow morning, Summerfield's breakfast room had become a temporary powder magazine, amid all the preparations for the officers' ball. There was simply no more time to waste.

"You're spending too much time cutting large sheets of paper down to size. I found long ago that the pages of this"—she flung a blue leather-bound book onto the table—"are the perfect size."

Charlotte stared at it. "But Miss Finch, that's *Mrs. Worthington's Wisdom*."

"Oh yes. It is."

"But you said it was a very useful book."

"It *is* a useful book. It's the perfect size for propping open windows. Its pages make excellent cartridges, and its contents are good for the occasional laugh. Beyond that? Don't ever pay it a moment's heed, Charlotte."

Opening the volume, Susanna mercilessly ripped out a page at random and smoothed it flat on the table. "First, make certain you have everything within reach and at the ready." She skipped her fingers over each item. "Paper, dowel, balls, powder, thread. Roll the paper around the dowel, forming a tube," she said, demonstrating, "and then use the ball to push the dowel through. When the ball's come almost to the end, pinch it off and give it a good twist. Then pour the powder."

Clasping the paper-wrapped ball between her fingers, she filled the rest of the slender tube with black powder, leaving a half inch of excess at the top. "No need to measure now, you see? Just stop pouring when the powder comes even with the margin of text. Another twist, and a bit of knotted thread . . . There." With a satisfied smile, she handed the cartridge to Charlotte. "With practice, you'll have the trick of it."

Charlotte took the cartridge and blinked at it. "May I ask you a question, Miss Finch?"

"Of course." Susanna ripped two more pages from the book and passed one to the girl. "So long as we work while we talk."

Cocking her head like a macaw, Charlotte peered at Susanna's ungloved wrists. "What's happened to you there?"

Susanna froze. Slowly, she flipped her forearm and regarded the exposed scars. She'd spent so many years carefully hiding them under sleeves and cuffs and gloves, or dismissing them with a lame excuse when someone stared or questioned.

Why?

Here she was, more than a decade later. Not a girl anymore, but a grown woman of sense and education. At this moment, she was literally ripping apart the restrictive teachings society foisted upon women, and showing a well-bred young lady the fine art of fashioning not painted tea trays, but black powder cartridges. Perhaps the world had left a few slashes on her, but she'd made her own small mark on the world. Here in Spindle Cove, where women were safe to be their best and truest selves.

She ran her fingers over the old, familiar map of pain. These scars were a part of her true self. They weren't *all* of who she was, but they were a part. And suddenly, there seemed no earthly reason to hide them.

"They're healed injuries," she told Charlotte. "From bloodletting. Years ago now."

The girl winced. "Do they hurt?"

"No." Her own smile caught her by surprise. "Not at all. I know they look impressive. But truthfully, sometimes I forget about them for whole days at a stretch."

As she spoke the words, she marveled at how true they were, and how much lighter she felt for saying them. Her affair with Bram was over, it seemed. He hadn't spoken to her in days. There'd been no further notes. Still, she would be forever changed by what they'd shared. Changed by him. He'd given her this precious, freeing gift—the courage to accept herself as she was. Scars, freckles, passions, and all.

In time, did a broken heart scar over? After a decade or

so had passed, would she be able to forget about Bram for whole days at a stretch?

Somehow she doubted it.

"Miss Finch!" Violet Winterbottom appeared in the doorway. "Miss Bright needs you in the hall. She wants your opinion on the decorations."

"I'll be there presently."

Susanna handed the cartridge-making supplies to Charlotte before rinsing her hands at the washbasin and leaving the breakfast room. She left her gloves behind.

She walked through the drawing room, where the militia volunteers stood like a field of scarecrows, arms outstretched, as pin-chewing ladies flitted and circled, marking final alterations to their uniforms.

When Susanna reached the hall, she found it similarly abuzz with activity. At one end of the long, narrow room, Kate Taylor was practicing on the pianoforte. Along the bay of plate-glass windows, Mr. Fosbury and two footmen were busy arranging tables for the buffet. Ladies and servants bearing flowers and furniture hurried this way and that, their footfalls clattering over the wood inlay floor. By tomorrow night, this scene would be a tableau of elegance—she hoped. But for the moment, it was the picture of chaos.

"Here," Sally Bright said, thrusting a wriggling baby into Susanna's arms. "Take Daisy while I climb the staircase. We have a few different choices for the swags."

Susanna waited patiently in the center of the room, staring up at the balustrade and bouncing the youngest Bright sibling in time to Kate's rapid scales on the pianoforte. Daisy had plumped in recent months. As the minutes passed, Susanna began to feel her arms would fall off.

"She loves you, Miss Finch!" Sally called, draping swags of fabric over the banister. "Now, this is the red.

It's striking, but maybe it will be too much, with all the uniforms in the room? And then we have this blue, but it's a touch dark for an evening affair. Which do you think best?"

Susanna tilted her head, considering.

"I agree wholeheartedly, Miss Finch," Mr. Keane called down, appearing next to Sally on the balcony. "Neither will do. We need something with more spark. I suggest gold."

"I told you, vicar," Sally said. "We don't have enough of the gold."

"You're right. Unless . . ." The vicar snapped his fingers. "I know. We'll combine it with the tulle."

"The tulle!" Sally exclaimed. "That's divine inspiration, that is. Just hold a moment, Miss Finch. We'll show you what he means."

They both disappeared, ducking to rummage in their boxes of supplies.

Susanna sighed, shifting Daisy from one arm to the other.

"There you are. I've been searching for you all over." Bram was suddenly at her side.

Thrown off balance, she juggled the infant in her arms. "You have?"

Save a few glances across the green, she hadn't seen him for the better part of three days. And of course, he *would* show up so dangerously attractive, wearing only an open-collared homespun shirt under his brand-new officer's coat. She tried not to look at him, but avoiding direct eye contact was the best she could manage. Instead, her gaze lingered on the strong angle of his jaw, the sensual set of his lips. Then dropped to the exposed wedge of his bare chest, and the dark hair curling there.

Was he *trying* to torture her?

"What, pray tell, are these?" He displayed his newly hemmed cuff for her, pointing out the brass buttons studded there.

"Oh, those." She bit back a smile. "Aaron Dawes made the mold and did the casting. Every proper militia needs a symbol."

"Yes, but proper militias don't choose a *lamb*."

"As I recall it, the lamb chose you."

His thumbnail traced the motto—a tiny crescent of Latin. "*Aries eos incitabit*. A *sheep* shall urge them onward?"

"Be careful, my lord. Your three terms at Cambridge are showing."

His mouth softened into that subtle hint of a smile she'd come to love. "Buttons aside, you've done a remarkable job. You and all the ladies. The uniforms, the training ..." He glanced around the room. "All these preparations."

His approval warmed her inside. "We've all worked hard. I happened to see part of drill the other day. Very impressive, my lord. Tomorrow will doubtless be a splendid triumph."

An awkward silence grew between them, until Daisy filled it with a wet gurgle.

"Who is this?" He nodded at the squirming infant in her arms. "I don't believe we've been introduced."

"This"—she swiveled to give him a better view—"is little Daisy Bright."

"Should have guessed it from the hair."

The towheaded babe stretched a chubby hand toward Bram, reaching for the shining buttons on his coat. Susanna yearned to reach for him, too. On impulse, driven by equal parts emotional distress and arm fatigue, she thrust the child at him. "Here. Why don't you hold her?"

"Me? Wait. I don't—"

But she left him no opportunity to object, settling little Daisy in the crook of his arm. The delighted infant grasped for a button and gave it a yank.

"Someone likes the buttons, see?" Susanna looked up at Bram. The poor man was frozen to stone, positively stricken with terror. "Do try to be calm," she teased. "She's a baby, not a grenade."

"I have more experience with grenades."

"You're doing fine." Relinquishing the button, Daisy grasped for Bram's thumb and squeezed it tight. "Look, she adores you already."

A lump rose in Susanna's throat as she watched him holding the infant so gingerly, viewed those stout little fingers wrapped secure around his thumb.

There he went again, with the torture. She'd never given it much thought before, but now . . . oh, how she wanted a child. She loved the image of her breasts and belly swollen with pregnancy. Loved the idea of staying up nights, feeling the babe kick at her from the inside. Loved dreaming about what the child would look like, wondering which of his parents he'd favor. She loved everything about the idea of carrying not just a child, but Bram's child.

Because she loved *him*.

She *loved* him. And perhaps he was too stubborn to admit it, but he needed her love. She couldn't let him walk away.

She did have one last hope, she supposed. There was the gown. A great ivory cloud of a gown, dripping with pearls and brilliants, currently hovering in her dressing room upstairs. She hadn't worn it but once, a few years ago in Town. But when she'd tried it on last week for fitting, the bodice stretched over her form like a second skin. The neckline pushed her breasts high and plump, and the sewn-in boning trimmed her waist.

She'd entertained this foolish vision of herself, floating down the grand staircase in that lovely, ethereal gown tomorrow night. In her imagination, Bram stood at the bottom of the steps, regarding her with a mixture of pride and sheer lust-struck wonder. Despite every indication that he wasn't much of a dancer in actuality, her Dream Bram claimed her hand and pulled her into a slow, romantic waltz. And there, before a crowd of admiring onlookers, he twirled her to a halt and confessed his undying adoration.

It was a lovely, silly dream.

But that was before they'd argued on the turret. Before he'd accused her of being mistrustful and afraid. Difficult to imagine simply donning a pretty dress would change his opinions on that. And if a pretty dress *was* all it took—she wasn't so sure she'd retain her respect for him.

"I need to speak with you," he said low. He turned a glance around the crowded room. "Somewhere else. Somewhere private."

"Private?"

Kate's piano scales suddenly ceased, and Susanna's heartbeat kicked into a faster rhythm than ever. The wainscoted walls began to press in on her, and she felt the scrutiny of every soul in the crowded room. She cast a glance around the hall, looking around at her assembled friends, neighbors, servants. Just as she'd suspected, everyone was watching them. Noticing. *Wondering.*

Well . . . good.

Not just good. *Excellent.* The anxious weight in her stomach dissolved into bubbles of giddy joy, fizzing through her like fine champagne. Suddenly, she knew exactly what to do.

"Dance with me."

He blinked at her. "What?"

"Dance with me," she repeated.

"Dance with you. You mean tomorrow night, at the officers' ball?

She shook her head. "No, I mean here. Now."

What kind of a modern woman was she, if she didn't reach for her own dream? Maybe it was time to sweep the man off *his* feet, for a change. She untied her work apron at the back and lifted it over her head, tossing it over the banister and smoothing the wrinkles from her blush-pink frock. It wasn't a voluminous, dazzling silk cloud, but it would have to do.

"Miss Taylor," she called, slicking back a stray lock of hair, "do play a waltz for us?"

Bram shifted his weight, eyeing her with what seemed to be genuine alarm. "I'm not much of a dancer."

"Oh, that's all right. Neither am I." She lifted little Daisy from his arms and passed the babe to a nearby chambermaid. "Kindly make it a slow waltz, Miss Taylor."

"Never had much practice at all, even before this." He gestured toward his injured knee.

"It doesn't matter." She took his hands and tugged him toward the center of the hall. "We'll manage."

Space cleared around them as the curious onlookers pressed to the margins of the room. Kate's talented fingers sent the first few measures of a melodic waltz lilting from the pianoforte.

Susanna stood in front of him in the center of the floor, lifting his left hand in hers and placing his other hand on her waist. "Now, let's see. How does this go?"

"Like this." His right hand slid, sure and confident, to the space between her shoulder blades, and a quick flex of his arm snapped her close.

Her breath caught in a gasp of delight.

He seemed to have realized that he had two options,

and escaping this dance wasn't one of them. He could either appear coerced and uncomfortable in front of all these people, or he could take control.

No surprise he chose the latter.

"Ready?" he asked.

She managed a nod.

With commanding grace and a slight, endearing limp, he waltzed her across the room.

And it *was* a dream come true.

They moved in perfect time to the music. Susanna suspected that was because Kate laid a syncopated pause on the third beat of each measure, to allow for their halting steps. So perhaps the music moved in time to them, but it was magical all the same.

He sent her into one turn, then another. Her flounced skirt swirled around her ankles, in little eddies of pink froth. And the sun, progressing on its slow slide toward the horizon, just then ratcheted a notch lower in the sky. So that its amber rays streamed straight through the bank of plate-glass windows lining one side of the hall. The ancient, warped glass took that day-worn light and made it precious, painting the room and all its occupants a glittering corona.

But no one caught more magnificence than Bram. Rosy fingers of light shone through the fine hairs at his brow. The melting afternoon lay like gold plate on his shoulders. Brilliant, shining armor. And he bore up under the weight of it beautifully, whirling her across the freshly waxed parquet. She heard more than one young lady's wistful sigh.

It was just like something from a fairy tale.

He stared deep into her eyes. Little sparks danced in his wide, dark pupils. "Are you going to tell me why we're doing this?"

She nodded. "You were right the other day, when you accused me of being afraid."

"I shouldn't have said—"

"Don't. You were right. I *have* been afraid. You see, I've always told the ladies that Spindle Cove is a safe place for them. A place where a woman can be her best and truest self, regardless of what anyone thinks. But for the past few weeks, that hasn't been the case for me. I've been hiding a part of my true self. This vital, growing part of me that holds all my feelings for you. I've been keeping it a secret from everyone, convinced I daren't tell a soul."

The music went on, but they twirled to a halt.

"But that's ridiculous, isn't it? And unfair to us both. When I looked at you just now, I knew. I knew in my heart, I couldn't conceal it one minute more. I wanted to dance with you. I wanted everyone to see us." A lump rose in her throat. "To see *me*, in love with you."

And for all this was her moment to be fearless and direct, she suddenly couldn't bear to meet his gaze. Instead she fingered the gold braid on his new red wool coat. Stroking her bare fingertip over the neat ridge. Cherishing him with her touch. "I'm not sure what to say. I haven't any practice with these things. I would tell you you're the best, bravest man I know. But considering how few men I know, that seems too small a compliment."

She finally mined some reserve of strength and raised her face to his. "So I will just tell you I love you. I love you, Bram. I want everyone to see it, and I want you to know . . . you're a part of this place now. No matter where duty takes you, Spindle Cove will always be here for you. And so will I."

He put both arms around her, pulling her flush against his chest. "You beautiful, brazen thing."

Then he went silent, just holding her gaze for what

seemed like eons. Nerves multiplied in her stomach with every passing second.

She swallowed hard. "Don't you have anything else to say?"

" 'Hallelujah' springs to mind. Beyond that . . ." He brushed a caress down her cheek. "Does this mean that if I proposed marriage to you right now, you might not make that twisty, unhappy face?"

"Try me and see."

And then a smile—a broad, boyish, shameless *grin*—spread across his face. It was a smile unlike any she'd ever seen him wear, forever defining the crescent as the shape of pure joy. She felt its mirror stretching her own cheeks.

He propped a finger under her chin. "Susanna Jane Finch, w—"

"Susanna Jane Finch. What's going on here?" The familiar voice startled them both.

Papa.

She beat down the impulse to hide, or to scurry from Bram's embrace. Too late for all that subterfuge, and no need anyhow. She wouldn't hide from her own father what she was eager to share with the world.

Still smiling, she caught Bram's hand in hers and wheeled on her slipper heel to face her father. "Papa, I'm so happy you're here."

But her father's expression did not read as happiness. As he approached them, moving across the hall in slow, even steps, he looked wary, at best. He turned his gaze around the room, surveying the shambles of half-finished preparations. Summerfield's servants jarred themselves into motion. In an instant, the bustle of moving furniture and hanging swags had resumed. Kate went back to playing scales.

Susanna bit her lip. "Is it the hall, Papa? I know it looks a true calamity at the moment, but just you wait for tomorrow. Everything will be perfect."

"I'm not concerned about tomorrow." His watery blue eyes fixed on Bram.

Susanna felt suddenly protective of the man at her side. She clutched Bram's arm. "Papa, we were only dancing."

One hoary eyebrow arched. "Only dancing?"

"You're right. It's not only dancing, it's more than that. You see, Bram and I have grown very close these past weeks, and . . ." She cast a fleeting glance at Bram. "And I love him." It made her so happy, just to say it. She never wanted to stop. "I love him, Papa. I do."

Her father looked at the floor and released a long, measured breath. She stared at him, oddly amazed. How could anyone breathe at a time like this?

Then he raised his head . . . and her heart fell.

She'd just told her father she was in love. For the first time in her life, in *love*. And he refused to even look her direction. From the distant expression on his face, she could tell Papa was going to receive this news in the same spirit he received all her other secrets and confessed emotions.

He was going to ignore it. As if he'd never even heard.

Oh Lord.

Had it been this way, all those other times? When she'd believed herself to be confiding to a distracted genius, had she truly been pouring out her heart to someone who just didn't care? The idea was nauseating. Unthinkable. Of course Papa cared for her. He'd saved her life. He'd given up so much to live here at Summerfield.

Bram cleared his throat. "Sir Lewis, we obviously need to talk."

"Oh yes. Indeed we do." Her father calmly reached into

his breast pocket and withdrew an envelope. "I was going to wait until after the field review tomorrow. But I think now is the ideal time."

Bram released Susanna's hand and accepted the folded paper. He opened the envelope and scanned its contents. "Bloody hell. Are these what I think they are?"

"Written orders," her father said. "Yes. I made inquiries with my friends in the War Office. More like strong suggestions. There's a navy vessel leaving from Portsmouth this coming Tuesday."

Susanna gasped. *"Tuesday?"*

Her father's demeanor was cool. "You'll be on it, Rycliff. And back with your regiment in a matter of weeks."

"That's . . ." Bram swallowed hard as he stared at the paper. "Sir Lewis, I don't even know what to say."

Say no, she wanted to scream. *Say you can't possibly leave so soon. Say you're marrying me.*

"No need for thanks." With his palm, Papa smoothed his wispy silver hair. "I view it as an even exchange. If not for your militia review, I'd never have this chance to demonstrate the new cannon."

"The new *cannon*?" Susanna turned to Bram, mortified. He'd given her his word he wouldn't involve Papa in the militia. Surely he wouldn't have lied to her.

"Yes, Susanna," her father said. "The new cannon. It will be unveiled tomorrow, as part of the militia review." He looked to Bram. "I do hope you've managed to whip those farmhands into shape? I'm counting on an impressive display, in exchange for the favors I pulled." He tapped the letter in Bram's hand.

"But—" Susanna shook her head. From across the room, Kate's plinking arpeggios hammered away at the last bits of her composure. "Bram, please tell me I'm misunderstanding this somehow. Tell me you haven't gone back on your word to me, in some underhanded ploy to regain your command."

He lowered his voice. "It's not like that. I can explain."

"Tell me I can trust you," she rushed on, emotion tweaking her voice. "Tell me you haven't been lying to me this whole time. Tell me I haven't made the most wretched, foolish mistake of my life, or . . . or I don't know how—" Her voice broke.

"Susanna," her father said sharply. "Stop embarrassing yourself. You know you're given to overwrought emotion. Whatever silly infatuation you've developed, it will pass. Tomorrow isn't about your girlish fancies, it's about legacies—both Bramwell's and mine. Perhaps we've humored you to a point, my dear. But there comes a time when men must be men. You can't keep holding us back."

—Chapter Twenty-four—

ursed cannon.

Colin wrestled with the ropes as he hauled the cannon into the wagon. For a scale model prototype, the thing was damned heavy. The barrel was thick as his thigh, fashioned of solid brass.

He straightened. "You. Don't touch those." From his perch on the wagon bed, Colin waved the Bright twins away from a pyramid of straw-packed crates. "Leave those be."

"What's in them?" one of the boys asked.

"Fireworks for tomorrow night. Don't touch them. Don't even breathe on them. Took more than a week for those to arrive from Town."

"Can't we help you with them?"

"No," he said, gritting his teeth. Those fireworks were meant to be *his* surprise, his own unique stamp on the day's festivities. Colin was going to produce the display himself, and he was going to do it well—prove to Bram he could be good for something. There wasn't much he could seem to get right in this life, but he did have a knack for artistic destruction. What better canvas than the clear night sky?

But first, to deal with Sir Lewis Finch's masterpiece. The cursed cannon.

He grasped a rope in both hands and rocked back on his heels, tugging with all his might. Being responsible for artillery had seemed a plum assignment, until Colin had realized just how much heavy lifting was involved. All day, he'd been hustling to and fro—taking powder to the ladies, then rolled cartridges to the armory, smuggling fireworks to Summerfield, and now carting Sir Lewis's prototype up to the castle. Loading the thing was taking longer than he'd planned. He was racing nightfall now.

"What's this one?" one of the twins asked.

Out of the corner of his eye, Colin saw Finn brush the straw from a noisemaker. Before he could object, the boy gave the cord a tug. The firecracker exploded with a sharp pop and a dusting of smoke.

"Cor," Rufus said, grinning. "Try another."

"I told you two to leave off," Colin bit out. He stood tall—just in time to watch Dinner scuttle off with a frightened bleat. The startled lamb squeezed under the fence that bordered Summerfield's gardens. "Now look what you've done. You've gone and frightened the damned sheep. You know how Rycliff dotes on the thing."

"Shall we fetch him?" Finn asked.

"No, I'll have to do it. He'll be scared of you now." Colin vaulted the side of the wagon. He clapped the fraying strands of hemp from his hands and wiped his perspiring brow with his sleeve.

Clambering over the fence, he entered the kitchen gardens, where the house's vegetables and savories were grown. He watched as the lamb trotted a path between two rows of turnips and squeezed under a second fence to enter a fallow plot bounded by meadow.

"Dinner," he called, giving chase again and entering the meadow. "Dinner, come back now."

When he reached the center of the field, he paused to catch his breath and scan the area for telltale tufts of wool. When the lamb failed to appear, he cupped his hands around his mouth and tried again. *"Dinner!"*

This time, his call earned an answer. Several answers. In fact, the ground shook with the collective bestial response. He spied several large, dark forms lumbering toward him through the twilight dusk. He blinked, trying to make them out. These weren't sheep. No, they were . . .

Cows. Large cows. Remarkably fast and menacing cows. A small herd of them, all thundering straight for him where he stood in the center of the field.

Colin took a few steps backward. "Wait," he said, holding up his hands. "I didn't mean you."

The beasts didn't listen to reason apparently. A shame, because they did have rather large ears. Or were those . . . horns?

He turned and made a mad dash for the fence.

Blighted idiot, he cursed himself as he pumped arms and legs, scrambling over the furrowed field. *Corkbrained fool.* What kind of imbecile entered a pasture at twilight and shouted "Dinner" at the top of his lungs?

One who hadn't left London in a decade, that's who.

"I hate the country," he muttered as he ran. "I hate it. I bloody damned well hate it."

In his hurry, he'd chosen a different route of escape than the way he'd entered the field. Rather than reaching a simple wooden stile, he ran smack up against a hedgerow. A thorny hedgerow.

"Hate it," he said, pushing his way through the bramble and twigs. "Loathsome, miserable, reeking, wholesome farmland. Feh."

He emerged on the other side of the hedge to find himself once again in the Summerfield gardens—the pretty bit, this time. He was scraped, but mercifully untrampled. He stood staring at the hedgerow a moment, picking bits of hawthorn from his clothing and cursing country life.

Then something odd caught his attention. A light smack on the head.

He wheeled around, batting blindly with a hand.

The next smack caught him across the face. A red burst of pain stung his already abraded cheek.

Good Lord, what *was* this? The Seven Plagues of Colin Sandhurst, squeezed into the space of one hour?

He raised his hands in defense, dodging the repeated blows.

"You villain," a female voice accused. *Smack.* "You deceitful cur."

Colin lowered his hands to get a proper look at his attacker. It was the middle Highwood sister. The dark-haired one. Miriam, was it? Melissa?

Whoever she was, she was hitting him. Repeatedly. With a glove.

"What on earth are you doing?" He dodged another smack, moving deeper into the gardens. He stumbled over a clump of daisies and narrowly missed a collision with a rosebush.

She chased him, still swinging away. "I want a duel."

"A duel?"

"I know all about you and Mrs. Lange, you . . . you rutting . . ." Apparently lacking either the imagination or the bravery to complete the insult, she moved on. "I never liked you, I hope you know. I've always known you for a worthless bounder, but now my mother and sisters will suffer the pain of the revelation. You'll have disappointed their hopes."

Ah. So that's what this was about. He was being made to answer for . . . for what, precisely? Flirting?

"Diana has no father or brothers to defend her honor. The duty falls to me." She slapped him across the face again. "Name your seconds."

"Good God. Will you stop with the glove?" He ripped the thing from her hand and tossed it into the thorny rose-bushes. "I'm not going to accept your challenge. There will be no duel."

"Why not? Because I'm a woman?"

"No, because I've seen the way you spinsters handle a pistol. You'd shoot me dead where I stood." Colin pinched the bridge of his nose. "Listen, calm down. I haven't touched your sister. Not in any improper way."

"Perhaps you haven't touched her improperly, but you've improperly led her on."

"Led her on? Perhaps I danced and flirted with her a bit, but I've flirted with every young lady in this village."

"Not *every* young lady."

He paused, stunned. As he stared at her, he felt a grin nudging his cheeks. "So you're jealous."

"Don't be absurd," she replied, much too quickly to be credible.

"You are." He wagged a finger at her, no longer on the retreat. "You're jealous. I've flirted with every young lady in the village but you, and you're envious."

"I'm not envious, I just . . ." She made a gesture of frustration. "I just want to hurt you. The way you hurt my sister."

The way he'd hurt *her*, she meant. If Diana Highwood had suffered one moment of pain on his account, Colin would swallow a Chinese dazzler. But this one . . . she was hurt.

Well, exactly how *did* she expect him to flirt with her?

Lines like "river of silk" and "sparkling diamonds" would never work on a woman like this. She was too clever by half. Moreover, such comparisons would be wildly inaccurate. Her hair was nothing like silk, and her dark eyes bore no resemblance to diamonds.

Cooled volcanic glass, perhaps.

"Listen," he said in a placating tone. "It's not like that, Melinda. You *are* a tolerably pretty girl."

"Tolerably." She rolled her eyes and made a dismissive noise. "*Tolerably* pretty. What kind of compliment is that? And my name's not Melinda."

"No, not tolerably pretty," he said, tilting his head for a better look. "Genuinely so. If only you'd . . ."

"Don't say it. Everyone says it."

"Everyone says what?"

She spoke in a low, mimicking tone. " 'If only you'd remove your spectacles, you'd be lovely.' "

"I wasn't going to stay that," he lied. "Why would I say that? What a perfectly stupid thing to say."

"I know you're lying. You dissemble as easily as you breathe. But my feelings aren't at issue here. This is about your cruel misuse of Diana."

"I assure you, I've not come close to using your sister, cruelly or otherwise. I apologized for all that business at the tea shop."

"Oh yes. You apologized quite prettily. You made them believe you were decent. That you cared. And then you took up with a *married woman*."

Colin rubbed the back of his neck. He really didn't have time for this. He had fireworks to set, a cannon to mount, and a lamb to catch. "I don't know what you hope to gain by pursuing this conversation. I tell you now, I won't offer marriage. Not to your sister, not to anyone."

"Hmph. I'd never allow you to marry her."

"Then what do you want from me?"

"I want justice! I want you to be responsible for your actions, instead of always weaseling out of them with a few pretty words."

Do you see? Colin wanted to say. *This is why I avoid you.* It was as if those spectacles gave her the power to see straight through him.

"You're starting to sound like my cousin," he said. "I do hope you're not planning to give me the same treatment you gave him."

She stared at him a moment. "What an excellent idea." With a swift, swooping motion of her arm, she drew back her reticule and let it fly.

Colin flinched just in time to take the blow on his shoulder, rather than his crown. Still, the cinched velvet purse landed with surprising force. Pain exploded through his shoulder. "What the devil is in that thing? Rocks?"

"What else?"

What else, indeed. How could he have forgotten her ridiculous obsession with geology? Vile harpy. "Listen, Marissa . . ."

"It's *Minerva*." She raised her hand to swing the rock-filled reticule again.

This time, he was ready. In a lightning-quick motion, Colin caught her wrist. He spun her around and pulled her to him. Her spine pressed flush against his chest, and he cinched his arm around her middle.

Her spectacles slipped from her face and tumbled to the grass.

She wrestled his grip. "Let me go."

"Not just yet. You'll step on them, if you don't stop struggling."

He wasn't sure he truly wanted her to stop struggling. From where he was standing, poised to look straight down her bodice, all that wrestling did wonderful things for her breasts. No cool, perfect alabaster to be found here. Just warm, womanly skin. And as enticing as she looked, she *felt* even better. So angry and alive.

"Hush." He pressed his lips close to her ear. Her hair smelled of jasmine. The scent swirled through his head, muddling his thoughts. "Be calm," he told her.

Be calm, he told himself.

"I don't want to be calm. I want a duel." She wriggled in his arms, and desire pulsed through him, as fierce as it was appalling. "I demand satisfaction."

Yes, he thought. This was a woman who *would* demand satisfaction. In life, in love. In bed. She would demand honesty and commitment and fidelity, and all manner of things he was unwilling to give.

Which was just the excuse he needed to let her go.

"Don't move, or you'll crush them." He bent to retrieve her wire-rimmed spectacles from where they'd landed in a clump of ivy. After brushing them clean of dirt and moss, he held them up to the moonlight to inspect them for scratches.

"They aren't broken, are they?"

"No."

She made a lunging grab for the spectacles, but he held them back. She stumbled, pitching forward to collide with his chest. As she looked up at him, blinking hard in her attempt to see clear, her lashes fluttered like thick, plumed fans. Her tongue darted out to wet her lips.

Good God. For a buttoned-up bluestocking, she had damned sultry lips. Luscious, plump, and a deeper red at the edges. Like two slices of a ripe, sweet plum. His mouth watered.

She leaned into him, cheeks flushed. As if she *wanted*

his kiss. More than that. As if she wanted *him*. Every incorrigible, rakish, broken part.

That couldn't be right.

"You know, they have a point," he said. "You do look different without your spectacles."

"Truly?"

"Yes. You look squinty. And confused." He fitted the spectacles back on the bridge of her nose, hooking the rims over her ears. Then he put a finger under her chin, tilting her face for his appraisal. "There, that's some improvement."

She blinked at him through the discs of glass, her gaze sharpening to that familiar, piercing ray of mistrust. "You are a horrid man. I despise you."

"Rightly so, pet." And just because he knew it would vex her, he touched a fingertip to her nose. "Now you're seeing clear."

─Chapter Twenty-five─

ram stared at the letter in his grip. This folded square of paper gave him back his command. For months now, this had been all he'd wanted. He'd worked tirelessly to recover his strength, pursued this one goal with single-minded determination. He couldn't have dreamed anything would make him happier than the very scrap of parchment he now held.

He wanted to throw it in the fire.

And then toss Sir Lewis Finch after it.

"I can't believe this. Oh my God." Susanna sobbed into her hand, and then ran from the hall before Bram had any chance to stop her.

"Susanna, wait." He started in pursuit.

Sir Lewis flung an arm in front of his chest, stopping him cold. "Let her be. She gets this way. All women do. I've found she always sorts these things out on her own, in time. If only you let her be."

Bram stared at the man, fuming. "Oh really. The same way you let her be, when she was distraught after her mother's death? Sending her to that ghastly torture in Norfolk?" With a curled finger, he thwacked the envelope containing his new orders. "How long have you had this, Sir Lewis? Days now? Weeks? Since before I even arrived in Spindle Cove, perhaps? Obviously, there wasn't any true need for a field review. Did the Duke of Tunbridge really ask you to muster a militia here, or was that a lie, too? I always knew you were a brilliant inventor, but perhaps you ought to try your hand at espionage."

The older man bristled. "I am a patriot, you ungrateful whelp. Tomorrow, before an audience of dukes and generals, I will introduce the weapon that could save many of your soldiers' lives. And what do you care if I engaged in some harmless exaggeration? You've got what you wanted, haven't you?"

"You mean this?" Bram shook the envelope at him. He lowered his voice to a growl. "This piece of paper has exactly one virtue right now. One quality that keeps me from crushing it under my heel."

"Oh? What's that?"

"It makes me free to say this. Go to hell."

Bram left the old man sputtering and hurried down the same path Susanna had taken when she'd fled the room. As he reached the end of the corridor, an open door to the gardens beckoned. Picking up speed, Bram charged through it.

And nearly collided with a stunned Minerva Highwood.

"Hold the cudgel," he said, raising his hands. "Did Susanna come this way?"

The bespectacled girl cast a glance over her shoulder. "I don't—"

"Thank you." Bram didn't wait for the rest of her reply. He simply followed the direction she'd indicated with her glance—a slate-paved pathway that disappeared around a tall, manicured hedge. As he rounded it, he caught a glimpse of Susanna's unmistakable hair as she dashed through a distant arch.

"Susanna!"

She paused, but didn't stop. She entered a square, ornate garden bounded by hedges on all sides and a trellis in each corner. Bram followed her, closing the gate behind him.

She heard the latch click and wheeled, knowing herself to be penned. Her eyes were wide with fear and disbelief. Of course she was terrified. Her beloved father—her only parent and protector for so many years—had just revealed himself to be an ambitious, selfish, unfeeling jackass.

"Listen," he said, raising his hands in peace. "Susanna, love. I know how upset you must be right now."

"You have no idea." She shook her head. "No idea." Her hands balled into fists, and she pressed them tight to her belly, as though afraid they might get loose.

"Will it help to hit something? You can hit me." Approaching her, he dropped his arms to his sides. "Go ahead, love. Do your worst."

No sooner had the words passed his lips than her fist met his gut, driving into his side like a mallet. A mallet with a knobby little row of knuckles. The blow came before he'd had the chance to prepare, to tense his muscles in defense.

"Oof." He clutched his side, reeling. "For God's sake, Susanna."

"You asked for it," she cried defensively, nursing her punching hand close to her breast and rubbing her knuckles. "You told me to do my worst."

"I know, I know." He straightened, blowing away the pain with a deep exhalation. "It's just . . . your worst was worse than I was anticipating."

"You should know by now, I'm just full of surprises." Her breath caught on a wild sob. She pulled back for another blow.

This time he intercepted it, easily catching her fist in his own. "Hold a moment."

"I'll hold nothing." She kicked him in the shin. His good shin, fortunately. "You've ruined *everything.* I'm furious with you."

"With *me?*" His head jerked back in surprise. After the callous, disgusting way Sir Lewis had just treated her in the hall, she was angry with *him?*

"How could you do this to me? You gave me your word. You promised you wouldn't involve my father in any of this."

"I didn't think I *was* involving him, not in the way you meant. I only agreed to demonstrate his new invention. It's not as though I put him in uniform."

"But don't you see how this is so much worse?"

"No. I don't see that at all." He put his hands on her shoulders and tried to soothe her with a brisk caress. "Susanna, I never meant to deceive you, I swear it. And regardless of how I feel about your father right now . . . Even I have to admit, his cannon is a brilliant idea. It should be made known."

"The cannon is a brilliant *idea.* But in practice, it doesn't work. Do you know how many prototypes he's tried? How many near-disasters we've evaded? The last one blew up, Bram. Practically in his face. He suffered a mild heart attack, remained abed for weeks. He promised me he'd discontinue experiments and send his drawings to colleagues for testing instead." She pressed the back of her hand to her mouth. "He *promised* me."

"Well, he broke his word. To us both." He cast a pointed glance at his breast pocket, where he'd stuffed the envelope. "He could have given me these orders weeks ago, don't you see? But he decided to use me while he had the chance. This event we've been working so hard to plan has nothing to do with the Duke of Tunbridge or defending the cove, and everything to do with your father's taste for glory. It's all a bit of gold braid and red-coated flash to set off the jewel that is his new cannon. He's manipulated us both. Not only us, but the whole damned village. For the sake of his pride, he's put all your work, all your friends at risk."

She squeezed her eyes shut and pressed her hands over her ears. "Stop! Stop talking. I don't want to hear any more. Just stop."

He knew her anger wasn't truly for him. The betrayal and devastation she felt were all to do with her father. That familiar, awful sense of helplessness descended on Bram, as he realized there was nothing he could do to alter the past. He couldn't mend this for her.

But he could be here, with her. He could listen, and hold her tight.

So he did. Bram wrapped her in his arms and clutched her close to his chest. She put her head on his shoulder and wept. He held her like that for several minutes, murmuring words of comfort in her ear. Lending her the warmth and strength of his body until the tremors ceased racking hers.

When at length she raised her head and drew a deep, shaky breath, he led her to one of the corner arbors. "Come, let's sit down."

"I'm so sorry. Your knee."

"No, no. It's not that." He pulled her down to sit with him. The arbor bench was narrow, and it would only accommodate the two of them if she sat half in his lap. He slid one arm about her waist. Her slender, stockinged legs twined with his knee boots. One of her slippers fell to the grass.

"Here." With his free hand, he wrested the flask from his pocket. He unscrewed the top with his teeth, then spat it aside. "Have a sip of this. It will help."

He raised it to her quivering lips, and she took a healthy swallow. Immediately, she seized up with a violent coughing fit.

"Sorry," he said, patting her back. "You're so proficient at shooting and Latin and so forth, I forget you haven't mastered every manly pursuit."

She cleared her throat and gave him a wry smile. "This is one I hadn't tried yet. As for the others . . . I just wanted something in common with him."

"I know, love. I know it well." He brushed the stray hair from her face. "It was always the same with me."

She rubbed her face with her hands. "He *promised* me, Bram. He promised me so many things, and I was such a fool to believe. He told me he'd look after himself, stop causing me so much worry. And now this cannon business." A bittersweet laugh broke through her tears. "He told me once, long ago, that Rycliff Castle was mine. Did you know that? It was my prize, he said. My reward for recovering. He encouraged me to store all my hopes and dreams there, and then . . ." She reached for the flask and took another nip of whiskey, swallowing with a grimace. "And then one afternoon, he just gave it away." Her tearful eyes met his. "To you."

"I didn't know. I'm so sorry."

"It's nothing. Only a girl's foolishness. But I'm a foolish girl, it seems." She sniffed and laid her head to his chest. "He promised me I'd be safe, that summer in Norfolk. That time spent there would be . . ." Her voice pinched. "Would be *good* for me. Now I know, he just wanted me out of the way. You heard him earlier. How he said I'm always becoming overwrought, holding him back. That summer, I must have proved too difficult to ignore."

"Hush, love. Hush." He pressed a kiss to her crown. "Don't distress yourself so."

Her fingers curled around his lapel. "And all this might be somehow bearable, if I had you. But now you're leaving. *Tuesday.* I don't know how I'll survive it. I love you so much."

Just like that, his heart danced a nimble little waltz in his chest.

She loved him.

She'd said as much inside the house. Four times, if he recalled correctly. But with every repetition, she only heaped more joy atop joy. He was well and truly wallowing in it now.

"Please don't go," she whispered, clutching his coat. "Don't leave me."

Her eyes held so much heartrending doubt. As if he would be the second man today to destroy her trust. He didn't know that he could find the words to convince her otherwise, so he answered with a kiss instead. He lowered his lips to hers, meaning to give her a chaste, reassuring peck.

But she had other ideas.

Her lips parted beneath his, inviting and lush. Drawing him in. Welcoming him home.

God. Yes. That first taste of her, after long days of separation, sent lightning forking through his body. A low groan rumbled from his throat.

They kissed hungrily, trading light nips and deep passes of their tongues. Susanna came alive in his arms, seized by some kind of sensual frenzy. She clutched his shoulders. Pushed aside his lapels to rub her breasts against his homespun-clad chest. Speared her fingers through his thick, cropped hair and twisted in his lap, driving their kiss deeper still.

Perhaps it was that small taste of whiskey—but in all their previous encounters, he'd never known her to be this aggressive. Her hands were bold. Her lips and tongue made demands.

Bram found he rather liked it. He liked it a great deal.

"Don't leave me," she urged, licking over his pulse. "Hold me, close and tight. Promise you'll never let go."

"Never." He slid one hand to her backside and pulled, hiking her higher onto his lap. But it wasn't enough. With one hand, she gathered and lifted the folds of her skirts. They made a sensuous rustle as she pushed up on her knees and moved to straddle him on the bench.

He slid a hand up her thigh. She was bare beneath her petticoats. Bare, and already wet for him. Their moans mingled as he explored her dewy cleft with his fingertips, finding and circling her swollen pearl. Her feminine spice mingled with the scent of roses, filling the air with an intoxicating, arousing perfume.

Her hand flew to the closures of his breeches front. She adjusted her weight, giving herself space to work the buttons free. The shift in her pose thrust her bosom in his face. Bending his head, he nuzzled the soft pillows of her breasts, greedily thrusting his tongue into the dark, fragrant valley between them.

As he kissed and licked the luscious curves, a needy whimper eased from her throat. "I need you," she said, reaching through the unbuttoned flap to stroke his aroused flesh. "I need you now."

She didn't need to ask twice. He worked his cock through the layers of buckskin and fabric, positioning the engorged, eager tip just at the entrance to bliss.

She lowered herself a fraction of an inch, then backed off—her slick heat lapping at the crown of his erection. He thought he would lose his mind, but he forced himself to be patient for a moment more, allowing his head to fall back so he could drink in the sight of her. The coils and wisps of her molten bronze hair, tumbling loose around her pale shoulders. Those full, berry-stained lips, swollen with his kisses. The flush of passion on her face. So beautiful, she made his heart twist.

He guided her hips, until she settled in just the right spot. And then he helped her sink by slow degrees. Inch by delicious inch. Until molten bliss enveloped him, all the way to the root.

They stayed that way for a long moment, each of them panting for breath, resisting the desire to move.

When the desire to move became an imperative, she rolled her hips. Slowly at first, but quickly accelerating to a brisk, urgent rhythm. He helped with his hands, clutching her backside tight and lifting, lowering . . . sliding her over his rigid length again and again. Faster, harder. Until their bodies met with resounding, erotic smacks of skin against skin.

Her brow fell to his shoulder. He could tell from the helpless whimpers of pleasure rising from her throat, she was close to the edge. He was already dangling over the edge, clinging to it by his gritted teeth. Pleasure buzzed up and down his spine, desperate for an outlet.

Hold out, he told himself. *Just a minute more.*

He needed to feel her body convulse around him, hear the cries she made when the pleasure hit. His pleasure would be meaningless without hers.

Knowing full well it would shred the last remnants of his control, he arched his hips for deeper penetration and quickened his thrusts. Her breath came hot and fast against his ear. Her nails bit into the soft flesh of his nape, and her breasts galloped against his chest. He was losing his battle for restraint, careening full-speed toward what was sure to be the most devastating pleasure of his life.

"Love, I can't hold back."

"Stay," she said. "Stay with me."

"Come," he forced through gritted teeth. "Come with me."

They stayed together, and they came together. Bucking, gasping, clutching each other tight. With the first tight, delicious pulse of her climax, she pulled him straight over the edge into bliss. Somehow her mouth found his, and they swallowed each other's cries of passion. Bram thought he would burst from his skin with elation. The blinding pleasure of his climax was only eclipsed by the fierce joy of filling her with his seed.

She was his now, forever. And he was hers, body and soul. They were one.

"Stay," she murmured, slumping forward and pressing her damp brow to his chin. "Stay with me."

His heart squeezed. He wouldn't desert her, ever. But he had orders now, and she needed to get away from this place. "Come," he said. "Come with me."

She made a sound of incredulity.

"I'm perfectly serious. It's not exactly a pleasure cruise, but I have guaranteed passage to the Continent next week. Come with me. As my wife."

Her brow creased. "But . . . I thought you believed women don't belong on campaign."

He forced down the instinctive surge of worry. "Most don't. But you're stronger than most. You know how to look out for yourself. We'll sail from Portsmouth, and the captain can marry us on board. We'll honeymoon in Portugal." He skipped a light touch up her spine, tangled his fingers in her hair. "It's beautiful there, Susanna. Vineyards and olive trees. An ocean so warm and blue. Groves of citrus, overburdened with fruit. Imagine, wading ankle-deep in lemons and oranges. The scent haunts you for days." He nuzzled her neck. "We'll let a villa by the sea. We'll make love on sandy beaches."

"I was thinking it might be nice to make love in a bed, just the once."

"I'll buy you the finest bed you ever imagined. Heaped with mattresses three feet thick. Sheets of silk and the softest down pillows."

"It sounds lovely, but . . ."

"But nothing. Just say yes."

She lifted herself off his flagging erection and resettled on his lap. Her lip folded under her teeth, and her eyes were downcast. Maybe he was pushing her too hard, too fast. He took his time refastening his breeches, giving her a moment to contemplate.

"I know this day has been devastating for you. You're feeling confused, overwhelmed, betrayed. But I'm here to tell you, there's only one decision you need to make right now. And that's to trust me. Trust me to look after your happiness, Susanna. I swear, I will not let you down."

"I do trust you. I'd trust you with my life. But think of the village, Bram. All the young ladies."

He caught her face in his hands, forcing her to meet his gaze. "Think of *you*. Brilliant, beautiful, remarkable you. You do great things here in Spindle Cove, but I know you're capable of far more. Let me show you the world, Susanna. More than that, let me show the world *you*. Don't let fear hold you back."

"I can't help but feel a little scared. You're asking me to leave behind everything and everyone I know, and you haven't even said . . ." She went silent.

Ah. So that was the problem. She was waiting to hear his feelings. He should have guessed as much. Hadn't labeling those emotions always been the sticking point with her?

At that moment, the air trembled with the force of a distant explosion. With a surprised cry, she huddled into the protection of his coat. Overhead, the sky burst into sparkling trails of gold.

She stared up in wonder. "Am I hallucinating, or are those fireworks?"

He swore with amusement. "Those can only be Colin's doing."

Another whistling rocket soared into the air, exploding into silver sparks. Bram's heart lit up like a Roman candle. This was just like the first time they'd met. She was in his arms, so soft and warm. The perfect place to land. And she trusted him to keep and protect her, while the world exploded around them.

He turned her face to his. Her pupils sparkled, mirroring the fireworks overhead. But even those glittering reflections couldn't outshine the emotion in her eyes.

Ridiculous, how damned nervous he felt. He was a big, strong man. All she asked of him were three tiny syllables. But somehow, it seemed easier to order his life around the sentiment than voice it aloud. What if he said the words, and they still weren't enough?

He wet his lips and steeled his nerve. "Susanna fair. I . . . God, how I—"

Boom.

His words were stolen by a fresh explosion—a louder, earthbound, bone-jarring blast.

After that, all they heard were screams.

Chapter Twenty-six

O h Lord." Susanna's heart stalled. "What's happened?"

There was so much noise, and she couldn't make sense of any of it. A loud ringing filled her ears. Her blood thundered in her chest. Frantic voices rose in indecipherable cries. Horses whinnied. The soles of her shoes slapped the packed-dirt lane.

She was running. When had she started running?

Bram paced her, loping at her side. His hand settled at the base of her spine, steadying her. Pushing her onward. They rounded the corner and joined the throng of people rushing toward the carriage house and stables.

There was blood. A great deal of it. She smelled it even before she glimpsed the spatter of red on the straw-covered ground. The pungent odor worked as a helpful antidote to the encroaching panic. She could not lose her head. Someone was wounded, and she had work to do.

"Who's injured?" she asked, elbowing a wailing Sally out of the way and pushing her way through the stable door. "What's happened here?"

"It's Finn." Lord Payne was there, pulling her through the crush of bodies, into an empty stall lit by a hanging carriage lamp. "He's been hurt."

To say Finn Bright had been hurt was rather an understatement. The boy's left leg was a raw, ragged horror below the knee. His foot, or what remained of it, dangled at a grotesque angle. White slivers of bone gleamed from the open wound.

Susanna knelt beside the boy. From the sickly pallor of his face, she could tell he'd already lost a great deal of blood. "We need to stop the bleeding, immediately."

Bram said, "We need a tourniquet. A girth or billet from the tack room will serve."

"In the meantime . . ." Susanna turned to Lord Payne. "Give me your cravat."

He complied, loosening the knot of his neck cloth with trembling, jerky motions and sliding the length of fabric loose. Susanna reached for it and wound it about Finn's calf just below the knee, pulling with all her might to cinch it.

That accomplished, she turned her attention to the boy. His breathing was shallow, and his gaze unfocused. The poor youth was going into shock.

"Finn," she said in a loud, clear voice, "can you hear me?"

He nodded. His teeth chattered as he whispered, "Yes, Miss Finch."

"I'm here." She put a hand to his cheek and tried to meet his gaze. "We're all here. We're going to have you put to rights just as soon as we can."

Aaron Dawes crouched at her side. "I'm readying a cart. We'll have to take him to the smithy for bonesetting."

She nodded her agreement. While Susanna dispensed salves and tinctures to the villagers, anything that required brute force—the setting of bones, the pulling of teeth, and so forth—all fell to Dawes, as the village blacksmith. Although, from the looks of Finn's wound, she wasn't at all sure this injury could be set. There was a very good possibility he would lose the foot entirely.

Assuming he lived.

She smoothed hair from Finn's sweaty brow. "Are you in a great deal of pain?"

"N-n-no," he said, shivering. "Just cold."

That wasn't a good sign.

Bram knew it, too. He handed her a buckled strap of strong, cured leather. As she wound the strap around Finn's leg, he found a horse blanket and draped it over the boy's torso.

"There now," he murmured. "Be strong, Finn."

Bram took the strap from Susanna's grip and yanked it tight, securing it much better than she could have done herself. Obviously, battle had given him a great deal more experience with wounds of this nature than with attacks of asthma. The blood loss instantly decreased.

Rufus knelt at his brother's head. Susanna could tell he was struggling to hold back tears. "Will he be all right, Miss Finch?"

"He'll be fine," she said, trying to convince herself. "But how did this happen?"

Lord Payne shook his head in dismay. "The fireworks. I meant them to be a surprise for tomorrow, but . . ." He turned his head to spit a violent curse. "Seems I can't touch a damned thing without ruining it. I was distracted, and the boys got it into their heads to test a few."

"But fireworks could not have caused a blast that strong. Could they?"

"No," he said. "That was the cannon."

"The cannon?" Dread sank like a stone to the bottom of her gut.

"After the fireworks, they coaxed Sir Lewis into a demonstration. The thing backfired."

Oh Lord.

"Where's my father?" Releasing Finn, she struggled to

gain her feet. She stood on tiptoe, craning her neck to view the group. "Papa?"

The men bustled about, preparing a cart to transport Finn to the smithy. Susanna forced her way through the crush of bodies. She found her father in the courtyard, picking through the cannon's wreckage.

"Damnation," he said in an anguished voice. "How did this happen?"

"Papa, don't!" She grabbed his arm just as he reached for a brass fragment. Leaning back with all her might, she tugged him away from the scene. "You'll burn yourself. You shouldn't be near this at all, with so much explosive still about."

Just then, a wafting spark landed in an open crate of fireworks, setting the packing straw alight and sending a rocket shooting sideways.

"Look out!" she cried, pushing her father to the ground and diving after him. She tripped and landed awkwardly, bouncing on her side. A half-buried rock crunched into her rib cage.

Ignoring her smarting ribs, she crawled to her father's side. "Are you well, Papa? Is your heart paining you?"

"How could it not?" Struggling up on an elbow, he lifted a handkerchief to his face, wiping away a mixture of tears and sweat. "What senseless destruction."

"It was an accident, Papa." *One that should have never happened.*

"I don't know what went wrong," he muttered. "Too much powder? A flaw in the casting? I was so certain this time."

"You've been certain several times before."

"Oh God," he moaned. "Such a tragedy. My beautiful cannon."

She stared at him, horrified. "*Papa.*" Smack. "To the devil with your cannon. Finn could die."

He blinked at her, stunned. Susanna was stunned, too. God help her, she'd cursed at her own father and smacked him in the face. It was awful. And satisfying.

"I'm sorry, Papa. But you earned that." She took advantage of his shock to press her hand to his throat and feel for his pulse. For a few horrific seconds, she couldn't find any heartbeat at all. But at last, her fingers located the elusive rhythm.

The beat was fast, but steady. Healthy and strong.

Tears of relief pressed to her eyes. Her father might be a selfish old man, enslaved to his ambition. Perhaps he'd never loved her the way a motherless, awkward girl yearned to be loved. But he had given her life. Not once, but twice. And he had given her this home she adored so much. He was her father, and she loved him. She didn't want to lose him today.

She flagged down a passing stable hand. "Take my father in to the housekeeper. Tell her Miss Finch says Sir Lewis must take to his bed and rest. No arguments."

With that settled, she turned back to the carriage house, where the men were hitching horses to the cart. The beasts stamped and whinnied, made nervous by the explosions and scent of blood.

The groom offered a hand, helping her into the cart to sit at Finn's knee. Her skirts crushed beneath her as she settled into the straw. Corporal Thorne and Aaron Dawes were already present, crouching on either side of Finn to keep him immobile. Thorne kept his hands clamped tight about the boy's calf, just above the tourniquet, adding the force of his grip to staunch the flow of blood.

"Go on ahead," Bram ordered the driver. He and his cousin prepared to mount their horses. "We'll catch you on the road."

The cart lurched into motion, turning off Summerfield

property and trundling down the dirt lane. They'd nearly covered the distance to the smithy by the time Susanna realized she wasn't the only woman in the cart.

Diana Highwood was there, holding Finn's head in her lap and wiping his brow with a lacy white handkerchief. "There, there," she murmured. "You're doing so well. The ride's almost over."

As they pulled into the smithy's small yard, Aaron Dawes vaulted from the cart and rushed ahead to throw open the doors. Bram slid from his horse and hurried to lift Finn in his arms and carry him inside. Thorne and Payne flanked him, to assist.

As Susanna alighted from the cart, she winced, feeling a sharp pain where she'd fallen. She paused for a moment, pressing a hand to her bruised side, until the pain subsided. Then she moved to follow the men inside the smithy.

Miss Highwood did the same.

Susanna caught the fair-haired beauty's arm. "Miss Highwood . . . Diana. This will be an unpleasant scene. I don't think you should be here." Susanna wasn't at all sure how *she* would make it through, herself. This went well beyond her usual realm of poultices and salves.

"I want to help," the young woman said, with clear-eyed resolve. "You all helped me, during my time of distress. You, Lord Rycliff, Mr. Dawes. Rufus and Finn, as well. I want to repay the kindness. I haven't the men's strength, or your knowledge, Miss Finch. But I'm not a swooning sort of girl, and I'll do anything I can."

Susanna regarded the young woman with admiration. Apparently, the delicate Miss Highwood was made of stronger stuff than everyone else had imagined . . . Susanna included.

Good for her.

"You'll be certain to step out, if it becomes too much?"

Diana nodded. "And I have my tincture, of course."

Susanna gave her arm a grateful squeeze before releasing it. "Then let's go in together."

Aaron Dawes hurried ahead of them all, clearing the tools from a long, wooden table and moving it to the center of the space. "Set him down here, my lord."

Bram hesitated for a moment, as if reluctant to let Finn go. But then he silently moved forward and lowered the moaning boy to the smooth, sanded surface. Thorne still held his viselike grip on Finn's wounded leg.

"Easy, Finn," Bram murmured. "We're going to take care of you." He turned to Dawes. "Laudanum?"

"I sent Rufus—"

"I'm here." Rufus dashed into the room, holding up a brown glass bottle. "Took it from All Things."

"I'll fetch a spoon or a cup," Miss Highwood offered.

"Save it for afterward," Dawes said. "He's already unconscious, and we can't wait for it to take effect." The smith poked gingerly at what had recently been a recognizable foot. "There's no saving it. I'll start readying the tools."

Susanna was saddened, but unsurprised. Even if the bone weren't splintered, the wound was an unholy mess—studded with bits of metal, boot leather, and other debris. It would prove impossible to clean thoroughly. If the blood loss didn't take Finn's life, infection would.

"What can I do?" Lord Payne asked. He stood at the edge of the room, his face ashen and drawn. "Dawes, give me something to do."

"Get the fire going. It's growing dark." The smith jerked his head toward the forge. "And there's a lamp in my cottage, across the way."

"I'll get the lamp," Diana said.

"Everyone, halt!" Bram shouted. He loomed over Finn,

his face hard and commanding. "No one is touching this boy's foot, do you hear me? I'm going for a surgeon."

Susanna winced. She ought to have known how Bram would receive this, after he'd so nearly lost his own leg. But that was a different sort of wound, incurred under much different circumstances.

Drawing up to his full height, Bram looked around the room and spoke with cool authority. "No one cuts into this boy. Not until I return. That's an order." He turned to his corporal. "Do you hear me, Thorne? No one touches him. You have my permission to use whatever means you must."

He turned and strode from the forge, leaving everyone stunned, staring blankly at one another. They all knew what Bram refused to admit—that preserving Finn's foot could mean losing his life.

"I'll talk to him," said Lord Payne, moving for the door.

Susanna stopped him. "Wait, my lord. Let me try."

A look of understanding passed between them. He nodded. "Stubborn fool never listens to me. Never listens to anyone, I'd wager. But he loves you, so perhaps there's that."

Susanna blinked at him, startled.

"Hasn't he said so yet?" Payne shrugged. "Cowardly bastard doesn't deserve you. Go on, now." He gave her a fond nudge.

Susanna rushed out of the smithy and into the yard, where Bram was readjusting his horse's saddle, preparing to mount.

"Bram, wait," she called, dashing to his side. "I know this is horrible for you. It's a tragedy, truly. But we can't wait on a surgeon's opinion tonight. Dawes must operate quickly, if Finn's to have any chance."

"I won't let you lame him. He's fourteen years old, for

Christ's sake. Full of a young boy's plans and dreams. Take that foot, and you take his whole future with it. The Brights aren't a privileged family. They work for their living. What kind of life is Finn going to have, with one leg?"

"I don't know. But at least he will *have* a life. If we delay, Finn will die."

"You don't know that, Susanna. I've seen a great many more wounds of this nature than you have. You may have a talent with herbs and such, but you're no surgeon."

"I . . ." She stepped back, feeling the sting of his rebuke. That ache in her ribs reasserted itself. "I know I'm not."

"Do you?" His jaw clenched as he tightened the saddle girth. "You seem eager enough to pretend. You'd sentence that boy to life as an invalid, just because you've been hurt in the past. You're letting your own fear of doctors put Finn at risk."

She grabbed his arm, forcing him to face her. "It's not my fears that are putting Finn at risk. It's yours, don't you see? You're still so caught on this notion that you can't be a whole man, can't be worth anything unless you prove you have two strong, perfectly functioning legs to carry you into battle. You'd even drag me along to Portugal before you'd admit otherwise. But this is not about you, Bram."

He shot her a defensive glare. "I hadn't planned to *drag* you anywhere, Susanna. I'd planned to take you willingly, happily—or not at all. Are you telling me you don't want to come?"

How could he put such choices to her, at a time like this?

"I love you. I want to be with you. But dashing off to Portugal next Tuesday, just because my father's a selfish, unfeeling old stick? It sounds romantic, to be sure . . . but also a bit juvenile. Aren't we both a little too old to be running away from home?"

"This may be your home, but it will never be mine."

"You're wrong, Bram. Home is where people need you." She gestured at the smithy. "And right now, the people in there need you desperately. Aaron Dawes needs every strong pair of hands to help. Finn needs you to stand beside him, and help him to be brave. To show him a man can be a man, whether he has two good legs or one. And after all is said and done, I'm going to need you to hold me. Because helping with this surgery is going to be the hardest thing I've ever done."

When he still didn't cease his preparations, a knot of fear formed in her throat. "Bram," she said, her voice breaking. "You can't do this. Not an hour ago, you promised to never leave me."

He ceased wrestling with the saddle and released an angry sigh. "Susanna. Not an hour ago, you claimed to trust me with your life."

"We're not off to a very good start then, are we?"

"I suppose we're not."

They stared at each other. Then he turned, placed his foot in the stirrup, and swiftly mounted his horse.

That pain in her side returned. Though logically, she knew the pain to be placed too low, she couldn't help but suspect her heart was breaking. "I can't believe you're actually going."

"I never had a thought of doing otherwise, Susanna." The horse danced under him, sensing its rider's impatience to be off. "The only question is whether I have a reason to return. If you let them take that boy's foot while I'm gone . . . I'll never be able to look at you again."

With that, he turned his horse and left.

She stood watching him until he disappeared into the darkening night. Then she turned and walked numbly back to the forge.

When she entered alone, all present turned to her.

"Lord Rycliff has gone," she said, although it hardly seemed to need saying. "How is Finn?"

"Weakening." Aaron Dawes's face was grave. "I have to do it soon."

Everyone looked to Thorne, who'd been ordered by Bram to stop them. The grim, stalwart officer who had once kept vigil at a wounded Bram's bedside, pistol cocked, ready to fire at the first gleam of a bone saw. Would he fight them now? Between Dawes and Payne, she supposed they had the corporal outnumbered. But even if they had a dozen men, the smart odds would still seem to favor Thorne.

"Corporal Thorne," she said, "I know you are loyal to your lord. But angry as he is right now, if he returns to find this boy dead, he'll be devastated. We must allow Mr. Dawes to operate."

She hadn't stopped loving Bram when he rode away from her. No matter what threats or ultimatums he'd given, she was looking out for Finn's well-being *and* his.

"Do you understand?" she asked. "We have to save Finn's life, or Bram will always feel responsible. We all care about him. And we don't want him to live under that burden of guilt."

Recognition gleamed sharp in the corporal's eyes. And Susanna found herself wondering just what burdens of guilt this quiet, ruthless man shouldered.

Thorne nodded. "Do it, then."

ram spent the three-hour ride to Brighton steaming with righteous anger, feeling like a misunderstood, maligned hero.

He spent the three-hour ride back to Spindle Cove swamped with fierce regret, feeling like a perfect jackass.

Daniels wasn't helping.

"Let me understand this," his friend said, when they stopped to change horses halfway. "Now that I'm more than half awake."

Daniels paced the lit area in front of the coaching house stables, pushing a hand through his wild black hair. "A boy got his foot blown apart in a cannon explosion. You had a capable blacksmith and an experienced apothecary all prepared to amputate. But you told them all to hold off for eight or nine hours. So you could ride breakneck to the Brighton Barracks . . ." He motioned to the right. "Haul me out of a warm bed, and drag me all the way back . . ." He waved the same hand to the left. "To do what, exactly? Pronounce the boy dead?"

"No. You're going to save his leg. The way you saved mine."

"Bram." The surgeon's flint-gray eyes were unforgiving. "A lone bullet passed *through* your knee in a straight, clean trajectory. To be sure, it tore your ligaments up—but at least it left edges that could be sewn together. Heavy artillery wounds are like shark attacks. All that's left is chum. You've seen battle. I shouldn't have to tell you that."

Bram scrubbed a hand over his face, absorbing the censure. "Just shut up and ride."

Joshua Daniels and Susanna Finch were two of the most intelligent people Bram had ever known. If the two of them agreed on something, that pretty well guaranteed Bram was wrong. Damn it all. If he hadn't torn off in such a hurry, he likely would have come around to reason, eventually. But he'd gone a little mad at the idea of just standing by helpless, allowing Finn to be permanently lamed. Susanna was right; after all his own struggles to recover his strength, it had hit too close to home.

But Susanna was stubborn, he told himself. Headstrong and brave. She'd never listened to him when it didn't suit her, so why should she start now? No matter what dire proclamations he'd made, surely she wouldn't have heeded them. Not if Finn's life hung in the balance. But then again, he'd told Thorne to use any means necessary to prevent an amputation. And Thorne had some formidable, ruthless means at his disposal.

Jesus Christ, what had he done?

Day was breaking as they rode over the crest and caught their first glimpse of Spindle Cove. His heart lurched at the sight. The charming little village, nestled snug in its valley. The ancient castle ruins, standing sentinel on the bluffs. The cove, calm and blue, studded with small fishing crafts. Warm, buttery sunlight melting over the ridge.

Susanna was right. He was lord of this quiet little nook of England, and there was pride in that. Spindle Cove had a claim on his honor and his heart. And for the first time in his life, Bram knew he had a true home. He could only hope she'd see fit to welcome him back.

They reached the smithy in a matter of minutes. He launched himself from the saddle the moment his gelding slowed to a walk. While the horses made good use of a nearby trough of rainwater, Bram led Daniels into the small, timber-framed building. They found the forge empty of all souls, save one. Finn Bright lay stretched on a long table in the center of the room, draped with linen from the neck down. Eyes closed.

The boy was as pale as the sheet that covered him. The smells of blood and singed flesh hung in the air. For a moment, Bram feared the worst had happened, and this new day would mean the boy's death on his conscience.

"He'll live." Dawes stood in the opposite entry, filling the entire doorway. He looked to have recently bathed. Damp hair clung to his brow, and he was still pulling down a fresh shirt. "Provided he doesn't go septic," the man qualified, "he'll live."

"Thank God." Bram sucked in a breath. "Thank God."

He knew he tossed out that phrase all the time, but this time he meant it. He was really, truly thankful to God. And unsure how he'd ever repay the debt.

"But there was no saving his foot, my lord. The blast had done most of the work already. I just did my best to make it clean."

"I understand. You did right."

Bram stared down at the boy's blood-drained, perspiring face. Fortunately, he looked to have been dosed with enough laudanum to take him beyond the pain. For now. When he woke, Finn would find himself in a vivid, burning hell. That much, Bram had experienced.

Clearing his throat, he introduced Daniels. "He's a surgeon and a friend of mine. He'll see to the boy from here."

Daniels threw back the linen drape from Finn's leg. Bram winced.

"It's not pretty, but it ought to heal cleanly," Daniels said, assessing the stump. "You do good work, Mr. Dawes."

Dawes nodded his thanks, wiping his hands on a small towel. Bram looked past the man, to the cottage adjacent. A fair-haired woman was sleeping at the table, her head bent over an extended arm.

He walked toward Dawes, giving Daniels some space to examine the boy. "Is that Miss Highwood?"

Dawes shot a glance over his shoulder and exhaled roughly. "Yes."

"What is she doing here?"

"Honestly, my lord? Damned if I know. But she's been here all night, and all the screaming and blood in the world couldn't persuade her to leave. Golden hair and an iron will, that one. Lord Payne's gone to borrow Keane's curricle, so he can drive her home."

"What about Miss Finch? Where is she?"

"Lord Rycliff." A thin, weak voice called to him. "Is that you?"

"Aye, Finn. It's me." Bram hurried back to the table and crouched at the boy's eye level. "How are you feeling?"

Stupid question.

"S-s-sorry," the wide-eyed lad scraped out. "My fault. I shouldn't have—"

"No, no." Guilt twisted in Bram's chest. "You're not to blame, Finn. It was an accident." An accident that should have never occurred. "Don't try to talk. There'll be time enough for that later."

He reached for the flask of whiskey in his breast pocket, with every intent of gifting it to Finn. The flask had nursed Bram through his own leg injury, and the youth had earned his right to drink like a man. But then he thought better of the gift, considering the absent Mr. Bright's struggles with liquor. He didn't want to send the boy down the same troubled path.

He gave Finn a warm pat on the shoulder instead. "I know it's hell, but you'll come through it. You're strong."

"I'm worried," Finn said through gritted teeth. "How am I to help Mum and Sally with the shop now?"

"In a hundred ways. We'll see you fitted with the best false foot possible—no pirate peg leg. You'll be walking and working again in no time. Or I'll send you to school, if you like. There are plenty of ways for a man to be useful that don't involve unloading crates." Or marching into battle, he thought.

"Cor, school? But I couldn't accept . . ."

"No arguments, Finn. I'm the lord, and this is my militia. I won't let it be said my wounded men don't have an excellent pension."

"One good thing's come of it." With a weak flash of humor, Finn glanced in the direction of his amputated foot. "No one will ever confuse me with Rufus now, will they?"

"No." A smile warmed Bram's face. "No, they won't. And I'll tell you a secret. The ladies find a wounded soldier hopelessly romantic. They'll be buzzing after you like honeybees."

"Suppose they will. Rufus may have two feet, but I'm still the one what danced with Miss Charlotte. Twice." He broke off, coughing.

Bram took the cup of water Dawes offered and held it to Finn's lips, helping him lift his head to drink.

"Does my mother know?" the youth asked, reclining again with a wince.

"Yes," Dawes said. "She was here earlier, during the surgery. But Sally and Rufus had to take her home, she was so overset."

"I'll take her word that you're well and asking for her," Bram said.

"Tell her to make certain little Daisy don't bang on my drum." The lad's eyes flew open. "Cor. The review. It's meant to be today, isn't it?"

"Don't you worry about that."

"But how can the men march if I can't drum?"

"They won't," Bram told him. "We'll cancel the review." Nothing lost there, really. After the revelation of Sir Lewis's deceit, he knew the militia never had much purpose, aside from providing fanfare for a doomed cannon's debut.

"But the review must go on," Finn said. "Don't call it off on my account. Everyone's worked so hard."

"Yes, but—"

With a grimace of pain, Finn struggled up on his elbow. "If the militia's found lacking, Miss Finch said the ladies would be called home. They need this place, and my family's store needs them. We've worked too hard to give up now, my lord. All of us . . ." He slumped back to the table, overtaxed by the effort of his speech.

"Rest, Finn." Bram dragged a hand through his hair. Guilt consumed him. After all their hard work, he didn't know how to tell the villagers the task had been rather meaningless all along. Just an exercise in bloated pride for a fool man.

Make that *two* fool men, if he included himself.

From outside the forge, hurried footsteps approached.

"You can't do this." That was Thorne's voice, rough and low.

"Yes I can." A female voice, drawing closer.

"Damn it, woman. I told you no."

"Well, let's see what Lord Rycliff has to say about it, shall we?"

The pair entered the smithy, and Bram's jaw dropped.

"I tried to stop her," Thorne said, throwing a gesture of disgust.

Her?

Her. Yes, of course. He recognized her easily by the port-wine birthmark at her temple. But in every other respect, Miss Kate Taylor was dressed the part of a drummer boy. With her petite height and her light, slender figure, she easily fit the militia uniform.

"What are you doing?" Bram asked. He waved at the red coat and buff breeches. "Whose are these?"

"Finn's, of course," she said. "I'm him today. You need a drummer, and I'm the only one who can stand in."

"Miss Taylor, I can't ask you to—"

"You haven't asked me. I've offered."

Thorne caught Bram's eye. The man steeled his jaw. "No," he said. "You can't allow it."

For more than five years, Thorne had served under Bram's leadership. He'd been not only Bram's right hand, but his right leg, when he'd needed one. And never—not once, in those five years of drilling, marching, digging, and fighting—had Thorne so much as hesitated to obey Bram's smallest command. He'd certainly never issued one of his own.

Until today.

"We're wasting time here," Miss Taylor said, earnestly approaching him. "We have only a few hours to prepare for the drill, and you must let me join you. Unlike the other ladies here, I have no family, no guardian. Spindle Cove is my only home, and I want to help in any way I can. I didn't do this for nothing."

With a dramatic sweep, she doffed her tall, black shako headgear to reveal her hair. Or the lack of it. The girl had clipped her chestnut-brown locks to collar length, and pinned them back to imitate a boyish crop.

"Christ Almighty," Thorne muttered. "What have you done to yourself?"

Miss Taylor touched a fingertip to her earlobe and bravely blinked tears from her eyes. "It will grow back. It's only hair."

It's only hair.

Bram's heart pinched in his chest. She reminded him so much of Susanna that day on the green, bravely offering her long, lovely hair if it meant keeping Finn and Rufus off the volunteer rolls. If only he'd listened to her.

Where was she? He was growing desperate to see her.

"Lord Rycliff," Miss Taylor said, "there are others, too. Everyone's gathered at the Bull and Blossom."

"The Bull and Blossom?"

"The tea shop," she explained. "And tavern. Since it's both now, the Fosburys made a new sign. Anyhow, what with the goings-on at Summerfield, we thought it best to move tonight's party there. And most of the village has assembled this morning. Everyone's waiting on your command."

"It's really not necessary," Bram said, halfheartedly.

"Perhaps not," said Aaron Dawes. "But maybe we want to see it through anyway."

What an idea. To go forward with this militia review and grand party today, not for Sir Lewis's pride or for Bram's—but for Spindle Cove's.

"We've all worked so hard, and looked so forward to today. We want to do it for ourselves, and for Finn. And for you, Lord Rycliff." Miss Taylor plucked at her sleeve. "Miss Finch said you'd be coming back, and we must be ready to do you proud."

"Susanna said that?"

"Yes." The girl clasped her hands in delight. "Oh, Lord Rycliff. I just knew the two of you were in love. I knew you couldn't leave her." She bounced on her toes. "This is all going to be so very romantic."

"With all that cooing, no one will take you for a boy," Bram said, chuckling. Truthfully, he was trying not to bounce on his own toes with excitement. "Where is she now?"

"She's gone home to have a rest and a change of dress, but she promised to meet us at the castle."

Straightening his coat and running his hands over his hair, Bram looked to the other men. "Then what are we waiting for? Let's go."

"Where is she?" Hours later, Bram stood impatient at the castle gateway, scanning the path for any sign of Susanna. All morning long, folk had streamed up the ancient road, traveling by cart, on horseback, on foot—some coming from ten or more miles away to watch the review. But none of them were the one woman Bram wanted to see.

"Most likely she fell asleep," Thorne said. "She worked hard all night."

"Perhaps I should ride down to Summerfield."

"I've already stalled for time as much as I can," Colin said. "If it were just a matter of the crowd, I'd say hold off. But generals and dukes aren't used to being kept waiting. And perhaps Miss Finch needs her rest."

Bram nodded his reluctant acknowledgment. The review itself wouldn't take long. If Susanna hadn't arrived by the end, he'd ride over to Summerfield straightaway.

Striding to the center of the green, he motioned for his men to fall in line. He surveyed them with no small measure of pride—his cadre of willing volunteers, all fitted out in their new uniforms and assembled to serve his command. What a band they were. Shepherds, fishermen, clergymen. A smith, a baker—no candlestick maker, but a boy, a young woman . . .

And a lamb. Dinner stood at his knee, tricked out in a jaunty red ribbon and bell.

Make no mistake, this *was* Spindle Cove.

Under festooned canopies, the visiting dignitaries and the ladies of the Queen's Ruby sat ready to observe. The assembled villagers and country folk lined the castle's perimeter. Children too short to see over the crowd had climbed atop the walls. Gaily colored banners flew from each turret.

With everyone in place, Bram mounted his horse and addressed his men. And woman. "I want you all to remember, we're not alone when we take to the field. There are others counting on us to succeed. All the ladies of the Queen's Ruby. Finn. And Miss Finch. Their faith in us— it's sewn into the linings of our coats, rolled into every powder cartridge. And it's in every beat of our hearts. We will not let them down."

He looked from one solemn, determined face to the other, making eye contact with every last one of his men. To Miss Taylor, he gave a smile.

"Vicar, say us a blessing, if you will." Bowing his head, he muttered, "We're going to need it."

Between the catastrophe yesterday and the subsequent lack of sleep, Bram wasn't sure how the men would perform. But despite his misgivings, the drill went surprisingly well. The wheel maneuvers that had given them such fits in recent weeks came off smoothly—even the backward one. There was a bit of a misstep with the obliques, due to Fosbury's persistent confusion of right and left. But with the firings, they ended on a high note.

Thanks to Susanna's tutelage, the men fired in swift, impressive unison—by file and as a company.

As planned, they capped the display with a *feu de joie*. All the men lined up in a single file, loaded their muskets, and fired in quick succession—much like opera dancers rippling kicks down the line. The wave of smoke and fire swept from one end of the file to the other.

When it cleared, the crowd broke into cheers and applause.

Bram looked from man to man. He could only imagine that they, like he, were quietly bursting with pride and relief. Only one thing could make this moment brighter.

"Bram!"

And that was it. Susanna's voice. She'd come. She was finally here, and she'd arrived in time to witness her friends' triumph.

"Bram!" she called again. Her voice was breathless. She sounded as excited as he felt.

He dismounted his horse and whirled on his boot heel, searching the crowd for her.

There she was, standing in a ruined archway near the gate. The previous night's trials had worn on her. She was pale, and shadows pooled under her eyes. Her hair was disheveled. Her Indian shawl drooped to the dirt. If someone had painted him this exact picture a year ago and said, *Someday, you will want to kiss this woman more than you want your next breath* . . . Bram would have laughed, and made some joke about artists and opium.

But today, it was the truth.

"Susanna."

As he approached, she leaned against the stone arch. "*Bram.*"

"I'm sorry." He had to get those words out first. "So sorry. I should never have said what I did. I shouldn't have left. I was an idiot, and you did just the right thing for Finn. Thank you."

She didn't respond. Simply stood there in the doorway, looking pale and stunned. Was a ready apology from his quarter truly that much of a shock?

Perhaps it was. He *could* be a stubborn fool.

He took a few more slow steps in Susanna's direction, stopping less than an arm's length from where she stood. It was killing him, not to take her in his arms. "I should have come to Summerfield earlier, just to say that. But Miss Taylor said you'd wanted to see this through . . ." He motioned around at the festivities. "Everyone's worked so hard, and . . . And they did it all for you, Susanna. It went brilliantly, and it was all for you."

She swallowed hard and pressed a hand to her side. She was silent for so long, he began to worry.

For good reason, apparently.

"Bram, I—" Her eyes went wide, and she drew a sharp, gasping breath. Where she clutched her side, her knuckles went white. "Bram, I feel so strange."

"Susanna?"

It was a fortunate thing he'd come within an arm's length of her. Because when she collapsed, he had only an instant to break her fall.

usanna loathed being ill. Absolutely despised and feared this sense of being out of control of her own body. And this . . . episode, or illness, or whatever it was . . . was worse than anything she'd felt in years.

The discomfort had been coming on all night, but it had worsened sharply after she'd left Summerfield. At one point, she'd stopped to sit by the side of the road, uncertain whether her feet could even carry her forward. But then she'd heard the sounds of the review floating down to her. Drumbeats, rifles firing in unison.

Bram.

Encouraged by the sounds, she'd somehow managed to gain her feet and stumble the rest of the distance up the path. But once she reached the archway, she couldn't take one more step.

She couldn't breathe. Her chest hurt, so very much. She'd forgotten this kind of pain existed. Pain that seemed a tangible entity all its own. A monstrous thing, made of sharp edges and bright colors.

But Bram was there. And despite his angry words at their parting, he *had* managed to look at her again. With a smile and apologies, even. His arms were around her, and his soothing whispers stroked away some of her fear.

"It's all right, love. It's all right. Just rest and let me help."

They carried her beneath a canopy and laid her on the ground. Cool grass and springy turf crushed beneath her weight. She opened her eyes. The slanting patterns of the canopy's striped canvas both amazed and overwhelmed her.

This couldn't be real. She couldn't be *dying*. Not now.

But perhaps she was. She heard people discussing her. That's what people did, when they thought you were dying. *Discuss* you, while standing right nearby. She'd been through this before.

"Poor Miss Finch. What's happened?"

"Perhaps she's just overtired. It was a hellish night."

"Miss Finch, overtired? I can't believe that, not her. She's too strong."

Well, if she had to die, at least it would be here—in her beloved castle, with Bram at her side, surrounded by so many people she loved. She could feel their concern, wrapping around her like warm cotton wool.

"I'm a surgeon," some newcomer said. He spoke with a Northern accent. "If you'd all clear out, I'd like to have a look."

Oh God. Not a surgeon. Bram's heat receded, and she clutched at his hand. *Don't leave me.*

"It's all right," he said. "I'm not going anywhere."

"Last night," she forced out, squeezing his hand. Every breath was pure, stabbing pain, made worse by how hard she had to fight for the torturous privilege. "By the stables, I . . . fell." Another painful gasp. "My ribs, I think."

"Her ribs," Bram said. "She says it's her ribs."

"Let me have a look, then."

Out of the corner of her eye, she saw a black leather satchel being opened. The very image made her want to scream. Nothing good came out of those satchels. Only pain, and more pain.

Someone cut, then tore her bodice into two halves. She felt so exposed. The instinct to struggle seized her.

"Be calm, love. Be calm." Bram stroked her hair. "This is Daniels. He's a friend of mine, and a brilliant field surgeon. He's the one who saved my leg. You can trust him. I do."

You can trust him. No, she didn't think she could. She tried to stay calm, drawing quick, shallow breaths as this Mr. Daniels listened and prodded and assessed. All the while, panic raced through her veins.

"You say you suffered some injury to your ribs, miss?"

She nodded. "Last night."

"But at the time, the pain wasn't this severe."

She shook her head.

"What's wrong with her?" Bram asked.

"Well, if you want my guess . . ."

"No, I don't want your guess," Bram said angrily. "I want the damned answer."

Mr. Daniels was unruffled by this outburst, which gave Susanna some reassurance. He and Bram truly must be close friends.

"I am certain," said Daniels patiently, "she has broken some ribs. But broken ribs alone should not cause this sort of difficulty and pain. Not suddenly, after so many hours. But if she's been going about physical activity since the initial wound, the broken bones may have caused her some bleeding, inside. Over the hours, the blood has been gathering inside her chest with no outlet. Now it's pressing on her lungs and making it difficult for her to breathe. It's called a hemo—"

"—thorax," Susanna finished. Hemothorax. Yes, she thought grimly. She'd read about that. It made perfect sense.

"Ah," said the doctor, in a tone of surprise. "So the patient is both lovely and clever."

"She's also mine," Bram growled. "Don't get any ideas. She's mine."

Susanna squeezed his hand. That sort of talk was so medieval and possessive. And she loved him for it.

"Yes, well." Daniels cleared his throat and reached for his satchel. "The good news is, this is all too common on the battlefield."

"How on earth is that good news?" Bram asked.

"Let me rephrase. The good news is, I've seen this many times, and there's a simple cure. It's a newer, controversial treatment. But I've used it in the field, with great success. All we need to do is drain the blood from her chest, and the condition will resolve."

"No." Wild with fear, she struggled to make the words. "Bram, no. Don't . . . don't let him bleed me."

"You can't bleed her," he said. "She had too much of that in her youth, and it nearly did her in." He turned her wrist scars-up for the surgeon's view.

"So I see."

And then Mr. Daniels did the truly astonishing. Something none of those doctors or surgeons in her youth had ever done. He crouched at her shoulder, where she could look him in the eye. And then he talked *to* her, not *about* her. As if she had a brain of her own, and full control over her own body.

"Miss Finch, if I can say it without risking a thumping from Bramwell here, you strike me as a very intelligent woman. I hope you will understand and believe me then, when I tell you this is no quack bloodletting. The pressure in your chest is unlikely to resolve on its own. If we do nothing, there is a good chance you'll die. Of course, there's always the risk of infection with such a procedure. But you're young and strong. I like your chances against a fever better than I like your chances against this." He thumped lightly on her distended chest, and it sounded strangely dull. "I won't do anything without your agreement, however."

Susanna regarded him with keen appraisal. He was young, it seemed. Scarcely older than she. His hair was unruly, but his eyes were calm and intelligent. Still, on this short acquaintance, she didn't know that she could bring herself to trust any man who carried one of those horrific black satchels.

But there was someone else. Someone she could always trust to protect her.

She looked to Bram. "Do you . . . trust him . . . with my life?"

"Absolutely."

"Then . . ." She pressed his hand and sucked another painful breath through a rapidly narrowing straw. "I trust you. *Love* you." She needed to say that, once more.

Relief washed over his face. "Do it," Bram told his friend.

She could bear this. So long as it was her choice, and Bram was beside her . . . she could bear anything.

Or so she thought, until she glimpsed the silver gleam of a blade, pressed against her pale skin. The sight made her recoil in horror. Her whole body flinched.

Daniels lifted the scalpel. "Where is that blacksmith? We may have to restrain her."

No. Please God, no. All the nightmarish memories came rushing back. The footmen, pinning her to the bed. The sharp fire of the lancet against her wrist.

"No," Bram said firmly. "No restraints. No one touches her but me." He turned her head to face him. "Don't look at what he's doing. Only look at me."

She obeyed, skimming her gaze over the handsome features of his face and letting herself sink into those familiar jade-green eyes.

He interlaced his fingers with hers. With the other hand, he stroked her hair. So tenderly.

"Now listen to me, Susanna. Do you remember that first night we met in the cove? I can refresh your memory, if need be. You were wearing that horrid bathing costume, and I was wearing a medieval torture device."

She smiled. Only he could make her smile at a time like this.

"That night, you suggested we make some promises to each other. Well, we're going to make them now. I'm going to promise not to leave. And you're going to promise not to die. All right?"

She opened her mouth to speak, but no sound came out.

"I promise to stay at your side," he said, "until this is all over. And for the lifetime after that. Now, make your promise to me." His eyes glistened, and his voice was rough with emotion. "Promise me, Susanna. Tell me you won't die. I can't go on without you, love."

She gritted her teeth, and managed a tiny nod.

Then the blade pierced her. And if there'd been any air left in her lungs, she would have screamed.

The pain was like fire. Burning and intense. But relief followed swiftly, like a quenching rain.

That first rush of air into her lungs . . . she was dizzied by it, turned upside-down. The world narrowed, and she felt as though she'd stumbled into a deep, dark well. As she fell down and down, she heard distant voices. Bram's. The surgeon's.

"I believe she's gone unconscious."

"Perhaps that's a mercy."

Yes, she thought, swirling and tumbling into the darkness.

Yes, it was a mercy indeed.

—Chapter Twenty-nine—

he'll recover soon enough. If she doesn't take a fever.

Those had been Daniels's words to him, after the procedure was complete. But it could not have been so easy. A few hours later—almost as soon as they'd seen her settled back at Summerfield— the fever had set in.

Now Bram hadn't left her side in days.

He kept an unceasing vigil at her bedside. He passed the hours tending her in small ways. Coaxing her to take spoonfuls of willow bark tea, or sponging the fevered sweat from her brow. Sometimes he talked to her. Read aloud to her from the newspaper, or told her stories of his childhood and his years on campaign. Anything that crossed his mind. Other times, he shamelessly pleaded with her, begging her to just wake up and be well.

He ate, when coaxed. The indefinite postponement of the village festivities had left Spindle Cove with a surfeit of Fosbury's cakes. There always seemed to be a tray of the pastel-iced things close at hand. Bram found himself developing a taste for them, in a wistful sort of way.

He slept, infrequently and fitfully. He prayed, with a regularity and intensity that would do a Benedictine proud.

Others came and went from the sickroom. Daniels. The housemaids. Sir Lewis Finch. Even Colin and Thorne came by. They all urged Bram to take a break now and then. Go downstairs for a proper meal, they said. Have a rest in the bedchamber they'd made up down the corridor.

He refused all their well-meant suggestions. Every last one. He'd made a promise not to leave her. To stay at her side, until this was done. And he'd be damned if he'd give Susanna any excuse to drop her end of the bargain.

So long as he stayed right here, she could not die.

Sir Lewis sat with him one afternoon, occupying the chair on the other side of the bed. The old man rubbed the back of his neck. "She looks better today, I think."

Bram nodded. "She is better. We think."

That morning, as he'd been adjusting the pillows beneath her head, his forearm had brushed against her cheek. Instead of scalding with fever, her skin had felt cool to his touch. He'd called in Daniels to confirm it, not trusting himself after so many hours of vain hoping.

But it seemed to be true. The fever had broken. Now it only remained to be seen if she would wake from it with no ill effects. The vigil was easier now, and yet unbearable in its suspense.

"Sir Lewis, there's something you should know." Bram took Susanna's hand in his. It lay wonderfully cool and limp across his palm. "I plan to marry her."

"Oh. You *plan* to marry her?" The old man fixed him with a watery blue stare. "That's how you ask a gentleman for his only daughter's hand? Bramwell, I would think your father had raised you better than that."

"Your blessing would be welcome," he said evenly. "But no, I'm not asking you for her hand. Susanna's wise enough to make her own decisions."

That was as close as he could bring himself to requesting Sir Lewis's approval. He damned well wouldn't ask the man's permission. As far as Bram was concerned, the moment Sir Lewis had lit that cannon fuse, he'd surrendered all responsibility for Susanna's welfare. The old man had endangered his daughter's work, her friends, her very life—and all in the name of glory.

Bram would protect her now. As her husband, if she'd have him.

"My only daughter, getting married. She is all grown now, isn't she?" With a trembling hand, Sir Lewis touched his sleeping daughter's hair. "Seems just yesterday she was a babe in arms."

"That wasn't yesterday," Bram said, unable to restrain himself. "Yesterday, she lay in this bed, burning with fever and hovering near death."

"I know. I know. And you blame me. You think me a self-serving monster." He paused, as if waiting for Bram to argue otherwise.

Bram didn't.

"One day," Sir Lewis said, pointing to himself, "this self-serving monster's greatest invention will be perfected, and it will see battle. That cannon will shorten the duration of sieges. Allow troops to attack from a safer distance. It will save the lives and limbs of many English soldiers."

"Perhaps."

"I love my daughter." The old man's voice went hoarse. "You'll never know the sacrifices I've made for her. You have no idea."

"Perhaps not, but I know the sacrifices she's made for you. And you have no idea what a remarkable person she's become. You're so absorbed in your own work, your own accomplishments. I've no doubt you do love Susanna, Sir Lewis. But you're bollocks bad at it."

Sir Lewis paled. "How dare you speak to me that way?"

"I believe I can speak to you any way I wish. I'm the Earl of Rycliff, remember?"

"I should have never secured you that title."

"It's not in your power to take it back. I'm the lord now." Bram drew a slow, deep breath, trying to calm his rage. He was furious with Sir Lewis for putting Susanna and Finn and all the others in danger. But with any good fortune, this man would soon be his father-in-law. For Susanna's sake, they would need to make peace.

"My father held you in the highest regard," Bram said. "So do I, on professional merits. You're a brilliant inventor, without question. Your creations have helped the British army prevail on many a battlefield, and as many times as I've lifted my Finch pistol in defense, I probably owe you my life. But your daughter, Sir Lewis . . ."

Bram turned his gaze to the sleeping Susanna and squeezed her hand. "Your daughter puts people back together. Young ladies, no less—who defy all rational formula. And she still finds time for the occasional washed-up, wounded officer. I may not owe her my life, but I owe her my heart."

His eyes burned at the corners. He blinked hard. "If you think that rifled cannon will be your greatest invention, you're a fool. Your greatest invention is right here, sleeping in this bed. Susanna is your legacy. And in your pride, you almost lost her."

Bram had almost lost her, too. He hadn't truly allowed himself to consider what that would mean, earlier. He'd been too focused on the next spoonful of tea, the new change of wound dressing, the fresh cloth for her brow. But now that her fever had broken, and Daniels had given her excellent odds for a full recovery . . . Jesus. The possibilities swept through him like a freezing, gale-force wind. A blast strong enough to strip the earth of everything warm and green.

He'd almost lost her. If this hellish ordeal had taught him one lesson, it was to never allow his pride to come between them again.

"You're right, Bramwell." The old man's eyes brimmed with tears. "I know you're right. I can only hope she'll find it in her heart to forgive me."

"Of course she will, good as she is. But hoping for her forgiveness is *not* the only thing you can do, Sir Lewis. You can try to deserve it."

The bed linens rustled, and he whipped his gaze to Susanna. Her bronze lashes fluttered against her cheek.

Forget birds singing, bells ringing, brooks quaintly babbling over rocks. Choirs of angels could go hang. Her voice, even scratchy and weak, was the most beautiful thing he'd ever heard.

"Bram? Is that you?"

Susanna's eyes fluttered open to what seemed just another lovely dream. Bram was there, beside her. And they had a proper bed, at long last. She'd had quite enough of loving him in coves and arbors.

"Bram," she whispered.

"It's me." He pressed a firm kiss to her hand, and several days' growth of whiskers scraped her skin.

She started to rise up on her elbow, but then some mischievous imp set the mattress spinning like a top.

"Don't try to sit up," he said. "You're weak yet."

She nodded, closing her eyes until the room stopped whirling.

"Do you want water?" He reached for a glass.

"In a moment. First . . ." With great effort, she turned her head. "Papa?"

Her father's work-roughened hands clasped hers. "I'm here, dear girl. I'm here."

She squeezed his fingers. "I want you to know I love you very much, Papa."

"I—" His voice broke. "I love you too, Susanna Jane."

"Good." To hear those words from her father was unexpected, and unexpectedly freeing. She drew a deep breath. "Now would you go down to the kitchen and ask Cook for some beef tea?"

"I'll send Gertrude right away."

"No, Papa. I'd prefer for you to fetch it. I'd like some time alone with Bram."

Her father sniffed and nodded. "I see."

"Thank you for understanding." She waited until he rose from his chair, wiping his eyes with the back of his hand, and made his way to the bedchamber door. When she heard the door latch click, she turned to Bram.

"Did you hear much of that conversation?" His gaze was wary.

"Enough of it. Oh, Bram. You were wonderful. I can't even tell you how much I wanted—"

He clucked his tongue. "Time enough for that later. For now, drink." He held a glass of water to her lips, and she took several cautious sips. "Are you in terrible pain?"

"Not too terrible," she answered, once he lowered the glass. She tried for a smile. "It only hurts when I breathe."

His answer was a stern rebuke. "Don't joke. It's not funny. I can't stand to see you in pain."

Dear, sweet man. "I'll be fine. Truly. The pain's so much better than before. How's Finn?"

"Recovering well, Daniels tells me. He's in a great deal of pain, but it's mitigated by a great deal of female attention."

She smiled. "I can imagine. What day is it?"

He rubbed his face with one hand. "Tuesday, I think."

Tuesday. There was something important about Tuesday.

"Oh no." She pushed herself up on the pillows, wincing. "Bram, your orders. The ship. I thought it left today."

He shrugged. "It probably did."

"But . . . you didn't leave."

"You didn't die." Finally, he smiled a little. "One kept promise deserves another."

He sat there, at her bedside, unmoving. As he likely had remained for days now. And she lay there, gazing at him in the warm light of day—his hair askew, shirt rumpled, jaw unshaven, and eyes rimmed with red. Only a man could be so unkempt and manage to look more endearingly handsome than ever.

"Goodness," she said with sudden horror. She reached up with one hand to investigate her hair. Just as she'd feared, she found it a hopeless tangle. And after all those days of illness—the blood loss, fever . . . "I must look a perfect fright."

"Are you mad? Susanna, you're alive and awake. You're the loveliest thing I've ever seen."

She pressed her cracked lips together. "Then why don't you touch me? Hold me?"

"It's not for lack of wanting to." He reached one hand toward her face, then hesitated for a moment—before finally brushing a single fingertip down her cheek. "Love, you have at least three cracked ribs and a chest wound. I'm not permitted to hold you. In fact, Daniels put me under strict orders if you awoke. I'm not to hold you, kiss you, touch you. I'm not to make you laugh, make you cry, make you angry, or excite your emotions in any way. Which means"—he inched his chair closer to the head of the bed—"that if we're going to talk at all right now . . ."

"Of course we are."

". . . we have to make this a very calm, completely dispassionate conversation."

She nodded, making her tone serious. "I can do that."

"You see . . ." He tenderly clasped her hand. "I have a question to ask Miss Finch."

"Oh." She adopted a formal tone. "And what would that question be, Lord Rycliff?"

"I'm wondering if you, Miss Finch, with your keen eye and discerning taste, would be so good as to help me choose some fabrics for upholstery."

She blinked at him. "Upholstery?"

He nodded. "I think it would be a safe enough occupation for you, while you convalesce. I'll have some samples sent over."

"Very well," she said slowly. "Is that all you mean to ask of me?"

"No. Of course not. If all goes well and your recovery permits, by next week perhaps you can advance to draperies."

"Draperies." She narrowed her eyes. "Bram, I know you've been forbidden to provoke me. But did Mr. Daniels say nothing about the dangers of confusing me?"

"I'll start again." He paused, staring down at their linked hands. "I've written to my superiors."

"About upholstery? Or draperies?"

"Neither. About my commission."

She gasped. "Bram, you didn't. You didn't resign."

"Hush," he warned, squeezing her fingers. "Very calm, completely dispassionate. Remember?"

She nodded, pausing to draw a cautious breath.

"I didn't resign." His thumb traced a circle on the back of her hand. "I accepted a promotion I was offered some time ago. I'll be assigned to the War Office, making sure the infantry regiments have the supplies they need at the front. It's not field command, but it's important work."

"It is. Oh, and you'll be brilliant at it. You've spent so much time at the front. Who knows better than you what they need?"

"There will be some travel involved. But for the most part, I'll be working in Town. So I'll need a house there, I suppose. I've never bought a house before. When you're well, I'm hoping you'd help me choose one. And then, I was hoping you'd help me make it a proper home. You know, with upholstery. And draperies. And . . . perhaps babies, eventually."

"Oh. Babies." A helpless giggle rose in her throat. "Do you plan to send over samples of those?"

"Don't laugh." He shushed her, putting a hand to her shoulder to keep her still. "Don't laugh."

"I can't help it." She stifled the impulse as best she could. Then, with a trembling hand, she wiped tears from her eyes.

Panic overtook his expression. "Bloody hell. Now you're crying. Daniels will kill me."

"It's fine," she assured him. "It's fine. The laughter, the tears . . . they're worth any pain. I'm so happy. Just miserably, painfully full of joy."

His dark eyebrows lowered, and beneath them his eyes went very grave. "You"—he squeezed her hand in both of his—"gave me the scare of a lifetime."

"I was frightened, too," she admitted. "But you helped me through it. And here we are. If we can survive that, I imagine we can come through anything."

He didn't respond, save to give her a long, affectionate look.

Surely he loved her. He didn't even have to say it. His

every action—from accepting the promotion in London, to the cool cloth he now swiped over her brow—told her so.

He didn't *have* to say it. But she was growing terribly impatient to hear the words, just the same.

He snapped straight and began adjusting the bed linens around her. "You need rest. Or tea. Or something. I don't know, you're the healer. If you were me right now, what would you do?"

"That's simple. I would go inform Daniels that his patient is awake. And then I would have a proper meal and a good, long sleep. And a bath and a shave. And I would not worry about anything."

He brushed a fingertip over her nose. "Little liar."

"But the very first thing I would do? Is give my future bride a kiss." When he hesitated, she cast him her most encouraging smile. "You've already broken all the other prohibitions. Don't go honorable on me now."

He leaned close, brushing the hair from her temple. "I never could resist stealing a kiss from you. Not since that very first day."

His lips touched hers.

And just like that first kiss, it was warm and firm, and then . . . it was over. Curse him, he was a model of restraint.

"Bram," she whispered, unable to resist, "do you think you could love me, just a little?"

He laughed. "Good Lord, no."

"No?" Susanna bit her lip, cringing inside. "Oh."

Oh dear. She dropped her gaze to his lapel, assessing her options. Could she bring herself to marry him, if he didn't love her at all?

Of course she could. The alternative flashed before her eyes—a future that appeared hopelessly lonely and grim.

She couldn't picture it too clearly, but she sensed it would involve a great many cats and peppermints.

Never mind love. She could make do with lust, or admiration, or whatever he offered her. Even tepid affection was better than fuzzy peppermints.

He touched her cheek, drawing her gaze back up to his strong, handsome face.

"No, Susanna," he said. "I cannot love you just a little. If that's what you want, you must find a different man." His green eyes were breathtaking in their intensity. His thumb brushed her bottom lip. "Because I can only love you entirely. With everything I am, and everything I ever will be. Body, mind, heart, soul."

Her heart soared. "Oh," she finally managed. "That's better. So much better." She pulled him close for a kiss.

He held back. "Are you sure?" he asked, looking serious now. "Think on it, love. Be certain you want this. I'm offering you everything I am. And if I do say it myself, I'm a lot of man to handle. I'll protect you fiercely, challenge you daily, and want you nightly—at the least. You won't be able to manage me the way you manage other men."

She smiled. "Oh, I think that's yet to be decided."

"I can be a beast, as you're so fond of calling me. Strong as a bull, stubborn as an ox . . ."

"But handsomer than both, thank goodness."

His eyebrows drew together in mock censure. "I'm being serious here. I want you to know what you're getting into."

"I know well what I've gotten into. It's love. And I've fallen so deep in it by now, I ought to have a bathing costume." She caressed his cheek. "I can't wait to be your wife."

He clasped her hand to his face, then kissed it warmly.

"Even though we'll reside in London, at least some of the time?"

"I would have followed you to the Pyrenees. London is just up the road."

"We will be here often, I promise. Christmas, Easter. Every summer, of course, so you can welcome your friends. I know for you, Spindle Cove will always be home."

"But not for you?"

He shook his head. "You're my home, Susanna. My home, my heart, my dearest love. Wherever you are, that's where I belong. Always."

Epilogue

Six weeks later

t was good to be home.

Just returning after a week's absence from the village, Bram paused outside the red-painted door of the establishment formerly known as the Rutting Bull. Which had been formerly known as the Blushing Pansy.

The gilt-lettered sign hanging above the door might be new, but when he threw open the door of what was now the Bull and Blossom, Bram encountered immediate proof that some things never changed.

His cousin remained a troublemaking idiot.

The entire tavern had been cleared of chairs and tables. Colin stood with his back to the door, directing men in two opposite corners of the room as they hoisted some sort of soldered frame toward the ceiling, using an elaborate network of pulleys and ropes. Bram had no idea what they were doing, but he knew it couldn't be good.

"Hold your ropes, now," Colin ordered, motioning with both arms like an orchestra conductor. "Thorne, pull it a hair or two closer to your corner. Not too far! That space will get smaller once the stage curtains are hung, and we need to leave the fair Salome plenty of room for her dance of the seven veils. Can't have her skimping and only giving us six."

Bram cleared his throat.

Colin wheeled in a brisk half turn. His countenance was purposely, studiously blank.

Bram could tell his cousin meant to look innocent.

He wasn't fooled.

"Salome and her seven veils? What, precisely, is going on here?"

"Nothing." Colin shrugged. "Nothing at all."

Behind him, the two men strained and sweated to keep the frame immobile. He viewed their guilty faces. Scheming bastards wouldn't even meet his gaze. He looked from Thorne, to . . . "*Keane?*"

The clergyman's face flushed red.

Bram glared at his cousin. "You're dragging the *vicar* into debauchery now? Good God, man. Have you no shame?"

"Me? Shame?" With a gruff noise, his cousin directed the men to secure their ropes. Then he turned back to Bram, wearing a resigned expression and scratching the back of his neck. "Bram, you weren't supposed to be here until tomorrow."

"Well, judging by this scene, it's a bloody fortunate thing I came early."

"I give you my word. Nothing untoward is going on here."

Fosbury walked into the room, wiping floury hands on his apron. "All finished with the cake, my lord. She's a work of art, if I do say it myself. Used almond paste for the skin tone; came out lovely. Nice, big bubbies of puffed meringue. Had a difficult time deciding whether to use pink rosettes or cinnamon drops for the nipples, though.

When it comes to those, a man does have his individual tastes, you—" The man finally took note of Colin's frantic "shut it" gestures. His gaze snapped to Bram, and he gulped with recognition. "Oh. Lord Rycliff. You're . . . here."

Bram fixed his cousin with an accusing gaze. "Nothing untoward?"

Colin raised his open palms. "I swear it on my life. Now if you'd only—"

At that moment, a breathless Rufus dashed into the room. "Lord Payne, your delivery's arrived. Where did you want the tiger?"

This time, Bram didn't bother waiting for a denial. He lunged forward and grabbed Colin by the lapels. "Didn't you learn your lesson after that first debacle? This is precisely why I won't give you a penny to live on elsewhere, you worthless cur. If you wreak this much havoc in quiet little Spindle Cove, the devil only knows what mischief you'd be up to somewhere else." He gave his cousin a shake. "Just what the hell do you think you're doing?"

"Planning your stag night. You dolt."

Bram froze. Then frowned. "Oh."

"Satisfied? Now you've ruined the surprise." Colin raised a brow. "Had it not occurred to you that your men might want to give you a party? Or had you forgotten you're getting married in a matter of days?"

Bram shook his head, chuckling to himself. No, he hadn't forgotten he was marrying Susanna in a matter of days. He'd spent the past month thinking of little else. And having only just returned to the neighborhood after spending a week in London, he was growing damned well desperate to hold his bride.

What the hell was he doing holding Colin, then?

Bram released his cousin's lapels. "Very well. I'm going to back out of this room the way I came. And pretend I never saw this."

"Excellent." Colin gave him a helpful shove to start him on his way. "Welcome back. Now get out."

Bram abandoned the long, curving lane to Summerfield and decided to walk overland instead, cutting directly across the bands of farmland and gently rolling meadow.

Just a week since he'd seen Susanna last. Lord, it felt like a year. How had he ever imagined he'd be able to leave her behind while he went to the Peninsula?

Despite the lingering pain in his knee, he picked up his pace as he crested a sloping, grassy hill. Here his path dropped into a little green valley, traversed by a stream. He cast his eyes downward, in order to choose his steps with care.

"Bram!"

Whomp.

Out of nowhere, something launched at him. A soft, warm missile that smelled like a garden and wore a sprigged muslin frock. He was caught off balance on his bad leg, and down they tumbled. He performed some heroic gymnastics to make certain he took the brunt of the fall, hitting the hillside with a dull *oof*.

She landed atop him. They tangled together on the ground, here in this small depression. The valley's low ridges walled out any distant landscape. His whole world was blue sky, green grass . . . and her.

"*Susanna.*" Grinning like a fool, he wrapped his arms around her middle and rolled a bit, so that they faced each other, lying on their sides in the tall grass. "Where did you come from?" He skimmed a touch down her ribs. "You're not hurt?"

"I'm fine. More than fine." Gentle fingers smoothed the hair from his brow. "How are you?"

"I don't know. I think I'm seeing double. Two lips, two eyes . . . a thousand freckles."

"Nothing a little kiss won't mend." A smile curved her sweet lips. Then those sweet lips touched his. "I heard you were down in the village, and I couldn't wait to see you. Why didn't you come to Summerfield straightaway?"

"I had to stop in the village first. Had some business with Colin and Thorne. And then I stopped by the forge."

"You went to see the *blacksmith* before coming to see me?"

He held up his hand between them and waggled his fingers. "Had to fetch this."

Her gaze fixed on the ring stuck firmly at the second knuckle of his little finger. She gasped. "Goodness."

She reached for it, but he teased her by holding the ring back. "Say you're sorry for doubting me."

The iris-blue hue of her eyes was sincerity itself. "I never doubted you, not for a second. I was merely impatient. Whether you go to the forge or to London or all the way to Portugal, Bram . . . I know you'll come home to me."

"Always." He captured her lips in a kiss.

"Wait, wait," she said, pushing away. "Ring first, kisses later."

He harrumphed and muttered something about feminine priorities. He worked the ring loose from his own finger and slid it onto hers, where it rightly belonged. He loved the look of it there, snug and sparkling. "I thought you might like to have a ring made here, since we'll be spending so much time in Town. This way, wherever we are, you'll always carry a little piece of Spindle Cove with you."

"Oh, Bram." She blinked furiously, as though she were holding back tears. He hoped they were happy tears.

Suddenly unsure, he pointed out the ring's features. "I had him use both gold and copper in the band, you see. Because your hair has both shades. And the sapphire reminded me of your eyes. Though your eyes are far more beautiful, of course." God, this all sounded hopelessly stupid, voiced aloud. "I think Dawes did quality work with it. But if you'd prefer something finer, I can take you to a jeweler in Town or . . ."

She shushed him. "It's perfect. I adore it. I adore you."

Ring first, kisses later, she'd said. He claimed his forfeit now, taking her mouth in a deep, thorough, passionate kiss. Letting her know just how much he'd missed her, every minute of every hour of every day they'd been apart.

Some time later, she rested her head to his chest and gave a contented sigh. "Do you know what today is?"

"It's Wednesday, Miss Finch." He stroked her molten bronze hair. "But you're not in the garden."

She lifted her head. "I didn't mean the day of the week. I meant, the significance of this particular day."

He considered. "It's . . . three days before our wedding?"

"What else?"

"Three days and two weeks before we move house to London."

"Yes. And . . . ?"

Good Lord, what kind of devilish test was this? "I know. Three days and nine months before the birth of our first child."

She laughed with surprise.

"What? I plan to be very industrious on our honeymoon. I hope you're well rested, because you won't be sleeping much that first week. You didn't plan on seeing any of the sights in Kent, did you?"

They would be letting a country house for a blissful fortnight before moving to London. In Town, he'd arranged a temporary suite of rooms in the best neighborhood—just until Susanna could choose their house. He couldn't wait to take her to London, as his wife. He looked forward to showing her more of the world, and watching Susanna come into her own.

"Today," she informed him, "marks exactly six weeks since my injury. I am not only rested, but officially healed. And that means . . ." Her hand slid coyly down his chest, and she looked up at him through downcast lashes. "We don't have to be careful anymore."

Part of him leaped eagerly at her implication. He did his best to ignore it. "Susanna, you know it's not a matter of how many days or weeks have passed."

"Mr. Daniels paid a call two days ago. He says I'm cleared to engage in any and all activity." One of her slender legs twined between his, and she pressed an open-mouthed kiss to his ear. Her tongue skimmed the delicate ridge. "Guess which activity I'm most eager to resume?"

Now, *that* invitation he was powerless to ignore.

They kissed hungrily, giving and taking in turn. He filled his hands with her, relearning her body. Cupping and shaping her every luscious curve. Her fingers did some bold exploring of their own, and he moaned his encouragement.

But when she reached for the closures of his breeches fall, he stayed her hand. "Really," he said, struggling for breath. "It's only three more days. I can wait."

"Well, I can't. I've missed you so much. And I'm tired of playing the invalid. I want to feel alive again."

A ragged sigh escaped him. How could he deny her that?

Arching her spine, she rubbed her body against his. She found his hand where he cupped her stockinged calf and drew his touch upward, past her knee and ribbon garter. All the way up to the silk of her bared thighs and the enticing heat between them.

He groaned. "God, I love you."

"I love you, too." She rolled her hips, pressing into his touch. "And I need you, Bram. So very badly."

They worked quickly then, the two of them. United in purpose and urgency, pushing aside bothersome folds of buckskin and petticoat, until nothing came between them. Nothing at all. At last he slid into her, fitting himself into that tight, sweet place where he knew he belonged, forever.

"*Yes*," she sighed, pulling him close.

It was very good to be home.

Afterword

egency-era medicine was a bloody business. While doctors surely had good intentions to help their patients, very little was understood about the origins and spread of disease. The preferred treatments of the day—bleeding and purging—had little, if any, real benefit.

Women's reproductive health presented an especially difficult puzzle, it seems. In researching Susanna's character, I read several Regency and early Victorian case histories of young women diagnosed with "hysteria." Their symptoms ranged from moodiness to muscle weakness, headaches to seizures. All manner of feminine complaints were attributed to irregular menstruation or some vague dysfunction of the reproductive organs. Prescribed treatments ranged from the standard bleeding and purging, to the application of pustule-inducing salves and leeches on . . . let's just say, delicate areas.

It all made me extremely grateful for my twenty-first-century doctors. But even with the advances in modern medicine, today's researchers are still striving to understand and cure diseases that affect tens of thousands of women each year. For that reason, I was honored to learn *A Night to Surrender* would be part of Avon's partnership with the Ovarian Cancer National Alliance, an organization dedicated to raising public awareness, finding a cure, and encouraging women to be their own health advocates. Please visit www.ovariancancer.org for more information.

Turn the page for a sneak peek
at the next delightful book in
Tessa Dare's Spindle Cove series,

A WEEK TO BE WICKED

hen a girl trudged through the rain at midnight to knock at the Devil's door, the Devil should at least have the depravity—if not the decency—to answer.

Minerva gathered the edges of her cloak with one hand, weathering another cold, stinging blast of wind. She stared in desperation at the closed door, then pounded it with the flat of her fist.

"Lord Payne," she shouted, hoping her voice would carry through the thick oak planks. "Do come to the door! It's Miss Highwood." After a moment's pause, she clarified, "Miss Minerva Highwood."

Rather nonsensical, that she needed to state just *which* Miss Highwood she was. From Minerva's view, it ought to be obvious. Her younger sister, Charlotte, was an exuberant yet tender fifteen years of age. And the eldest of the family, Diana, possessed not only angelic beauty, but the disposition to match. Neither of them were at all the sort to slip from bed at night, steal down the back stairs of the rooming house, and rendezvous with an infamous rake.

But Minerva was different. She'd always been different. Of the three Highwood sisters, she was the only dark-haired one, the only bespectacled one, the only one who preferred sturdy lace-up boots to silk slippers, and the only one who cared one whit about the difference between sedimentary and metamorphic rocks.

The only one with no prospects, no reputation to protect.

Diana and Charlotte will do well for themselves, but Minerva? Plain, bookish, distracted, awkward with gentlemen. In a word, hopeless.

The words of her own mother, in a recent letter to their cousin. To make it worse, Minerva hadn't discovered this stinting description by snooping through private correspondence. Oh, no. She'd transcribed the words herself, penning them at Mama's dictation.

Truly. Her own *mother.*

The wind caught her hood and whisked it back. Cold rain pelted her neck, adding injury to insult.

Swiping aside the hair matted to her cheek, Minerva stared up at the ancient stone turret—one of four that comprised the Rycliff Castle keep. Smoke curled from the topmost vent.

She raised her fist again, pounding at the door with renewed force. "Lord Payne, I know you're in there."

Vile, teasing man.

Minerva would root herself to this spot until he let her in, even if this cold spring rain soaked her to the very marrow. She hadn't climbed all this distance from the village to the castle, slipping over mossy outcroppings and tracing muddy rills in the dark, just to trudge the same way back home, defeated.

However, after a solid minute of knocking to no avail, the fatigue of her journey set in, knotting her calf muscles and softening her spine. Minerva slumped forward. Her forehead met wood with a dull *thunk*. She kept her fist lifted overhead, beating on the door in an even, stubborn rhythm. She might very well be plain, bookish, distracted, and awkward—but she was determined. Determined to be acknowledged, determined to be heard.

Determined to protect her sister, at any cost.

Open, she willed. *Open. Open. Op—*

The door opened. Swiftly, with a brisk, unforgiving *woosh*.

"For the love of tits, Thorne. Can't it wait for—"

"Ack." Caught off-balance, Minerva stumbled forward. Her fist rapped smartly against—not the door, but a chest.

Lord Payne's chest. His masculine, muscled, shirtless chest, which proved only slightly less solid than a plank of oak. Her blow landed square on his flat, male nipple, as though it were the Devil's own door-knocker.

At least this time, the Devil answered.

"Well." The dark word resonated through her arm. "You're not Thorne."

"Y-you're not clothed." *And I'm touching your bare chest. Oh . . . Lord.*

The mortifying thought occurred to her that he might not be wearing trousers either. She righted herself. As she removed her spectacles with chilled, trembling fingers, she caught a reassuring smudge of dark wool below the flesh-colored blur of his torso. She huffed a breath on each of the two glass discs connected by brass, wiped the mist from them with a dry fold of her cloak lining, and then replaced them on her face.

He was still half-naked. And now, in perfect focus. Devious tongues of firelight licked over every feature of his handsome face, defining him.

"Come in, if you mean to." He winced at a blast of frost-tipped wind. "I'm shutting the door, either way."

She stepped forward. The door closed behind her with a heavy, finite sound. Minerva swallowed hard.

"I must say, Melinda. This is rather a surprise."

"My name's Minerva."

"Yes, of course." He cocked his head. "I didn't recognize your face without the book in front of it."

She exhaled, letting her patience stretch. And stretch.

Until it expanded just enough to accommodate a teasing rake with a sieve-like memory. And stunningly well-defined shoulders.

"I'll admit," he said, "this is hardly the first time I've answered the door in the middle of night and found a woman waiting on the other side. But you're certainly the least expected one yet." He sent her lower half an assessing look. "And the most muddy."

She ruefully surveyed her mud-caked boots and bedraggled hem. A midnight seductress she was not. "This isn't *that* kind of visit."

"Give me a moment to absorb the disappointment."

"I'd rather give you a moment to dress." Minerva crossed the round chamber of windowless stone and went straight for the hearth. She took her time tugging loose the velvet ties of her cloak, then draped it over the room's only armchair.

Payne hadn't wasted the entirety of his months here in Spindle Cove, it seemed. Someone had put a great deal of work into transforming this stone silo into a warm, almost comfortable home. The original stone hearth had been cleaned and restored to working order. In it blazed a fire large and fierce enough to do a Norman warrior proud. In addition to the upholstered armchair, the circular room contained a wooden table and stools. Simple, but well-made.

No bed.

Strange. She swiveled her gaze. Didn't an infamous rake need a bed?

Finally, she looked up. The answer hovered overhead. He'd fashioned a sort of sleeping loft, accessible by a ladder. Rich drapes concealed what she assumed to be his bed. Above that, the stone walls spiraled into black, cavernous nothingness.

Minerva decided she'd given him ample time to find

a shirt and make himself presentable. She cleared her throat and slowly turned. "I've come to ask—"

He was still half-naked.

He had not used the time to make himself presentable. He'd taken the chance to pour a drink. He stood in profile, making scrunched faces into a wineglass to assess its cleanliness.

"Wine?" he asked.

She shook her head. Thanks to his indecent display, a ferocious blush was already burning its way over her skin. Up her throat, over her cheeks, up to her hairline. She hardly needed to throw wine on the flames.

As he poured a glass for himself, she couldn't help but stare at his leanly muscled torso, so helpfully limned by firelight. She'd been used to thinking him a devil, but he had the body of a god. A lesser one. His wasn't the physique of a hulking, over-muscled Zeus or Poseidon, but rather a lean, athletic Apollo or Mercury. A body built not to bludgeon, but to hunt. Not to lumber, but to race. Not to overpower unsuspecting naiads where they bathed, but to . . .

Seduce.

He glanced up. She looked away.

"I'm sorry to wake you," she said.

"You didn't wake me."

"Truly?" She frowned at him. "Then . . . for as long as it took you to answer the door, you might have put on some clothes."

With a devilish grin, he indicated his trousers. "I did."

Well. Now her cheeks all but caught fire. She dropped into the armchair, wishing she could disappear into its seams.

For God's sake, Minerva, take hold of yourself. Diana's future is at stake.

Setting the wine on the table, he moved to some wooden shelves that seemed to serve as his wardrobe. To the side, a row of hooks supported his outerwear. A red officer's coat, for the local militia he led in the Earl of Rycliff's absence. A few finely-tailored, outrageously expensive-looking topcoats from Town. A greatcoat in charcoal-gray wool.

He passed over all these, grabbed a simple lawn shirt, and yanked it over his head. Once he'd thrust his arms through the sleeves, he held them out to either side for her appraisal. "Better?"

Not really. The gaping collar still displayed a wide view of his chest—only with a lascivious wink instead of a frank stare. If anything, he looked more indecent. Less of an untouchable, chiseled god and more of a raff-ish pirate king.

"Here." He took the greatcoat from its hook and brought it to her. "It's dry, at least."

Once he'd settled the coat over her lap, he pressed the glass of wine into her hand. A signet ring flashed on his little finger, shooting gold through the glass's stem.

"No arguments. You're shivering so hard, I can hear your teeth chatter. The fire and coat help, but they can't warm you inside."

Minerva accepted the glass and took a careful sip. Her fingers did tremble, but not entirely from the cold.

He pulled up a stool, sat on it, and fixed her with an expectant look. "So."

"So," she echoed, stupidly.

Her mother was right in this respect. Minerva con-sidered herself a reasonably intelligent person, but good heavens . . . handsome men made her stupid. She grew so flustered around them, never knew where to look or what to say. The reply meant to be witty and clever would come out sounding bitter or lame. Sometimes a teasing remark from Lord Payne's quarter quelled her into dumb silence altogether. Only days later, while she was banging away at a cliff face with a rock hammer, would the perfect retort spring to mind.

Remarkable. The longer she stared at him now, the more she could actually feel her intelligence waning. A day's growth of whiskers only emphasized the strong cut of his unshaven jaw. His mussed brown hair had just a hint of roguish wave. And his eyes . . . He had eyes like Bristol diamonds. Small round geodes, halved and polished to a gleam. An outer ring of flinty hazel enclosed cool flashes of quartz. A hundred crystalline shades of amber and gray.

She squeezed her eyes shut. *Enough dithering.* "Do you mean to marry my sister?"

Seconds passed. "Which one?"

"Diana," she exclaimed. "Diana, of course. Charlotte being all of fifteen."

He shrugged. "Some men like a young bride."

"Some men have sworn off marriage entirely. You told me you were one of them."

"I told *you* that? When?"

"Surely you remember. That night."

He stared at her, obviously nonplussed. "We had 'a night'?"

"Not how you're thinking." Months ago now, she'd confronted him in the Summerfield gardens about his scandalous indiscretions and his intentions toward her sister. They'd clashed. Then they'd somehow *tangled*—bodily—until a few cutting insults severed the knot.

Curse her scientific nature, so relentlessly observant. Minerva resented the details she'd gleaned in those moments. She did not need to know that his bottom waistcoat button was exactly in line with her fifth vertebra, or that he smelled faintly of leather and cloves. But even now, months later, she couldn't seem to jettison the information.

Especially not when she sat huddled in his greatcoat, embraced by borrowed warmth and the same spicy, masculine scent.

Naturally, he'd forgotten the encounter entirely. No surprise. Most days, he couldn't even remember Minerva's name. If he spoke to her at all, it was only to tease.

"Last summer," she reminded him, "you told me you had no intentions of proposing to Diana. Or anyone. But today, gossip in the village says different."

"Does it?" He twisted his signet ring. "Well, your sister is lovely and elegant. And your mother's made no secret that she'd welcome the match."

Minerva curled her toes in her boots. "That's putting it mildly."

Last year, the Highwoods had come to this seaside village for a summer holiday. The sea air was supposed to improve Diana's health. Well, Diana's health had long been improved and summer was long gone, yet the Highwoods remained—all because of Mama's hopes for a match between Diana and this charming viscount. So long as Lord Payne was in Spindle Cove, Mama would not hear of returning home. She'd even developed an uncharacteristic streak of optimism—each morning declaring as she stirred her chocolate, "I feel it, girls. Today is the day he proposes."

And though Minerva knew Lord Payne to be the worst sort of man, she had never found it in herself to object. Because she loved it here. She didn't want to leave. In Spindle Cove, she finally . . . belonged.

Here, in her own personal paradise, she explored the

rocky, fossil-studded coast free from care or censure, cataloging findings that could set England's scientific community on its ear. The only thing that kept her from being completely happy was Lord Payne's presence—and through one of life's strange ironies, his presence was the very reason she was able to stay.

There'd seemed no harm in allowing Mama to nurse hopes of a proposal from his lordship's quarter. Minerva had known for certain a proposal wasn't coming.

Until this morning, when her certainty crumbled.

"This morning, I was in the All Things shop," she began. "I usually ignore Sally Bright's gossip, but today . . ." She swallowed hard, then met his gaze. "She said you'd given directions for your mail to be forwarded to London, after next week. She thinks you're leaving Spindle Cove."

"And you concluded that this means I'll marry your sister."

"Well, everyone knows your situation. If you had two shillings to rub together, you'd have left months ago. You're stranded here until your fortune's released from trust on your birthday, unless . . ." She swallowed hard. "Unless you marry first."

"That's all true."

She leaned forward in her chair. "I'll leave in a heartbeat, if you'll only repeat your words to me last summer. That you have no intentions toward Diana."

"But that was last summer. It's April now. Is it so inconceivable that I might have changed my mind?"

"*Yes.*"

"Why?" He snapped his fingers. "I know. You think I don't possess a mind to change. Is that the sticking point?"

She sat forward in her chair. "You can't change your mind, because you haven't *changed*. You're a deceitful, insincere rake who flirts with unsuspecting ladies by day, then takes up with other men's wives by night."

He sighed. "Listen, Miranda. Since Fiona Lange left the village, I haven't—"

Minerva held up a hand. She didn't want to hear about his *affaire* with Mrs. Lange. She'd heard more than enough from the woman herself, who'd fancied herself a poetess. Minerva wished she could scrub her mind of those poems. Ribald, rhapsodic odes that exhausted every possible rhyme for "quiver" and "bliss."

"You can't marry my sister," she told him, willing firmness to her voice. "I simply won't allow it."

Beautiful and elegant, Diana Highwood—as their mother was so fond of telling anyone who'd listen—was exactly the sort of young lady who could set her cap for a handsome lord. But Diana's external beauty dulled in comparison to her sweet, generous nature and the quiet courage with which she'd braved illness all her life.

Certainly, Diana *could* catch a viscount. But she *shouldn't* marry this one.

"You don't deserve her," she told Lord Payne.

"True enough. But none of us get what we truly deserve in this life. Where would God's sport be in that?" He took the glass from her hand and drew a leisurely sip of wine.

"She doesn't love you."

"She doesn't dislike me. Love's hardly required." Leaning forward, he propped an arm on his knee. "Diana would be too polite to refuse. Your mother would be overjoyed. My cousin would send the special license in a trice. We could be married this week. You could be calling me 'brother' by Sunday."

No. Her whole body shouted the rejection. Every last corpuscle.

Throwing off the borrowed greatcoat, she leapt to her

feet and began pacing the carpet. The wet folds of her skirt tangled as she strode. "This can't happen. It cannot. It *will* not." A little growl forced its way through her clenched teeth.

She balled her hands in fists. "I have twenty-two pounds saved from my pin money. That, and some change. It's yours, all of it, if you promise to leave Diana alone."

"Twenty-two pounds?" He shook his head. " Your sisterly sacrifice is touching. But that amount wouldn't keep me in London a week. Not the way I live."

She bit her lip. She'd expected as much, but she'd reasoned it couldn't hurt to try a bribe first. It would have been so much easier.

She took a deep breath and lifted her chin. This was it—her last chance to dissuade him. "Then run away with me instead."

After a moment's stunned pause, he broke into hearty laughter.

She let the derisive sounds wash over her and simply waited, arms crossed. Until his laughter dwindled, ending with a choked cough.

"Good God," he said. "You're serious?"

"Perfectly serious. Leave Diana alone, and run away with me."

He drained the wineglass and set it aside. Then he cleared his throat and began, "That is brave of you, pet. Offering to wed me in your sister's stead. But truly, I—"

"My name is Minerva. I'm not your pet. And you're deranged if you think I'd ever marry you."

"But I thought you just said—"

"Run away with you, yes. Marry you?" She made an incredulous noise in her throat. "Please."

He blinked at her.

"I can see you're baffled."

"Oh, good. I would have admitted as much, but I know what pleasure you take in pointing out my intellectual shortcomings."

Rummaging through the inside pockets of her cloak, she located her copy of the scientific journal. She opened it to the announcement page and held it out for his examination. "There's to be a meeting of the Royal Geological Society at the end of this month. A symposium. If you'll agree to come with me, my savings should be enough to fund our journey."

"A geology symposium." He flicked a glance at the journal. "This is your scandalous midnight proposal. The one you trudged through the cold, wet dark to make. You're inviting me to a geology symposium, if I leave your sister alone."

"What were you expecting me to offer? Seven nights of wicked, carnal pleasure in your bed?"

She'd meant it as a joke, but he didn't laugh. Instead, he eyed her sodden frock.

Minerva went lobster red beneath it. Curse it. She was forever saying the wrong thing.

"I'd have found that offer more tempting," he said.

Truly? She bit her tongue to keep from saying it aloud. How lowering, to admit how much his off-hand comment thrilled her. *I'd prefer your carnal pleasures to a lecture about dirt.* High compliment indeed.

"A geology symposium," he repeated to himself. "I should have known there'd be rocks at the bottom of this."

"There are rocks at the bottom of everything. That's why we geologists find them so interesting. At any rate, I'm not tempting you with the symposium itself. I'm tempting you with the promise of five hundred guineas."

Now she had his attention. His gaze sharpened. "Five hundred guineas?"

"Yes. That's the prize for the best presentation. If you take me there and help present my findings to the Society, you can keep it all. Five hundred guineas would be sufficient to keep you drunk and debauched in London until your birthday, I should hope?"

He nodded. "With a bit of judicious budgeting. I might have to hold off on new boots, but one must make some sacrifices." He came to his feet, confronting her face to face. "Here's the wrinkle, however. How could you be certain of winning the prize?"

"I'll win. I could explain my findings to you in detail, but a great many polysyllabic words would be involved. I'm not sure you're up to them just now. Suffice it to say, I'm certain."

He gave her a searching look, and Minerva marshaled the strength to hold it. Level, confident, unblinking.

After a moment, his eyes warmed with an unfamiliar glimmer. Here was an emotion she'd never seen from him before.

She thought it might be . . . respect.

"Well," he said. "Certainty becomes you."

Her heart gave a queer flutter. It was the nicest thing he'd ever said to her. She thought it might be the nicest thing *anyone* had ever said to her.

Certainty becomes you.

And suddenly, things were different. The ounce of wine she'd swallowed unfurled in her belly, warming and relaxing her. Melting away her awkwardness. She felt comfortable in her surroundings, and more than a little worldly. As though this were the most natural thing in the world, to be having a midnight conversation in a turret with a half-dressed rake.

She settled languidly into the armchair and raised her hands to her hair, finding and plucking loose her few remaining pins. With slow, dreamy motions, she finger-combed the wet locks and arranged them about her shoulders, the better to dry evenly.

He stood and watched her for a moment. Then he went to pour more wine.

A sensuous ribbon of claret swirled into the glass. "Mind, I'm not agreeing to this scheme. Not by any stretch of the imagination. But just for the sake of argument, how did you see this proceeding, exactly? One morning, we'd just up and leave for London together?"

"No, not London. The symposium is in Edinburgh."

"Edinburgh." Bottle met table with a clunk. "The Edinburgh in Scotland."

She nodded.

"I thought you said this was the Royal Geological Society."

"It is." She waved the journal at him. "The Royal Geological Society of Scotland. Didn't you know? Edinburgh's where all the most interesting scholarship happens."

Crossing back to her, he peered at the journal. "For God's sake, this takes place barely a fortnight from now. Marietta, don't you realize what a journey to Scotland entails? You're talking about two weeks' travel, at the minimum."

"It's four days from London on the mail coach. I've checked."

"The *mail* coach? Pet, a viscount does not travel on the mail coach." He shook his head, sitting across from her. "And how is your dear mother going to take this news, when she finds you've absconded to Scotland with a scandalous lord?"

"Oh, she'll be thrilled. So long as one of her daughters marries you, she won't be particular." Minerva eased her feet from her wet, muddy boots and drew her legs up beneath her skirts, tucking her chilled heels under her backside. "It's perfect, don't you see? We'll stage it as an elopement. My mother won't raise any protest, and neither will Lord Rycliff. He'll be only too happy to think you're marrying at last. We'll travel to Scotland, present my findings, collect the prize. Then we'll tell everyone it simply didn't work out."

The more she explained her ideas, the easier the words sprang to her lips and the more excited she grew. This could work. It could really, truly work.